ELEGY BEACH

ELEGY BEACH

A Book of the Change

STEVEN R. BOYETT

ACE BOOKS, NEW YORK

THE BERKLEY PUBLISHING GROUP
Published by the Penguin Group
Penguin Group (USA) Inc.
375 Hudson Street, New York, New York 10014, USA
Penguin Group (Canada), 90 Eglinton Avenue East, Suite 700, Toronto, Ontario M4P 2Y3, Canada
(a division of Pearson Penguin Canada Inc.)
Penguin Books Ltd., 80 Strand, London WC2R 0RL, England
Penguin Group Ireland, 25 St. Stephen's Green, Dublin 2, Ireland (a division of Penguin Books Ltd.)
Penguin Group (Australia), 250 Camberwell Road, Camberwell, Victoria 3124, Australia
(a division of Pearson Australia Group Pty. Ltd.)
Penguin Books India Pvt. Ltd., 11 Community Centre, Panchsheel Park, New Delhi—110 017, India
Penguin Group (NZ), 67 Apollo Drive, Rosedale, North Shore 0632, New Zealand
(a division of Pearson New Zealand Ltd.)
Penguin Books (South Africa) (Pty.) Ltd., 24 Sturdee Avenue, Rosebank, Johannesburg 2196, South Africa

Penguin Books Ltd., Registered Offices: 80 Strand, London WC2R 0RL, England

This is an original publication of The Berkley Publishing Group.

FIRST EDITION: November 2009

Library of Congress Cataloging-in-Publication Data

Boyett, Steven R.
    Elegy Beach : a book of the change / Steven R. Boyett.—1st ed.
      p.   cm.—(The change ; bk. 2)
    ISBN 978-0-441-01795-9
1. Regression (Civilization)—Fiction.   2. Magic—Fiction.   I. Title.

PS3552.O896E44   2010
813'.54—dc22
                                                            2009031015

PRINTED IN THE UNITED STATES OF AMERICA

10   9   8   7   6   5   4   3   2   1

The boys cast stones at the frogs in jest,
but the frogs die in earnest.

—BION, 100 BC (CITED BY PLUTARCH)

[...] Cities of light, long summers
Of leisure were not to be ours; for to come as we had, long after
It mattered, to live among tombs, great as they are,
Was to be no nearer the end, no farther from where we began.

—MARK STRAND, "MORNING, NOON, AND NIGHT"

PART ONE:
SPELLWARE

ONE

The last thing in this world I wanted to see was another damned unicorn. They were the big deal for schoolgirls in Del Mar this year. Gaggles of them came into Paypay's shop wanting their vewwy own unicorn that would wait for them outside Mrs. Cowardan's school with tail swishing to walk them home. Some women wanted one in the livingroom like some sort of knick knack. They could have one too, for a half a pound of coffee, a couple ounces of chocolate, a jar of decent homebrew, or whatever else Paypay was trading for this week.

It seemed pretty hollow to me. Maybe unicorns had been common as cockroaches back in the days just after the Change, but clearly they'd long since left for greener and more hospitable pastures. If we were what they had to rub elbows with, who could blame them.

Older ladies always moaned about this while I made the charm in Paypay's shop. Poor widdle unicorns, them all go byebye, how sad, could you make it shinier, please? I smiled and nodded. They were customers.

Today it was Mrs. Gloster who wanted her unicorn shinier. "I just like having them around the place," she said. "They make things feel so warm and friendly." She smiled at me. "Inviting."

Mrs. Gloster was a regular, went through about a unicorn a week—pretty good deal for Paypay, considering their trade value and the fact that they only last a couple of days. I smiled and nodded and uncapped the potion thermos. I'd taken to mixing up the unicorn potions in big batches first thing in the morning and pouring doses into thermoses. It saved a lot of time. Paypay was oldschool and hadn't thought of this. He did castings without wondering how they worked or why, or figuring out ways to make the whole messy process more efficient. I wish I'd thought of the thermos trick last year when everyone had wanted lawn gorgons. I wondered if Mrs. Gloster would be as happy to trade dear for her shiny unicorns if she knew I brewed them from readymix.

"My guests just love them," Mrs. Gloster was singing on. "Your work is so accomplished, Fred."

"Well, I'm glad you like them." I lit the campstove. Propane was one of the items we traded for. More Paypay logic: trade castings for items you use to make castings that you trade for. How do you get ahead that way?

I held up a finger for her to be quiet and turned to recite the charm. Paypay liked castings to be dramatic and in full view of the customer. "Customer think magic belong on stage, you know? In movie. Make exciting. Make big."

Whatever; I'd never seen a movie. And it was hard to act excited when I'd recited the unicorn charm so many times that I once woke myself up saying it in my sleep. But Paypay was my boss, so when he was around I did the whole bit, raised arms and flourishes and dramatic voice.

But he wasn't around now. I cracked my knuckles and made the passes over the cauldron—really just a saucepan on a rusty old campstove—and recited the charm. Just because I said it ten times a day didn't mean that I couldn't still mess up, and when castings go wrong they tend to go memorably wrong. My first unicorn charms had been these horrible lopsided skinless popeyed mutant horselike things that had gimped around the back of the shop braying and falling down a lot for two days before fading out. Well if casting were easy everybody'd do it.

The door jangled as another customer came in while I was reciting the charm. I'd asked Paypay could he please lose that damned bell—it could throw you off at a crucial moment, and it seemed to jangle only at crucial moments. Paypay'd just shrugged and said, "You get used. Concentrate is good."

The eidolon unicorn was taking shape in front of me. Mrs. Gloster liked her unicorns small and shiny, goldenhorned and glossy—more like ceramic ornaments. I'd learned to leave some things out so she could make helpful suggestions and feel she'd contributed a creative hand. Everyone's an artist if they only had the time. Well what was the harm.

This week's unicorn was "a cute little one for the upstairs." I made it doe-sized and made the head too big for the body and the eyes too big for the head and gave it thick black lashes. Mrs. Gloster asked could I make it shinier. I added faint blue to the coat to give it more glow indoors and made the tail fluffier and backed off on the eyes and lashes. You've got to have some standards.

The charm was finished and the unicorn likeness was starting to look solid. Its tail swished and it stared up at me reproachfully. I frowned at it and turned away. "There you go, Mrs.—"

Two girls were watching me. For ten seconds all I could do was stare. The fact that they were strangers was worth a few seconds by itself. You don't see a whole lot of new faces in this big old empty world. They were gutpunch gorgeous and seemed quite tall until I realized they were wearing blades. I'd been so involved in the charm I hadn't heard them come in.

"Right with you." I tried to sound professional but my voice broke.

"Freddie does such nice work," Mrs. Gloster told the girls. "I hope Mr. Papadopoulos appreciates him."

It makes you feel funny when someone with bad taste likes what you create. And calls you Freddie in the process. But she meant well. I shrugged and smiled lamely and opened the countertop for the unicorn. It could have walked right through it but it wasn't good business to spoil the illusion before the customer was even out the door.

Mrs. Gloster beckoned to it with a ring-barnacled hand and said, "Come here, baby. I can't wait to put you in the solarium."

The unicorn looked at me. I really should have backed off more on those eyes. I spread my hands and shrugged at it. It wasn't alive or even real but I still felt sorry for it.

I added the unicorn charm to Mrs. Gloster's tab. She had some arrangement with Paypay that I wasn't privy to. But she did tip me a hunk of foilwrapped chocolate. Where do people get this stuff.

"Thanks, Mrs. Gloster."

"Thank you, Fred." She hesitated at the door and eyed the two girls up and down, her customary obtuse expression replaced by one of pure appraisal. She looked like a swap meet trader considering a haggle. She seemed about to ask them something but then the look vanished and she smiled at them vacantly and held the door open for her new charm, which looked back at me again before leaving the shop and going on to meet its horrible domestic fate.

The bells jangled and the Gutpunch Girls looked at me like I'd pissed on their lunch.

"That," said the redhead, "is so sad."

"It's what she paid for," I said even though I'd been thinking the same thing.

"How could you let her leave with that creature," said the blonde.

"It's not real," I said—then realized the creature she meant was Mrs. Gloster. "It's just a charm. It'll only last a few days."

"Poor thing." The blonde shook her head at the door.

"Well maybe I can brew up something you won't find so—"

"Cheesy?" said the redhead.

"I was going to say obvious."

"Actually," said the blonde, "we wanted to know if we could put a flyer in your window." She gave me one. It had a crude line drawing of a man and a woman facing each other with hands joined and a radiating ball floating between them. Despite the bad art it was nicely printed.

safe circle presentz

shelter

del mar racetrack

dusk to dawn

solstice

I looked up from the flyer. "I don't think my boss will let this stay up till June. But leave one with me and I'll put it up on the community board at the racetrack. No one's seen a printed notice on that board in like thirty years; it'll get looked at. Where'd you get it done?"

"There's a woman living at this old bookstore in Carlsbad," the redhead said. "On Woodley."

"Bizarre," said the blonde. "Wacko strange-o."

"I think she's just a witch," the redhead said. "Anyway she has this oldtime press with a big—" She mimed turning a big screw. "She said it was in the store when she squatted it. Like a decoration. She taught herself how to use it."

"Wow. Good for her." I indicated the flyer. "It sounds like fun. Are you guys gonna be at the, um . . . Shelter?"

"Vibe. It's a vibe." The redhead's smile was somewhere between appreciation and Nice Try. "And I will most definitely be there."

"I'll look for you. I haven't been to a vibe in a long time."

"It'll be epic."

"We should get going," the blonde said.

The redhead took a flyer from her and gave it to me and said Thanks a lot.

"Glad to help. I'm Fred."

She smiled. "Freddie does such nice work."

I laughed. "Ouch."

This time the smile was real. "See you next summer."

I started to say Count on it but decided it would be just the other side of pathetic, a border I had probably breezed across as it was, so I just said See you. Which would turn out to be more true than I could have expected or wanted.

They went out into the warm October day and the bells were still jangling as I heard them start to laugh. "I haven't been to a vibe in a long time!" I heard the blonde say as the door shut slowly. "What, when you were twelve."

———————

Parts of Paypay's lunch still clung to his patchy gray beard. He put on his apron and wiped his hands on it. His nostrils widened and he sniffed and looked around. "You make unicorn?"

"Mrs. Gloster."

He nodded.

"Can we work on binding spells today. We were supposed to a couple weeks ago but—"

"Is late today. Learn tomorrow."

"It's just after lunch."

"Fred."

I took a deep breath and tried to let it go. I was turning into more of a store clerk than an apprentice. My education seemed to have slowed down a lot lately. I tried to be patient but there was more to casting than I could learn in ten lifetimes. How Paypay had done it, sloppy and slipshod as he was, without turning himself inside out, or embedding himself half in rock, or sending himself some horrible where, or leaving a big hole in the ground where he used to be, or any of ten thousand other things that can go mortally wrong when you start speaking dead languages inside a pentagram, was a total mystery to me.

My father told me that after the Change suddenly everyone and his brother was a caster. Talismans, charms, Summonings, you name it. Even he had tried it, though he wouldn't say much about it. People quickly figured out you could get killed playing with this stuff and I guess that took all the fun out of it. The guys who kept at it got really good. You know they were good because they were still around to do it. And let's face it, you've got to be pretty decent to be even a shitty caster.

Paypay was the only full-on caster in Del Mar unless you count the coven down at the old youth hostel. He was well regarded and a local fixture and he didn't seem to need much but he seemed to just get by. People used his services but I think they found it hard to take him seriously. Casters are supposed to be haughty otherworldly guys who inspire fear because they can kill you with a word, not shuffling overweight guys with tobacco-stained fingers and food in their beards.

But then he'd unpack his kit and get down to it and suddenly he was focused and economical and meticulous, even graceful. He knew his shit even though he wasn't always able to say what it was he knew. Before I could learn casting from Paypay I'd had to learn how to learn from Paypay. It was a separate education.

The bells jangled intermittently through the rest of the afternoon. Mrs. Abney wanted a vase uncracked, which epic casting was of course handed to yours truly. There was no shortage of dusty vases lying around for the taking but apparently this thing was some fabulous family heirloom, blah-dee blah, could you just uncrack it and stop making helpful suggestions that will send business away from the shop, Fred. Mr. Akbash wanted his dog's leg fixed. I taped it and sent him off to Dr. Ramchandani down the highway.

Then school let out and we got one more unicorn charm (no thermos; Paypay watched me like a hawk); a request from Joey Binauer for something to keep him awake for three days to study for a test, which was a bad bargain for Joey because he couldn't pass so much as a meal if he worked on it for three months; a glamour from Lucinda Welter, who had a crush on Dylan Rondomaki (I warned her that glamours aren't target-specific and everyone would pay attention to her, which for Lucinda would be like putting a hex on herself, she was so painfully shy). You learned more about your town than was good for you in this job.

The day slogged on. I said no more to Paypay about binding spells.

Just before dark I hung my apron on a nail in the doorframe leading to the back room and stuck my head in Paypay's office to tell him I was heading home. He wore his reading glasses as he leafed through an old book by the light of a lone candle. He grunted in my direction and turned a page.

I watched him a moment and wondered if he'd put my education on the back burner because I wasn't measuring up, or if I had done something wrong.

I left without asking him. He'd tell me or he wouldn't. Nothing was going to rush him.

Halfway out the door I remembered the flyer and went back in and grabbed it from behind the counter. shelter. solstice. On the way to Yan's I realized that one thing the redhead hadn't left was her name.

TWO

Yanamandra Ramchandani's family lived on the third floor of an old apartment building on a hill above a cliff with an incredible ocean view. It had withstood any number of quakes before and after the Change, including the big one nine years ago that had sagged the building south of them and sent the one north of them halfway down the slope. The buildings downslope had burned down years ago. How their own place had avoided going up like a tiki torch is anybody's guess. Wind direction maybe. My father had joked that Dr. Ram had burned them down because they'd obstructed his view. Apparently other people had done this. There wasn't a law against it—there wasn't a law against anything really—but it was generally frowned upon. People who'd done it had been politely asked to move on and then impolitely asked if they refused.

The Ramchandanis' building was only a mile from Paypay's and I bladed there before full dark. The lobby was pitchblack but I knew my way by heart. The stairwell door had been removed long ago.

The Ramchandanis' block of apartments was about the only livable place in the building. Long ago the pipes had burst a few floors up and it was only a matter of time before the rot worked its way down to them. Until then they were quite at home. Dr. and Mrs. Ramchandani's apartment served as a sort of common area for the family. Yan had a small apartment across from theirs and his sister Nan's apartment was down the hall. Between Yan and Nan's was a nursery where Parmita grew shade spices and on the roof a small greenhouse where she grew even more. She used them for cooking and Dr. Ram used them for medicines or trading with the wiccans. What they didn't use they traded at the swap meet. Half of the spices in Mrs. Halobagian's breads came from Mrs. Ramchandani's apartment garden.

I was jealous of the Ramchandanis' setup. My father and I shared a small inland house with a tiny yard that always needed cutting with a huge scythe that I just knew was going to kill me someday. We did have nice fruit trees in back though. Orange and plum and peach. They'd gotten us through our share of lean months.

In the dim hall I knocked on Yan's door. The door across the hall opened and Yan's mom grinned at me. "Fred. We knew it was you. Come in." She opened the door wide.

"Hi, Parmita. How'd you know it was me."

"Because," a voice called out from inside, "no one else has your instinct for other people's dinnertimes."

Parmita led me into the dining room and slapped the back of Yan's head and then mussed his hair.

"Oh, are you eating. I'll come back later."

"When we're having dessert," Yan agreed.

"Which tonight is gulab jamun," said Nan, across from him at the table. "So sit down, Frederick."

Nandita was incredibly beautiful and unfairly intelligent and inhumanly graceful, and she had a voice like an underwater bell. Or what I think an underwater bell would sound like. Or should. Or—look, I didn't think too straight around her, which I guess is pretty clear. Her eyes in the dining-room candlelight didn't help. She always called me Frederick, pronouncing all three syllables, even though I was just plain Fred. Yan still sometimes called me Freddum long after everyone else realized I had outgrown it.

Dr. Ramchandani handed me a plate of garlic naan as I sat down beside Nandita. "I really don't come over to mooch," I told him as I took two pieces and passed the plate to Nan who set it down without taking anything.

"Of course not," said Dr. Ram. "You come over after Mr. Papadopoulos closes for the day. Which he does every day at dinnertime. Eat."

"How'd it go today, Fred," Yan asked. "Did you erect any floating castles, summon any demons, curse any evildoers."

"Two unicorns, one healed vase, one study charm, one glamour that I talked the customer out of, and a dog."

"You made a dog?" Parmita looked impressed.

"Not even a fake one. He had a hurt leg. We sent him to you, Dr. Ram."

"Oh yes, Mr. Akbash's dog. Infected cuts. They really should not let that dog out at night. Next time he may not be so fortunate." He wrote a note in a pad he always kept in his shirt pocket. He was the only man I ever saw who wore buttonup shirts, with a collar and everything. Any time of year however hot. The Ramchandanis kept their place open and nicely aired and they burned nag champa incense, a smell I would always associate with them and with Yan. There weren't a lot of windows but there was a sliding glass door opening onto a tiny balcony with a glorious ocean view. Still the room had a boxy stuffiness that made it feel small. In the old days people must have believed outside air was bad for you. Or maybe before the Change it had been.

Dr. Ram returned the notepad to his pocket. "I keep forgetting to bring up the raccoon foragings at the town meeting."

Yan raised his eyebrows. "There are raccoons foraging at the town meetings?"

"Yan," Parmita said.

But Dr. Ram replied as if Yan had spoken seriously. "The raccoons are becoming very bold. I am concerned about rabies."

"I'd think the hyenas and wildcats would take care of the raccoons," I said.

No one said anything, no one registered anything, but I swear even the candlelight changed. I stared at my garlic naan and felt like a fool.

Nan handed me a plate of peas in some kind of rich yellow curry sauce. "It's very good tonight," she said.

My face felt very hot. "It's good every night."

"Especially tonight." Her slight knowing smile meant just for me.

I gave my plate my full attention.

"Well I did not heal so much as a vase today," said Dr. Ram. "Though I gave two excellent haircuts." He shook his head and gave his own small private smile. "What was interesting at Mrs. Cowardan's today, Nan."

"We learned about the Internet. I think half the students didn't believe any of it."

"Which half are you in," Yan asked.

"I take her word for it but I don't quite understand it. So I want to say I'm in the believer half but I'm not comfortable believing in something I don't understand."

"She is your daughter all right," Parmita said.

Dr. Ram crossed his knife and fork over his plate. "Mrs. Cowardan is an excellent teacher but I do not understand why she dwells on these irrelevancies. Perhaps I should talk with her."

"It's history," Yan said with a confidence I envied. "You're all always going on about us having no history. Now you don't want us to learn it?"

"There is history and there is nostalgia. I see no use in teaching nostalgia."

Yan waved his knife at the apartment, somehow indicating as well the great decaying expanse beyond. "We live in what's left of a world that's only twentyseven years away and most of us have no idea what most of it was for. Do you, Fred."

"I see it so much that I don't really see it." This argument between Yan and his father was worn pretty thin and I didn't want to weigh in. Dr. Ram was one of the few older people who thought the Change had been a good thing for the human race in the long run. Yan was one of the few people my age who was obsessed by that lost world and its accomplishments. I fell somewhere between them: impressive accomplishments that had little to do with me or the world I lived in.

"We could learn a lot from then that would make our lives better," Yan said.

"Digging around in graveyards will not teach you how to live."

"It was Lucinda Welter who wanted the glamour," said Nan. "Wasn't it."

"It wouldn't be right for me to say."

"Lucinda Welter. She has a crush on Dylan Rondomaki."

"You can do that, Fred?" Parmita asked.

"Sure. Glamour charms are easy. But you can't aim them at a specific person. I put a glamour on Lu—on a customer, and everyone will want to hang out with her. Or, um, him." I colored and everyone laughed and I breathed a private sigh of relief.

———————

"Yan, man, I am so sorry."

In the hallway outside his apartment he made the passes that unlocked his door and I nodded approval at his improvement. He'd spent a few nights on his parents' couch because he couldn't remember how to unlock his door. "Sorry about what."

"About mentioning . . . you know. How dangerous it can be at night. I wasn't thinking."

"Oh, the hyenas." He shrugged as the door opened. "No one thinks you meant anything, I'm sure."

"You don't have to mean it to step into a big pile."

He looked at me. "It's been three years."

"He was your brother."

He shrugged. "Sudama was mean to me. Come on, we have stuff to do."

The first thing you saw when you walked into Yan's apartment was a tacked-up poster of a sneaker print in gray dirt. Yan claimed it was a picture of a bootprint on the moon. And maybe it was, but pre-Changers were always whining so much about it—We went to the moon and now look at us!—that it was hard to be impressed.

Yan slept in the small livingroom. The bedroom was a workroom full of things I couldn't quite imagine working. Models of wasplike metal airplanes that made war on people and cities and other planes. Containers the size of gumsticks that had supposedly held libraries of books and weeks of music. Cellphones with tiny gray glass squares that had contained moving pictures. Shiny rainbow mobiles of compact discs. A picture of a treelike cloud above a desert that Yan claimed was an entire city or something blowing up. A structure the size of a building erupting in flame at the bottom. Square machines on steel wheels scraping at red dirt. Enormous ships that held more warplanes. Tiny cylinders that had shone light bright enough to see for miles that supposedly could cut through metal. And even more stuff whose purpose was unimaginable to me. Pre-Changers had liked things really big and really small.

Yan's workroom stank of potions gone wrong. The carpet had got so freckled with burn marks and spill stains that Yan and I tore it out and refinished the wood beneath, good oak that by now had acquired its own share of burnmarks, stains, and pentagram traces. The desk and bookcase were piled with catalogs from department stores and electronics sellers.

Yan lit a lamp off an incense stick he'd brought from his parents' and yellow light reflected from dozens of shapes scattered around the room like eyes in a storybook forest. Yan turned the lamp up and the room glittered with familiar shapes made strange by being mirrored. Baby dolls, Barbie dolls, buttons, boxes, frogs, all reflecting themselves and us in recursive distortions that made you feel funny if you stared at them long enough.

The frogs creeped me out the most. Goggle-eyed and veiny, perfect down to the smallest wart. Their eyes reflected everything and held nothing. And they would do so forever. Yan called them sacrifices in the name of the New Science. I was so uncomfortable with the idea that I had threatened to walk out on our research if we used any more live subjects, and Yan had finally relented.

Yan opened the windows and the ocean got louder and cool salt air blew in. We sat on swiveling office chairs near the window. Silvered frogs of several sizes glinted moonlight on the sill. I picked one up. It was the size of my fist. African toads, my father had said; they'd been dying out before the Change. Maybe so but they'd recovered to a fault. Nighttime was deafening because of the big ugly bastards. Them and everything else that hooted, howled, croaked, chirped, barked, roared, bugled, or screamed.

My head reflected flat across the big frog's wide mouth, tiny in its bulging eyes. "Poor Froggum," I told it. "All alone in the dark."

"Fred," Yan said, "it isn't in the dark."

"Light won't get in there. That means it's dark."

"Time won't get in there either. So even if frogs could have a clue, that one never will. If we figure out how to cancel the stasis tomorrow or when we're eightyseven, no time at all will have gone by for him."

"If it's tomorrow at least his friends will still be the same age."

"Fred. It's a frog."

"What about gravity. What if he's all weightless in there."

He shook his head and smiled indulgently. "Same thing. There's no time, so if he's weightless it'll never affect him. He won't experience anything because he's cut off from any kind of experience we can measure."

"How about ones we can't."

The smile became a smirk. "You don't know it Freddum but that question was quite a big deal in the old physics. They could only observe by interfering, which wasn't really observing at all. It made them nuts."

"From what your dad says they interfered with everything and they already were nuts. I don't know why you're so in love with them."

"They figured out a lot more about their world than we've bothered to learn about ours."

"They had a lot more time than we have."

"True. But that's why we're doing all this, isn't it. To figure out how it all works now. To be the New Scientists."

I nodded. Magic wasn't science yet. That was why it was so hard to learn, why spells were so hard to duplicate, why so many people made so many tragic and comical mistakes. Casting in the dark. No one was making any kind of organized investigation of it. How it worked. Why it worked. Most casters just learned by rote and taught the same way. They didn't question, didn't innovate, didn't like to share their secrets or the ways they'd learned them. The only reason Paypay'd taken me on at all was because Casey Yu, his first apprentice, had run off to Los Angeles with the Harpers' oldest girl, Aymee.

Yan had set us on the path to understanding the how and why of casting. He wanted to apply those newfound principles and sell tons of products and live like a king. Or like kings were supposed to have lived. If we did I was all for it, but if we didn't I was fine with just knowing.

Stasis spells were our first big project. Our goal was simple: figure out how to open one. Once we did we'd get all kinds of attention and make a name for ourselves and acquire fundamental knowledge no one else had. Our ingenious scheme had only one major obstacle: since the beginning of time no one had ever undone a stasis spell.

Things in stasis are mirrored because they reflect absolutely everything. Light, sound, heat, gravity, time, inertia, magic—nothing can get through. The object is cut off from the universe. So any casting meant to undo a stasis spell just comes whizzing back at you or goes into the neighbor's roses or heads for Jupiter or into the nearest coyote.

Yan was certain we would figure out a way around this. He believed the solution would prove as simple as the stasis spell itself. So far his certainty was all we had to go on. The whole point of putting a stasis spell on something was to make sure that nothing, no force in the universe, including your own magic, could get to it from then on. The casting itself was simple but rarely performed because it was unchangeable and irreversible and fundamentally useless except maybe as a very labor-intensive weapon. Casters weren't organized but they did have some consensual taboos. Don't mess with the power found in death and dying. Don't summon anything you can't banish. Don't screw around with stasis spells.

We thought undoing a stasis was a worthy project. Which was why Yan's workroom was littered with spotless mirrored Barbie dolls and toy soldiers and pencils and coffee cups and infinitely patient African frogs all reflecting each other in infinite reduction.

Yan had libbed a portable wipeboard from some real estate office and set it up opposite the big french windows in his workroom. He used it to work out castings, a trick he'd learned from the science books he devoured. For a couple of hours we wrote stasis-spell variations on the board and took them apart and put them back together. Like unicorn charms by now I could write stasis spells in my sleep.

We broke once for coffee and went at it a while longer, until moonset made me realize how late it had gotten and I told Yan I had to go. My father was going to be so pissed.

I picked up Froggum again and tapped his head. "I'm afraid you're gonna be a reflecty frog a while longer, bud."

"We'll break it," Yan said.

I held the frog away from him. "You wouldn't dare."

"The spell, Fred. We'll break the spell."

"Sure."

Yan walked me downstairs and through the nightblacked lobby. The marine layer had moved onshore and the night was chill. We listened to the great frog congregation around us. "You can stay," Yan said.

"I've gone home this late plenty of times. I'm more worried about my father than anything else."

He started to say something but seemed to change his mind. I didn't press. My father was something of an issue for just about everybody.

We kissed goodnight and I started away and then felt something in my hoodie pouch. "Forgot to give this to you," I called to Yan and underhanded it to him.

He caught it and frowned and turned the foil wrapper in his hand and suddenly grinned.

"Save a bite for Nan," I said and went my homeward way.

The frogs were holding a vibe of their own in the hills. I was cold but didn't put my hood up because I wanted to listen unobstructed. The marine layer now was thick and general and the cold night grayed and damp. Everything changes when the sun goes down and the air grows thick and moves like specters round you turning all the decomposing cars to crouching waiting shapes containing who knew what within the subtle eddies. It didn't help that some of them could be crouching shapes waiting. The tricks imagination plays are nothing next to those the world performs.

The booming surf receded as I walked uphill from Yan's and crossed the old Pacific Coast Highway with rollerblades across one shoulder banging time with my walk. I knew that road like it had been tattooed on my eyes but there was no way I was blading home in this soup.

Farther on I decided to bypass the Interstate 5 onramp and get onto the freeway by walking up the embankment. My shins got soaked from trampling the waist-high grass. The nightsounds faded as the fog grew thicker until all I heard was the strange ringing night mist seems to bring with it, a distant tinkling not quite heard but somehow sensed.

I stepped over the concrete retainer wall and onto the freeway.

Home was only a mile inland but distances get longer in the dark. Large shapes thickened from the mist as I advanced. Cars and trucks and SUVs. I could always sleep in one if I really felt caught out. My father would be worried though. Or angry. They showed up about the same in him.

Not that he didn't have good reason to be either. Wayward Son had stayed out far later than was sensible and was moving between the ordered cars stopped inexplicably and forever in their crumbling treegrown lanes, hoping nothing would rob him or eat him or take his parts home to the family. Right now Wayward Son was cold and trying to breathe quietly and tell himself that what he heard behind him and to the right wasn't footsteps.

Wayward Son's unwayward father lived by his sword, ate by his sword, slept by his sword, and would probably die by it. It was a pre-Changer thing. Wayward Son himself felt there was a better way to go through the world than by wearing your fear in a scabbard for all the diminished world to see, so Wayward Son didn't carry weapons. He spent his days making unicorn charms and healing vases. Maybe if a hyena attacked him he could send it to Dr. Ramchandani.

At the foggy moment Wayward Son was coming up on a van with peeling vinyl decals. Like nearly every other car in the world it was covered in birdshit and its tires were dryrotted and its windows and lights were busted out. For all that Wayward Son knew he himself had busted them out years ago. Like nearly every other boy in the world. Wayward Son walked casually till he passed the van then stepped in front of it and squatted. His ears would have gone flat to his head if they'd been able to.

Crouched before the cockeyed van I listened for footsteps, breathing, growls, skate wheels, hooves, claws, whatever. After a few minutes I decided I'd been hearing things or that if I really had heard something it wasn't anything threatening. Cockroaches probably sound loud on foggy nights.

I stood and stepped away from the van and nearly ran into the dark shape of a man who stood there waiting for me. I said gaah and jumped back. He didn't move at all. Moonlight glimmered on curved metal in front of him. There came a small cough I knew quite well and my father resolved from the fog. "Thought it was you," he said, and sheathed his sword.

THREE

People who remember the Change are different. There's something in their eyes. The things they had to witness or endure or commit just to stay alive. For each of them a day had come when everything they knew about the world and how it worked was suddenly horribly wrong. And there was no going back.

They tend to look hard and lined and worn. They share a tacit misery. You feel it when they get together. Which they don't do all that often, unlike my generation who pile on each other like blind bunnies as my father once complained. And that it was a complaint was telling.

Recoverable tragedies can knit communities tighter. I've seen it happen after earthquakes, stormfloods, fires. But the Change was irrevocable as far as they knew and its first citizens had wandered its still and depopulate realms like wraiths.

But however they handled the memory of their lost world now—mourning it, forsaking it, grieving and then coping—the awful meridian of that transmuting day and its ensuing chaos still abided in their eyes.

———

Apparently my father'd had it pretty rough when the Change occurred. He didn't talk about it much—he didn't talk about anything much—but over the years I'd pieced some things together. He'd lived on the east coast. When it happened he'd been younger than I am. He'd lost his mother, his brother, his friends. Not uncommon for those days.

He had wandered. He was attacked, beaten, robbed. He'd fought to protect himself and even killed. He'd come out west. I don't know why he'd thought California would be any different. People still jacked each other for their food or for their squats or for no reason at all. Animals that had escaped from zoos and adapted and bred still hunted in packs. Supernatural creatures showed up and wreaked havoc.

I don't think my father had been alone when he'd headed out. Whoever she was it hadn't lasted and, big surprise here, he didn't like to talk about it.

It took him well over a year to reach the west coast. He stayed away from cities and people whenever possible. How he managed to meet my mother is anyone's guess. But meet they did and I was a result and a few years after that Mom got sick and died. I have memories that might be her but I'm not real sure. I hope they are.

After he met Mom my father tried to become a farmer but it didn't take. I remember a little fenced yard of chickens. They were dirty and stupid and the rooster was scary and mean. One of my earliest clear memories is of looking up at a cow towering over me while Dad squatted next to it milking. Or trying to anyway. For all my father knew about cows it had been a bull and he'd only been making it happy.

My father told me he'd left farming because it wasn't good for me to grow up isolated. Maybe so but I also think he was lonely. Something he never would have admitted even if he'd realized it. In any case he'd turned the livestock loose and put me in a super deluxe baby stroller. He told me he'd come to the coast because he'd rather throw a hook in the water for dinner than plant seeds in the ground and wait half a year.

Beach communities had formed and thrived. Who doesn't want to live on the beach. In Del Mar we'd squatted a small house with a small yard in good shape about a mile inland and my father fixed it up. He said he didn't want the hassle of living on the beach. For years I assumed he meant the repair and maintenance but after Dr. Ram told me about what happened to the Hendricks I wondered if he'd been worried about something like that as well.

So I grew up in the ocean community of Del Mar. Warm and pleasant and easy and beautiful. Sheltered.

The northern boundary of my childhood forays was delimited by the canted rusting wreck of a supertanker that had careened on Carlsbad Beach in Encinitas decades ago. Drowned corpse of some foundered god. When I was ten a group of us kids went exploring in it despite being strictly forbidden to. Or maybe because of that. The inside was a cramped dark slanting metal maze above a manmade grotto slick with algae dank with water rank with oil. And inhabited. Squatters lived in its tilted upper decks, skinny Asians in ragged clothes fishing off the sides and for all I know eating kids too stupid to keep out. When we saw them we fled screaming and laughing. They cursed us in some catlike language and threw things as we splashed into the water and slogged ashore. Yan claimed they were the tanker's original crew or descended from them. I never went back there but its iron corpse loomed throughout my childhood like a haunted house, the way the concrete vastness of the Del Mar racetrack dominated it like a storybook castle.

Our lives were governed by the ocean, by the shore.

Strange things washed ashore sometimes. Giant nets and thick cables, countless plastic bottles and saltpolished wood, bottle glass and airline seat cushions, rusting drums of industrial chemicals, carcasses of sea serpents, one time a rotting mansized mass some people claimed was a mermaid though I never saw it and can't say either way.

Summers were social and soft and easy. In June families would load picnic backpacks and head for the cliffs at Seagrove Park to watch the sea serpents mating. Huge as railroad tunnels and equally improbable there in the crumpled bright water with scales gleaming strawberry red tinged with vibrant yellow they fanned their parasol gills, dead-man's eyes and built-in leers giving them permanent expressions of goofy fanged delight. A quartermile offshore the males would rear and hiss and bite each other, churning the water and getting knotted as a ball of rubber bands and then sorting themselves out and starting all over again.

Some of the older adults were uncomfortable with us kids watching because sea serpents were big and scary and new—they hadn't existed when our parents were kids—and they were having sex after all. Though how you could tell in all that thrashing I don't know.

One time my father told me sea serpents were clearly related to dragons, and Mr. Binauer, who ran the Stopon Inn—really just a bar he ran out of what was left of the L'Auberge hotel—asked How the hell do you know and my father said Because I killed one once and that shut him up even though I don't think he believed him. And maybe he shouldn't have. Sometimes Dad just wanted people to shut the hell up.

After mating season there was usually a corpse or two washed ashore. That was bad. You couldn't eat the meat—it wasn't poisonous, it just tasted awful—so the corpses would just lie there festering and swelling and attracting dogs and clouds of birds and flies. They were too big to move and sometimes they bloated up until they popped like some kind of monstrous zit that sent rotting meat and guts flying fifty feet in all directions. But at least after they popped you could get rid of most of the corpse. Sometimes they just kind of deflated. The smell was unbelievable. I mean you could smell it half a mile away. They rotted fast after that but most Julys I was actually glad I didn't live near the beach.

Despite this a lot of adults and older kids would surf, which I thought of as a beautiful but complicated form of suicide. Why not just tie a rope to a big hook and put it through yourself.

Winters were gray whale migrations. Hundreds of them ancient and unknowable swimming out there off the coast. My father said they had almost all died out before the Change, killed off by hunters, by getting tangled in discarded fishing nets, by industrial chemicals in the water, by military experiments with underwater sound for some unfathomable reason. All of this was hard to imagine especially when you saw those dark encrusted backs break surface and spout, little geysers on tiny islands. Mr. Binauer once said They look like living submarines and I asked What's a submarine and the look he gave my father was a combination of pity and contempt us kids had seen so many times we really didn't see it anymore. It said You haven't been teaching him. My father had nodded toward the water and said to me but so Mr. Binauer could hear, "Subs were big warships, Fred. They moved underwater and carried people and weapons. They're still out there too. The *Titanic* wreck. There's still satellites up there looking down at us and up at the stars. A space station. Pioneer Ten, Voyager, Hubble, Mars rovers, Saturn probes. Who knows what else. All our teevee shows still spreading out among the stars. The Mona Lisa covered with fungus."

The Binauers left soon afterward. So did a few others. My dad the buzzkill.

One December when I was seven we were up at Seagrove with some other families, wrapped against the cold and eating smooshed chunks of Mrs. Halobagian's flatbread spread with Mr. Fayelle's honey, leaning into erratic gusts of chilly offshore breeze. Dad wore his sword of course. Older people found it hard to leave the house unarmed. Someone had got hold of a baby Salamander and us kids chased it and shrieked when it shocked our hands trying to burn us with a ferocious power it would not possess until it reached adulthood. The Salamander was hard to hold onto. Slippery and elusive and not quite really there it seemed, and it moved in quick small random hops that sent us bounding after it and often crashing into one another. The adults watched us in much the same way they watched the whales. As if we were aliens. Well we were. We had grown up on a different world.

I had been catching my breath between rounds while the Salamander regenerated, changing colors in the grass. Out on the dark ocean a whale surged up between its fellow travelers and slapped down hard on the water. The splash was enormous. The whale sank slowly until its tail flukes upended. "Dad, look," I yelled. "It's doing a headstand."

"So I see."

I tried to do a headstand and kick my feet like tail flukes and I fell over. "Whales are cool," I said.

"Whales are way cool," my father said. "They did me a big favor once."

"They help you kill that dragon?" Mr. Binauer asked, and a couple of grownups turned away so my father couldn't see them trying not to laugh.

"Dragon was already dead," my father said.

I sat up in the grass and looked at him, certain he was pulling my leg. He liked to deadpan ridiculous statements and he was very good at it. But whatever I was going to ask or say was lost in my startlement. Mr. Binauer was looking away in sudden awkward embarrassment and my father's eyes were bright with heldback tears.

Then the Salamander regenerated and turned yellow-white again and Casey Yu got hold of it and yelped when it shocked him. He wrung his hand and the Salamander squirmed loose and jumped my way and we were off again. I got too close to the cliff edge and my father yelled at me and I forgot about whales and favors and bounding after baby Salamanders for a decade, until I wrote this down just now.

FOUR

Mist ebbed around me and my father as we walked home on the freeway. He was okay with walking along in awkward silence but I wasn't.

"Sorry I'm late." My voice strangely flat in the fog.

His only reply was a grunt. He was probably annoyed at me for talking. Enemies in the Fog, Fred.

"You eat," he finally asked. Quietly.

"The Ramchandanis fed me."

"You shouldn't eat there so much."

"Dr. Ram likes having me over. And it makes it easier on you."

He stopped beside me.

"What?"

He started walking again. "Raj works hard for his food," he said.

At home he put his sword on its stand by the front door and lit lamps and checked all the rooms. When he was satisfied we weren't going to be savaged by hiding werewolves he set a lantern on a shelf and turned it up high and sat in his chair and picked up a book from the stack beside it and started reading. And there I knew went the rest of his night.

Books were my father's living and luxury. Our place was littered with them. He used books as bookmarks. Every weekend he pushed a shopping cart full of liberated books to the swap meet to trade with other book nuts, most of them pre-Changers. While everyone else bartered bread and eggs and poultry and fish, veggies and spices and fruits and herbs, dubious medicines and debatable remedies and dodgy canned foods, coffee and chocolate and booze and pot and jams and colored rock candy, a few men and women with a certain hungry look clustered around my father's table to haggle over books. A lot of them like Mrs. Cowardan wore taped and beatup glasses. They spoke well but were hard to understand. They dealt with my father because books on gardening, farming, metalwork, canning, preserving, hunting, trapping, carpentry, husbandry, and repair were either moldering in bookstores and libraries or long gone from them.

My father had a talent for finding books. He had long ago libbed the nearby libraries and stripmall bookshops and now ferreted out private collections in abandoned houses and storage bins and garages. So many had succumbed to mold and mildew and silverfish and rain. If you asked him where he found his books he'd just look back and grin. He had kind of a mean grin.

Rumor was his past was violent. He was awfully good with his sword and he kept it with him always. He never backed down and he wasn't afraid of anybody. I think a lot of people thought he was crazy. There was no shortage of crazy people around. People who never recovered from the Change or who grew up after it without any rules.

I didn't think my father was crazy. I think he just didn't like being around people. His every interaction seemed a kind of compromise. He relied on himself and didn't ask anything from anybody.

But oddly enough I also think he was lonely. If you gave him a warehouse full of books and a full larder and a chamber pot he'd be happy as a dog rolling around in something dead, but I suspect that sooner or later he would get a hankering to see some people. Even if it was just to have someone to argue with. Books were surrogate company. They were people without the messy parts. You're never alone with a book, he used to tell me.

Half the kids I knew could barely read. It was debatable how much they needed to. In my father's house it was a requirement, and though I'd felt like a total dork half the time I'd grown not only grateful I knew how but fairly enthusiastic about the whole thing. Besides the obvious advantage of knowing what was marked poison when you scrounged, the fact that I could write down castings in a grimoire and read from other grimoires as well as track my experiments with Yan was pretty valuable. But I regarded books themselves as mere notes in bottles from a sunken continent. Novels, biographies, sports, computer and science books? Long and boring epitaphs composed by the dead themselves.

Watching my father reading after our strained walk home I noticed that he held his book a lot closer to his face than I did. He looked tired. He kept himself in good shape—my arms would never have muscles like his and probably not scars like his either—but tonight he seemed kind of used up, like he hadn't been sleeping. There were circles under his eyes and his face seemed loose on its bones. I realized he was getting old.

He saw me studying him and shut his book around a paperback to mark his place. "Fred, I don't want you going back to Mr. Papadopoulos' shop for a while."

"Huh?" This had come out of nowhere. "How come."

"I need you to help out around here. This place is falling apart."

I couldn't believe what I was hearing. "So what. There's like ten thousand other places within a mile of here. Let's move to one of those."

"That's not the point."

I thought about what I was about to say and decided to say it anyway. "You just don't want me casting."

"I don't like you casting but I wouldn't stop you unless I thought it was getting out of hand. Mr. Papadopoulos doesn't think taking a hiatus will—"

"You talked to Paypay about this?"

"He says it won't hurt you to take some time off and he can run the shop without you."

"Paypay said that? I don't believe it."

"Don't call me a liar, Fred."

"But I don't understand. Paypay wouldn't—" I took a deep breath and changed my tone. "I can't see Paypay saying that. I help him out a lot. He likes teaching me."

"He does. He says you're a good student and a fast learner. Maybe too fast."

"What's that supposed to mean."

"He's concerned about some things he's seen. So am I."

"What things. Come on, Dad, if I'm supposed to quit casting I should at least know why."

"Fair enough." He set his book back on the stack and leaned forward in his chair. His head went in front of the lantern and I couldn't see his face. "Paypay says it's become obvious you're learning casting from someone else." He held up a hand. "He knows you wouldn't go to a competitor. Not that he really has one here. But he also knows, and so do I, that you're smart and young and impatient and you tend to go off halfcocked."

"I don't know what halfcocked means."

"It means you try to do things before you're really ready for them. Mr. Papadopoulos doesn't approve of the direction some of that is going. Frankly I don't either."

"What direction."

"It just seems clear that you boys are getting ahead of yourselves."

"You mean me and Yan."

"I do."

"Dad, Paypay can't afford to take Yan on as an apprentice, so I'm teaching him what I learn. What's wrong with that."

"I'm not worried about what you've been teaching him."

"Then what?"

He held out my grimoire.

"Son of a bitch."

My father raised a split eyebrow. "Come again?"

"You read my grimoire?" Never mind that I'd put a binding charm on it that should have kept him from being able to even open it; I was so insanely angry at the sheer betrayal, the utter breach of my father holding my most private book in his hand, that I couldn't think straight. "How would you like it if I read your journal."

"I don't keep a journal, Fred, but that's not what we're—"

"You don't keep a journal." I went into his room and got it from under his pillow and came back holding it up. "What's this, *The Three Musketeers*?"

"Put it away, Fred."

But there was no stopping me now. "I wonder what it says. I'll bet it's more interesting than some stupid apprentice caster's spellbook. What do you think." I started to open his journal and got my next big jolt: it was spellbound too. I gaped at him.

"We're not talking about what I've written and what I've done," he said. "We're talking about what you're trying to do. I have a duty to keep you from getting into certain kinds of trouble."

"What trouble. We're just trying to learn things Paypay's going to end up teaching me anyhow."

"Really." He held out my grimoire and made the correct pass over it and said *inexpugnabilis est*. And opened it easy as you please.

You can go crazy without a sound. Without a motion. I crossed that line so easily I didn't even know it was there until much later when it was well behind me and there was no going back. I held out my father's journal and passed three fingers over it in an outward spiral and said *erumpo liber* and it opened up.

He didn't knock the crap out of me, didn't knock his book from my hand. He did something worse. He looked down at my grimoire and started reading out loud. "Yan says yearling blood but how will we know. Any older deer blood should work just fine for pentagrams. I'm sure as shit not going out hunting a young deer and definitely not going to cut its throat and carry its blood around in some old bottle. Maybe from the swap meet? Plenty of deermeat there. Like whatever we Summon is going to know the difference or care." He looked up.

Screw it. I began blindly thumbing through his journal. My own name caught my eye and I stopped. Sure, let's give this one a try. "I know it ought to make me feel closer to Fred," I read aloud, "but it doesn't. It only pushes me further away. He looks so much like her. She's gone but there she is, her ghost on my son's face. It reminds me of too many things I've lost. I want the past to stay in the past. It isn't—"

"Fred."

"It isn't his fault but I still resent it and I resent him and I hate myself for it. My mind knows Fred didn't—" I looked up at him. His look said don't do it, don't go on. I looked back down. "My mind knows Fred didn't mean to kill her. But my heart knows she's just as dead regardless and every day I have to see her face in the person who took her from me. I know it isn't right. Fred lost her too. But there it is and it won't go away. Some days when he's off at Paypay's I tell myself I could just leave. Fred's nearly grown. Older than I was when I got left on my own. He'd be fine. Probably relieved. It would be so easy. Just leave and don't look back. A part of me loathes myself because I know I'm capable of it. Because I've done it before. Because I might yet."

I looked up from the journal.

"So now I guess we both know," my father said, "why people keep secrets."

"I guess we do." My voice sounded odd. I was shaking. I wanted to ask about what I'd just read but no way was I going to give him the satisfaction.

"Fred, it's not what you—"

This time I held up a hand to stop him. "I'll save you the trouble. I'll leave. In fact I'll be happy to." And I did.

FIVE

found a sleeping bag in back of a camper van and tried to sleep in back of an SUV but the fight with my father kept replaying itself in my mind. It had been brewing for a while I suppose but did it have to boil over like that?

Okay so he'd read that we'd planned a Summoning. What he hadn't known was that I didn't date my entries, since half the time who knows what day it is much less the date, and that entry was over a year old. We'd decided against the Summoning long ago when we became obsessed with creating a reversible stasis spell. But that wasn't why I couldn't sleep.

So Paypay didn't like the things I was learning with Yan. But the only stuff of ours I'd used at the shop was shortcuts and timesavers, nothing wrong or dark or god forbid competitive. More likely Paypay had figured out I was teaching Yan and was annoyed because he wasn't getting anything out of it. Which come to think of it didn't seem unreasonable. It was a pretty good deal for Yan, who got to learn what I learned without having to pay my dues. But that wasn't why I couldn't sleep.

So my father wanted me to quit learning casting. Okay, he had his own reasons not to like casters. Fine. But what I was learning would shape the rest of my life. And the important word there was *my*. But that wasn't why I couldn't sleep.

Cars had controls that said HEATER. You'd pushed a button and it made you warm. That would've been nice. Even with a sleeping bag and my clothes I was chilly in back of the SUV. The night was quiet. The mist and cold had even kept the coyotes and dogpacks and hyenas off the prowl. There was ringing fog and croaking frogs and chirping crickets and nothing else. But that wasn't why I couldn't sleep.

My mind knows Fred didn't mean to kill her. That was why I couldn't sleep.

Almost everything I knew about my mom I learned from my father. Including what she looked like. I had a few memories but I wasn't sure how much they reflected the reality. I remember her holding me. Waking up as she carried me off to bed. I can almost hear her voice, like a call still echoing in a room someone has left. I think she liked to sing.

She died when I was four. All my father ever said about it was that she got sick and it happened fast and he couldn't do anything about it. We were living on the farm back then, no doctors or wiccans or midwives around, and most of the old drugs and antibiotics had gone bad a long time ago. Mom had gotten sick and my father couldn't help her and she died.

My father gave up the farm soon after that. We came here to Del Mar but my father brought with him the most unavoidable reminder of his dead wife there could be: me.

That cold night inside a thin sleeping bag in back of a weathered windowless and rusting Chevy Tahoe dead for nearly thirty years was one of the longest nights of my life. My father thought I'd killed my mother. I'd been four years old for god's sake.

I must have gotten sick and Mom had caught it from me and I got over it but she died. Would my father really blame me for making Mom sick?

Maybe not in his mind. But in his heart he did. He'd written as much.

First light found me bleary and aching. The freeway that had seemed so ominous last night was a harmless weedgrown ruin strewn with useless rusting carapaces and stubborn trees.

I drew the sleeping bag around me and got out of the car. The marine layer was burning off but the day wouldn't warm up for a while. I hadn't thought to bring my blades last night and I'd have to hike to the shop.

I stretched and yawned and wondered how I'd scrounge up breakfast. Then I stopped in midyawn. It occurred to me that I would have to scrounge up breakfast for the rest of my life. I shrugged and set out for Paypay's.

Which wasn't open yet but I had a key. In a world where you can lib a lot of what you need, a lot of people don't bother to lock up. Other than perishables what people trade for is services. Hard to steal services.

But casters don't like sharing their trade secrets and some ingredients are quite hardwon. Paypay locked the old iron security gate over the door and slept in back of the shop. The place was in an old pedestrian mall off what was left of the Coast Highway. The counter and cash register were still there and a big plateglass window that got west light. Mornings the room was dark and cold, afternoons bright and hot. Before the Change the shop had been a music store. That is it had sold objects that contained music. Grooved vinyl platters and smaller compact discs. These were mirrored and shiny like some kind of stasis spells that contained music and let it out when you—

I stopped with my key halfway to the lock. Stasis spells. That held music. What if. What if. I stared at the key. It had been right there, my mind had touched the answer Yan and I needed. What had it been.

I shrugged. It would come to me or it wouldn't.

Then I tried to unlock the gate and my key wouldn't work. I don't mean that Paypay had changed locks, I mean my key would not go in the thing. Every time I tried it deflected like opposing magnets. Paypay had charmed the lock.

I put the key back in my pocket and stared at the gate lock. How much effort would Paypay take to charm his store lock. I should just lib a pair of boltcutters and open it. Cast this, motherfucker.

Screw that. I'd rather beat him on his own turf.

Paypay was righthanded. I'd watched him work castings for the better part of a year and I knew his habits and patterns. I moved my right hand around the lock and said *ex obfirmo*. I got it on the third try.

And was halfway into the dim shop before it occurred to me to wonder what exactly I was going to do now. Start work? I'd broken in, for god's sake.

In the doorway I hesitated. First my father wants me to take an open-ended break from my apprenticeship. Then he says Paypay doesn't like my extracurricular learning. Then I show up for work and the lock is charmed against my key. What do you want, Fred, writing in the sky.

And decided hell with it. If Paypay was going to fire me he would have to do it in person, not by charming locks against me.

I went into the gloomy shop.

Paypay sat on the counter in his ratty L'Auberge hotel bathrobe. He must have heard the gate rattle open. Something glinted in his hand and I thought he was about to put the whammy on me but it shifted and I saw he was holding an aluminum baseball bat. I was relieved and then suddenly wary again. You can put a most prodigious whammy on someone with a baseball bat.

"Paypay." Goddamn if my voice didn't crack. I just hate that.

"Fred." He didn't hop down from the counter. "Why you so early."

"I had a fight with my dad and I slept in a car. I woke up early so I came on in."

"You fight with you father?"

"Just an argument. Not, you know—" I held up my fists.

He shifted on the counter. The picture window faced west and most of the shop was dark. Paypay was mostly a big shape in the room. "You don't come here now," he said.

"You want me to come back in a few hours? Sure, I'll—"

"You don't come here now. Not in a few hours, not no more. You finish."

"Finished. Paypay, look—" I stepped forward and remembered the bat and stopped. "I don't know what my father told you but I haven't done anything, I'm not going to do anything. I just want to learn from you."

He unshouldered the bat and looked at it. "You don't learn from me only."

"I practice with Yan. What's wrong with that."

A fingernail rang the metal.

"I do everything you ask. I find herbs, I dry them, I grind them up, I make your potions and keep your books, I trade off with the Chandlers for your black candles. I do a ton of things you don't even notice, just to help—"

"I notice." He slid off the counter and propped the bat against it. I was relieved when he walked away from it. "Come here, Fred."

I didn't move. "Where."

I knew he was hurt by my suspicion. Yeah well you try getting locked out of your day job big guy. After a moment he shrugged and rummaged behind the counter and came out with something bright and metallic and I remembered having left it there just as he thumped it on the counter.

"You know what is here?"

"It's a frog in a stasis spell."

"Stasis spell." He snorted. "Listen Fred. You good helper. You listen. You learn. You do good casting. One day you be good caster." He held up a hand. "Already you are good. But good not good enough. You don't got gray hairs, you know? You in big hurry. Sixteen and you want make building fly, make earth shake. You play but you don't learn rules. You hurt somebody."

"I haven't hurt anybody. I'm not going to hurt anybody."

He looked at the mirrored frog.

"It isn't hurt. It'll be good as new when we unlock the stasis."

He made a brushing gesture. "Show."

"Okay, we don't know how yet. But we will."

He pointed at the frog. "What if it is boy. What if it is you. You fix then?"

"We'll reverse it."

He shook his head slowly. "This very bad, Fred. You don't do this things. You know? This things is very bad. Much I could fix for people with this spell but I don't. Caster don't do this spell."

"Why not. If we can fix it, what's wrong with it."

"We." He folded his arms and looked down at me.

I wanted to argue but I had said we, hadn't I.

Paypay jutted his jowly chin at the mirrored frog. "Spell is send him somewhere spell don't bring back. Spell don't work where he is."

"What if I promise not to do it again."

"You friend promise too?"

I hesitated. I knew Yan better than that. And suddenly I felt a defeat that was strangely calm, like a luffing sail turned suddenly out of the wind. "What do you want me to do."

He said one word and changed my life. But really my life had already changed. Was changed before the fight with my father. Was changed even before I started my apprenticeship. Was changed years ago when I became friends with Yanamandra Ramchandani.

"Go," he said.

I didn't argue. I left.

SIX

We bladed south on PCH, bent a little forward to offset our loaded packs. The pavement eroded by storms and cracked by decades of tremors and sprouted weeds and grass and trees. It wasn't too bad if you kept to the middle. Rough as it was the road was smooth as glass compared to the sidewalks and surface streets, which were potholed, overgrown, fragmented, storm-damaged, and pushed to crazy angles by earthquakes and tree roots.

Yan wouldn't tell me where we were headed and I kept my suspicions to myself. He kept up a constant chatter while we bladed. He didn't seem to need me beyond the occasional grunt or uh huh or oh really. Which was fine by me. I was nervous enough about the weight in my backpack. About what we'd done that afternoon.

It had felt weird to be home during the day. It had felt even weirder to be there while my father was gone. Yan kept glancing around and I realized he had never been there before. Come to think of it nobody had. My father didn't exactly encourage it. I'm not even sure anyone knew exactly where we lived.

Yan started to pick up one of my father's samurai swords—not the main one; that one never left my father's side—but I knocked his hand away. He looked surprised, even combative. "My dad's funny about people touching his swords," was all I said, and put the sword back on its stand.

Funny, yeah. I once saw him knock a guy six feet for touching the scabbard of his sword. He'd been cleaning the blade behind his folding table stacked with books at the swap meet. I'd never seen the guy before, some city scavenger who'd showed up to trade. A lined hard scarred and scary son of a bitch, but my father shot up and books scattered and the guy went flying like someone yanked him backward on a rope. He came up pissed-off blustering and ballfisted and nearly ran himself into the point of my father's sword suddenly leveled at his chest unwavering. All my father said was Please don't do that again and he sheathed the sword without looking and went back to sitting behind his table. I hadn't even seen him draw the thing. The guy had looked like he wanted to go after him anyway but Mr. Ripney put a hand on the guy's arm and shook his head just the smallest bit. The guy got tightfaced but backed off. My father wore a look of calm speculation like I don't want you to come after me but I kind of do.

In the livingroom Yan grinned at the main bookcase, which filled a wall. "My what a very lot of books."

"The ones we want aren't in here. We better hurry. If he finds us here he'll put our heads on broomhandles at the swap meet."

"No he won't."

I glanced at him. "You don't know him." I went into my father's bedroom.

"I'm not sure you do either, Fred." He opened his backpack as he followed me in.

Now we bladed past the Del Mar horsetrack where the swap meet was held every weekend. The old track so large and so present that it had become practically invisible to me. Ivy crawled its faded spanish style walls. I'd practically grown up inside them. Playing Stop the Zombie in its dim and rotting corridors. Scavenging its dilapidated rooms for anything interesting or useful though anything valuable had been libbed long ago. Tagging along with my father as he bartered books with neighbors and strangers on the concrete pavilion at the swap meet. It had been built to hold fifty thousand people. That was hard to believe. I didn't think there were that many people left on the west coast. Maybe even in North America. Even harder to imagine was that all those people had come here to watch horses run in circles. Such wealth and capability and insanity confounded me even while that wealth and capability and insanity loomed decaying and indisputable around me. As the pre-Changers themselves confounded me, and decayed.

South of the track the highway veered inland. The afternoon was gorgeous clear. Yan led us to the next exit ramp and down the long incline we squatted low and gave our legs and backs a rest and picked up speed with blades clattering rough asphalt. Ramps are cool.

At the end of the ramp a semi had been making a left turn for decades beneath a stoplight gibbeted on drooping wires. The truck's back gate stood open, the boxes inside long weathered to mush. A plastic bag read FROZEN PEAS. They used to turn food to ice so it would last longer. Why didn't they just eat it when they got it.

As we neared the ocean the road began to climb. We took off our blades and put on our shoes and slung our blades across our packs and marched up the rise.

A few optimistic surfers paddled out on the chop. Disconsolate seagulls pecked. On the beach something large glittered and moved. At first it looked like a man with huge translucent wings and then he squatted but the wings didn't move and I realized it was someone getting ready to windsurf. Probably Ron Golecki on one of his homemade boards.

Yan grinned and waved at the hopeful windsurfer and yelled Hey serpent bait. It was still eight months till serpent mating season but I agreed. There were things out there that would use you to pick other meals out of their teeth.

What houses hadn't burned up or slid down the hillside were weathered and rotting. Between them and the beach was a grassy berm inlaid with railroad tracks. We walked among them balancing on the crooked rails or walking through thick overgrowth and on the rotted crossties in between. Hard to imagine trains running along these rails. Hard to imagine trains at all. I'd seen pictures of them. They looked like one good push would send them over.

"Father says the whole country was covered with these," Yan said. "You could walk this thing all the way down to Mexico, or up to—to wherever it goes."

I stepped over a broken upthrust crosstie. "Why didn't they fly."

"Maybe there were things that were too heavy to fly."

"How could there be. I mean airplanes were too heavy to fly. If they could get those in the air they could lift anything."

"Seems reasonable."

A minute later I blurted, "Where were they all going."

"Who."

"People in trains. People in planes. What did they have to do a thousand miles away that they couldn't do down the street."

"Maybe they just liked going different places. The world is big, Freddum. Don't you want to see more of it. Cities and lakes and islands and canyons. Fly over mountains and through clouds. Look down on—I don't know. On everything."

Now this may sound strange but until that moment I'd had little desire to go anywhere or see anything. The part of the world I'd seen you could cover with your hand on a roadmap. The rest of the world existed in books and in stories the pre-Changers told, and they argued about those so much that you didn't know how much to believe. The world beyond Del Mar was an idea that lived in maps and fading pictures in musty books and the unreliable memories of old people.

But there really were manmade islands covered with buildings a quartermile high. Giant canyons. Skies that glowed in shimmering curtains. Dragons in the Appalachians. Continents of ice. All of it out there, really out there beyond the vanishing point of those barely visible iron rails.

Suddenly dizzy I grabbed Yan's shoulder and felt the strange mix of fear and challenge you get at the edge of a cliff. Yan turned to ask me what was up but stopped at the look on my face.

"I want to see where these tracks go. I want to fly. I want to—" I laughed "—to look down on things." It rushed in on me. The unexamined, unexplored possibility of my life. Of life itself. "I want to stand on a mountain. I want to go skimming down it."

"Skiing."

"Whatever. I want to see ice. Stand on it, eat it. You can eat it, right? I want to see one of those cloudscrapers. Maybe climb one. There's—there's. . . ." The entire rest of the world got caught in my throat.

Yan grinned. "You mean you don't want to be the best caster in all of Del Mar anymore?"

We were just north of La Jolla, farther south from Del Mar than I'd ever been. Maybe three miles. When the train tracks split we followed the inland set to a small railyard with a large aluminum shed with chainlocked sliding doors on either end. The tracks went right into the shed. Yan tried an unlocking spell but thirty years of weathering had fused and rusted enough metal that mere unlocking wasn't gonna do the trick.

A length of iron rebar did the trick.

We pushed the tall door aside and Yan marched into the shed and I followed. It was cool inside. After a minute my eyes adjusted and I realized there was a train car in the shed and that Yan stood by its opened doorway, arms folded and looking smug.

I trailed my fingers along the car as I headed toward Yan. It was big of course. Bare aluminum on the bottom third, blue and white paint scheme above. Other than the dust it looked brand-new. Even the windows were intact. Lettered toward the back was AMTRAK SURFLINER SLEEPING CAR.

In a patch of sunlight I looked at my palm dark gray with decades of dust. "This thing used to move?"

Yan grinned. "It's got wheels doesn't it."

The sleeping car had that odd and alien stillness that surrounds something not used in many years. Downstairs had closets for baggage and a shower and tiny bedrooms. Upstairs had larger better bedrooms that were still tiny. Two could be connected to make a kind of suite. The chairs unfolded into beds and trays unfolded over chairs to make a kind of desk. Bathrooms and a little coffee station. Large curtained windows. We opened the windows and doors and the seabreeze circulated and the huge metal thing felt almost homey.

"We could clear out some of the rooms," Yan said. "Get rid of the cobwebs and nests and take out a wall upstairs and make a workspace. Rig a cistern and gravity feed on top so the toilet will work. Even a solar shower. What do you think, Freddum. Train sweet train?"

"I think it's cool. But it's kind of far away."

He put his hands on his hips and smirked. "It is now."

SEVEN

"You ready?" Yan called down.

I looked up at the bright square of winter daylight in the ceiling where we'd removed the plastic skylight. "Ready as I'm gonna be."

Most of the floor space in the Surfliner's conjoined upstairs rooms was now a casting circle containing me and the miniature track we had meticulously built after several expeditions to the gloriously untouched Hobby Lobby. I knelt in front of the potion simmering in a saucepan over a folding campstove. Little plastic saucecups around it held ingredients. I closed my eyes and took a deep breath and felt myself fall from my self. Ready? Yes.

Into the potion went thick grease from the Surfliner's bearing case. I stirred the mixture with a stick until it started smoking. I held hand sinister palm-out and traced the pattern with hand dexter as I spoke the spell we had devised. I made the passes and stuck a paintbrush into the pan and picked up the model railcar. Yan had painted it to resemble the Surfliner, even lettering AMTRAK SURFLINER SLEEPING CAR on the sides. I coated it with the thick potion and turned off the propane burner under the campstove and set the sticky Surfliner Jr. in place on the miniature track. I put out hand sinister again and traced the final inverted cross with hand dexter and said *abjuro*. I squinted up at the bright skylight and yelled Hold on.

"What the hell else am I going to do," the voice came down.

I set my hand on the little train and moved it as slowly as I could. And caught my balance as the sleeper car around me lurched.

Three months of hard work. The first week we swept out cobwebs and wasp nests and packrat nests of shredded paper and fabric, scraped mold off walls and scrubbed and dusted everything several times. We made an upstairs bathroom and the downstairs shower operational. We tore out chairs and walls on the upper level to make a large central workroom. At first Yan went home in the late afternoons and I slept in one of the deluxe compartments but it wasn't practical for him to keep blading out every morning and he moved in with me. It was great having him there but privately I missed the hot breakfast and thermos of hot sweet chai he'd bring, compliments of Parmita.

We worked sixteen-hour days. At night I'd lie in my ingenious fold-down bunk and worry about the new path I was making for myself and think about the one I'd fled. We had big ideas and big plans for them. Why be mere casters competing with the Paypays of the world for the trade of a thousand Mrs. Glosters when we could be the New Scientists and delineate the New Science of casting.

The Surfliner came to embody that ambition. If we managed to move the massive railcar along the tracks to the Del Mar racetrack it wouldn't just become our home, shop, school, and laboratory. It would be a new thing on the landscape—something that didn't happen often in our world. Here for all to see would be our journeyman work, the shingle we hung out to announce that we had set up shop. If we didn't get killed doing it.

But we couldn't do a thing until the Surfliner was able to roll. In theory those cars were so well balanced and lubricated that two guys could push one along a level track. We tried it. Yeah right.

One day I was nosing around the repair shed and found big cans of thick and sludgy grease and I asked Yan what it had been used for. He said They probably packed bearings in it and we looked at each other. A forehead-slapping moment. We located the bearing cases in the Surfliner and spent an afternoon getting filthy up to our elbows repacking the bearings and slathering grease on anything that looked like it was supposed to turn or roll. And you know what? Two guys really can move one of those railcars. A couple dozen feet anyway.

So the Surfliner would roll. Now it needed something to roll on. Three miles of track between here and Del Mar racetrack were overgrown and offkilter. At one point a goddamn tree had grown between the canted rails.

We used up two drums of weedkiller until we actually read the labels and realized they'd long ago lost their potency. We thought about hoeing the whole mess down to the crossties. Then we said hell with it and dug a firebreak just south of the racetrack and poured drum after drum of gasoline along the tracks and burned that shit down.

Clearing it down to the crossties was still a pain in the ass. The crossties were in bad shape under that greenery, rotted by weather and splintered by branches. We hammered and pried for weeks and still I thought they looked pretty dodgy. "Not to worry, Fred," Yan said. "We only need them to work once."

"What do we do when the rails just slide aside as we plow down the track."

"We'll cross that bridge when we come to it."

I looked along the burned length of rickety track. "Or we won't."

So the Surfliner would roll and the track was cleared. Now all we needed was a spell that would move a ten-ton railroad car along three miles of decrepit track. We agreed that our casting should be based on a basic blunt-force spell. If you need to knock something down or get something going, blunt-force spells are your best friend.

Yan could theorize on a wipeboard forever but I needed things I could move around. Models. I'm limited like that. So I libbed a metal railroad set from the Hobby Lobby and set it up in our workroom and we tried scaled-down versions of blunt-force spells on it. Our first attempts knocked it ass over front off the track.

"Well," said Yan, "you said you wanted to fly."

We toned it down and tried again and it went over sideways on turn one. I pictured little Yans and little Freds jumping off to hit and roll in a forest of carpet.

Eventually I could get the model railcar as far as the backstretch. Anything harder just sent it off the rails on turn one, which was as far as Yan ever got. The problem was that the blunt-force spell was a single discharge of energy, a whack with a magical bat.

"We need to spread the force out somehow," Yan said after failure number twentyfive or so. "Keep it constant."

"It's called pushing."

"So we need a pushing spell."

I shrugged. "Don't know one. Never heard of one."

"So we need to invent one." He picked up the toy railcar and examined it. "I'm starting to think that intent plays a role in casting."

"I'm starting to think we should be carpenters. Any blunt-force spell strong enough to knock this thing from here to the racetrack is just gonna cause the first train derailment in like thirty years."

Yan drummed his fingers on the padded arm of one of the comfy passenger chairs we'd left bolted in. The afternoon was cloudy and the sunset looked promising. I was annoyed at being cooped up all day so I was taking it out on the model by pretending to push pins into it and imagining the big sleeper car shuddering and groaning around us.

Yan's fingers stopped drumming. "What are you doing."

"I'm punishing our sleeper car for not cooperating." I pushed in another imaginary pin. "Arrgh."

Yan sat up.

———

Now I moved the little car along the little track with all around me shrieking iron as the railcar lumbered groaning and unlikely from the workyard after nearly thirty years of silent stillness. I kept a hand on the floor and my mind on what I was doing. Intent. Focus. "You brain must be mirror," Paypay used to tell me. "You heart must be mirror." When you perform a casting you are just a conduit for forces in the universe, a lens for what's already there. You are its opportunity to manifest. Get in its way and you filter what comes through. The lens distorts the image. Take your self out of the picture, desire hope anger greed ego all of it, and it shines through. I knew this but it wasn't something you knew, it was something you did. It was hard for me to shut my brain up long enough for the universe to get through.

A loud cheer from up on the roof. Sitting lookout Yan had wind in his face and a stunning ocean view while I inched across the pitching floor in the smokey room pushing a little voodoo train along its little voodoo track. We'd lined sections of the model track with items from the areas they represented, sand and stones from beaches between here and Del Mar. At the far end of the track stood a faded picture of the Del Mar racetrack taken from a book. I was driving our railroad car along the tracks toward the real thing. Me, using magic on a model railroad car.

I curbed my sudden excitement. Make your mind a mirror. Full commitment, utter detachment. The little railcar wobbled and I caught myself with my free hand as the Surfliner gave a sudden lurch.

Yan banged the roof. "Easy, will ya."

"You all right?"

"Yeah. You?"

"Yeah."

"First bend coming up."

"Got it." Our sleeper car was on the only section of coastal track between here and Los Angeles with any appreciable curves. The worst were the one coming up and the last one just south of the racetrack. If we were going to derail those two spots were the most likely. If we got past these we had the rail bridge hard by the racetrack to worry about. It was made from the same thing as the crossties after all.

I had no idea how fast we were going. I'd never moved at more than twelve or fifteen miles an hour and I wasn't good at judging speed.

I guided us around the first curve and felt the little car push hard against my hand. Metal shrieked as we leaned out of the turn. Yan scrabbled overhead. I held on with both hands and kept us moving and tried to keep us from flying off. I imagined tiny casters inside the model railcar making tiny fools of their tiny selves as they tried to make their own fleasized railcar move along threadsized tracks.

Then we were out of the first curve and on a series of much gentler curves heading northwest. We'd picked a swap meet day for maximum exposure. If it went off right it would be glorious. If it went off wrong it would happen in front of pretty much everyone we knew.

The ride was rough. Downstairs things fell and clattered. The model railcar resisted as its huge imago forced its way over crossties uneven and rotted and barely holding the rusted iron rails above them. We were massive hurtling and rickety. The hardest part was keeping my hand steady while I crawled along the bucking floor. Any bump threatened to build into something Yan had called a feedback loop: I rock the model and the real train rocks and so I rock inside the real train and I jerk the model even more. Which jerks the real train even more. Which doesn't end up anywhere good.

Yan must have had a lot of faith in me because he'd let me handle all of it.

Above me I heard Last curve and I was startled. No way we had come most of three miles. I looked down the miniature tracks on the shaking floor. About a yard away the final curve. Sharp, northward, beachside, just south of the narrow railroad bridge between the racetrack and the beach. I took a deep breath and held it and forced my hand steady. My fingers were cramped and my arms were tired. The miniature's resistance and slow response reminded me of leaning into Mr. Villaraigosa's fishing boat to push it from its berth.

I let out the breath and pushed us into the turn. Metal screamed as twenty thousand pounds of train car leaned out of a sharp curve. The model railcar pressed against my hand. If I let go we would come off the rails in a large loud way. Full commitment, utter detachment. The train leaned and the wheels screamed and the walls thudded like something big demanding to be let in. Then the weight left my hand and we righted and the metal shriek subsided as we came out of the curve.

Yes! came from above.

I squinted up at the bright square of sky and replied Thank you god.

From there on it was a nice straight line toward the racetrack. We had walked it, sawed it, burned it, hoed it, poisoned it, and called it a lot of bad names. I had more faith in my sympathetic magic than I had in those rails.

"They see us," Yan yelled down. "They're coming to look."

I risked a glance out the window. The huge and vinespread grandstand was about half a mile ahead. Windowshards gleamed afternoon sun. The train tracks ran between the grandstand and the beach. You could see them from the grandstand and the field that had been the parking lot led right up to the railroad bridge. Two, three hundred people from communities as much as twenty miles away would see us coming.

"Fred, slow down."

I'd been running blind since we'd lurched out of the workyard but I didn't need to see where I was going, I needed to see where to stop. Yan was my eyes. He was the captain, or whatever you call a guy in charge of a train.

"Better?"

"Yes. Everyone's watching. I'm waving ba—"

We barreled onto the bridge and in my hand the little railcar seemed to buck. I checked an urge to yank my hand away or bat the train aside. Wouldn't that have been something.

Later people said it was the damnedest thing they ever saw. First someone yells Holy shit there's a train coming down the tracks. And sure enough a railcar with no locomotive comes swaying up the ruin of beachside tracks. Then people see Yanamandra Ramchandani riding on top of the thing. The railcar starts to slow down near the bridge but then it seems to hit a bump. Its wheels lock up. Metal tears and sparks fly and it screams and teeters onto the bridge and then stops right in the middle with startling suddenness as if it hits an invisible wall. Things inside it bang forward. One of them is me. Yan shoots off the roof and flips in midair, lands on his feet and rolls and stands upright on the tracks in the middle of the narrow bridge to face the gaping crowd.

I held onto Surfliner Jr. the whole time and I swear the model train pulled me forward about a foot and a half. I lay still for a moment and waited to hear more crashes and bangs and grinding metal. Nothing. Then I heard people yelling. I looked at the Surfliner Jr. My hand still clutched the top of it on its little track. I carefully let it go and held out palm sinister and opened the fingers of palm dexter like a flower and said *libero*. I hurried to the edge of the casting circle and scratched it in four equidistant places with an iron nail and went back to the model railcar. I hesitated and then flicked it with a fingernail. It tinged. The little car wobbled and the big car didn't.

"You okay?" I called up.

Nothing. Oh shit he's dead was my first thought. Fell off and got busted up on the tracks. Oh this is bad. Oh Yan don't be dead. I hurried downstairs and stopped halfway out the entrance when I saw we'd come to rest on the narrow railroad bridge. I held my breath and listened for creaking wood or groaning iron. Nothing. The bridge was holding. The rails were hot beneath me and hot metal air wafted from the undercarriage of the car.

The swap meet crowd reached the edge of the lot and came over the hedge fence to the railway embankment. They were cheering. I had never heard a large crowd cheer. I started to feel embarrassed and then I saw Yan standing in front of the Surfliner. Bowing before them and basking. Mrs. Rondomaki, Mr. Guevera, even Mr. Binauer. A few of the older people were crying. Mrs. Villaraigosa, at the meet to sell her husband's catch as always. Old Mr. Hayliss. People I'd known most of my life applauding and cheering.

My father was there. It was the first time I'd seen him since our argument. He wasn't cheering. Another still point in the surging crowd was Paypay. At the swap meet to buy herbs and ingredients for the shop. He stood at the back of the crowd like a somber graying bear just looking at me and Yan with great disappointment as if his worst expectations had just been confirmed before his veteran eyes.

I didn't have much time to dwell on it right then. I was beside Yan and the crowd flowed up the embankment and onto the bridge and started squeezing our arms and slapping our backs. We were heroes. Arrogant damnfools but heroes.

Yan grinned. "Take a bow, Fred."

I never did bow but it didn't matter. We were alive and nobody got hurt and our new home was parked on its new home, the narrow bridge between the racetrack and the ocean. We had arrived all right.

EIGHT

We set up shop. Yan had barely thrown his things into his sleeping compartment before he wanted to get right back to solving the stasis-spell problem. I insisted we get the Surfliner into shape first. A lot of things had shaken loose on the Voodoo Short Line and I wanted to make the place presentable. We needed a respectable place of business.

We also needed to eat. I wasn't an apprentice getting two meals a day anymore. My father wasn't going to bring home dinner he'd hunted or libbed or traded for. Without customers we could clean and paint and work on spells and watch the sunsets on the beach all we wanted, right up to the time we fell over from hunger. I was nobody's hunter or fisherman and neither was Yan.

At first Nan brought us charity baskets of Parmita's cooking, which I only later realized were also an excuse for her to visit me. I finally told her she was welcome anytime but she had to stop bringing food. "I can't keep living on your family's charity," I said. Yan looked at me like I'd grown horns. But in a sense living on their charity was exactly what I ended up doing because next time Nan came by she wasn't bearing a basket but an offer from her father.

"You young people are excellent at finding things," Dr. Ramchandani said when I asked what my new job was. His office was a former barbershop, sunny and clean and just down the hill from his family's apartment, and Dr. Ram served as a barber whenever anybody wanted. "I need herbs, medicines, plants, supplies. Sometimes I need a finger on a knot while I tighten it." He laughed. "You are not squeamish, are you."

It also meant trading with the coven living in the old youth hostel on Ocean Boulevard. They made good medicines, cheesecloth bags of roots, leaves, barks, flowers, mushrooms. Nectars from blooming plants picked at midnight by full moonlight and crushed in goatskull mortars by pestles made from condor thigh.

Dr. Ram said wiccans had once been kind of fringe, but with the Change their knowledge of medicines was suddenly much greater than his. He sent them pregnant women and infertile couples and women with severe menstrual cramps and they sent him swollen tonsils and broken bones and parasitic infections. He respected and appreciated the wiccans, even deferred to them. But I think the part of him that had gone to an expensive school for years to learn his trade was affronted by the effectiveness of what he'd been taught to regard as pure nonsense. It's hard to get past your training even when it's wrong. Especially when it's wrong. Funny enough it was Dr. Ramchandani who taught me that.

———

Most days Dr. Ramchandani let me off around lunchtime. He didn't care when I came in or how long I worked as long as I got things done. Those of his patients who paid him at all paid in food and staples, so I always had plenty of good food to take home in exchange for my services. Even coffee. A few people had tried shade-growing coffee, but Mrs. Ngokami was the only one who'd had any success. Her four kids and husband were regular patients and barber customers, and Dr. Ram was kept wellstocked with her latest roasts. Usually I drank coffee only when I was visiting the Ramchandanis, or those rare times when my father brought some home. Now that it didn't cost me a week of indentured servitude I developed a taste for it, which Dr. Ram seemed to find amusing.

I was blading home one clear cold bright blue cloudless early February afternoon with a backpack holding coffee beans and oranges and figs and a fresh loaf of Mrs. Halobagian's bread. A big flock of green parrots with yellow necks screamed overhead. I had a sudden impulse to stop by Paypay's shop. Curiosity? Gloating? In any case I rolled on by. And naturally as I did the bell clanged and the door opened and Paypay came out with a sage cigarette in one hand and a pushbroom in the other. He stopped when he saw me.

"Paypay."

He nodded and leaned the broom against the window. He was wearing his apron, which looked like something dragged by hyenas. He pulled on the handroll and breathed out smoke and looked at me pointedly.

"I was just going home." I indicated my backpack like I was offering proof. "To the train car. The one we moved. Me and Yan. By the racetrack."

His mouth worked and he turned his head and spat a fleck of tobacco.

"I'm working for Dr. Ramchandani."

He nodded slowly and flicked ash from his cigarette.

"I'm learning a lot about casting now too." It sounded pointed even to me. But I was on a roll now. "I'm getting really good. Yan and I are about to open our own shop."

He shrugged. "Is you business."

"We don't want to take anything away from you. Business, I mean. You know? We're going to do different things."

"Different already."

"You got another apprentice?"

He blew smoke. "Don't need."

"Good. That's great, Paypay. I'm glad things are going well." I indicated my pack again. "Well, I have to get home. Wish us luck."

"You talk to you dad."

"Have I talked to my dad? No, I—"

"You should. He come looking."

"He knows where I am."

He nodded again and finished his cigarette and then dropped it on the weedcracked pavement and ground it beneath his tennis shoe. "Everybody know," he said and picked up his broom.

"There were electric grinders before the Change," Yan said as I ground the beans in the mortar.

"Yan, there were electric pencils before the Change."

He laughed. "Electric pencil sharpeners anyway. And no they didn't sharpen electric pencils. They were electric devices that sharpened regular pencils."

I shook my head. Those people had been either unimaginably lazy or unbelievably pressed for time.

Yan nodded at the mortar and pestle. "But before they had electric grinders they used hand ones."

I set the pestle in the mortar and flapped my hands. "Why don't we get one of those then. This is like grinding pebbles."

"They don't work either. They had gears." He glanced into the mortar. "You don't have to make powder out of it, Fred. We're making coffee, not paint."

"I'm an overachiever."

"You've made too many potions for Paypay."

"Can't argue with that." I stared at the grounds. Dr. Ram had said Mrs. Ngokami divined with coffee grounds. He called it javamancy. But he'd been grinning when he said it. Still I wondered what Mrs. Ngokami would see in mine. "I saw him today. Paypay. On my way home."

"I'm sure he sends his love."

"It was awkward."

He took the pestle from me. "Well it can be very stressful to encounter the evidence of your mistakes."

"I wasn't a mistake."

"Firing you was."

"Oh."

He upended the ground coffee into a baggie and gathered the blankets and nodded for me to pick up the kettle and the thermos. The onshore breeze was starting up so I put on a hoodie but kept my cargo shorts on.

"You need to forget about Paypay, Freddum." Yan led the way out of the Surfliner. "He's the competition now."

"You shouldn't forget about your competition."

He glanced back at me. "True."

We rounded the railcar and headed up the dune toward the beach. I glanced back at the Surfliner and I stopped and said Hey Yan.

I heard him stop up the dune. After a moment he said Goodness.

The Surfliner's new paint and cleaned aluminum glowed in the late afternoon sunlight. The plastic windows shone. Its shadow stretched toward the grandstand rising across from the trampled lot. The grandstand's concrete walls shone pale yellow through the dark green twining vines. Myriad glass shards sparked in windowframes. Above the overgrown infield a wedge of starlings turned as one in the salt breeze.

Yan did not look away as he said, "Photographers used to call this magic hour."

I nodded. Sometimes magic's there already. You just have to look.

We'd set up a brazier on the beach between two chairs taken from the Surfliner. We spread a blanket on the cool sand before them and Yan got a fire going and set the kettle on the wire grill. I sat in my blue fabric chair gritty with sand and put my hands in my hoodie pocket. Offshore a bluegray wall of marine layer awaited nightfall before invading the land. I closed my eyes. Salt air. Pounding surf. Soon the hissing kettle. Yan took it from the grill and poured boiling water into the french press he'd screwed into the sand. He sat in his makeshift beach chair and kicked off his flip-flops and dug his dark feet into the sand. The onshore breeze grew chill as the sun went down.

A few minutes later I smelled coffee and opened my eyes. Yan was holding out the thermos cup. "First pour."

I accepted the cup and held it under my nose and breathed deep. "Smells like your mom and dad's place."

"Their place smells like nag champa."

"Yeah. But it also smells like coffee. It smells like home. But yours, not mine."

"Your father doesn't drink coffee?"

"He likes it but doesn't like to trade for it."

Yan poured coffee into a white cup that had a sun and CALIFORNIA printed on it in gold. He sat back in his Amtrak beach chair and sipped and nodded out to sea. "There's Mr. Vee."

I hooded my eyes and peered out across the water. Against the dull red blob of sun setting behind the marine layer was the telltale outline of Mr. Villaraigosa's sleek twomaster heading back to shore. "Out late. Wonder what he's caught."

"I've eaten more of that guy's fish." Yan shook his head and pulled a rubberbanded baggie from a pocket.

"Everyone has." I watched him unband the bag and unroll it. "You crewed for him didn't you."

He snorted. "Who hasn't."

"I only crewed for him a few weeks."

He fished a little book of papers out of the baggie and opened it. "How come."

"He found out I couldn't swim." I sipped coffee.

He turned from the wind and pulled a paper from the book and shook the baggie over the paper. "Everyone should be able to swim."

"Everyone should be able to fly too." I could feel the coffee waking me up. "This is really good."

"Doctors always get the good shit." He rolled the paper tight and got up and went to the brazier and held a stick to it and then held the stick to the roll in his mouth and snuffed the stick out in the sand. He pushed his chair closer to mine with his foot and sat down and threw the blanket over both of us and passed me the joint.

I coughed. "So they do." I handed it back.

"Father would rather have the coffee. It's more valuable anyhow."

"What's your problem with your dad, Yan."

"I might ask you the same thing."

"I don't have a problem with your dad."

"You have a problem with yours."

"Well yeah. Your dad's a standup guy. My dad's whacked."

"Your father is from the east coast."

"What, people from the east coast are whacked?"

"I don't know. I've never met another one. Not one who came here after the Change anyway. No one here has. Do you have any idea what it must have taken for him to get out here?"

"A year and a half. Something like that."

"Freddum I love you, but at times you can be awfully obtuse."

I shrugged. "I don't know much about any of that. My father doesn't talk about it."

"He doesn't have to. Everyone already knows about it."

"Knows about what."

He lowered his coffee cup. "You're kidding, right."

"Knows about what."

But Yan shook his head. "I'm not going to be the one to tell you."

"Tell me what. Damn, Yan—"

"I mean it, Fred. You should hear it from him. Or from Father. He knows the story better than I do. Him and your dad are old friends."

"They are?"

He laughed and pulled a paperclip from his pocket and fitted the roach onto it. "Does everyone in Del Mar know more about your father than you do? Your father and mine were really close friends years ago."

"What happened." I felt very conscious of the crashing of the waves, the way the sound sometimes spread left and right at the same time as they broke, the way if you shut your eyes and listened to that it felt like the world was getting wider.

"Nothing happened." Yan blinked. "They're still friends. Just not like before."

"You think that'll happen to us?"

"No way I'm going to be here twelve more years."

"I mean not staying best friends."

He put an arm on my arm under the blanket. "Fred Fred Fred. Friendships like ours are ordained. Don't you know that. We'll be connected our whole lives. We don't have a choice."

"We're friends whether we like it or not, huh."

He laughed and laid his head on my shoulder. "You are the world's innocent. It's why the girls all love you."

"Sure they do. Look, here they all come stampeding down the beach while I sit here with your head on my shoulder."

Suddenly he stood and threw off the blanket and pointed down at me. "What do you want, Fred. What."

"I want my blanket. What do you want."

"I want this." He pulled me to my feet and turned and kicked sand toward the waves, the rose patch of sun dissolving into gray. "All of it." Yan yelled at the ocean. He turned to me with hands on hips. Redeyed and wild, some skinny zealot returned from a wasteland to force baptisms on a foreign shore. "Why do you want to learn casting."

I took the roach from him and took the last hit and snubbed it out in the sand. "Because I like it."

"But why."

"Why do I like it or why do I want to learn it."

"What's the goddamn difference," he shouted over the waves. Suddenly he rushed me and tackled me. With his arms around me I couldn't catch myself as I fell backward and slammed my head on the hardpacked sand. "There's no difference, Fred," Yan yelled into my face. He stayed on top of me and propped up on his elbows. "You learn things so you can know how they work. You like them because you know how they work."

"I like you and I don't know how you work."

"You will like me less if you do." He laughed and kissed me and then pushed off me and stood facing the low gray wall advancing from the sea. I retrieved the blanket and shook it out and wrapped it around myself and stood next to him and held it out to cover both of us but he stepped away.

"I read," he said quite calmly, "that there is enough energy in one set of crashing waves to run an entire city for a day. One of the old cities." He turned and looked at me. "That's what I want."

"To run a city?"

"Yes. No. Crap. I don't know." He turned away from me again and pointed at the sea. "I want that. The power of those waves." Suddenly he made passes and yelled *confuto* and spray kicked off the crest of the nearest wave. I wouldn't have noticed it if I hadn't been looking where he pointed. He turned back to me. "I would like," he said in a clear and reasonable tone I found more unnerving than his zealot's stare, "to be able to stop every wave on the beach for just an hour."

"For what."

He looked at me. "Fred, don't you want to do something just to show you can do it. Don't you want to know how it all works. To know why you can say a word and wave your hand and light a stick on fire. That's what scientists used to do, you know. Figure out the laws that lay under everything. And then use them."

"To stop waves."

"Yes. You're joking but that's exactly what they used them for. They stopped the waves. They made lightning. They brought the sun into their houses. We could do that, Fred. If we found the patterns under it all. The new natural laws. We could fix the whole world."

"Not everybody believes it's broken, Yan."

"Really. Walk through a city with me. Go to Los Angeles, go to San Diego."

I shook my head. "They're changed. Changed isn't broken. Don't you listen when pre-Changers talk about it? It doesn't sound any better than this."

"They went to the moon."

"They used machines to sharpen pencils."

We stared at each other. I remember it not as an angry moment but a sad one. When my best friend became a stranger.

He tried another tack. "Fred, all those other casters. Those Paypays. They're just repeating what they learned from books and other people. They don't understand it any more than a dog does. But once you know how it works it isn't magic anymore. It's science. And you can apply it. You can change the world with it. Why else have we been doing all this."

"Let's go in. I'm getting cold."

We picked up the blanket and french press and thermos and walked in separate silence from the evercrashing waves. Before us on its slender bridge the sleeper car rested dim and strangely new, the grandstand behind it rising dark and familiar.

As we hiked up the berm toward the bridge Yan came up beside me and put an arm around me. "Doctors always get the good shit."

I laughed despite myself and he squeezed my shoulders and laughed with me and things were okay again for a while.

NINE

"Do you know what software was."

I looked up from my weighty copy of Blakely's *Charmes of the Antiente Wyrld*. "Sure. Computers used it. It was like fuel they burned so they could do . . . computer things."

Yan set his computer-programming book on the foldout tray of his chair and leaned forward. "Software was instructions in a madeup language that told a computer how to do things. There were different languages that did different things. But they had to be logical and consistent or the computer wouldn't work right."

"Okay." I looked back at my Blakely.

"What is casting, Fred. I mean at its most basic what is it."

I waggled my hand but did not look up from the book. "Ooh, I know this one. Casting is a process you go through to make magic happen. Potions, talismans, spells, gestures."

"It's a set of instructions. A madeup language that tells the universe how to do things."

"You think casting is like software."

"No. I think casting is software."

I marked my place in the Blakely and closed it and looked at him.

"What happens if you say a spell wrong. If you mispronounce a word, screw up the timing, forget a motion, say the wrong line."

"The spell doesn't work. If you're lucky."

He tapped the software book. "When they gave these programming languages to the computer, if they were written wrong the program didn't work. If they were lucky. Sometimes the computer got stuck. It was called a crash. Sometimes the computer worked wrong. Then they said it had a bug in it."

"A fly in the ointment."

"Exactly. Only the fly wasn't in the machine. It was in the language."

"And by some amazing accident the universe speaks casting language."

He smiled. "It's the other way around. By some amazing accident there's a language the universe responds to."

"That's quite a coincidence."

"But it's not really coincidence, it's opportunism. Look, did you ever use a magnifying glass to start a fire. Burn ants, maybe."

"Just for fires."

"So the universe lets light go through a lens and focus in a way that makes fire. Was the universe built so lenses could do this? Of course not. Its rules permit it, that's all. Those rules happen to favor lenses. We can take advantage of the rules and use lenses to make fire."

"So what's the lens for magic."

He sat back in his chair and folded his slim hands across his chest. "Language itself."

"Language. Language is a lens."

"Certain language. Certain words said certain ways. Just as certain lenses in certain shapes in certain circumstances make fire. You know in the old physics they'd started to think that observation and intent were real forces that influenced events."

"Intent again."

"Language communicates intent. Language is the lens. The thing the new laws permit to influence things."

"Software was a language for programming computers. Language is a lens for programming the universe." I bit my lip. I was on the edge of it. I could feel it. I could glimpse its edges. Flaws in the lens distort the image.

Yan's grin was a little scary. "Do you know what they did with those programs, Fred."

"They ran computers with them."

"They did. And they used the computers to run the world."

I remembered the light in his eyes that evening on the beach a week ago. "What if I don't want to run the world."

"But what if you didn't just know some of the words of the language that could run the world. What if you understood it. Had a grammar for it."

I shrugged. "Haven't thought that far."

"They had computer programs that recorded what you programmed and played it back when you pressed a button." He grinned. "Or said a word."

"How nice for them."

"What if you had a spell that could record spells and play them back whenever you wanted."

I tried to wrap my brain around the idea. "I could record a spell and then cast it later on by saying a word?"

"Later on, somewhere else, someone else can say the word and cast it." He waggled the book. "They called them macros."

"Software macro spells. Spellware."

He clapped his hands. "Spellware. Exactly. Yes." He jumped up and let his book thud onto the floor. He paced back and forth in the carpeted workroom, wildeyed and excited. "You see? You see it now?"

I hated to bring him back down to earth but he needed some kind of tether nailed to the real world. "It wouldn't work," I said.

He stopped. "What do you mean it wouldn't work. Why not."

"To record a unicorn-charm casting I'd have to perform a unicorn-charm casting."

"So."

"So that would make a unicorn charm. See. Performing a casting makes the casting happen. To record it you'd need something that would contain the energy as well. Like my thermos."

He cocked his head.

"I keep potions for unicorn charms in a thermos at Paypay's. So I don't have to keep making them every time."

"My clever Freddum." He picked up Froggum and looked at his gleaming warty surface. "So you'd need to contain the macro spell in some kind of bottle."

"Yeah. Something that could hold the energy and then release it later. I don't know what could do that. It would have to hold a spell but not be affected by—" I stopped. Yan was holding out the mirrored toad. "Oh," I said. "Oh dear."

Yan's grin widened behind the stasis-field toad. The light in his eyes was not reflection. "Look who just caught up."

After one fruitless session a week later Yan stared at the latest burnmark on the railcar wall and said, "If we figure out how to do this the world is our oyster."

"I don't like oysters."

"It's just an old expression. It means you can do whatever you want. No one has anything like this, Fred. The Paypays, the wiccans, they'll all be bedroom casters after this. New Scientists my ass. We'll be gods."

"Gods who make unicorns for Mrs. Gloster."

"When it comes to dealing with the Mrs. Glosters of the world you already are a god, Freddum."

"She was actually a good customer. Kind of whacked but very nice. Also very loyal. We'll never get her away from Paypay."

"Our enterprise will sustain the loss."

I reclined my blue fabric Amtrak chair and kicked up the footrest. "She was the only one who ever tipped me. A pack of gum or a piece of chocolate or something. I have no idea where she got it. It's not like she's some big scavenger or something."

"No, but a lot of her clients are."

"Clients?"

"Sure." I must have looked befuddled because Yan shook his head. "Fred, how have you gotten even this far in the big mean world."

I unreclined my chair. "What are you talking about."

"Mrs. Gloster runs a whorehouse."

"That old lady? Are you out of your mind."

"She's not that old. And I didn't say she's a whore though she used to be. I said she runs a whorehouse." He cocked his head. "You really didn't know."

I sighed and leaned my chair back again. "I'm sheltered. I'm a sheltered boy."

"What do you think she was trading for Paypay's services."

I sat up without straightening the chair. "You're kidding me. Paypay and Mrs. Gloster—"

"She probably just handed him off to one of her employees. Like he always did to her."

I could only stare. "Do you know how many unicorn charms I must have made for that woman."

Yan couldn't stop laughing. "Poor Fred. Chewing gum and eating chocolate when all this time he could have been—"

I sat back again. "How do you know it for a fact. Have you been there."

"Well—yes. Certainly."

"And you just never mentioned it to me. You're so full of shit."

He shrugged and went downstairs and came back with coffee beans and mortar and pestle and french press. He poured beans into the mortar and handed them to me. "You shouldn't ask questions you don't want answered," he said. I straightened the chair again and began grinding the beans. Yan lit the campstove I used for potions and put a pan of water on it.

I wasn't bothered so much about finding out Mrs. Gloster was a, a whorehouser or whatever you called it. What bothered me was that I hadn't figured it out. All that time she'd brought me hard-to-find items people hoarded. Disposable razors. Tiny little liqueurs from before the Change. Sugar. Candies wrapped in colored cellophane, not those rock candies on a string that Mrs. Binauer made. One time she gave me a handful of little coneshaped chocolates wrapped in foil. "Kisses for my Fred," she'd said as she dropped them onto the counter. I must have looked confused or maybe flustered because she'd explained, "That's what these were called, chocolate kisses. I remember eating them when I was a little girl."

Astonishingly the chocolates hadn't gone bad. The foil must have protected them or maybe they'd all been sealed in something. They were wrapped so that a little tail of paper stuck out. HERSHEY was printed on it. You pulled on the little paper strip and the foil unwrapped and there was the little chocolate cone shape fresh as—

Fresh as.

Yan was looking at me funny. He started to say something but I held up a hand. Fresh as? I was picturing a lock, a key trying to fit but being warded off. Paypay's lock that had been charmed against me. Why was I remembering that now.

"Fred—"

"Shut up." I'd been trying to figure out the charm Paypay'd put on the lock. Early morning. I'd been thinking about how Paypay's place had been a music shop before the Change, a store that sold recorded music, objects that contained music. Shiny objects reflective like stasis spells. Shiny objects like foilwrapped chocolates.

In front of Paypay's that morning I had thought I was close to something that had to do with stasis spells. And here it was again right in front of me. If I put it together right.

Mirrored objects that contained music that could be released on a machine that could read it like a book. Little chocolates wrapped in shiny foil with a little paper ribbon that stuck out a bit so you could unwrap them.

Suppose the foil was the stasis around the object, the reflective impermeable container, and the paper strip wrapped with it was a flaw in the stasis, a deliberate imperfection built into the foil so that the foil could be—

I stood up and spilled ground coffee all over myself and I looked at Yan and said I've got it.

Yan looked me up and down. "You've got something. I just hope it isn't contagious."

TEN

The other traders had been hawking their wares for a while by the time Yan and I had carted our folding table and box of goods to the racetrack and set up. Oh, look, little Yan and Fred have a lemonade stand. How cuuute.

But other than smiling and nodding goodmornings after curious looks they left us alone. Yan ran off to Mrs. Halobagian's booth for some sweet-buns while I sat behind the folding table draped with black fabric on top of which lay an assortment of small mirrored objects, twiddling my thumbs and watching everyone make sales but me.

Ron Golecki saw me sitting there and I guess I must have looked pitiful because he left off planing a foam surfboard blank and came over. "Fred M. Garey," he said like it had been ten years since he'd seen me instead of a few weeks. Tall, muscular, athletic, goodlooking, easygoing, affable, and either indifferent or oblivious to his appeal. You wanted to hate him for it but he was so damn nice you hated yourself for thinking it. Ron built surfboards. When he wasn't surfing on a board he was building, repairing, designing, or talking about one. Golecki boards were supposed to be some special deal, which I guess they'd have to be in a world where surfboards were free for the taking.

Ron's calloused hand enveloped my own. "First you're railroad guys, then you're swap meet guys. What are you two up to."

"Setting up shop. Plying our trade." I smiled at the Surfliner gleaming on the narrow bridge just past the grass lot.

He followed my gaze. "That was a hell of a thing. So that's your shop. You guys are making—" he picked up a little mirrored disk and it slipped from his fingers and fell onto the black cloth "—jewelry?"

"Not exactly." I wished Yan would hurry back. "They're talismans."

"Goodluck charms?" He grinned again. Perfectly even teeth perfectly white in his sunbrowned face. "Love potions, things like that?"

"They're like bottles that hold spells."

He picked up the disk again. "Slippery."

"Not a lot of friction."

He looked thoughtful. "Really. What's in this one."

"Light."

"Like a lantern?"

"Like a bottle full of light. Here, hold it up." He complied and squinted at the mirrored poker chip reflecting morning sunlight.

I said *ka-pow* and suddenly Ron was holding the sun. He made a funny yip and dropped it and it left a pulsing green afterimage that moved with my gaze. I picked it up. A poker chip, unmirrored now. When I straightened I realized everyone was staring at us. Those who weren't rubbing their eyes or blinking and shaking their head.

"You could warn a guy."

"Sorry." I felt like an asshole.

"Ron, hello." Yan hurried to us. "I see Fred has been demonstrating our merchandise. In fact all of Del Mar sees it. Sticky bun?" He held out a paperwrapped bun glistening with glaze. Ron stared a bit off the mark and I realized he was still seeing the pulsing green afterimage. "I was just looking at your most recent boards. The paint jobs are amazing. How did you do the lace pattern on the blue one."

"Trade secret." Ron would have talked surfboards if his optic nerve had been burned out with a hot poker. "Three coats of metalflake base, then DuPont Pearlescent Opal using a lace tablecloth as a stencil."

"You brush stenciled that?"

Ron looked thoughtfully toward his work area where hardened resin and stiff fiberglass-cloth remnants and wood and foam shavings lay around sawhorses on which a foam blank rested. "Sure is a pretty day today."

Yan grinned back. "Okay."

---

minded the table while Yan went to hawk customers. I was wondering how we could capitalize on the lightbottle act when a shadow fell across me and I looked up to see Paypay studying the talismans. I watched him a moment but couldn't tell what he was thinking. "Hi Paypay."

He didn't look up. "You figure out stasis."

"I—yeah." I was about to tell him how we'd done it, to show him how all-fired competent we were and how much better off I was without him, but reason prevailed. "We figured it out."

Paypay sighed. "No good come."

"They're just talismans. They hold the same charms I made for you a thousand times, only covered with stasis spells. We learned how to unlock them so the talisman will play out the spell it holds."

He kept frowning down at them.

I picked up a mirrored Hot Wheels car. It really was slippery. "Here, look. This one holds a Salamander. You just open it and tell it what to burn." I picked up a mirrored dollhead. "This one holds your unicorn charm."

"How you make."

I shrugged. "It's not hard."

And the funny thing was it wasn't hard. The problem with the basic stasis spell was that it was perfect. It did its job right and couldn't be opened. Whereas our stasis spell was deliberately flawed. We left an opening, a crack, and into that crack we placed another tiny spell embedded like the paper strip that unravels the chocolate kiss. And what the tiny spell, the paper strip, did was deactivate the stasis spell. A deliberate crack that let you pry the whole thing open.

But I wasn't about to tell Paypay any of that. "All I have to do," I said as I held out the mirrored dollhead, "is say the key phrase that unlocks the stasis, and bam: instant unicorn. No more potions, no more burned flooring, no more lopsided horses from bad pronunciation."

He looked at it like I was offering him a cockroach. "Is cheat. Not magic."

"I made it with magic. It holds magic inside. It took a magician to make it. Why isn't it magic."

"Anyone say, or just caster?"

"Anyone. That's how we can sell them."

"What is word to make work."

"If I say it it'll play the spell."

He pulled his reading glasses from his shirt pocket and put them on and fished a little notepad from the same pocket and pulled a short pen from its spiral binding and handed them to me. "Write."

Well what could it hurt. I wrote down the key and handed it back to him. He glanced at it and lowered it and looked around. I saw Yan nodding distractedly at Ron's booth while Ron waxed on about surfboards. Mrs. Villaraigosa shooed flies from her baskets of gleaming fish while her kids chased each other around the table. Ananda Fayelle pushed a dented grocery cart on wobbly wheels. Paypay caught Ananda's attention and waved her over.

Ananda and I had been classmates for the two years I had gone to school. I always thought her quietness seemed less shyness than easy confidence. Like she knew things but didn't need to say them. Her father was a beekeeper and sold the only honey anyone could get. He must have been selling off some stock; you didn't usually see the Fayelles at the swap meet in March.

Ananda's beatup cart clattered up to my table. "Hey Mr. Papadopoulos. Hey Fred."

"Hi Nanda." I wanted to ask how she'd been and how her little brother George was. When he was eight George Fayelle had fallen off a skateboard on a curve of crumbled coastal road and tumbled down an incline. For three days he'd clung to a root and called out for help, unable to move because of a broken ankle, but no one heard him yelling. Finally Mr. Villaraigosa had been heading in with his day's catch and spotted him desperately waving his shirt on the steep cliffside. George was bad off by the time a rescue party got to him. His break had been exposed and gotten infected and then turned gangrenous and Dr. Ram had to amputate.

Paypay held out the notebook to Ananda without so much as a hello. "Nanda, what this says."

She frowned at Paypay but took the notebook. Past her I saw Yan at Ron's worktable no longer nodding at Ron's surfboard soliloquy but frowning my way. I shrugged. Ananda held up the notebook and said *allah kadjim* and the mirrored dollhead silently exploded into a ponysized unicorn charm. Ananda yiked and jumped back. Paypay looked mildly interested. The unicorn blinked and swished its tail and looked fairly ridiculous on the folding tabletop.

I grinned. It was as good a charm as any I'd ever made for Mrs. Gloster. Better. I hadn't gussied it up with doodads and fluffy bunny swirlies. I'd kept the thick lashes though. It really was a good effect.

The unicorn lowered its milky spiral horn and gave a somewhat ungainly hop off the table. The only thing missing from the illusion was weight.

Ananda looked expectantly at Paypay but he only frowned at the unicorn so she looked at me.

"We had a bet," I said.

"You win or lose?"

"Um, not sure yet. Sorry if it scared you."

"I'd say startled. Not scared."

"Important difference." I grinned.

"Is to me. Are you done with me." She didn't sound irritated at all.

"Um, sure. Thanks. We'll talk later. Can we talk later."

Now she grinned and left and left me wondering.

"Hey Nanda." The rickety shopping cart stopped and she looked back. "You can have it if you want." I gestured at the unicorn pretending to graze on the pavilion concrete. "It'll only last about three days but you can take it."

She didn't look away from me. "That's terrible."

"It isn't alive. It's just a charm."

The unicorn picked that time to look at me and blurt soundlessly.

"You can take it to George."

"All right. I'll do that." She looked at the unicorn.

"Go on." I made shooing motions. "It's okay."

Ananda shook her head and pushed on. The unicorn trudged behind her rattling shopping cart. I got the impression it was faintly disgusted with the whole business. If vapor could feel disgusted.

By now Yan had returned to our table and Paypay was standing with his arms folded. "See. Is cheat."

"How is it a cheat."

Paypay replied to Yan but looked at me. "Anyone do. Anyone can say word. Where is caster. Where is magic." He shrugged.

"There is no caster." Yan indicated the mirrored objects on the table. "The magic's all in there bottled up and waiting for anybody who knows the word to uncork it and let it out. People don't have to travel half the day to some caster every time they want a lawn gorgon or a vase healed or whatever. They can buy half a dozen from us and use them whenever they want." After the light bottle and the unicorn charm people were watching us. Yan took advantage of the fact and raised his voice. "That's the beauty of spellware, Mr. Papadopoulos. Once a spell is bottled up anyone can use it anytime they want."

Paypay was remarkably unperturbed. "Still not casting."

Yan smiled meanly and nodded. "No sir it isn't. It's commerce. We're not selling services. We're selling products. Buy them from us and take them home. Use them right away or put them on a shelf. Buy a sixpack of room coolers for the worst week in August. Buy three emergency lights to give to your kids. If they never use them they can give them to their kids. They'll still work. Guaranteed." He wasn't looking at Paypay anymore but addressing the dozen onlookers who had gathered. One of whom was my father.

"Put one of our bottled fireseekers in your kitchen," Yan said. "It'll sit there good as new until the moon stops going around the earth. Or until the day a fire breaks out and you say the key and put the fire out—" he snapped his fingers and smiled "—like a light." A few people laughed because the saying was just a saying to people our age.

All the products Yan was hawking were news to me.

Paypay raised an eyebrow. "You think these things is what caster do."

"They're what you do."

"Not only."

"They're portable. They're cheap. They're there until you want to use them and you don't have to call a caster to your house in the middle of the night to make them work. They don't need house calls because they're already home." He picked up a mirrored lego block and turned it to catch the light. "The spell's already in there. It never breaks and there's nothing to go wrong." He tossed the lego block and caught it. "Fred and I have changed everything, Mr. Papadopoulos. Everything."

"Everything already change." Which got a laugh from the over-thirties. He scribbled on his little notepad and looked at Yan over the rims of his narrow reading glasses. "Nothing go wrong."

"Nothing." Yan folded his arms and appeared to dig in his heels. "Once the spell's in there it's in there till you uncork it. Like I said, guaranteed."

Paypay tore a page from his notepad and spat in it and folded it into quarters and lit it with his cigarette and then flicked the burning paper away and said *aperio*. A piercing banshee cry brought people's hands to their ears as the folding table erupted in an impossible menagerie of surly lawn gorgons, thrashing gargoyle room sentinels, bigeyed baby dragons, multicolored flames, and an enormous column of smoke that solidified into a veined white marble column that began to glow with bright red letters that read 50 FIFTY CASTING.

When it all died down and disappeared our table was covered with ordinary unmirrored bricabrac. People were laughing and even my father was grinning and Yan was standing with clenched fists and a murderous expression.

Paypay calmly removed his reading glasses and folded them and put them in his shirt pocket along with the notepad for which I had developed a sudden and profound respect. He gave Yan a little shrug and said, "I find keys."

A week later his shop burned to the ground.

ELEVEN

Yan was in a lather. Our casting had been *hacked.* We had to *build in security.* We needed *password protection.* I told him that what Paypay had used to make us look like monkeys had been a garden variety reveal spell. Diviners used them all the time to find lost things. I pointed out that any spell that revealed the key would also yield the password so what was the point. Yan insisted we voicekey the stasis bottles so that only paying customers could unlock them. I pointed out that customizing every stasis bottle pretty much negated the whole mass-production thing. At which point he stormed out of the Surfliner and stomped off the bridge to walk north along the early evening beach. I put on some coffee so it could be waiting for him when he got back.

An hour later I got tired of waiting and poured myself a cup and sat downstairs and stared out the window thinking. I'd just taken the first sip when someone outside said, "Um, hello? Anyone here?"

I set down the mug and heaved open the sliding door. Ron Golecki stood in bright floral shorts and a hoodie. "Hey Fred. Hope I'm not bothering you."

"Ron. What's up."

He grinned and pointed to a tall yellow surfboard he'd leaned against the railcar. "Want a customer?"

———————

"Those mirrored things you guys make." Ron set down the coffee I'd given up waiting for Yan to come and drink. "They're very slippery. Hard to hold."

"Stasis spells don't let in anything from the outside world. Heat, light, anything. Yan thinks even time and gravity."

"So they're frictionless."

I frowned. "Well to be honest I'm not sure." I shrugged. "They take up space, so there'd still be wind resistance. Even so there'd definitely be less drag than if it wasn't—" I glanced toward the door, where his surfboard leaned against the wall outside. "Oh."

He grinned. "That fucker would glide, dude."

———

Ron stared at his distorted reflection in the oval, thick in the middle and pinheaded. My own fatbellied pinheaded reflection came up beside his and said Gonna try it out now?

"Tomorrow morning. Tide's out now."

The newly mirrored board was slippery and Ron had a hard time carrying it back downstairs. I walked out with him. Shadows were lengthening and the grandstand was ochres and umber and black vines. The dying day quickly chilling in the onshore breeze. The surfboard an oval cutout of evening sky against the side of the Surfliner. "So what do I owe you Fred."

"Haven't the slightest. Let me talk to Yan. We're just getting established, so maybe indentured servitude would be good."

"If this thing rides the way I hope it does it might be worth it."

———

I cleaned up the workroom before it got dark. Yan had left some books lying around and I put them into his compartment. Even now I wonder at my own motives. Would anything have changed if I hadn't gone in there. Useless question. I did. I did go in.

———

Yan came back just after full dark and made coffee for himself. He seemed in a better mood, drumming the counter as he heated a cup of water, and didn't reference our earlier argument. Which made it harder to get around to what I wanted to ask him about.

"Ron Golecki came by while you were gone."

"A visitor. How encouragingly social."

"Wasn't a social visit. It was business." I told him about Ron's new mirrored surfboard.

"So you're telling me that our first customer hired us to do the spell we've killed ourselves learning how to break."

"Pretty much."

"I would cry if it weren't so funny. I take it you made it for him."

"Of course I made it for him. What, did you want me to say, Begone, pissant customer, thy needs are beneath our skills."

"What did you charge him."

"I told him I'd discuss it with you."

"So he hasn't paid yet."

"No."

"But he does have a nice mirrored surfboard."

"Yes."

He shook his head and turned his back to strain his coffee. "Fred Fred Fred. How shall we ever make an entrepreneur out of you."

"Speaking of inexplicably mirrored objects."

He kept his back to me and poured his coffee. "Ah. The nut of the matter." He turned to me with the mug steaming in front of his face. He blew across it and looked at it. "What's really on your mind, Freddum."

"I cleaned up the workroom after Ron left."

"You're annoyed because I don't do enough cleaning?"

"I put some of your books away. Into your room."

"Ah." He wasn't going to give me anything.

"I wasn't snooping on you. I—"

He raised a hand. "We don't need preambles, Fred. I know you aren't the snooping type. What did you find."

"A cat."

He looked bemused.

"A mirrored cat."

I swear to god he looked relieved and suddenly I was much less worried about what I had found in his room than what I had not. "Oh. I forgot about the cat."

"You forgot about a cat in stasis in your sleeping compartment."

He nodded. He still didn't seem very troubled. "I did it a long time ago. When we first started all of this."

"You lived in your parents' building when we first started all of this."

"Yes."

"And you brought the cat with you here and then forgot about it."

"I brought it because I felt bad about it and I wanted to figure out how to undo it. That was what we were working on, undoing it."

"You can't undo the perfect stasis spells."

"I'm well aware of that, Fred. I'm not very happy about it either."

"We agreed we'd stop working on animals."

"I did this before we decided that."

"And you didn't tell me."

"I felt guilty about it. If I had told you you would have been mad and I would have felt even worse and we still wouldn't have been able to do anything about it." He spread his hands. "I am evil incarnate. Put me in a sack full of snakes and drop me off a cliff before I unleash more terror upon the innocent globe."

"It isn't funny."

"Fred." He put a hand on my arm. "I am genuinely sorry about the cat. I felt terrible when I did it and I felt worse when we learned that those perfect stasis fields could never be undone. But your reaction is exactly why I never told you about it."

I was about to say okay, I understand, it's over, I just wanted to know what it was about, when he sniffed and said, "It's just a cat, Fred."

"Not anymore it isn't." I went outside. My turn for a cooldown walk on the beach.

A plume of dark gray smoke rose from Del Mar near the shops.

I went back inside. "Get your blades. Something's burning."

———

Ten minutes later I stood with Yan and half the Del Mar community and watched Paypay's shop burn down. The rest of the old untenanted shops in the row went with it. It had blazed well past the point of no return by the time a bucket brigade could be assembled. All we could do was stand back and watch and hope the wind didn't pick up and take half the town with it.

Paypay was in the crowd unharmed and staring at his life on fire there before him. I thought about what was in those burning rooms. Books and notes and ingredients, much of it irreplaceable. He saw me looking at him and I knew what he was thinking and I shook my head. I don't know if he believed me. I had nothing to feel guilty about but I felt guilty anyhow.

The Ramchandanis had seen the smoke and come to see if they could help. Dr. Ram saw me waving at them and he pointed me and Yan out to Parmita and Nan and they came over. "How did it start," Dr. Ram asked. "Does anyone know."

"We just got here," said Yan.

"How terrible." Parmita shook her head at the coruscating flames. "Poor Mr. Papadopoulos."

The wind shifted and the heat pressed our faces and we all stepped back. The crackling sound a giant stumbling through a brittle forest.

Dr. Ram went to Paypay and asked him questions. Paypay shrugged and answered and never took his gaze from the burning shop. Dr. Ram put a hand on his shoulder and then came back. "He says he was in back of the shop when he smelled something burning in the front room. He went to see what it was but the room was completely on fire and he ran out the back door."

"Did he get any of his kit out."

Dr. Ram looked at me blankly.

"His ingredients. Chemicals, grimoires. They're worth a lot more than the shop."

He shrugged. "I did not ask. He did not say." He turned to the huge loud burning. "But even if he did not he is very fortunate I think."

I nodded and kept my thoughts to myself.

Late that night I woke up and slipped from my room and crept downstairs in my socks and eased the door open. Cold salt air blew in while I sat in the doorway and put on my sneakers and tied the laces of my rollerblades together and slung them over my shoulder. I slid the door shut and walked along the railroad bridge in bluewhite moonlight. Past the racetrack lot I traded sneakers for blades. I looked back at the Surfliner silver against the dark ocean sky and held still and listened. No motion. No light. Beyond the railcar gleaming waves crashed as they always would.

I zipped my hoodie and bladed north.

The remains were still hot. Every now and then something popped. Ash-rimmed surfaces in moonlight. The front door a smokeblacked ruin of melted glass and slagged metal. Its mail slot still identifiable. I pictured sticking my hand in and tossing an object to the left or right. I'd want it to land someplace unobtrusive. In a corner or behind something. And I wouldn't be able to throw it very far.

I poked around with a charred broomhandle near the mail slot and found it to the left of the door behind the white-edged char that was all that remained of the wooden shelves that had held jars. It was burned but not beyond recognition. The metal was still hot. I gloved my hand in my hoodie and picked it up and wiped off soot and held it up to the moonlight. Glanced around the dark ruined shop snapping restless around me. Slagged aluminum and melted shop glass. That fire had been whitehot, lightning hot. Most people would assume that chemicals and arcane ingredients had ignited. A casting must have gone wrong and Paypay should thank his lucky stars he hadn't been blasted off the planet or turned inside out or worse. It had happened to plenty of casters better than Paypay. Everyone would believe that or something like it unless I did something about it.

In my hand was the ability to do something about it. It was small, burned black, halfmelted, but still recognizable as a Legends Hall of Fame Ed "Big Daddy" Roth Beatnik Bandit Hot Wheels car. The last time I had seen it, it had been in Yan's room. Last time I'd seen it, it had been completely mirrored.

TWELVE

I didn't even try to sleep when I got back. I snuck into the workroom and lit the propane stove and by its faintly bluish light I redrew my pentagram and gathered ingredients and made my preparations.

I had to work at Dr. Ram's that day. I picked some ingredients from the bottles and bags on the workroom shelves and put them in my daypack and then put on my blades and headed out before Yan got up. I was waiting when Dr. Ram opened his office. He didn't comment on me being there so early. I think he assumed I'd spent a restless night because of what happened to Paypay. Well he wasn't wrong.

I wanted to tell him about Yan. He of all people deserved to know. But I couldn't, not just yet. I had to give Yan the chance to prove me wrong before I got a bunch of people riled up about him.

Paypay had stayed in Dr. Ram's apartment building last night and was already setting up a new shop a block from the old one. People had gathered food and clothing for him and were helping him clean and move libbed furniture into his new digs. The coven on Ocean Boulevard had collected basic ingredients to give him a kind of starter set for casting. I gave Dr. Ram a bundle from my pack and asked if he would drop it off at Paypay's on his way home today. "It's some stuff he could use that the wiccans may not have thought of."

Then Mr. Hayliss came in with a bad cut and we got to work. The day seemed to go on forever. I kept wondering how it would go this afternoon. I kept thinking about that day we'd gotten wasted on the beach, that light in his eyes. *I would like to be able to stop every wave on the beach, even for just an hour.*

I'd grown up with Yan. I loved him. I thought I knew him deeply. Had I been wrong.

Well. I'd find out this afternoon.

———

He put his book away quickly when I came in. "How's Paypay."

"Fine. He stayed in your parents' building last night."

"Oh good. That means Mother fed him this morning."

"He's already setting up shop again."

He nodded. "I'd be surprised if he wasn't."

"Let's go upstairs. I want to work on something."

He had this faint smirk as if I were telling a joke he already knew the punchline to. "Aren't we the industrious one."

"We are indeed."

———

Upstairs I gathered what I needed to cast a stasis. Yan watched from outside the pentagram. "Flash of inspiration? Solution to our problems?"

"I have a theory."

"Put it in the water and let's see if it floats."

The pan on the unlit burner before me. The small pentagram around me. Safe circles casters sometimes called them. In a pocket of my cargo pants was the burned Hot Wheels car. In another pocket was an Eveready AAA battery I had put in bottle stasis early that morning. Batteries had once stored power. It seemed fitting.

"I want to make a macro spell in a stasis bottle."

"Sounds good."

I kept working. "I want to try adding something new to the tail." The tail was what we called the deliberate flaw in the spell, the little paper strip that let you unwrap the chocolate kiss.

"Interesting. What do you want to add."

"I want to build in a delay."

He blinked. "Delay how?"

"I want it to open at a fixed time after I say the password. Do you think that's possible."

He studied me. "Sure. Why not. Time delay spells are possible by themselves, aren't they."

"I don't know any. But I know they exist."

"It's a great idea. Think of the possibilities."

"I've been thinking of them all day. I'll bet you can think of some too."

"Why don't you name some."

"Do I have to."

"I think you do."

"Okay. In fact I'll show you one." And from my pocket pulled the blackened Hot Wheels car.

He said *plan b* and light flared from a corner of the room where a mirrored pen had lain on the shelf.	I said *snap* and the pentagram glowed sudden red as a spot of air flared whitehot above its rim.

Heat dissipated around the perimeter of the pentagram. The workroom air suddenly stifling. We began to sweat.

Saved by a syllable's difference.

"My goodness. Our first casting duel. Fred, you continue to surprise me."

"You son of a bitch."

He still sat in his chair like we were talking about the weather. "Well. What now."

"You have two choices."

"Really."

"You can come with me to Paypay and your father and let the town decide what to do with you."

"Let's hear choice two."

"Leave."

"Leave."

I nodded. "Pack up, leave town, leave the whole goddamn area. Don't come back."

"What would the town do with me do you think."

"You tried to kill Paypay. You tell me."

For the first time he looked something other than amused or smug. He looked embarrassed. "He was supposed to have been at the swap meet. It went off too soon."

"Oh. So you weren't trying to hurt Paypay, you were only trying to burn down his shop. Maybe you'll only have to write an essay."

He snorted. "The least they'll do is give me your leave-town option."

"My leave-town option doesn't include being tarred and feathered."

"There is that."

"Your dad will intervene. I don't think he could stop them throwing you out but he might be able to keep them from hurting you. But I don't care if the town wants to give you a parade. I want you to leave."

The outright glee in his eyes was our friendship's epitaph. "Fred. That's as close to a threat as I've ever heard you make."

"It wasn't supposed to be close."

He laughed. "Well look who grew a pair." He glanced around. "I like our little mobile home, Freddum. What if I don't want to leave it."

"I don't care what you want." I was tired of kneeling in the pentagram so I stood and faced him. "I'm the one who does the casting. I did all Paypay's work and cleaned his shop and learned his trade and handed it to you with a bow around it. You just have ideas about casting. I've lived with it for years. I'm pretty good at it."

"Better than me?"

"One way to find out."

"I might surprise you."

"You already have."

His fingers drummed the arms of his chair. I tensed. He saw it and laughed. "Not today I think."

I did not relax. The pentagram had expended its energy and I hadn't prepared another warding spell. I had no idea what I would do if he called my bluff and sent another thunderbolt my way.

Suddenly he stood. I flinched. I know I flinched. But he didn't notice and it occurred to me he was at least as nervous as I was. He just put up a better front. He hadn't expected me to be ready for him or to be his equal if I had been. "So I'm to be a prince in exile." He grinned. "A prophet without honor. The open road calls my name."

"I think it's pretty much yelling it."

The grin vanished. "Do you really hate me so much already."

"You fucking burned down Paypay's shop. You could've killed him. You could've burned down the whole town. Jesus fucking christ, Yan, your parents live near there. Do you even give a shit."

He frowned. "You know," he said. "I really don't think I do."

He put rolled pants and shirts and socks into his daypack.

"Do you want to go by your mom and dad's."

"I said goodbye to them when I moved in with you. You can tell them for me." He smiled tightly. "You're family."

"All right."

He closed the pack and slung it on one shoulder and looked at me.

"That all you're taking." I felt like a wall.

"I would be much obliged if I could take half the coffee."

"Take all of it. I can get more."

He nodded. "Okay." He picked up his blades and slung them with laces tied across the daypack. "You don't mind if we walk, do you. There's no poetry in blading into exile."

"We can walk."

Downstairs I put the coffee into a baggie and gave it to him. He stuffed it into a daypack pocket and we went outside. He patted the Surfliner affectionately. "I will miss this. Where will I go, I wonder."

"It's a big world."

He turned and looked at me. "You have no idea." He started off and then stopped suddenly and said he'd forgotten something and ran back inside. I ran after him. Forgot, my ass.

He was already ransacking his compartment when I got upstairs. He plowed past me and knocked me against the wall and hurried into my compartment. He'd opened out the bed and lifted up the thin pad by the time I got there. "Where is it." He looked wild. He wasn't faking this, he was near panic.

"Where's what."

He ransacked my room. I didn't try to stop him. I wasn't hiding anything and I didn't care what he wanted to take with him. When he didn't find what he was searching for he pushed past me and went into the workroom. I followed and watched him make a shambles of that too. I didn't care. I could clean it up. And after it was clean he would be gone. That was all I wanted right then. Him gone.

"If you'll tell me what you're trying to find I'll help you look for it. I might even know where it is."

He laughed. "That's good, Fred. That's funny."

"I might."

He stopped with a chair cushion in his hand. "If you know where it is I'll kill you."

"Well. Lucky for both of us then."

He dropped the cushion and walked up to me and grabbed two handfuls of my sweatshirt and pulled me close. I didn't resist. He studied me a moment and then he let me go. "You don't have it. You wouldn't know what to do with it if you did. It doesn't matter."

"I don't have it. And it's time for you to go."

———————

We walked the tracks along the coast through Del Mar north toward Cardiff-by-the-Sea. The sun grew blighted as it lowered behind the offshore marine layer to enmolten a dull metallic corridor of ocean. The onshore breeze blew late March chill in the growing gloom.

When the broken tanker hove into view in the shadowed distance near South Carlsbad Beach I stopped walking. Ahead the tracks sank into marshland and the tide had made the going wet. I was so tired.

Yan walked on a few paces before he noticed I'd stopped. "This as far as you take me, sheriff?"

I didn't know what a sheriff was but I nodded. "You can go on from here."

"What if I come back."

"You won't."

"You don't know what I will or won't do."

"I know you won't come back."

He smiled.

I nodded at the overgrown uneven track that ran north from our town beyond the rusting supertanker we had run away from years ago and through the dead eroding sprawl of Orange County and L.A., up the unknown coast across mountains and over bridges that might or might not have held up all these years and finding its unguessable end out there. A rusted iron path across a vastened world made strange. Yan was right. I had no idea how big the world really was. Or what abided there.

"One last sunset together, Fred."

I shook my head. "I want to be back before full dark."

"Ah. It's like that then."

"It's like that."

"Remember that day we found the Surfliner? When we walked along the tracks and you realized you wanted to see where they lead."

I nodded. My throat tightened at what was coming. God damn him. "I wanted to fly."

"You wanted to fly. You wanted to look down on things. Ski down a mountain."

"I'm not coming with you."

He grabbed my arm. "Why not. Fred, why not. Look what we've been doing. Look what we've learned. There's nothing for you in Del Mar. You just don't see it yet. Del Mar is a zit, a scab. It's nothing compared to what's out there. But we're huge, Fred. We could own the world. The one outside Del Mar."

"An hour ago you tried to kill me. Now you want to divvy up the planet between us. Your way of looking down on things is different from mine."

"Oh Fred. People love you because you're a pure soul. I love you because of it. But you are so dull." He let go of me and smoothed my sweatshirt and shook his head in pity at his own judgement. "Your father wrote a book," he said.

"A book." I felt stupid.

"My dad has a copy. You should read it. That's my last bit of sage advice before I brave the great unknown."

I studied him. If there was some underlying meaning I didn't know what it was. "All right."

"All right." He put out his hand. "You've been a good friend, Fred. Be seeing you."

I looked at it, then took it. "I don't think so."

"You don't think you've been a good friend?"

"I don't think I'll be seeing you."

He smiled and let go my hand. "I know you don't. That's because you haven't thought this through."

"Don't come back, Yan."

"That's not what I meant." He let go my hand and I let go of him.

---

zipped my hoodie and tightened the hood around my face as I walked back. The sun succumbed to the waiting gray and the wind grew bitter cold. I kept asking myself how I felt about all this. It was like throwing a rock into a well and not hearing it hit. I kept looking for some other way it could have gone but couldn't find one.

Waves crashed on my right the whole way back.

I was okay right up to the moment I saw the Surfliner in the distance on its narrow span of wooden bridge beside the dark and epic ruin of racetrack. Then I sat down on the tracks and cried. Cried like a landscape overtaken by a sudden storm. Cried in a way I knew I had not since the day my mother died.

PART TWO:
SYMPATHETIC VIBRATIONS

THIRTEEN

They'd been setting up at the racetrack all day. A crew had cut down the tall grass beyond the concrete pavilion where the swap meet was held and now they were finishing up work on two wooden platforms between what had been turns one and two. Others were attaching bright plastic streamers to some kind of maypole. From the Surfliner I watched them through a small telescope I'd libbed from a camera shop. There must have been nearly a thousand people there, more than I'd ever seen in one place, and it was hours yet before the vibe was supposed to start.

I grabbed a hydration pack and put a mirrored penny in my pocket and went out.

A group of five people was walking south on the overgrown railroad tracks toward the racetrack. One of them carried a guitar case and one had a long wooden tube painted with red and yellow designs. All wore daypacks. They'd been about to step onto the bridge but stopped when I got out of the Surfliner.

"Anything good left in there," the tallest one called out to me.

"I hope so. I live here."

"No shit."

They walked onto the bridge and we hugged and traded names. Taylor, a darkhaired girl with cracked black nail polish, folded her arms and said, "That wasn't here before, was it."

"Nope. We moved it here about six months ago."

"We."

"Me and a friend."

"You and a friend. Moved that." The tall guy, Sean, was good at these question-and-observation lines.

I asked where they were from.

"Temecula," Sean said.

"Don't know it."

"About thirty miles northwest. Big valley, very nice."

"Long walk."

He shrugged. "Two days. It's not—"

The first throb hit us and we all turned toward the racetrack.

"Shit howdy," said Eric, the thin blond guy with the big stick thing. But he was grinning.

"They're still setting up," I said. "I guess they probably have some—" The second throb shook the nearer wall of the Surfliner. "—adjusting to do."

"Omigod," said Trace, a thinner, shorter copy of Taylor down to the cracked nail polish. Little sister maybe.

Everyone laughed but it was goodnatured. "It's her first vibe," Taylor said.

I smiled at Trace. "Mine too."

She linked arms with me and stuck out her tongue at the others, who laughed again.

"One of the guys spinning is a friend of mine," said Eric.

"Let's don't keep him waiting then." I fished the mirrored penny from my pocket and held it out to the Surfliner and said *grunion surfliner* and suddenly we were looking at our distorted reflections and the reflected grandstand and green hills in the mirrored surface of the sleeper car.

"Um, okay," said Eric.

I grinned and offered Trace my elbow again. "Shall we." This time she hesitated before slipping her cracklenailed fingers around my arm.

———————

The sun was its own breadth above the water and everything looked buttered and basking as I led them off the bridge and down the berm. We stepped into our shadows as we made our way across the cracked and weedgrown lot. The grandstand pale golden tan. Darker patches where plaster had fallen. Bright green ivy nearly glowing in the fading light. I glanced back at the mirrored Surfliner gleaming unearthly on the bridge and thought about what had and had not changed since March.

I'd had to tell Dr. Ramchandani that his son had burned down Paypay's shop and that he'd left town for good. After his initial disbelief Dr. Ram just kind of collapsed in his clothes and started sobbing deep soundless sobs the way I had cried on the railroad tracks after escorting Yan out of town. I'd closed up shop for him and walked him home. I offered to go up with him while he told Parmita and Nan but he just held up a hand and shook his head. I wanted to help, to say something that would fill some of the plug I'd torn out of his heart. But I just watched as he staggered into the dim lobby of his apartment building, fallen in on himself and looking, for the first time in my recollection, old.

From there I went to Paypay's new shop. Either the same goddamn bell or one just like it was on the front door. Paypay looked up at me when it jingled.

"Paypay. Can I talk to you a minute."

———————

Paypay never said a word about the fire or Yan or my extracurricular education. I was grateful for his silence. I knew I was on probation, but in his silence I also heard a slow forgiveness as well. I did the work he set me without complaint and I learned. Then I went home and worked on the castings I wanted to work on. Cautiously, patiently, without the urgency and ambition I'd felt when Yan had been pushing me.

The only thing unsatisfying about it was that I had no one to share what I was learning. At first I missed Yan terribly despite everything. When I found another use for a stasis bottle spell I'd look forward to telling him about it and then I'd remember. When I lay awake at night the Surfliner would seem too quiet and I'd remember. When I made coffee and ground enough beans for two people, when I walked to the beach to watch the sunset, then I'd remember.

I threw myself into my work, into working for Paypay and helping Dr. Ram.

One day Dr. Ram said, "Parmita would like to know why you have not been over for dinner, Fred. To tell you the truth I would like to know as well."

"Well I guess I thought you wouldn't want me over."

"Why would that be." He was studying his little notepad, I think so I couldn't see his eyes. "We all need all the family we can get, you know."

At one of those dinners my father had been a guest. He arrived after me and I'm ashamed to admit that as he pulled his scabbarded sword from his beltloop and set it politely by the front door my initial reaction was resentment at Dr. Ram's manipulation. At dinner my father had passed me the naan and said So how've you been, Fred. It wasn't until that moment that I remembered that Yan had told me that my father had written some kind of book. A lot had happened and I'd had a lot on my mind. Or maybe I'd been avoiding it. I don't know. But I realized that I missed him. We kept it light, both of us circling around the thing between us that was too big to take on just yet. Still I was glad we'd made some initial effort however tentative.

One night I was reading a book by the light of a glowspell above my little Surfliner bed, the sound of crashing waves accompanying the cool salt air through the opened ceiling vents, and I marked my place and told the light to go out and stared past the ceiling and listened to that timeless crashing and wondered at the emotion I was feeling until I realized that I hadn't recognized it because I hadn't felt it in a long time. I was happy.

Walking toward the grandstand with the group from Temecula I smiled suddenly, remembering that night, that feeling. "Hey, what is that thing."

Eric hefted the painted wooden tube. "Didgeridoo."

"Do what."

He grinned. "Do this." He set the large end on a chunk of asphalt and put his mouth against the waxed end, and—well, I don't know what he did to it. Blew into it or sang into it or talked through it. Maybe all three. Whatever he did the sound that came out was a deep organic thrum that felt strangely familiar to something primal in me. I hadn't heard much music. Mr. Guevera's guitar. Singing. Drum circles on the beach. Somehow this was outside all that. He played the thing for about a minute and then sounded a hornlike toot and took his mouth from it and grinned.

"Wow. That was. . . ." I shook my head. "Wow."

He laughed. "Just wait."

Five guys played hackysack in a ring beside the old fountain in the little plaza before the main entrance to the grandstand. Past them was the highgrassed oval promenade where horses used to be displayed before races. A lot of people milled around talking or smoking cloves or sage or weed or whatever and passing flasks or bottles. Others tethered horses in the little stable stalls. There was a lot of yelling as people recognized each other. I got the impression many of them had last seen each other at other vibes.

As we went from the promenade to the pathworn grassy entrance tunnel into the grandstand Trace and Taylor let go of me so we could all hug people. There was a great feeling in the air. A sense of wanting to touch and be touched, of contact just for its own sake. The tunnel was jammed and I was hugged and patted and passed along for a solid ten minutes before emerging onto the concrete walkway leading to the stands. Eric spilled out behind me looking happily dazed. We saw each other and started laughing. We hugged each other as a kind of coda. All the contact in that joyous gauntlet had polished my senses. My skin was vibrating. I realized how little I'd been touched these last months.

"This is gonna be so great," Eric said as our hug broke.

"It already is."

The next throb washed over us. The grandstand shuddered and then rang after the throb had stopped. A tattered cheer from the diffuse crowd. Eric laughed and took my arm. "Come on. The others'll find us."

We followed the trickling crowd along the path through the highgrassed band that had been the track and onto the enormous oval infield. What had been a lake in the middle of the infield was now a tiny island of tall grass from which tall bare palms projected.

We walked past the sunbleached scoreboard scrawled with ivy, following the trampled path across the old front stretch toward the concrete pavilion. Beyond that were the platforms set up for the vibe. People ran yelling and laughing from the paths to stalk each other through the tall grass. Groups spread blankets across the freshcut infield grass. Small groups lounged in the folding seats up in the grandstand. I couldn't get over all the new faces. Every swap meet there'd be a couple of people I'd never seen before come to trade from ten or twenty miles away or stopping by as they traveled along the coast. But here were a thousand new faces from places I had never heard of. Temecula. Fallbrook. Escondido. I remembered that widening feeling I had felt the day that Yan first led me to the Surfliner. The sudden vertigo of perspective. And now inhabitants of that real and larger place beyond Del Mar prevailed throughout this wasted icon of my childhood. More strangers in my field of vision than there were people in my town.

Many of the pavilion's walls were ivy covered and many terracotta roof shingles were broken or missing. Otherwise it showed little sign of wear. My father had said it would outlast the pyramids. I'd seen pictures of pyramids and didn't know what the fuss was about. Office towers were a lot more impressive.

Eric and I approached the two platforms erected between turns one and two. Ten feet square and three feet high and fifty feet apart. Each with pentagrams carefully drawn and westaligned and nicely edged. Between them something shimmered in the air.

In the center of the lefthand pentagram a skinny guy wearing a checked overshirt knelt before a saucepan on a folding campstove. Tattoos vined his neck to spread at his bald head. He made a pass and put a black feather in the saucepan and said something. The shimmer gave a shudder and the next throb nearly knocked me down. Not a musical note. You felt it. Everything for a mile had to have felt it.

One of the Safe Circle crew stacking scrapwood for a bonfire well back from the platforms grinned at the caster working in his pentagram. The caster shrugged back like it was no big deal but then grinned.

"That's Wedo."

"Your friend who's spinning."

Eric nodded.

"What's the other platform for."

"That's right, you're a virgin." Before I could thank him hugely for yelling it out he said, "That's so cool. You're gonna have the time of your life, I swear. Your first vibe's always the best. Do you know how all this works." I shook my head and he nodded, excited. "You're a caster, right. You'll like this." He indicated the caster on the platform. "Wedo's doing a spell that makes a sort of energy ball in the air."

"A force cage."

"He spins the energy ball and makes it vibrate really fast and it starts pushing the air around it in all directions. He spins the ball and then, he says this is the tricky part, he contracts and expands it in rhythm. Boom, big masses of air spread out. Boom, big low notes go all over the place."

"With you so far."

"Okay. Here's where it gets very cool. Another spinner does the same thing on the other platform. So now you've got two big spinning balls of energy vibrating like fuckall. The spinners tune them in and synch them up and then they start playing with them. Different speeds, different rhythms, different harmonics. The vibrations start to get complex, like—" he nudged his didgeridoo with a foot "—like this, but huge. Epic."

"Vibe," I realized.

He folded his arms and smiled. "There ya go."

I shook my head. "I thought it was called a vibe because of the whole together-as-one thing. You know, the vibe. Duhh."

But Eric's smile broadened to show teeth. "Oh but it is."

I looked around. For some reason I couldn't have named tears stung my eyes. Eric set a hand on my shoulder. "Welcome to the tribe, Fred."

———————

Eric raised his didge and Wedo saw him and waved us over. Eric introduced me and Wedo grinned. He had an infectious grin. "Like that last one?"

"I think people in San Diego probably liked that last one."

He laughed. "Bringing the sounds to the people." He jutted his sharp chin at Eric's didge. "We gonna try that thing?"

"Hellyeah. Sam here yet?"

"Somewhere. She better be here soon, I'm about ready to roll."

"We'll get out of your way then."

Wedo clapped his shoulder and they touched foreheads. "Come back when we've been going a couple hours, okay? We'll do the thing." He saw my expression and grinned. "Secret. Big surprise."

"If it works," said Eric.

"If it works," said Wedo, "that's the surprise."

———————

Eric joined some drummers and I listened to them for a while. People danced. I just swayed and watched. Somehow Eric played his didgeridoo for fifteen minutes without stopping to breathe. Or somehow he breathed and blew into it at the same time. However he did it the drone never stopped. What he played was complex. Rhythm and counterpoint and syncopation, harmonics and harmonies, toots and growls. He made that hollow log do five things at once. It sounded great with the drums.

A blue-eyed girl with beaded cornrows pulled me deep into the dancers. Someone passed a flask. I took a swig and took another one. Some kind of tequila? After a while I hugged the girl I was dancing with and hugged another girl I realized we had been dancing with and waved to Eric and wandered off.

The grandstand was a blacker wedge against the indigo sky. I looked for people I knew from town but it was getting too dark to recognize anyone. I sat in a stadium chair near the front just as the bonfire lit. A cheer went up. I put my feet on the seatback in front of me and watched the shadowplay of dancers before the fire. Synchronized hands of redlit drummers. Wedo casting in his pentagram beyond. A scene as old as people.

The next throb made the bonfire flinch. My arm hair flattened. By the bonfire light I dimly made out people scattered about in the seats. Resting watching smoking drinking. On an upper level a girl was calling Andy? Aaaaan-deeee?

Another throb went out from between the platforms. Just as powerful but the tone had changed. I looked toward the firelit platforms and saw someone in the righthand pentagram now. Wooden barricades had been set around the shimmering energy cages. A ball of air between the platforms glittered firelight. It brightened and rushed toward a common center and then rushed away. The throb hit. Glitter contract expand: the second tone hit.

Then both cages pulsed and both tones sounded.

I was on my feet and yelling before I knew what I was doing. I couldn't hear my own voice. The tones continued, rich in harmonics and enveloping me and enclosing everything. I could lean against that sound. The tones ended and I heard myself yelling and I realized everyone around me was yelling too. Around the bonfire primal shadows raised their spectral arms. People streamed from the grandstand. Drawn to the fire, drawn to that sound. I was one of them laughing and stumbling in the tall grass, holding on and being held. When I was halfway there the massive throbbing opened up again and pulsed a steady beat. By the time I reached the bright bonfire a second, syncopating beat wound round the huge relentless pull of godlike fundamental throb.

Spinners sheltered in their circles, crowd around me lost in rhythm, ring of motion round the fire, tribal movement unifying. Fire's heat against my face. Bodies surging all around me. Weight and press and warmth and life, massive sound from throbbing cages pressing on my sensile skin, pulsing air that flapped my clothes. Swimming in the lake of sound we laughed we yelled we touched. We danced around the bonfire with our thousand other selves surrendered to the overwhelming rhythm that made moths of our connected souls.

———————

Refilling my hydration pack from a big dispenser set up near the front stretch. It was hours later, or not. Someone threw a cup into a trashcan and patted my sweatsoaked shoulder and walked back toward the fire. I tried to place the figure and the long tube he carried. Caught up to him and touched his shoulder and said his name. He turned. The light in his eyes was odd and even frightening but I knew I had it in my own because it was in everybody else's. He grinned and pointed toward the righthand platform and I nodded and he led me through the pullulating crowd.

I staggered into someone and apologized and realized I was really drunk. I laughed and closed my eyes. Opened them and realized I was kissing someone. Leaned away. She smiled and set crackled black fingernails against my mouth. I pointed to Eric standing at the edge of the pentagram and Taylor nodded and we held hands and went to stand beside him. From behind I put my hands around her waist and tried to tell her that the smell of her hair could bring me from my sleep to stand before her door however far away her door might be. But she wouldn't have heard me and I wasn't making much sense anyway.

Eric waited for the spinner to see him as she knelt above her own small campstove fire. She and Wedo faced each other and watched each other's distorting figures through the shimmering air and played off each other's gestures as they worked the very air around them. A footwide miniature of her energy cage floated in the air outside her pentagram. This was what she was controlling and its motions were amplified into the energy cage beyond. Very clever: slave the larger to the smaller and manipulate the smaller. Less work, less risk, more control.

I liked watching them, liked the power funneling from them to the energy cages and then out to the crowd which gave it back. And their responses entered the tonic rhythms that washed across the crowd. It was a kind of looping collaboration. It looked hard and dangerous and fun.

The spinner, Sam I guess, saw Eric waving and nodded. Eric grinned at me.

A few minutes later the two spinners brought the rhythm to a head and then brought it down again until what remained was only Wedo's initial steady throb, slow insistent chthonic creature straining at its leash. Sam broke the pentagram at the cardinal points with a piece of rebar and motioned to Eric who jumped onto the platform and stepped cautiously across the painted border as if stepping across a crevasse which in a way he was. Sam hugged him and asked some questions and then looked at me and showed no recognition. Maybe I was backlit by the bonfire.

Eric left the pentagram and headed for the shimmering space between the platforms that still pulsed in time with Wedo's gestures. He rested the bell of his didgeridoo on a rickety folding tray before that massive array of energies. He nodded at Sam and she rejoined her pentagram and tied back her red hair and touched her toes and shook her legs before resuming her position. When she re-formed her energy cage what she conjured this time wasn't a ball but a ring. Its vibration threw back shards of firelight.

Close before me Taylor twisted round. "Have you seen this."

I shook my head. "Virgin."

She ruffled my hair and laughed. "We'll be gentle."

Eric put his mouth to the didgeridoo and then lifted his mouth and shook his head and spun a finger at Sam. The vibration increased. Eric drew a huge breath and put his mouth to the instrument and blew again and the dancers nearest him fell down. Something pushed my left side and I staggered holding Taylor as the bonfire flames blew back and the grandstand groaned and rang.

Taylor laughed and broke away and pulled me stumbling toward the surge of dancers. Some of them still picking themselves up startled but unhurt. Eric ghostly through the pulsing lens of coruscating air. He blew again. A long deep growling heartfelt purr. All around me people laughed or smiled or kissed, moving touching laughing. We danced.

In the grandstand drinking water and trying to catch my breath. Three or four A.M. Soaking wet and cold. Around me people resting drinking smoking fucking sleeping. Overhang reverberating with the massive infield rhythm. Mist encroaching on the infield. I shut my eyes and grinned. I could sleep. Did I want to sleep. What would I miss if I slept. This was the first time I'd stopped moving since the sun went down. I laughed and opened my eyes and stood uncertainly and knocked the folding seatback up behind my legs and wavered a bit. Oopsy. "I'm not as drunk as I look," I told the chairback.

"Well I hope not."

I turned. "I'm just clumsy. It works out about the same but doesn't hurt as bad next day. Hi Sam."

She leaned from shadow with a joint brightening as she inhaled. Her hi came out all smoke and without recognition.

"I work at the casting shop. You and your friend were handing out flyers for the vibe."

"The unicorn guy. The charmer."

"Um, that day, yeah. Usually, though, I—"

"What are you, Eddie, sixteen?"

"Fred. Eighteen."

"Fifteen."

I folded my arms. "Seventeen and that's my final offer."

"Sold." She tossed the roach and crabstepped into the aisle. Halfway down the steps she looked back. "Going once, going twice."

I nearly fell over getting out of the row. Clumsy, drunk. It works out about the same.

A narrow path led through the infield overgrowth to the taller grass island where the center lake had been. Sam seemed to know her way through it as she led me deeper in. I couldn't decide if her familiarity toward me and with the path we took intimidated or excited me. Maybe both.

In the center island the dry grass and shrubs were higher than my head and rustled with the pulsing bass as if some monstrous creature beat the bushes flushing quarry. Ahead of me Sam turned a corner. I hurried to catch up and turned the corner and then stopped. No Sam. Dry grass shivered rhythm but no wind blew or body passed amid the overgrowth. There was no moon and I could barely see the path before me.

"Sam." I felt foolish. Dry grass whispered hisses. "Sam."

From the grandstand someone called out Annn-deee.

I held my hands before me and walked slowly, dragged my feet to feel the narrow path. Thrumming through my shoes. Overhead the high grass drooped to form a canopy of black. Three hundred yards away a thousand people danced to music moving dry brush all around me yet I might as well have been alone out in the woods.

The sound around me broadened and I realized I had come into a clearing. Kneehigh dew-wet grass. Low and drifting overcast faint orange in the bonfire light. Deep abiding rhythm, dry grass rustling reply. I tried to find the grandstand but could only see the top outlined against the mist. I was in a slight depression, the bed of the vanished lake. Dew had wet my pant legs and my legs were cold. The rhythm seemed stronger. I thought about calling Sam again and decided hell with it. I was drunk and it was late and I was tired and it was dark and I was cold and this was weird.

I turned to find the path and make my way back to the warming fire and dancers' heat. Motionless before me Sam stood alabaster in the diffuse light, bundled clothes held draped before her.

"Aren't you cold," I said. Like an idiot.

She dropped her bundle and stepped toward me. I couldn't see her face. Beyond the bonfire deep undinal throbbing thickened. Right then I really needed to see her face. See if it was serious or mocking or filled with heat or condescending or just plain stoned and nothing more. The rhythm came from all around us now. As if generated by our meeting in this clearing.

Behind her bushes parted and a unicorn emerged. Ghostly silent huge and blackeyed. Gossamer mane and silver hooves and spiral horn. Muscular. Almost luminous in the clearing's dark. It saw us and stopped.

Unaware of it Sam took another step toward me. "What kind of magic can you make with this." And brushed back her red hair.

I could see she thought the look of pure stunned wonder on my face was because of her. Then she realized I was looking past her and her self-assurance faltered. She said What and turned to see what I was looking at.

I can't say how long we stood there in our strange tableau with that deep rhythm shaking everything around us. Sam naked beautiful and cold in flesh and heart and staring in that timeless stillness. Me damp with sweat and dew and shivering cold and staring at the heartbreak beauty of the unicorn stately at the clearing's edge. I did not move. Sam did not move. As if motion would dispel it like a mist.

The surrounding rhythm grew louder and discordant. Hissing grass a random susurration. A breeze blew Sam's hair and fluffed the unicorn's gossamer mane. I think the sudden wind made Sam aware of being naked. I think the knowledge made her feel ashamed. In any case she bent and got her clothes.

The unicorn flashed across the clearing and into the brush without a sound and gone.

Sam straightened and turned to me with clothes pressed tight against her. I could see her face just fine now. "You fucking asshole."

"You're the one who moved. I didn't make it go anywhere."

"You're just the one who made it, period."

"What?"

"What. What." She started putting on her clothes. "Charm boy. What the fuck was I thinking." She put on her jacket and zipped it up with unmistakable finality and said fuck you and left me standing there.

"I wasn't laughing at you," I told the space she'd occupied.

Still I did not move. I felt privileged and diminished. Finally I wiped my sleeves against my eyes and thought about how to find my way out of the overgrowth. I skirted the clearing's edge and found the path again but hesitated.

Something was wrong with the music. The dry grass was no longer beating in rhythm. The pulsing metronome had been broken. Like the sound was hitting a distant wall and weird echoes had started returning out of synch. It had taken on an oddly threatening edge.

I felt an overwhelming urge to run.

Screw the path. It's just grass. I crashed through the overgrowth and waved my arms as if swatting bees and knocked stalks aside and pushed through the dried and brittle brush.

I came out facing the grandstand. The enormous structure shuddered with the broken rhythms. I remembered reading that soldiers once were ordered to break stride when they marched across wooden bridges because if enough of them walked at a certain pace it could start a resonance that could wreck the bridge. Sympathetic vibration it was called.

I ran toward the pentagrams.

The painful sound was screwing up my equilibrium. It was hard to run in a straight line, like I was being slugged with pillows. The dancing had stopped and people were holding onto each other or pressing their palms to their ears, which helped relieve the piercing dissonance but not the body blows of sound. The concrete and iron grandstand was protesting. People stumbled down the steps beneath the trembling overhang and struggled toward the exit as if fighting a gale. It didn't help that most of them were wasted. Many of them ran into the tunnel and then ran back out. It probably felt like the whole thing was about to come down on them. Maybe it was.

I went around turn two and came up behind the platform where Wedo had been spinning. He had yielded his spot some time ago and from what I could tell the new spinner was trying to shut down the energy cage and it was having none of it.

If you're fighting something that you're casting either your pentagram was poorly made or something wants in real bad. Either way I couldn't help him without knowing what spells he was using and breaching the integrity of a pentagram while a casting is underway is pure suicide.

I looked around. No sign of Wedo or Eric. Even Sam would have been a welcome sight right now. I wondered if I could figure out the casting from the ingredients around the campstove in the empty pentagram at turn one.

I fell once as I ran to it. The pentagram was still broken at its cardinal points. The length of rebar lay nearby. I stepped in and quickly rejoined it and then knelt before the campstove and looked for matches to relight it. A woman yelled and I looked up to see Sam outside the circle looking scared and angry and definitely wanting in. I broke the circle again and she hurried in. She said something and I pointed to my ears and shook my head and she put her lips against my ear. "Get. The fuck. Out. Of my. Circle."

I pointed at the other spinner struggling for control inside his pentagram and shook my head and yelled into her ear. "What. Spell. Is it."

She didn't want to tell me and I didn't want to argue. A deep grinding filled the air and I looked past the north end of the track just as the roof collapsed on the far side of the grandstand.

I grabbed Sam's shoulder. "Spell!"

The massive roof rippled like a flag and she relented and yelled "Bolus."

Even in the midst of all that chaos I could only gape in disbelief. The bolus is one of the first spells anyone learns. Casting 101. A little ball of energy you conjure up to prove you can. But at some point someone had realized you could slave a bolus to a really big bolus and fluctuate it to push air around and make rhythms.

Buffeted by sound I lit the stove and threw in a crowfeather and sulphur and the rest of the ingredients. Sam spoke the incantation and the air began to shimmer again beside the pulsing ball the other spinner fought. Sam got it going and I indicated that I wanted to take over. Clearly she didn't want me to. Just as clearly she had no better idea herself. I put my hands over her hands and she slid aside and I took her place. It felt like I was trying to hold a floating ball of water. You had to handle it a certain way. There was surprising resistance because I wasn't manipulating the bolus but the larger energy cage beyond the platform. Tiny movements yielded big results. My first few gestures made a sonic horror that was worse than what I was trying to fight.

I glanced at the other spinner in his pentagram and something wrenched the bolus from my control. My hands flew from a common center as if I'd tried to grab a spinning wheel.

I got the bolus under control and held it spinning steadily. The huge energy cage slaved to it hummed with its velocity but sent out no more throbbing notes. Sam yelled something but I ignored her. The dissonance was increasing. The bonfire flinched in the gale of sound. Across from us the other spinner was losing his wrestling match with his energy cage.

I closed my eyes and felt the rhythm with my hands and not my ears and what I felt was someone else's casting trying to take over. What I felt felt familiar.

I opened my eyes and twitched my fingers and the bolus contracted and expanded. Fighting it would probably cause more damage than letting it take over. I needed to do to the unseen caster what he was trying to do to me and use my own bolus to control his. Work it into his broken rhythm and then start messing with it.

Paypay's visualization exercises paid off now. I imagined my bolus was a marble and the energy cage was a beachball. I imagined a wide rubber band stretched around the marble and the beachball so that if I turned the marble back and forth the beach ball turned as well but its motion was amplified. Now here comes another caster with his own marble and he stretches his own rubber band around my beachball and starts turning his marble and taking control of the beachball himself. I imagined my senses extending through my hands into the bolus and through the energy cage and out along the lines of power into the unseen caster's bolus. I tried to glean a pattern and anticipate the next movement. The hardest part was not fighting it.

The spinner on the other platform caught on to what I was doing and struggled with his own bolus until its pattern matched mine. He probably thought bringing it in line would negate the influence of the interloper. I couldn't blame him but I wanted him to stop, now and fast, but I couldn't stop what I was doing without making things worse. He got his pattern aligned with mine and instead of occasional violent peaks from our battle with the interloper we got a savage thrum torn from the core of the world as the two giant balls of energy began to resonate. Soldiers must break stride.

Glass blew from the grandstand skyboxes and rained shards down on the infield. Girders in the center began to bend.

Something wrenched my hands off of the bolus. I yelled and wrung burned palms. Okay, he knows I'm here.

The energy cage spun faster outside the pentagram. Somehow the interloper was feeding energy into it. The spinning ball now glowed a dull red as the air around it heated.

It was getting hot inside the pentagram too.

I leaned close to Sam and yelled that I was going to open the pentagram so she could get the hell out of here. I picked up the rebar and Sam punched me in the jaw and tried to take it. I couldn't really blame her. She thought I was going to kill us both by opening our pentagram and subjecting us to the forces outside it. Well maybe I was. But if the unknown caster kept feeding power to the energy cage it would soon overcome the spell that constrained it and blow apart and the bolus inside our pentagram would probably go nova too. So I put a foot behind Sam and tripped her and before she got back up I used the iron bar to break the pentagram at the four cardinal points. And was nearly knocked down as the sound pressure wave washed across me like a tide. My bones rang with it. My brain concussed against my skull. The deep thrum pulsed so quickly now that it was a constant pressure, the pushing spell Yan and I had wished for when we'd moved the railcar.

Yan. Oh son of a bitch.

The contracting energy cage had flared from red to orange and was humming like a tenfoot hive of angry bees. The containing spell couldn't hold much longer. Just outside the breached pentagram the small bolus paled to yellow. I shoved Sam from the pentagram and pointed toward the exit to the promenade. She hesitated and then ran.

Outside the pentagram was bedlam. The grandstand roof was buckling in the center, taking the skyboxes with it in a broad V down to the mezzanine. Glass had blown everywhere. Bonfire sparks had set the dry grass burning. I saw a few people running and a few on the ground but it looked like most had made it out.

The other spinner breached his own pentagram made a break for it and he yelled at me as he ran by. I guess he thought I was crazy. I'm not sure he was wrong. I sealed my pentagram again.

Magic flows along a path like water in a pipe. Yan said electricity had worked like that and that a pentagram was like a Faraday cage. All I knew was that pentagrams aren't for casting so much as they're for protecting casters from the castings they make by keeping the energy outside the circle. Two things will quickly turn a casting graveyard bad. The pentagram gets breached from outside and all the casting's energy blows out the breach at once. Or the pentagram gets breached incorrectly from inside and the casting's energy eventually overcomes the pentagram and it tears apart at its weakest point. Either way the pentagram itself is where the energy gets channeled.

I could let the spinning ball of energy go critical and stay in my pentagram and hope it held while the discharge blew the shit out of everything else for miles around.

I could incorrectly breach both pentagrams knowing that the casting's energy would discharge out the flaws and hope that I could aim the discharge somewhere harmless.

I could incorrectly breach my pentagram and aim the flaw at the other pentagram and then haulass into that one and seal it before the breached one discharged into it, and hope the one I sealed would stand up to the blast. If it worked it would absorb the energy and I'd be safe and Del Mar would still be part of the coastline. If it didn't work—well it wouldn't be any worse than my other two options would it. Which meant there really was no other option.

I looked down at the length of rebar. You sure about this, Fred?

The energy cage was whitehot now and hissing as it burned air.

Fuck it. I scraped away the yard of my pentagram closest to the other platform and then ran out. The spinning ball of air was now a little sun a few yards wide, blinding white and keening. I winced against its heat and my armhair singed as I ran like hell around it to the other platform.

Brush burned all across the infield now and false dawn grayed the eastern sky. Metal girders screamed above the grating keen of spinning orb. The remainder of the buckled grandstand roof rippled and collapsed. Pieces flew and dark dust billowed.

I jumped onto the turn two platform and into the pentagram. The spinner had tossed out his potion and shut off the campstove before he'd run like hell. Got to admire good work habits. I grabbed his squeezebag of blessed blood and paint—a nozzled confectioner's bag, very clever—and hurriedly rejoined the cardinal points and spoke the standard invocation that would seal the pentagram as hand dexter traced the fivepointed star in the air and then hand sinister traced the circle round it. If I had done a shitty job sealing the pentagram I'd be less than toast when the energy cage discharged.

A dome around me lit up white before the shockwave knocked me to my hands and knees. The pentagram was protected but the ground beneath it shook as rolling thunder filled the world. I lay prone and shut my eyes and held onto the surging platform and rode out the inferno, held on until the light dimmed and the platform stilled.

I opened my eyes. Starklit palmtrees bent back as if craning to look up at a geyser of white light that rose above the infield fires. A ring of blackened grass leaned away from it. The force of the explosion had blown out most of the infield fire.

I watched my shadow fade as preternatural daylight gave way to genuine dawn. Then I got up and turned in a complete circle and felt a hard click in my throat when I swallowed.

The platform was charred black and smoking except for a perfect circle of unmarred pine within the pentagram. The platform at turn one was gone.

I found the rebar and breached the pentagram. Correctly.

From the grandstand's tunnel entrance I saw people picking themselves up on the promenade. The structure groaned and shook around me. Ahead of me my shadow wavered from the burning infield light behind. I knew I shouldn't be standing here waiting for a thousand tons of building to fall on me. I wasn't indifferent, I was numb. I had no room for more.

The back side of the grandstand had survived but shards of glass and terracotta had rained everywhere. Across the oval courtyard people had sought shelter in the tiny bare stalls where horses were tethered. Across from me a large-eyed girl stared up at the lightening sky. Tall gangly wild-haired and swallowed by a U.S. Marines coat. She brushed herself off absently and turned around as if looking for someone. I thought her hair was dyed in dark streaks until I saw the streaks grow longer and saw her hand gleam as it lowered from brushing back her hair. She seemed oblivious and kept dusting herself off as if cleaning her dirty jacket were the most important thing.

I glanced up at a lengthy sound of creaking. Swaying on a huge-linked chain an enormous chandelier winked orange infield fire. I walked out of the tunnel and onto the grassy promenade. Nothing crashed behind me.

The bleeding girl stood looking at the dawn sky as if puzzled by it. I went to help her. She gave no sign she saw me as she put her hands to her mouth and took a deep breath, and even before she yelled it out I knew the name she'd call.

People said it was a miracle no one was killed. I couldn't disagree. Dozens had been hurt. Cuts, scrapes, concussions from falling tiles. Most had hearing problems for weeks afterward. My ears rang for days.

The town held a meeting and decided that any future events held at the track other than the swap meet required town approval. I didn't tell anyone my suspicion about Yan. It would have required revealing that Yan had burned down Paypay's shop, though I think most people suspected that anyhow with Yan suddenly absent from Del Mar, and I tried to convince myself it didn't matter because Yan was gone and what had happened at the vibe was just his little parting gift. Even though the parting itself had occurred three months ago.

Be seeing you.

I don't think so.

That's because you haven't thought this through.

Dread reunions, wands on the hill at dawn. Thunder and lightning, scorched earth. Thou nemesis my ancient. The whole pointy hatted ball of wax.

I was going to have to learn more defensive casting.

FOURTEEN

ARIEL: A BOOK OF THE CHANGE. Gold letters unevenly embossed on a plain black cover. No author name.

I looked up at Dr. Ram. "My father wrote this?"

"I have no reason to believe he did not."

"That's not quite an answer."

He shrugged. "Some people believe he did and some do not."

"What does he say."

"I have never asked him. And to the best of my knowledge he has never said, to me or to anybody."

I thumbed through pages. "Why not."

"Read it, Fred. Read it and decide for yourself."

I read the opening line and snapped the book shut and said You have got to be fucking kidding me. Dr. Ram was consulting Mr. Lee in private and the room was empty. Not that I'd been talking to anyone. I looked at the book as if staring at it could somehow change what I'd just read. I took a deep breath and opened the book again and reread the first line.

I was bathing in a lake when I saw the unicorn.

---

read it all that morning whenever Dr. Ram didn't need me, and that afternoon whenever Paypay wasn't looking over my shoulder.

My father had been sixteen when the Change occurred. He'd been at his school somewhere in south Florida for something called a debate tournament when everything stopped at fourthirty in the afternoon. It was a story I'd heard many times. Cars had stopped moving, electricity had stopped, batteries failed, most mechanical and electronic devices simply wouldn't work. Their whole world had depended on these things and now they were useless.

He'd made his way home and found it being looted. A girl who came with him got killed. Soon after that he saw a manticore, a creature that had not existed in the world he'd known. It had wandered to a canal not far from his house. That was when he realized that things—technology, the principles by which technology worked, the rules, the laws, the world— hadn't just stopped. They had Changed.

All my life I'd heard about how dangerous the first years after the Change had been. Anarchy and survival and chaos and blah blah blah. I had no idea how ugly it had been. How, I don't know—raw.

My father had struck out on his own. He lay low and learned to survive and camped in libraries and read books on hunting and weapons and self sufficiency. One day he was bathing in a lake when an injured unicorn approached the shore. He tended it and befriended it and named it Ariel. It was about as different from one of my unicorn charms as I could imagine.

It grew up and grew huge. We're not talking dainty doe-like waif here. We're talking Appaloosa. It was smart. It could talk. Worse, it learned to talk from my father, and when he was young he clearly wasn't the tightlipped hardass he would become. They were friends and they loved each other.

You had to be a virgin to touch a unicorn. It didn't take a genius to realize none of this was going anywhere good.

They wandered north to Atlanta where they met a man named Malachi Lee. Which finally explained the middle name I had been saddled with. Malachi Lee had squatted a house in the city and lived as if he were some kind of feudal Japanese samurai. I thought he was a couple ingredients shy of a potion but my father clearly admired him. Lee taught my father how to fight with a sword, and presented him with a sword of his own. My father named it Fred. Kind of as a joke.

I had been named after my father's sword and some nutjob who thought he was an ancient samurai.

I shut the book and walked around a while.

———————

At Paypay's that afternoon I read more when Paypay was busy or when he thought I was.

While he was in Atlanta training with Malachi Lee and naming swords Fred my father learned that a caster had offered a reward for an alicorn, the horn of a unicorn. Alicorns are some of the biggest mojo there is, and this guy wanted one so he could become the Big Kahuna Caster. He was in Manhattan, which was a big city that was also an island. This was back when the cities had started to run out of food, but apparently caster boy liked his skyscraper view too much to turn farmer himself. So he ran some kind of protection racket on the outlying farm communities that had begun to form, taking food by threatening them through a musclehead whose biggest claim to fame was the huge and hugely nasty griffin he rode.

Malachi Lee set out for Manhattan to kill the caster and keep Ariel safe. Supposedly. I think he was just bored and had nothing better to do. He told my father and Ariel to get out of town and lie low while he took care of things. Naturally they ignored this and set out after him. I don't know why he didn't save time by blading. He mentioned it but never said why he didn't do it. Maybe he didn't know how.

Along the way they acquired two people. A sweet but dim kid named George who'd been sent by his father to kill a dragon in the Adirondack mountains and a strongwilled but abrasive girl named Shaughnessy who didn't seem to have anything better to do than follow them. Seeing a pattern here?

It was obvious from the start that the girl was trouble. That my father couldn't see it coming is more evidence that he was a little thick about such things, which is probably how you end up still a virgin at twentytwo in the first place.

In the mountains in North Carolina they killed a dragon by puncturing its hydrogen-filled gasbag with arrows about the time the stupid thing landed on their campfire. Boom: dragon steak everywhere.

I remembered the embarrassed silence that time my father told Mr.

Binauer he'd killed a dragon. Everybody thinking my father was full of shit or crazy.

They sent the George kid back home after the dragon business. The main roads north were being watched so they diverted to Chesapeake Bay, where they made a drydocked sailboat seaworthy and set out for Manhattan. At sea Ariel palavered with dolphins and they fetched three humpback whales that towed them the rest of the way to the island city. Could I make this up. More to the point, could my father. Mr. Binauer had once made fun of him for telling me that whales had done him a big favor a long time ago. But that only proved my father had read this book, not that he'd written it.

I couldn't stop reading the thing. I don't know if it was the story itself or the thought of it happening to some nearly inconceivable younger version of my father. It was hard to believe this was him talking to me from a quarter century ago. This guy sounded so young. Vulnerable and emotional and smartassed and strangely naive. I'd hang out with the guy in this book any day. What had happened to him? How had he turned into my father?

I stayed up all night and found out.

At one in the morning I read how my father and Ariel were captured the moment they arrived in Manhattan. They were taken to the Empire State Building, a skyscraper the caster had squatted. My father escaped but without Ariel.

Around two A.M. beat up and half starving in the city he fell in with a group that took him back to Washington D.C., which apparently had been America's headquarters before the Change. The group belonged to a farming collective who'd been paying protection to the caster guy in Manhattan. They'd had enough of it and had regrouped in Washington and were scouting Manhattan to plan an attack against the caster's halfassed fortress skyscraper, which was really only occupied on the very top and bottom floors.

At twothirty my father gave the Washington group information about the caster's organization that led to the craziest scheme I'd ever heard of. A small team using hang gliders to attack the barely defended upper floors of the skyscraper. The idea being to kill the caster while the rest of their army, if you can call a couple hundred people an army, attacked the ground floors and fought their way up. My father was in this team. So was Malachi Lee, who had found the Washington bunch before my father did.

At three A.M. they flew their hang gliders onto the Empire State Building and the fighting began. My father killed a lot of people. Malachi Lee killed himself instead of letting himself be killed when he was surrounded.

At four A.M. Ariel killed the caster. Shish-kebabbed him with her horn. Yow. Half crazed from captivity she fled during the confusion of the raid. My father left everything behind to track her down. Shaughnessy came with him as he scoured the countryside and in one inevitable night of loneliness and weakness he succumbed to a burning older and deeper than the one in his heart and he changed everything irreparably and forever. Because even when he finally did find her he couldn't have her back. She had gone half wild and crazed and he had irretrievably crossed a line. Too bad, so sad.

I finished the book in the cold hours before dawn and sat thinking and awaiting the light.

It was true. I believed it was true, all of it. I believed it entirely because the man who wrote it sounded nothing like the man I knew.

What had happened to my father. I gripped the book tightly. This. This had happened to him.

FIFTEEN

Dr. Ramchandani jumped when I dropped the heavy book onto his coffee table. He looked at my face and frowned. "Please go home and sleep, Fred. I don't need you today. Not this much anyway."

I yawned and nodded. "One question."

"It is never one question with you. What is it."

"Where did this come from." I set a finger on the book's plain black cover. "I mean how did you get it. Who printed it, how did it end up in California."

"You see. Four questions."

"Dr. Ram."

He shrugged. "A woman named Roxanne printed it. I believe she used to be part of the coven here. Somehow she acquired a very old screwtype printing press and occasionally she undertakes commissions or peculiar projects. I understand she herself is somewhat peculiar."

"She live in Carlsbad?"

"I believe so, yes. But I would lay very good odds that she set it from a copy someone gave her, a copy that had been printed in similar fashion."

"It's like four thousand miles to North Carolina."

"It has also been nearly twentyfive years since it was first written. I do not know how the original manuscript was printed but it was. As to how it has spread so far—" He shrugged. "I do not think your father was trying to be any kind of historian, Fred. I think he was only trying to tell about these events that happened to him. His Change, if you will. But I know of no other book of any consequence that describes the Change and the time immediately following."

"Is it possible that my father is just someone who's nuts for this book. So that he named me after one of the characters and got a samurai sword and all of this stuff. I mean it could be that, right."

"Your father is hardly a follower, Fred."

"A lot of it just seems . . . out of character."

He smiled. "Some people do not like your father. He is blunt and he does not suffer fools gladly. Some people think he is a bit, well. . . ."

"Crazy."

"Unwavering in his beliefs. But when George Fayelle fell from the cliff that day and Mr. Villaraigosa saw him clinging to a root it was your father who brought him up from there. Your father got there ahead of the rescue party and found George holding on by a thread. By a root really. He did not wait for the rescue party to arrive, he climbed down thirty vertical feet with no rope and he brought George back up. The rescue party met him and brought George to me. The difference of those few hours may have saved George's life."

"He never told me."

"Why would he. I imagine you probably do not know about the Hendricks family either."

"They're the ones that were murdered when I was a kid."

He nodded. "They lived in the big white cliffhouse that the Lees live in now. A group of strangers decided to squat it." He shook his head. "A hundred empty beach houses here and yet they had to have this one. So one night they simply walked in and killed Bob and Janona and their two children. They cut off their heads and threw the bodies down the hill and put the heads on the fence outside the house."

"Jesus christ."

"We had a town meeting about it. We cannot allow this, we must send men to make them leave. You know. Your father simply walked out of it. The next day a group of us went to the house to force them out. When we got to the Hendricks' house there were four pikes out front, I think they were actually ski poles, and on them were four heads. Not the Hendricks I should add. Inside the house there was a great deal of blood on the furniture and the walls and a most terrible stench. But nothing else." He smiled thinly and gave a little shrug. "Your father came to my office the next day but he said nothing about it and I never asked him."

"But you still think it was—wait a second. Why did he come to your office."

He looked sheepish. "I stitched a moderate laceration on his forearm. Somehow I misplaced the billing. I am a good doctor I think but I am a terrible accountant."

The next day I was mixing a potion in back of Paypay's shop and I was tired and wishing I hadn't promised not to use stasis bottles to shortcut my work. I heard the doorbells clang and sensed a certain stillness fall in the shop outside. A woman's voice asked something I couldn't make out and I heard Paypay's indistinct reply. It was late afternoon, Mrs. Gloster's usual time for coming by and ordering up another in her endless series of—

"Fred," Paypay called from the front of the shop. His voice curiously flat.

"Right there." I got up and cracked my knuckles and set the half done potion on a shelf.

Paypay stuck his head through the curtained doorway. "Someone here for you."

"For me?" Maybe Sam had come to apologize for her behavior at the vibe. I nodded at Paypay and wiped my hands on my apron. Paypay didn't go back up front but regarded me with strange appraisal. He probably didn't approve of girls visiting me while I was working. It hadn't come up much before.

"I am back here," he said and stepped past me into the workroom.

"Okay." I squeezed past him and went into the bright sunlight of the front room, squinting and putting on my Customer Face. "Hi, what can I—"

Something large blotted out the afternoon sunlight in the front windows. I blinked rapidly. Looked left. Looked right. Glanced back at the doorcurtain still moving from Paypay going through it. Swallowed hard and turned to the front of the shop.

"Howdy," said the unicorn.

SIXTEEN

"Umm, umm. Hi?"

The filament tail threw sunlight across the shop as it swished. "Take your time. Take it all in." Husky voice from an impossible, unmistakable silhouette. "Get used to it. Then get over it. Okay?"

"Are you. I mean is this. Do." I had absolutely no idea what to say.

"Can we maybe go outside. It's kind of stuffy in here." The long head tossed on the powerful neck. The spiral horn starred sunlight. "I'm a lot prettier in the light anyhow."

What stood before me in the bright afternoon light outside that worn-down stripmall real as the vinegrown benches on the cracked and weedy walkways rendered language pitiful. To describe her now is to trap in language what was never meant to be confined.

She was large. Not deerlike, not fragile or slender or delicate. Built like a draft horse muscular and strong. But she did not move like a horse. She could be still, stillness surrounded her. Her pure white coat was nearly glossy. Faint rainbow refractions played on her hide when she moved and when she moved her motion was deliberate and graceful. Bright metallic hooves. Fine mane that played in the onshore breeze. Her tail looked combed, always looked combed, and never once moved to brush away a fly. There was never a fly to be seen around her. The yardlong alabaster horn that augered from her forehead showed opalescent depths and faint pastels in certain light. It was hard not to stare at it when she spoke. The eyes my father wrote about decades ago regarded me from several yards away, black and observant and intelligent, acute but holding a tiredness he had not described. It seemed out of place in the timeless features that regarded me.

"You smell like him."

"Like my father?"

The tail swished. "No, like Shiva, Destroyer of Worlds. Who do you think." The eyes narrowed. "Don't look much like him though."

"Is that why you're here."

"For your father?"

"No, for Zeus, hurler of thunderbolts. Who do you think."

"Ah, there we go."

"There we go what."

"Now you sound like him."

I snorted.

Wind and light played across her in the ensuing silence.

"That was you at the vibe. At the racetrack."

"Never been near the joint."

"But. I saw." I took a deep breath. "A few nights back there was this—"

She laughed and a chill went down my spine. It was simultaneously the most beautiful and alien sound I ever heard a living creature make. "I'm just fucking with you. It was me." I swear to god she smirked. "Sorry I interrupted by the way. I'm famous for my timing."

My face got hot. "Oh, that was—um, it's okay. You probably did me a favor."

"Uh huh."

I looked both ways down the grassy street and looked back at the shop. No one was around.

"You haven't asked me why I'm here."

"Oddly enough I think I have some idea."

"Oddly enough it's not about your father."

"No. You're here about Yan. Yanamandra Ramchandani."

"Dark as you, dark straight hair, skinny, a little older than you, two inches taller, gold eyes with green, permanent smirk?"

"That sounds about right. What did he do."

The horn rose, the nostrils flared. The eyes were holes. "He killed my mate."

I got my stuff and told Paypay I was going to have to leave early today. He nodded. "You back tomorrow, Fred?"

"I think so. I'm not sure."

"You tell me, okay."

I slung my blades over my shoulder. "I will, Paypay."

He nodded again but looked worried. Beyond that you'd never know a real unicorn had walked into his shop twenty minutes ago.

I am going outside to walk with a unicorn. I am excited. I am afraid.

Outside Paypay's shop I looked her up and down and shook my head. She hadn't moved.

She snorted. "Yah, still here. What, did you think you ate the wrong mushrooms?"

"My father didn't do you justice."

The horn flashed sunlight as she nodded. "You're telling me."

We headed inland. I asked where we were going.

"You know where."

I stopped walking. "Okay, let me try to put some things together." I ticked them off on my fingers. "Yan killed your—your mate. I was Yan's friend. You and my father were once—you were his Familiar. You're going to see my father because you want us to go after Yan."

She studied me. "It's more than just Revenge of the Unicorn."

"Like what."

"Tell you when we get there. Living it once has been bad enough, I sure as hell don't want to have to tell it twice. A little patience for now? Pretty please with sugar on top?"

"But why me. Why didn't you go to my father first. He's your—"

"I know that would seem to make more sense. But you gotta believe me when I tell you that the connection to your father is the biggest accident in this whole farce. I was down this way because I was sniffing out your buddy pal's trail and I could feel him all over his little recital at your big party the other night. I sniffed you out because I could feel him all over you too. I was going to confront you with all of it at the racetrack. Who is he, what do you know about him. But you caught me by surprise."

"Because of the girl?"

"Because you smelled like your father."

"You didn't know?"

She dragged a hoof across the broken road and sparks flurried. She turned away and resumed walking. I had to hurry to catch up. "I had no faintest glimmer of an idea," she said as I drew beside her. "And I'm sure as shit not happy about it."

I glanced at her. Wondered for the first time could I touch her. "Did you know my father wrote a book about you."

"Your father wrote a book about your father. I was just in it."

"He never told me about it. About the book, about anything that happened to him. About you. I only just read it."

"Can't say I blame him. The past is a graveyard, Fred."

"Ah, there we go."

"There we go what."

"Now you sound just like him."

We made our way among desolating cars cluttering the freeway exit ramp and onto the surface street. Near my father's house I watched her pick her silent way among vinecovered cars rusted cockeyed there. The sun below the cliffs, our surroundings redgold, our shadows leading east. Hers outlined by a shimmer. I glanced at her and drew a sharp breath. She was glass reflecting fire. Colors moved with her muscles and played burning highlights all along her glossy coat. Yellow highlighted curves deepened to orange on broader spaces. Her horn looked the way I imagined machines had looked when electricity had once flowed through them, iridescent and alive.

She caught me looking and snorted. "The sun makes light of me."

I shook my head and gave no rejoinder. Only later did I realize she might have meant son.

———————

Tree roots corrugating sidewalks demarcating leafcarpeted lineaments of streets. Undifferentiated yards a riot of tall grass and weeds and creeping vines. Birdshit everywhere. Brokenwindowed houses missing tiles. Sagging roofs draped by powerlines or fallen limbs. Insides rotting wood and waterstains, peeling wallpaper and spreading mold, paperthreaded nests and skeletons of dogs and cats.

Then the startling order of my father's house. Cut lawn and trimmed hedges and patched roof. Porch swept and windows replaced. Sigils of occupation. A place carved out of the obdurate world. I hadn't come this way since the day Yan and I stole some of his books.

I started to go to the front door but my remarkable companion shook her head and said He's in back. I only nodded and led her to the back yard.

He was practicing. He practiced a lot. Cargo shorts and running shoes, no shirt. Tan and fit and sweating and scarred. Lean arms welldefined. The beginnings of paunch but mostly in much better shape than I would probably ever be.

The sword flashed as it moved in precise and deadly arcs and thrusts. It never wavered. It was part of him. Had been part of him longer than I had been alive. Had killed a lot of people. My father had killed a lot of people. I still wasn't sure how to feel about that.

We halted at the corner of the unattached garage out of his line of sight. My strange companion watched my father steadily and did not move or even blink. I hadn't learned to read her face. After a minute she glanced at me and I nodded and walked forward and cleared my throat and said Dad.

He looked surprised to see me. Started to say something. Then saw her. Went rigid. Stepped back. The sword lowered. He looked at me with more questions in his eyes than I would ever be able to answer. And fear. For the first time in my life I saw fear in my father's eyes. I could only shrug.

She came forward then, flowing silent in the ochre light. Her gaze flicked brief acknowledgement as she passed me. Brief acknowledgement.

She stopped before him he. Swallowed hard I. Stayed very still.

He sank to his knees in the freshcut grass. Tired gaze on tired gaze. Held out the sword. Lowered it to the ground with the handle on the left and the edge toward him. He looked like a boy. My father looked like a child lost in wonder and pain. "My name." His voice cracked and he cleared his throat and tried again. "My name is Peter Garey. And I would. I would." He looked at the sword.

She stepped forward and lowered her head to touch her glimmering horn to the sharp curved metal. She shut her eyes and held her horn there a moment and then lifted her head and looked at him.

He nodded. He did not look delighted or relieved at this reunion. He looked aggrieved. Picked up his sword and returned it to its scabbard silently and without looking. Set it aside and looked at his hands in his lap and then brought them up to cover his face.

"Oh Pete," said Ariel.

SEVENTEEN

"I wandered. Blindly. Wildly. I wasn't sane I think. The captivity had driven me somewhere I was never supposed to be, and seeing you with—well all I knew was running. I ran for a long time. Weeks I think. Years in a way.

"One day I was drinking from a stream and looked up and saw a harpy on the wing circling me and I realized I had no idea where I was. How I'd gotten there. How long I'd been there. I had never been lost in my life and suddenly my soul had lost its own magnetic north.

"I wandered. I think I was looking for my own kind. We're pretty hard to find. And you know it's not like there's a unicorn registry anywhere. I just wandered and knew that one day I would know when they were around. I kept away from the things of man. They had done me little good and my kind wouldn't be found among them anyhow. There were plenty of places where humans aren't.

"One day I watched a bird die. I was somewhere in the midwest in midwinter. It was barren and beautiful and a mirror to my soul. I saw something fluttering on the ground and went to it. It was a crow that had been clawed by a wildcat. Fastened to the ground by its frozen blood but still alive. It quieted when I came to it but it was breathing fast and opening and closing its beak. I could do nothing for it. I stood beside it only just touching it to let it know something was out there for it. After a while it died. That was all really. And I saw that it was horrible and beautiful and utterly necessary. If the wildcat had died of starvation for not having found the crow would that have been less sad.

"In the natural world things die. In the natural world things kill to live. The bread you eat is alive. The ground you tread on is alive. In your bodies entire nations invisible to the eye wage war. Eventually all of it must yield. The only way to postpone that loss is to hasten it in something else. There is no escape. No argument. No remedy. Ignore it and be a fool or accept it and lose your foolish innocence.

"But I am not natural. I will never age. Never sicken. I have killed to stay alive but I do not have to kill to live. I knew then I had taken much for granted. Humbled and humiliated before the simple bloody truth of one dead bird I understood the tragic great machinery of being. My heart was cored there on that empty plain and I was stark undone.

"And free. Finally free. Because at last I understood that what had happened to you was necessary. You are mortal. You must kill or die. You must grow or die. You must change or die. And Pete you killed. You grew. You changed. I am eternal and unnatural and did not want you to change. I loved you and love is selfish. But out there on that barren plain I understood that one day you will face that horrible beautiful necessity as well and that I had fled that truth as much as I had fled from any act you had committed.

"I was not cured but that was where I began to heal. To feel anything at all after so long was a beginning. And eventually I buried you, Pete. I buried you. As in the decades since then you have buried your heart's claimants in the reclaiming earth. I see it in your eyes. I wish it were otherwise. But I cannot escape it. Cannot argue with it. Cannot remedy it. Cannot ignore it. All I can do, all anyone can do, is stand beside you on that windswept plain when your time comes and let you know you're not alone.

"I ranged north to snowbound lands where the sun hovered above the horizon for days on end. I went south until the constellations changed and wind and cold grew unabating. I saw creatures never cataloged by man or myth. Ruins of cities built by creatures that had never seen a man. Fledgling empires ruled by necromancers building monuments with legions of the shambling resurrected dead. I saw men on the backs of rocs in harness gliding in and out of threads of mist in the foothills of the Andes.

"In the Yucatán I acquired a companion, a girl whose parents had been killed in some attack by creatures she remembered only dimly. I found her living on a farm outside a massacred village that was running out of food. I was more friend than Familiar to Mila, more guardian than parent. I taught her to read, to hunt, to grow food. I protected her from jaguars and centaurs and men. But she grew older and her body changed and I could sense that it grew curious about men even as her mind sought my protection from them. I knew what this would bring about one day and realized I would have to put her back in contact with her own kind to acquire social graces and a place among them and eventually a mate and I did these things and so did she. Perhaps I remain a fire story for her children. I felt that she had been entrusted to me and that I had been a proper steward to that trust. I enjoyed the time that she was with me and I did not miss her after she was gone. Mila was not my adventure. I was done with adventures.

"After that I spent a month in a colony of demons in Panama. They were pacifists, pariahs among their own kind who had fled persecution to forge a new life here. They had a little community in the forest and were trying to teach the trees to grow into buildings and houses. Their colony was hard to find and tended to be discovered only by those who needed to recuperate from one thing or another. They had become a kind of informal halfway house for soulsick creatures. They told great stories and threw great parties. One of them told me he had heard of unicorns along the western coast of North America. When I left them that was where I headed. But I wasn't in the hurry I had been in. My need had lessened. Plus unicorns are immortal. I could look for my people until the sun went nova if I wanted to.

"In New Mexico I found a city of tipis. Many of the plains Indian tribes had merged and begun a huge migration eastward. Back to Virginia and the Carolinas on a collective dreamquest to reclaim the forests that had been theirs hundreds of years ago. Their magic was strong. I kept some distance from them but I know I was seen because they made offerings to me. I'm sneaky but some of those guys could steal fleas from a cat.

"In Utah I nearly got captured again. A party on horseback came after me outside Salt Lake City. Sons of bitches actually herded me down the streets. They had nets, rope, wire, lassoes, crossbows, longbows, and for all I know unicorn repellant. Include me out, thanks. I outran em, barely. I have no idea what they wanted with me and I don't give a shit.

"Five years later I was in Yosemite. I'm happy to report that the trails and picnic tables are completely overgrown and the cabins and buildings are mostly forest mulch. Reclaiming. That's our theme for today. Oh there were construction cranes and microwave relay stations and the cliffs and boulders are gonna be chock full of pitons and pickholes till the next ice age at least. But you all haven't made the impact you think you have.

"It was pretty country. Mountains and waterfalls and springs, elk and moose and fluffy bunnies. I thought I might just stick around for a while.

"I first saw him drinking water from a strangely bowlshaped growth that I realized was a dish antenna covered with weeds. I watched him for five minutes and still wasn't sure I could believe it. You have to remember that I'd never seen a unicorn before. He looked fake. He was bigger than me. He moved like he was made of mercury. I watched him drink and I thought I could watch him drinking for days and then the wind shifted and he looked up and saw me and suddenly he just wasn't there. Damn we're fast.

"After all my searching there was no way he was getting away from me. I spent weeks trying to track him down. It never occurred to me that these were his woods and this was his countryside and he wasn't gonna be found till he was good and ready.

"So he tracked me tracking him until he decided to show himself. It wasn't the stuff of great drama I can tell you. I was in a clearing wondering which direction I should head next and he just walked out from the trees and stood there. For all I knew he'd been standing there half an hour. He was a lot better at this than I was.

"First shock: he didn't speak english. He didn't speak anything. His body was language, his face was meaning. I kept saying Hey, hi, hola, güten haben, konnichi-wa, whuddup and he just stood there patiently until I got it through my pointy little head that he was talking to me, just not with words.

"Which led to shock number two: I knew fuckall about how to be a unicorn. Most of my language had been learned from an adolescent boy. My education took place in the books of human beings and within their society. I did not act, react, move, communicate, or even perceive like one of my own kind. I was stunted. Shit, I had raised a little girl and taught her how to be a goddamn human being. That's how much of a unicorn I was.

"I can't tell you his name because it wasn't words. Joe, okay? Joe had lived in Yosemite as long as he could remember which meant since the Change. Unlike me he had seen other unicorns. Also unlike me he had known to let them be. It turns out us unicorns are a very localized, territorial, solitary, and unsocial species. We find a piece of ground that speaks to us and we staple ourselves to it. We adopt it, protect it, defend it, nurture it, love it. We're just gardeners really. We don't go out to unicorn bars on Saturday nights and get plastered and wake up next to each other with stinky breath. We're immortal. We're patient. We don't need to breed to carry on the line. We are the line. We always will be.

"Joe taught me Basic Unicorning. How to be invisible through pure stillness. How to read the trees for growth, disease, occupants, coming weather. Hear the earth turning. Feel a shadow touch my hide. Make a small place mine, make my place a garden. There was a lot I can't put into words.

"Eight or nine years went by in which I saw not one human being, traveled no more than a dozen miles. Joe's garden was my world and my senses, my identity, extended into it. And eventually, inevitably, into Joe.

"He never asked me about my life with humans or why I was so lousy at being a unicorn. I don't think he'd have understood if I had explained. He lacked the sophistication. Well, not lacked. He didn't need it. Hi, I'm Joe, this is my garden, would you like to be a gardener too? That was enough.

"One day in Joe's garden I watched a crow attack a finch. The crow didn't kill it but left it with a broken wing, which is only a delayed death for a bird in the wild. It happened in our garden and the crow was part of our garden and the finch was part of our garden and I thought of my dying crow on the midwinter plains years ago and knew that Joe would never need the lesson I had learned there. It was factory installed. It inhabited his every cell. And all around me were things feeding on living things and growing on living things and living on living things. And feeding and growing and living on dead things. I didn't play favorites, I helped find balance. I was a caretaker not an owner.

"And I was happy. I knew it couldn't last. Being a gardener was enough for Joe. It was what he was meant for. But something in me needed change. Wanted the new. I had started off very far from that garden path and it had marked me. I felt the old urge to wander.

"Joe knew it before I did. I expected some bittersweet parting. Country

Mouse and City Mouse say farewell. Surprise surprise: Joe asked could he come with me. Could he? Fuck yes.

"So we left Yosemite. My mistake was to forget that Joe didn't think like me. He thought like a unicorn. He envisioned happy fluffy versions of himself overseeing pocket gardens everywhere and he wanted to see how they grew. Compare composting techniques, swap seed catalogs, all like that. He trusted me to lead him along the primrose path of the outside world. Innocent of him and very stupid of me.

"That demon in Central America had told me there were unicorns on the coast so we ranged northwest until we reached Eureka. Funny, huh. There's a big bay there, very rough and pretty, and we started making our way down the coast from there. We always did want to see the Pacific Ocean, didn't we, Pete. No wonder. It's wild and raw and teeming. It sang to me and I sang back. Whatever else happened on our little road trip I told myself I was gonna find a garden of my own by the ocean and tend it. Yosemite was glorious, bucolic and timeless. I'd understand if Joe wanted to go back. But the Pacific was a collision between the ocean and land that made a kind of violent beautiful Coleridge poetry and it spoke to me.

"We started seeing human beings. Along the coast they'd done pretty much what you've done here, formed little beach communities, learned trades, kept their lives simple, learned to enjoy the new world. Dozens of little towns with a few hundred people. We found some that had been abandoned and a few where everyone had been butchered. There are things out there that don't like you guys much. Centaurs have really got it in for you. We didn't see many people on the road. You all stay safe in your little enclaves now, strung out along a thousand miles of coastline. When you're looking for unicorns you don't go where the people are so we stayed more inland as we headed south.

"The Mendocino Forest stretches north to south for hundreds of miles. Joe saw signs that unicorns had been in some of the areas we passed through. A certain esthetic to the growth, a kind of natural arrangement if that isn't an oxymoron. But any unicorn gardeners that had been there had moved on. It puzzled Joe.

"North of Santa Rosa we ran out of forest. Joe may have been nature boy but he didn't know jack about geography and had never heard of a map. Geography wasn't my strong suit either or I'd have known to keep going north when we hit the coast back at Eureka. It's solid forest from there all the way up into Canada. Story of my goddamn life.

"So we could head farther inland to the Sierra Nevadas and cut north through some of the same ground again or head to the Sierra Nevadas and work our way south through Yosemite. Joe was the first to admit he was only really familiar with his patch of ground there. For all he knew there was a weekly meeting of the Unicorn Local Fortyseven within twenty miles of him.

"I picked south because there'd be less forest to cover. If we couldn't find any country cousins there we'd know it fairly quickly and could light out for the big coastal forest to the north. Joe was fine with that—he was fine with most everything—and we went east. We hit postcard heaven: the Sierra Nevadas, Yosemite, Sierra Forest, King's Canyon, Sequoia. No unicorns.

"The shit hit the fan outside Bakersfield. We'd run out of forest again and decided to head west to the Los Padres Forest and follow that up the coast and retrace some of our steps until we got north of Humboldt again. Only we didn't. We got ambushed crossing I-Five. I don't know how many of them there were. Ten or twelve. They had horses, longbows, crossbows, shit I don't usually worry about. We outran them. But they had these mirrored balls and they triggered them by yelling phrases and next thing I know Joe isn't running with me anymore. I look back and he's down. But he hasn't just fallen, he's a mirrored statue and he's fallen over in midstride. I started to go help him but all I was gonna do was end up the same way if I went back. I thought I could help him more by running away and coming for him later. So I ran.

"There isn't a goddamn thing to hide behind in the San Joaquin Valley. My choices were pretty much run twenty miles to the mountains or find a truck or something to get behind. The people chasing us lost interest in me once they got Joe so I found a harvester in the middle of what had been a field and I waited behind it until dark and got closer and took a good look at them.

"Shaved heads and tattoos, saddlebags full of weapons and drugs and booze. Their horses were tattooed. It's nice when people accessorize. They set up tents and got a fire going and two of them mounted up and one headed back toward Bakersfield and the other one headed north. The others stood Joe in the middle of their camp and highfived each other and patted Joe a lot. That was really fun to watch. Though of course they weren't touching him at all. Joe was beneath that mirror. Time had stopped for him, would never start again unless I could get him out of there. Meantime Joe reflected the fire and didn't move.

"Late that night the Bakersfield outrider came back pulling a small U-Haul flatbed trailer converted for harness. They loaded Joe on. It took all of them to pick him up. I was nervous he'd break. Funny, huh. Joe could have survived orbital reentry inside that thing. Half of them were falling-down drunk and I figured they'd wait till morning but they broke camp and headed out.

"I followed them north for three days. Thought about picking them off one at a time but that would leave me in the middle of the Central Plain with Joe caught in a spell no one had ever broken. These assclowns sure as shit didn't know how to do a casting that would bind a unicorn. Someone else had made those mirrored balls. Made a shitload of them and handed them out with a promise of a big fat reward if someone brought back a real live unicorn. Which meant someone had figured out how to break stasis spells. So I decided to see where they were taking Joe.

"North of Bakersfield they cut over to State Road Fortysix and headed northwest toward San Luis Obispo. Old wine country, not much left of the road, but the easiest coastal access on the Central Plain. Not that they ever got that far. Just east of the foothills that second outrider came back carrying a passenger. Dark and darkhaired, not a day over eighteen and not a bit nervous about meeting up with a bunch of gangbangers. He barely even glanced at them. He only had eyes for Joe. He gave Joe a quick inspection on the trailer and turned down a bottle of tequila and gave the gangbangers a bag of mirrored objects. They seemed pretty happy about that. They un-hooked the trailer and left it there with Joe still on it and they headed back toward Bakersfield.

"I stayed where I was. They were assholes and I wanted them dead but I wanted Joe back a lot more. Somehow this guy was going to release the stasis, I knew it. But I also knew he was only going to release Joe because he wanted something from him and there's generally only one thing a caster wants from a unicorn and it isn't help holding a jumprope.

"He dug out some more mirrored things and said a word and suddenly one of the mirrored things wasn't mirrored anymore and there was a pen-tagram around him on the road in front of Joe. Cute.

"He waited for night before he started casting. I knew the spell. It had been tried on me in New York and I had killed the son of a bitch who tried it. It was a cage of energy about a yard long and he wove it around Joe's horn. If I didn't stop him he would complete the cage and release the stasis and take Joe's horn before Joe knew what was happening. I didn't have a plan, I had an image of me running into him until my forehead hit his fucking back. So that's what I tried to do. But I was crazy and panicked and not thinking about sneaking up on anybody and he must have felt me coming because he turned to me just as I jumped. I knocked him ten feet but he dodged my horn. He yelled something and then he disappeared and I was falling down and it wasn't night anymore but noon.

"I don't know how he did it but somehow it was half a day later. The pentagram was still there. The trailer was still there. Joe was still there too. I found him in front of the trailer where he'd fallen. He was out of the stasis and he was alive and where his horn had been was just a circle of raw bone. He wasn't bleeding. Didn't even seem to be in pain. He was trying to get up but he couldn't. He didn't seem to recognize me.

"I didn't know what to do. If I went after the caster I would have to leave Joe. But even if I got Joe's horn back I couldn't fucking glue it back on and make everything all better again. This wasn't something that could be undone. There was no going back.

"I wanted to run and not stop running until the person who had done this was dead by my doing. I wanted to kill every human being I ever saw again.

"I stayed with Joe. Got him upright and stood beside him. Stayed there till the sun went down, stayed there all night long. He shivered with the cold. No unicorn does that. In the morning he could walk if he leaned against me so we headed out. Away from cities. Away from roads. Away from the ruins and ruin of man. We headed northwest back toward the forest.

"He got worse as we traveled. His coat got dirty and matted. His eyes were dull. Flies lighted on him. He made noise when he walked. He was weak and disoriented. He stumbled and fell and took an hour to get back up. I helped him as best I could. It rained two nights in a row and after that he was sick. Disease sick. I could hear him breathing. Soon he was feverish and shivering. I think the only thing that kept him going was that somehow he knew where I was taking him.

"A few days later he just stopped walking. I waited with him, thinking he was resting, but he didn't go on. He lowered his head to the grass. He was trying to touch it with his horn. To bless it. My heart was flayed. I went to comfort him but he sank to the ground and wouldn't move. I waited near him and finally I looked away from him and realized we were less than a hundred yards from where I'd first seen him drinking water from a satellite dish antenna laced with weeds. He'd known it right away.

"Joe stayed on the ground and I stood beside him. I talked to him all day. Talked to him after he went to sleep. Because all I could do was stand by him in his garden and let him know he wasn't alone. And after a while it was time and then past time and I said goodbye to him and left him in the garden he had taught me how to tend.

"After that was not a time of blind wandering. Not a time of running from the horror of mortality and change. Crows had taught me lessons about dying, one on a winter plain and one in a summer garden, and those lessons are embroidered on my soul. I am wandering now but I am not blind. I am running now but running toward.

"I have come because someone powerful and without conscience has come into possession of an alicorn, the horn of a unicorn, most powerful of talismans. It will lend him power deep and fundamental. With it he will touch you. With it he will touch your world.

"I have come to tell you I must find and kill him. You will think I am unseemly vengeful. And I am. I am shamed by retribution and diminished by desire to want the death of anything alive upon the earth.

"I can live ashamed. I can live diminished. But I cannot live while such a creature also lives. He was friend and more to you I know. But he has killed a unicorn, my mate, my friend, and taken his horn, and now nothing will be restrained from him which he has imagined to do. So I have come to ask your aid."

EIGHTEEN

Leaving the Surfliner wasn't hard. It would be safe in its stasis and everything exactly the way I'd left it when I got back. If I got back.

Leaving Del Mar wasn't hard either. Sure I'd grown up here, it was the only home I could really remember. But it wasn't home.

Leaving people wasn't hard. There were plenty I liked but none were really friends. My only friend had already left. That friend was why I was leaving.

Packing was hard. I was about to hunt down a caster a lot smarter than I was who wouldn't hesitate to turn me inside out if it came down to him or me. What ingredients should I bring. What spells should I make ready in stasis bottles. Should I bring weapons. What weapons.

I made myself calm down. My father and Ariel would be here in a few hours. I had to think clearly and prepare myself.

I went into the workroom to get my father's grimoires. They might have spells I could use and I needed to return them to him anyway. I pulled them from the shelf and something they'd been pressing against the wall fell behind the bookcase. I nudged it out with a yardstick. A thick, worn spiral notebook. I flipped through it. The pages were covered with lists, notes, marginalia, underscores, exclamation points, formulas, all in Yan's frantic handwriting. From what I could make out I was reading a book of incantations and I was also reading one of those software manual things Yan had consumed voraciously. Symbols arcane and alge-

braic, nested phrases, ingredients. Yan had come up with his own nota-
tion for castings.

If you know where it is I'll kill you.

"Well hey howdy hey," I whispered to it. I had found Yan's grimoire.

———————

I dug out the campstove and some pentagram bottles and went upstairs and
made coffee and put together some casting basics and sealed them in stasis
bottles along with a few other spells I thought I might need in a hurry. I was
just cleaning up and repacking when someone pounded on the Surfliner. I
glanced out the window toward the beach and noticed the sun. Holy crap.
I'd spent a lot more than two hours making stasis bottles.

I grabbed my backpack and went downstairs and took a deep breath
and slid open the door and looked down at an annoyed man looking up
and a curious unicorn looking evenly at me. "Sorry. I had a lot to—"

Ariel poked her head in. "Do I smell coffee?"

———————

"You packed?"

I indicated the backpack leaning against a reclining chair. Ariel
watched patiently, filling up the entryway of the Surfliner. There wasn't
room for her anywhere else.

"Bring socks?"

"A few pair, yeah."

"Bring more."

I stared at him. "Can I make my own mistakes."

"On your own time, sure." He untied and unzipped my backpack
and emptied it on the floor and repacked it again. He hesitated over the
grimoires he knew were his but put them in without comment. He asked
about the mirrored talismans and what kind of access to them I needed
and I realized I probably didn't need access at all. Just say the password
and it should do its thing. He put them in a flap pocket and finished
repacking. I got the feeling he'd been looking for something and hadn't
found it.

I put on the pack and he adjusted the shoulder straps.

"Let your back do it, not your shoulders."

"How do you skate with these things on."

He tightened a final strap. "Not our problem."

"We're not going to skate."

He shook his head.

"Why not. She can keep up."

Ariel tossed her mane. "Homey don't skate."

My father adjusted the waistbelt. "Anything else?"

"Magic wand?"

He started to look around, then stopped. "This isn't funny, Fred."

"Thus my absence of laughter, Dad."

"You ready."

"As I'll ever be."

"All right then. Let's go."

I took a last look around. I patted a foam headrest. We left.

Outside the car I thought of something. "Thirty seconds," I said, and ran back inside. I put grounds in the french press and used one of my pre-made spells to heat a pitcher of water and poured it over the grounds and set the lid with the plunger on top and set a coffee mug beside it. I smiled at it a little and went back outside. I got a mirrored penny from my pocket and said *grunion surfliner* and the railcar was mirrored and would stay that way until I returned or the universe died, whichever came first. I threw the copper penny toward the shore.

———————

"We have to stop by Paypay's," I said as we began to walk north along the trestle bridge.

"No we don't."

"I told him I'd let him know what I was gonna do. Paypay took me back, the least I can do is—"

"We already stopped by there. Which your father could have said at the outset."

My father cast her a withering glance. "I told Paypay about Yan and the fire. I told him what we're doing."

"Oh. Well I wish I could've said goodbye to him. Paypay's been pretty good to me."

"He had a piece of advice for you," said Ariel.

"What was that."

We stepped off the bridge and onto the fragmented coastal highway.

"You can not use magic too." Her imitation was spot on. "I have no idea what it means."

"Knowing Paypay it could mean four or five things."

"I do know Paypay," said my father. "And he probably means all of them."

––––––––––––

In the distance someone sat on the hood of what had been a convertible. My father glanced at Ariel.

"Five ten, one sixty, dark skin, dark hair, dark eyes, nice teeth. Button-up shirt. Big mole on one cheek."

My father shook his head. "The surprising thing is that I'm surprised."

A few minutes later we stood silent and windswept before Dr. Ram-chandani. Ariel was starting to display rainbow contours in the setting sun and I have to say Dr. Ram did a pretty impressive job of not giving her any more attention than he did the rest of us.

"Hey Raj."

"Good afternoon Peter." Dr. Ram would have been polite to his hang-man. "I believe you are setting out after my son."

My father's mouth pressed tight and he nodded. "He's caused a lot of harm, Raj. I'm sorry but he has. Burned down Paypay's shop, trashed the grandstand. We're pretty sure he killed my friend's mate." He nodded at Ariel. "We have reason to believe he isn't finished yet."

"Even so he is my son."

"Everyone who ever lived was someone's son." Mister Diplomacy, that's my father.

"Only one of them is mine."

My father regarded him a moment. "Raj. I've known you since I came out here. We've always been friends. But you know I can't let you stop me."

"It had not occurred to me to try."

"Then—" My father cocked his head at his old friend.

"He wants to come with us," said Ariel.

My father looked at the grassy pavement. "Parmita and Nan know you're doing this?"

Dr. Ram allowed himself a little smile. "It was all I could do to keep them from coming with me."

"What do you expect to accomplish by coming with us, Raj."

"What do you expect to accomplish by going."

"We expect to confront Yan. We expect to prevent him from causing even more trouble than he already has."

"Have you brought manacles of any kind. Shackles or a straitjacket?"

"No, why would we—"

"Then you do not plan on bringing Yanamandra back." He looked at all of us. "You are leaving to kill my son and you would expect me to stay here and treat scrapes and give shaves?"

"We're leaving to find out if your son is the one who killed Ariel's mate. If he is it's probably because he's going to use the power he gained from it to hurt even more people. We're pretty sure the racetrack collapse was his doing. If we're wrong—well, no harm no foul, Raj. I wouldn't kill him because of Paypay's shop or the grandstand."

"Pete. Let him come."

He gave her a look that had more years behind it than I've been alive.

"He's going to follow us anyway. Aren't you."

Dr. Ram shrugged. "I have not thought that far."

"Jesus Ignatz Christ on a waterslide." He looked accusingly at Ariel. "We haven't even left town and we're acquiring people."

"Everyone has a part to play. In their drama if not in yours."

"Oh fuck off." He pushed on ahead of us. Ariel glanced back at us briefly and then caught up to him.

I touched Dr. Ram's shoulder. "I'm glad you're coming with us, Dr. Ram. No one wants to hurt Yan." It occurred to me that I was carrying a backpack full of items expressly designed to hurt Yan.

"Thank you, Fred. I am grateful to be in your company."

Ahead of us Ariel and my father conversed in low whispers for the next mile.

NINETEEN

We got all of four miles north of Del Mar before sunset. We tried three motels before we found one we could sleep in. Water damage ratnests bugs and shit were the standard decor. Pawprints in the lobby. I'll pass, thanks.

Motel Number Four was just off the highway in Encinitas within sight of the broken supertanker rusting slanted on the shore. It had bowed ceilings and peeling wallpaper and curling linoleum but had escaped weathering and occupation by more than cockroaches and spiders and silverfish. Walls once bluepainted with waves or maybe whales were covered with ivy. We chose rooms and stood mattresses on end and beat them with broomhandles and put them back upside down on the boxsprings and jumped back coughing in the dust billows.

Dr. Ram wished us all a polite but trenchant goodnight. As he went to his room I realized he hadn't brought a backpack or any kind of gear. Just the clothes he was wearing and a waterbottle.

My father and Ariel went to their own room. I had enough questions to keep them up all night, about our plans and about their separate and mutual pasts, but they clearly wanted to speak privately.

My father and I hadn't spoken much after Dr. Ram joined us and we said only perfunctory goodnights as we headed to our separate rundown rooms. Not the most auspicious start for an expedition. Mission. Posse. Whatever you want to call it. Well, we'd be walking all day tomorrow. Plenty of time to talk then.

My body was tired but my brain would not shut down. I duct taped the opaque curtains to the wall and lit a glowspell and took Yan's grimoire from my backpack and brought it to the huge bed. Outside the window the waves crashed and always crashed.

An hour later I was about as far from sleep as I have ever been and Yan had graduated from reckless or greedy or sociopathic to being one of the most dangerous people in the world.

"Fred. Fred. Wake up, Fred." A husky feminine voice, sexy but a bit of an edge. "Rise and shine and all that shit."

I opened my eyes. "Um. Huh." The room was dark. A large white something stood beside me.

"Wow, you sound more like your father by the minute."

Unicorn. Yan. Leaving town. Motel.

I sat up. "Um." I rubbed my face.

"When you get to opposable thumbs and upright posture you can join us in the lobby." She looked down her long pale snout at me. "We'll even let you hold a coffee cup."

"I have the coffee."

"Your value to this expedition has already increased."

"What time is it."

"Five thirtyseven."

If she was kidding it didn't show. "Why's it dark."

"You slept all day. It's night now."

I swung my legs over the side of the bed. "How come it's cold."

"The earth stopped rotating and the sun never came up. This side of the earth is encased in a thick sheet of ice. We need you to go chip out some fish for dinner."

"I don't believe you."

Her tail twitched. "Suit yourself. But I'm not sharing my fish with you." She walked out without a sound.

It was fivethirty in the morning and everyone looked it except Ariel of course. Dr. Ram and my father were being polite enough to each other but their very civility was a sign of tension.

I made coffee on my little campstove and everyone but Ariel had a cup. Apparently she just liked the smell.

True dawn found us on the road. The breeze was offshore and the marine layer quicky dispersed in the growing light and heat. I kept glancing back at the wrecked supertanker growing smaller behind us. This was the farthest north from Del Mar I had ever ventured.

The grassy highway was overgrown and crowded. I tried to strip away the greenery and rebuild it in concrete, repaint it and repopulate it and fill it with motion and noise and light and then hurtle these useless shells forty or fifty miles an hour only feet apart from each other with music coming out of them. I couldn't imagine it.

In Encinitas we passed a sprawling white building with weathered gold minarets and gold lotuses on square columns set in a low white wall with a metal plaque that read ENCINITAS SELF REALIZATION FELLOWSHIP. Inside the walls tall palmtrees towered. Six men squatted before the wall discussing an unfolded gas station map weighted with rocks and a serrated KA-BAR. Close at hand were dowel spears, a crossbow, a speargun, nailbats, binoculars, and backpacks.

"Should we go up another street," asked Dr. Ram.

"Won't matter now. They're either gonna let us by or—" my father spread his hands "—or they won't let us by. Just be nice. We're walking down a street on a nice summer day. They'll stare at Ariel more than at us."

"They have weapons."

"So do we. And those little mirrors in your pack don't all make coffee. It's a mean old world. Let's cut them the same slack."

They fell silent as we walked by them in the middle of the road, following a path that had been worn in the grass between the cockeyed cars. They stared at Ariel. A flap of their weighted roadmap lifted and the map blew off. No one moved to retrieve it. My father nodded at a guy wearing binoculars who did not nod back. We kept walking. I got a cold itch between my shoulderblades. Three blocks away they probably heard me when I swallowed.

Dr. Ram let out a long breath. "If nobody minds I should like to stop in a well-equipped sporting-goods store."

"Gonna give in and get a backpack, Raj?"

"Oh that too, yes. But I was thinking of projectile weapons."

We turned right at what was left of the next major intersection and trudged inland through the tall grass toward I-5. A few blocks later Ariel said to my father, "You know they're following us, right?"

"Figured they would."

"Gotta ask ourselves why."

"Already did."

"Déjà vu all over again."

I couldn't help glancing back. They were half a mile back and not bothering to hide.

"You know, I really did walk four thousand miles to get away from this shit."

"You should have gone four thousand miles north," said Ariel.

He smirked and shook his head. "How you want to play this."

"Split and flank."

"Sure. You want Fred or Raj."

"Fred. I think you've worked with the good doctor before."

"Yeah. But I thought we'd put that kind of work behind us."

Half a mile ahead was an onramp arcing out to an overpass that was the 5 Freeway. On the corner before the onramp was a Big 5 Sporting Goods store.

"See, Pete," said Ariel. "The universe likes us."

"I think the jury's still out."

She laughed. "Come on, Fred." She walked faster.

"Um. Where are we going."

She looked back at me. "Shopping."

Any place with camping, fishing, and hunting supplies, usable weapons, or freezedried food had been ransacked about fortyfive minutes after the Change occurred. The Big 5 was no exception. The chromed lug wrench that had smashed the front window still lay amid shards of dusty glass. The hole it had left wasn't big enough for Ariel so she stood aside while I busted out the rest with an aluminum bat. The sound must have carried a mile. I decided to hold onto the bat until something more comforting presented itself.

Inside the store was musty dim and cool. Ceiling panels collapsed in back and waterstains on those remaining. Scattered warmups, hoodies, running clothes, shoes, ratnests. Discount tables overturned. Empty boxes by the register had held nutrition bars. Faint shoeprint outlines in the dust had long ago filled with dust again.

Ariel's shadow filled the storefront. "See what happens when you rely on loss leaders."

"What now."

She cocked her head. "Well, bad guys are after us so we're going to try to stop them."

"I'm down with details."

"They saw us split up but they'll still come here because they saw me go in." She surveyed the store in a practiced and precise way. "So we have until they show up to get you and Doc a good weapon or six."

"How are we going to get the weapons to Dr. Ram."

"Him and Pete are the flank part of split and flank. You really need to pay attention if you want to retire somewhere with an ocean view."

"It's not my fault I haven't done this before."

"True. What kind of weapon do you think the doctor prefers."

"How should I know. I only ever saw him try to fix people, not break them."

"Okay. Well, he said projectile weapons, which definitely narrows the field. At least there's still a fine selection of baseball bats. You look left and I'll look right. Meet you in back by the shoes. I'd say we have about five minutes."

Left was Camping Hunting Fishing. Rifles in cases behind a glass counter near the front of the store, dusty ammunition boxes. Most knives were gone. I loaded what remained into a blue plastic handbasket. Propane canisters. I shook a dozen and found two that felt promising. A better thermos than mine. No more hunting bows or hunting arrows or crossbows or bolts. I found a kids' fiberglass target bow in a package with three bright yellow target arrows with plastic fletchings. Well it was better than nothing. I hoped.

From the back of the store I heard Yo and hurried to where Ariel stood calmly among scattered boxes of Nikes and Nevados.

"Well aren't you the little ninja assassin."

"I'm working with what I've got here. Do I need to add that I'm scared off my ass."

"Goes with the territory."

Patterned pounding came from the direction of the stockroom. "You might want to go let your father in." She shook her head. "Your father. Can't get used to saying that."

I frowned at her but she only looked down at me with those unfathomable dark eyes so I hurried through the dusty cluttered stockroom kicking aside old packrat nests. At the back door I hesitated. Well she'd said it was him. I opened the door and Dr. Ram squinted in at me. My father stood behind him with his back to the door and a hand on his sword handle. They hurried in and my father checked the lock when it shut. "Weapons?" he said as I led them through the stockroom.

"Knives, bats, darts. This." I showed him the Superscout Action Bow Set.

He lifted a corner of his mouth. "Raj?"

"Some time ago I was not embarrassing with a bow." He took the mostly toy bow and arrows from me and frowned down at them. "But even so."

"Bad craftsmen blame their tools, bud. Come on."

We hurried to the front of the store.

"Think they saw you?" said Ariel.

My father shrugged. "We went pretty wide and came all the way around that freeway entrance." He hurried to the gun counter I had already canvassed and took a large blister pack from a wall display and cut it open with a Buck knife that had seen a lot of use and pulled out a black metal foamcovered wristrocket slingshot. From behind the counter he got a box of .45-caliber shells. He caught Dr. Ram's eye and pointed to the other side of the broken window and Dr. Ram hurried there with an arrow already fitted into the strung bow. Which didn't look as if it could shoot through cardboard.

"Other side of the register, Fred. We don't want to drop one right away or the others will stay outside. We lose a waiting game in here. So we let the first one come in and give the okay. They'll leave two outside if they're smart but the others will come in fast, so you'll have to deal with any that me and Raj—" He held up a hand and then pointed to Dr. Ram. I hurried to the other side of the island of counters that formed the register. Ariel stood in front of me between the register and the broken window. My father knelt behind the gun counter on the right with slingshot in hand and sheathed sword on top of the case. Dr. Ram crouched in a circular rack of baseball jerseys on the left.

I had a clear view through the shattered window when the six of them came into view. They were over a hundred yards from the storefront, out of bowshot and not bothering to hide. They all wore dark sunglasses. So much for being sunblind when they got inside. Mostly I was looking at a speargun and a crossbow and a nailbat and three spears. I had an aluminum baseball bat and a filleting knife. My balls pulled up to somewhere around the pit of my stomach and I wanted to throw up. Ariel glanced back sternly and I realized I was breathing loudly and tried to calm myself. My hands were sweaty on the bat grip.

Outside the men talked and then nodded and spread out until only Crossbow Guy was framed in the broken window. He cocked the crossbow and headed toward the store. He was still about ten yards away when two of his buddies ran in from either side of the shattered window and tossed aside their sunglasses and crouched low. The one on the left tripped on the lug wrench and fell on his ass. His partner glanced back at him and the second he looked away my father slingshotted a .45 round past his head and he whipped back around to where my father was already vaulting the counter and drawing his sword.

Dr. Ram let fly at the guy who had fallen as he was getting back up. He missed but hit the guy my father had missed with the slingshot. The arrow dangled near his floating ribs and then fell out. The guy made a pained face that looked like a grin and faltered and my father ran him through the chest and twisted the blade and pushed him off it with his knee.

Dr. Ram threw a baseball bat at the guy he'd missed. The guy tried to block with his spear but the bat hit him in the shoulder. It had to have hurt but he held onto the spear. Then he remembered my father and reversed the spear and thrust. My father had already moved to his blind side and now he slashed up and cut through overshirt and nothing else, so he reversed the slash and cut off the first yard of spear and the hand that held it. The pain had just started to register on the guy's face when my father ran him through at the kidneys.

"Front," called Ariel.

With the handle of his sword my father held up the dying man clutching his sudden stump and turned him toward the front of the store. The remaining hand grabbed the protruding blade and sliced open at the palm. The body jerked and as my father pushed it off the blade I saw six inches of crossbow bolt sticking out of the left side of the dead man's chest.

Dr. Ram grabbed a fallen spear from the floor and my father picked up the other one and shook off the severed hand still clutching it and they faded back to their former positions.

My father had just killed two men in five seconds and no one had made a sound.

Ariel's head twitched and I heard a snap. She had blocked a crossbow bolt with her horn. She stepped into the light. "Hey, asshole, call it a day, willya? Write it off and go home."

Crossbow Guy cocked his crossbow and raised it and fired again and Ariel batted the bolt aside and said Best three out of five?

Crossbow Guy lowered the crossbow. Sunlight starred his mirrored shades as his head cocked to one side. He motioned to his three remaining buddies somewhere out of sight and reached into his robe and pulled out a ball a few inches wide and perfectly mirrored. Oh shit oh shit. He took a deep breath to say a password and I tried to remember the password to one of the stasis bottles in my backpack and as he opened his mouth to speak I yelled *calliope* and Crossbow Guy became a perfectly reflective statue of himself. It was hard to look directly at him in the noonday sun.

The other three ran off. After half an hour my father went out the back and around the building to make sure.

"Do you think they went for help, Peter?" Dr. Ram asked.

"We turned their buddy here into a lawn jockey. What would you do."

"I would not have come after us in the first place."

We stood outside before the mirrored form of Crossbow Guy. Mirrored binoculars hung around his mirrored neck. A mirrored crossbow held low in his mirrored hand. A mirrored ball upheld in his other hand's mirrored fingertips. Mirrored mouth open to reveal mirrored teeth and tongue. Two distorted humans and a distorted unicorn reflected along many shapes on many hardened folds.

"Good man, Fred," my father said.

"We should go," said Ariel.

"I would like to pick up some items," said Dr. Ram. "My feet are throbbing grievously. I came very ill equipped for such traveling, I am afraid." He smiled tightly. "Yes yes I know, be quick about it."

My father watched him go back into the Big 5. "Three fourths of Del Mar owes that guy more than most of them will ever know," he said. "But I swear we're going to regret bringing him."

"Would he kill you to stop you from killing his son," asked Ariel.

"I would."

"That ball he's holding was a stasis spell," I said.

He studied the mirrored figure. "So your buddy's still handing out samples. Fucking great."

"He probably gave out a bunch of them some time back. They're still out there. They're probably the same casting that captured Ariel's, um, friend."

"Swell. How many of these could Yan have made."

"Dozens. Hundreds even. They're easy to make. Sorry."

He shook his head. "The hits just keep on coming, don't they."

"I can let him out and we can ask him where he got it."

He looked at the gleaming man reflecting everything around him and then raised an eyebrow at Ariel.

Who swished her tail. "The crossbow would be nice too."

───────────────

I said *hyperion zeus* and Crossbow Guy unmirrored. He flinched and his look of triumph vanished as he realized he was lying down staring up at a ceiling when an instant ago by his reckoning he had been standing beneath a sunny sky. He flinched.

My father took his crossbow from him and stepped back.

Crossbow Guy sat up and looked around. A dead buddy on either side of him. Severed hand on the carpet. He brought his hands up and stared at the slathered dark on them and realized he was sitting in a sticky pool of congealing blood. What had been a mirrored ball in his hand was now a pingpong ball. He dropped it and it stuck in the thickening blood without a bounce. He patted himself and left brownish red handprints all over his clothes.

Ariel stepped forward. "Howdy, Sparky. Where'd you get the nifty mirrors."

Crossbow Guy grew absolutely still. He was in his fifties at a guess and hard fifties at that. Lean and scarred and wrinkled, bad teeth, eyes that gave out nothing. "No speak."

My father raised the crossbow. "Speak this?"

The man looked at the wall. Ariel said something to him in a language I'd never heard. He looked surprised but shook his head. She asked him a question and he glanced at the crossbow and nodded.

"Someone gave them the mirrored balls," she said.

"What language is that," I asked.

"I don't know. It's language."

We interrogated the guy through Ariel for half an hour. His group had not met Yan but had traded for the stasis bottles from another group. This group said they had gotten them from a very young caster who was offering huge rewards to anyone who brought him a unicorn. They believed the stasis bottles worked but there were no unicorns. A member of Crossbow Guy's group knew someone who had seen a unicorn many years ago and he said it was worth a gamble so they traded for the mirrored balls. This had happened near Los Angeles several months ago. No, he did not know where the other group had gotten the stasis bottles from the young caster though he knew they had come from the north.

We asked where they were supposed to take a captured unicorn. He said they'd been told to head north on I-5 or the 101 and they'd be met.

"Screw it," said Ariel. "I liked this asshole better when I could see myself in him."

"I don't think I can do that," I said.

"Can't or won't."

"Okay, won't."

She tossed her head. "I vote we do unto him as he tried to do unto us."

"What happened to the whole I don't advocate killing anything philosophy."

"Left it in Yosemite." She walked out of the store.

I watched her stand out in the sunlight and I thought about what I had read in Yan's grimoire last night. "So what do we do with him."

"One third of his party is dead," said Dr. Ram. "I do not know that raising it to one half will present more of a deterrent."

My father frowned and told Crossbow Guy to get up. The man stood and my father pushed him out of the store. Ariel stood facing the distant sliver of ocean and didn't look at us as we came outside. My father pointed at the coast. "If I see you again I'll cut your stomach open with a knife dipped in my shit." He glanced at Ariel. "Tell him, will you."

She didn't look away from the ocean. "He got the gist."

My father pushed him. Crossbow Guy glanced back at the Big 5 and looked as if he wanted to say something. Then he took another look at my father and thought better of it. He tugged his pack straps and tried to leave with some shred of dignity even though his clothes looked like the paper on a butcher table at the swap meet. We watched him go until he was out of sight.

"Think we'll see him again," I asked.

"I think we'll see more like him." He went to Ariel looking out at the pale blue crayon line of ocean miles away.

"We said we'd come to California," she said. "After everything was over."

He nodded slowly. Hot wind blew his hair. Her mane.

"I think I knew you'd be here. The whole time Joe and I were looking. I think I knew."

He reached out a hand to her that stopped suddenly and lowered. "I think," he said, "that's what you were really looking for."

On the curving overpass walking north again I shook my head and started to laugh and once I started I couldn't stop. Ariel glanced back at me but said nothing. My father's look was much more reproving. Finally Dr. Ram asked if I was all right. I shrugged and could not answer for laughing. He traded a look with my father and my father let me catch up and walked beside me.

"You gonna do this all day."

"No. I'm as surprised by this as you are."

He glanced at the twined handle of his sword sticking up from his belt-loop. "Were we supposed to not kill them, Fred."

"No. Honestly no. I don't feel bad about it. I really don't. They would've killed us to capture Ariel. They got what they deserved. You even let one of them go and you didn't have to. This is just—" I shrugged again. "I don't know."

"Hard to take in. Is that it."

Ahead of us Ariel snorted. "How quickly they forget."

"Meaning. . . ." my father said.

"Exactly," she told the road ahead of us. "How quickly they forget meaning."

TWENTY

In Oceanside we scavenged food and found rooms for the night. After Oceanside was the seventeen-mile stretch of Camp Pendleton and there would be no towns or shops or convenience stores or gas stations to scavenge along the way. "There'll be a decent chance of finding water in some of the vehicles and a slim chance of food," my father said, "but I wouldn't want to bet on it and I'm not going to. It's most of a day across Pendleton so we'll scavenge what we need for the trip now and leave early in the morning."

Oceanside stood out from the undifferentiated towns we'd passed through. What architecture remained was mostly mission style, the stucco grimy where it hadn't flaked off entirely. The sides of many buildings had been painted with ocean scenes now too faded or overgrown to make out.

My father left with Dr. Ram and I was with Ariel.

"So where to," I asked.

She made an oddly horselike blurt. "I dunno. You're the one that eats."

We were in front of something called a bowling alley. Across the street was an overgrown lot that had apparently been a cemetery. North on the coast the huge concrete cube of the Encina power station owned the cliffside, massive gray smokestack rising like a blinded lighthouse. Patient pelicans hovered above sagging buildings, subtle wing movements keeping them in one place in the shifting breeze.

"You have a lot more experience at, um, foraging than I do. For food anyway."

"That was when I was helping look for stuff that hadn't gone bad after six years. After thirty years—" She blurted again. "Would you eat something that could last thirty years?"

"Depends. How long do cows live."

Her laugh rang like a fork on crystal and I smiled.

Which made her scowl. "What."

"Nothing. You have a nice laugh. Come on."

Naturally I found nothing. And naturally my father and Dr. Ram found enough to last everyone several days.

I heard them coming down the street from the direction of I-5 well before I saw them. A growing rhythmic rattle and clank. My father was pushing a canfilled shopping cart that jounced and tottered on the broken weedgrown road. He stopped before us and grinned.

Behind him Dr. Ram shrugged. "One exit north of here there is a Denny's that nobody has scavenged."

"There's a Denny's here? There's one not far from the racetrack."

They laughed. "There was a Denny's everywhere, Fred," my father said.

"The only things edible are canned," said Dr. Ram. "Chili and soup and peaches and pears. Fruit cocktail. No vegetables. I had hoped to find pancake batter mix, but it was all in packages and eaten by bugs." He looked so forlorn that I had to laugh.

"I hate packing cans in backpacks," my father said. "But most freeze-dried stuff went bad a while back too." He picked up a large brown can of Yuban coffee. "Not sure how much I trust these either though."

"We still have a while before dark," said Ariel. "Where do you guys want to sleep."

"I hear Tahiti's nice."

Dr. Ram frowned down at a can of chili in the cart. "There must be many places in the world where the Change was not so much of a change at all you know. Tribes in Africa and the South American rain forest, aborigines in Australia and here."

"Except that their magic works now," said my father. He pulled a can opener from his back pocket.

"How come we didn't bring horses," I asked suddenly.

My father raised an eyebrow at Ariel and grinned.

"Screw you. I'm as much horse as you are chimpanzee." She squinted at him. "Less."

He snorted.

Dr. Ram opened a can of chili and stirred it and sniffed it and shrugged and ate two bites with a spoon and then passed it to my father who stirred it and ate two bites and passed the can to me. "I can't fight on horseback."

"Huh."

"Why we didn't bring horses. Or skates."

"He can't fight on skateback either," said Ariel.

"Oh." The chili wasn't that bad. Or that good. "You can run away on horseback."

"Only from slower horses."

I started to offer Ariel the can of chili but stopped when she shook her head. "It makes me fart."

"But unicorn farts smell like the first snowfall of winter," said my father.

"I only hung around you because you appreciated me."

I offered the chili to Dr. Ram.

"Holy journeys are made on foot," said Ariel. "That's why."

I sensed we were nearing dangerous territory here and kept quiet but my father asked How is this a holy journey.

She looked at him and looked suddenly forlorn. She shook her head but didn't reply.

"Let's find a hotel around here," I said.

"If I threw a rock," said my father, "I'd only hit about twelve."

"I double dog dare you," said Ariel.

We scouted likely places to crash from the ocean side. Buildings weathered waterlogged and rotted. One hotel had a loose pile of smashed chairs and old clothes and garbage and shit beneath two balconies.

Ariel walked on the wet sand without leaving hoofprints.

That night I had a room to myself on the third floor of a luxury condo. Curling wallpaper and ocean view and nice breeze. The sound of the ocean had accompanied most of my life and I could not imagine its absence. A waxing crescent moon hung in a clear sky. Pale beach breakers faintest green.

I opened a glowspell and opened Yan's grimoire and caught up on my reading.

The moon had set by the time I finished the spellbook. I needed to rest for the long hike tomorrow but there was no way I was going to rest after taking another crawl through Yan's mind. Tomorrow's hike and Yan's notes weren't unrelated. I was worried about what we might find tomorrow.

No use fighting it. I repositioned the light and upended the bed and got out my works and opened a pentagram stasis bottle. Dawn was graying before I finished. That Yan, he's a page-turner.

My father wanted us out of Camp Pendleton and in San Clemente well before nightfall. I made the last of Mrs. Ngokami's coffee and we drank it as we headed back toward the freeway.

Camp Pendleton was a gray area seventeen miles long between Oceanside and San Clemente. Near the north end was San Onofre State Beach and a nuclear reactor. Yan's notes had mentioned it. If Yan had gone there as I was sure he had there was a chance he'd gotten killed. If he hadn't gotten killed he might have gotten hold of something that would make our mission much more urgent. I was keeping quiet about it until I saw for myself.

The marine layer blew off quickly and by midmorning it was hot and humid. Inexplicable metal frameworks and giant growth-covered dishes adorned browning hillsides. A gated station near the beach contained a battered and birdshit-covered geodesic dome, weathered Quonsets, barracks, low buildings. A desiccated metal framework my father thought had been a helicopter. Dr. Ram explained that this had been the largest stretch of undeveloped land in California, then had to tell me what undeveloped meant. Apparently it meant not yet transformed beyond its natural appearance for human use. Dr. Ram said the Marines used to conduct massive beach exercises here with landing boats and mock assaults. I tried to picture a boat that could land but what I came up with didn't seem very likely.

The freeway here was very wide. You could almost figure out the lanes from the positions of the cars but it was hard to be sure because so many had pulled over when their engines had stopped.

We passed a pale yellow sign that read CAUTION with pictured silhouettes of a man pulling a woman pulling a child and then a sign that read WEIGH STATION RIGHT LANE NO PICKUPS NO SERVICES. Then another that read SAN ONOFRE INSPECTION FACILITY. I asked Ariel what time it was and she said two twentyseven.

A quartermile ahead a range of hills sloped gentle toward the ocean until it was interrupted by the cut of a concrete structure built over the road. A line of semitrucks off the highway to our right. Several glassless highway patrol cars parked near a small building off the road.

We passed the inspection station and rounded the base of the hills. Another triangular yellow sign with a running family rusting. The land beyond it strangely barren as if burned some time ago and not yet recovered. Stunted trees. No birds and no small creatures rummaging the tall dry grass. Wind, dry grass rustling, insects, distant waves. Nothing else.

Ariel stopped walking. "Bad. Big bad. Way bad. The really not-good kind of bad."

In the distance massive wicketlike structures were strung with many thick power cables that bowed across the freeway. No bird sat on any line. Near the ocean something glimmered through the sickly trees. Dr. Ram frowned at this but said nothing.

"I feel funny," said Ariel. Her snout furrowed between her eyes and her gaze looked inward.

"What's wrong," my father asked.

"I don't know. The land. Me." She shook herself out of her reverie and looked at my father. "Everything tastes like metal. I feel like I'm falling."

Dr. Ram pointed at the glimmer through the trees up ahead. "That is the San Onofre Nuclear Generating Station. I think it is very possible there was a meltdown. The land here may be dangerously radioactive."

"Son of a bitch." My father shook his head. "Son of a bitch."

"It could have been the Change. But these lightwater reactors were designed for containment in the event of power failure. The fuel rods were supposed to drop back down into the coolant tank from gravity if the power failed. And there is no shortage of seawater for cooling." He frowned. "I think it may have been the big earthquake nine years ago. If the containment tank were ruptured, radioactive steam may have escaped and spread inland."

"How far."

He shrugged. "It is anybody's guess, Peter. It depends on so many things. The explosion, wind, amount of steam, you know. The Chernobyl meltdown contaminated many thousands of square miles."

"If we walk through here are we gonna die."

"Without a geiger counter there is no way to know."

"It probably wouldn't work anyway." He frowned. "Fred, is there anything you can do."

"The only thing I can think of would be to put you guys in stasis bottles and haul you through here and then unlock them when we're in the clear. Wherever that is."

His frown deepened. "That's—shit, I don't like that."

"Peter," said Dr. Ram. "I think it is possible that we human beings will be all right if we go quickly. Ariel may be more susceptible to radiation than we are."

"Ariel?"

"Not a clue, buddy boy. This is a new one on me. All I know is that everything around me feels just plain wrong."

"Can you walk."

"Right now I can."

"Then let's walk right now."

We walked. Past the stunted trees we saw the San Onofre Nuclear Generating Station. Two huge domes each with a conical cap on top like a giant pair of breasts, which apparently everyone who ever saw the thing had observed. Only now they looked like two giant mirrored breasts that twinned the sky and sun, so bright I couldn't look directly at them even through my sunglasses. Several nearby silo-shaped structures were also mirrored. The whole facility was in stasis.

"This cannot be good," said Dr. Ram.

"Why would he do this," my father asked. "What was the point."

"He didn't want me coming after the uranium," I said.

———————

It was stifling hot in back of what had been a refrigerated Ralphs grocery semitruck. Its frozen vegetables had long ago melted rotted mummified or turned to dust. We'd thrown out a bunch of boxes to make room for all of us and used a small box to block the door from shutting. Ariel said she didn't feel as bad inside the truck. Dr. Ram said the metal walls blocked some of the radiation. I barely understood what radiation was.

My father squatted avoiding the hot metal walls and supported himself with both hands on his sword before him. Dr. Ram sat on a towel. We drank bottled water and poured sweat. Ariel did not sweat of course. She stood watching me calmly though from her silence and stillness I could sense she was not feeling well.

"In this world," I began, "alicorn, the horn of a unicorn, is one of the most powerful materials for conjuring. In the world before the Change one of the most powerful materials for generating power was uranium."

"Uranium can't be used for generating power anymore," my father said. He frowned. "Can it."

"Not for generating electricity. And probably not for making big bomb things. But if you consider it as an ingredient for casting I think it's still powerful. More important Yan thinks so too." I glanced at Dr. Ram but couldn't read his expression. "Look, why are we going after Yan. Not because he smashed up the racetrack or burned down Paypay's shop. We're doing it because he's gotten hold of one of the most powerful objects in our world and we don't think he's going to use it to make butterflies and bunnies. And now he has one of the most powerful relics of the old world too."

"Why would he want them," asked Dr. Ram.

"I've been reading Yan's grimoire. His book of castings. He left it behind, I found it the day we left. It's full of ideas about things we were working on. Casting as science. The new physics, he called it." I took a long drink of water to buy some time. Despite the undeniable evidence of the mirrored containment domes not two hundred yards away I was still hesitant to say what I thought. No, what I knew.

But I capped the waterbottle and took a deep breath. "I think Yan wants the world to go back to how it used to be. I think he wants to reverse the Change."

Ariel nodded. My father and Dr. Ram stared at me. Outside the sweltering truck the sun moved imperceptibly along the double domes of sky.

My father looked at Ariel. At Dr. Ram. I could sense him trying to pick from among a lot of questions. "Do Yan's notes say this. That he wants to change everything back."

"Not directly." I fidgeted beneath his intense gaze. "I think he got the idea from me."

Yan threw a stick out on the water. "I've never heard anyone say anything about the fact that the Change happened at fourthirty pee em."

"Why's that any more interesting than any other time."

"It's not the time that's interesting. It's that it didn't happen everywhere at the same time."

"Huh? Fourthirty is fourthirty."

He shook his head. "It used to be that when it was fourthirty on the west coast it was seventhirty on the east coast."

"Huh? How could we get to fourthirty three hours before them. It's like time travel."

He laughed. "You have it backward. They got to fourthirty before we did, so that by the time we got to fourthirty they'd been there three hours ago."

I couldn't wrap my brain around it. He showed me with a rock by marking east and west coasts on it and turning it so that the east turned into the light before the west did. Everything in the world is always turning east only we never give it a thought.

"So what does this mean for the Change."

"Think about it, Fred. People in California say it happened at fourthirty, but people in Florida also say it happened at fourthirty. If it had really happened everywhere all at once it would have happened at fourthirty here and seventhirty there."

"So it didn't happen all at once?"

He shook his head and threw the rock. "Fourthirty there and fourthirty here means that it started somewhere and then spread across the planet as the world turned. Or that it happened in one fixed spot in space and the world turned into it."

"But. But."

He grinned. "Makes your head hurt, doesn't it. You know about the Big Bang, right."

"A seed containing everything there is that exploded all at once." I knew what it was but I wasn't sure I believed it. I sure as hell couldn't picture it. If everything was in the seed then what was outside the seed. Where was the seed.

"Physicists were pretty sure that just before the Big Bang happened there weren't any laws at all yet. There was so much heat and pressure that everything was constantly changing. Nothing had been set. It was all just potential. Like a bottle spinning around. Where it's going to point isn't set yet. It's a lot of potential that changes every instant. The laws of the universe were like that in the instants before the Big Bang when heat and pressure were so great that anything like the laws we now have couldn't have existed. No laws could have existed. But when it exploded it hit a point where the heat and pressure let off enough to fix the laws in place. To stop the bottle. It took nanoseconds, tiny fractions of a second. But the point is that where the bottle stopped wasn't inevitable. It could have pointed a little to the left or right of where it did. It could have aimed somewhere totally different. Some people thought there were lots of Big Bangs and lots of bottles but most of them pointed places that were too unstable to last. Only the ones that could persist persisted."

"Okay. And this has what do with fourthirty."

"What if someone moved the bottle."

"Say what."

"Look, the Change sweeps across the planet, right. That means the Change must have had a starting point. Started somewhere specific. So it makes you wonder did someone cause it."

"Cause it how."

"I don't know. Maybe it was an accident. Maybe some physics lab fired particles in a chamber and tore open a wall between our universe and another one with different laws and theirs won. Some of them anyhow."

"I don't know what any of that means." I grinned. "Maybe someone just did a casting that made the rules Change."

He smirked. "Fred, a casting wouldn't work before the Change. The Change was what made casting work. See."

"Well maybe someone found a loophole. A foot in the door. You know, a tail. Like we did with the stasis spell."

He stopped walking.

"The whole universe was just a tiny seed once. Maybe it was mirrored. Maybe there was a password."

He had stared. Just stared. Then he'd suggested we head back home.

TWENTY-ONE

"You shouldn't feel a thing," I said. "In fact when I unlock the stasis you won't even know any time has passed. So we'll have you out of here in literally no time at all as far as you're concerned. You ready?"

Ariel nodded. The fact that she didn't add a smartassed reply gave some indication how bad off she must have been.

We were alone in the back of the grocery truck. I was soaked with sweat and dizzy from heat. "Okay," I said. "Give me a few minutes. I'll yell when I'm ready."

She nodded again. I reached out to pat her and she flinched and her horn hit the side of the truck and I snatched my hand back. I hadn't touched her. Could I touch her. I should be able to. Shouldn't I.

She saw the question in my eyes. Her whisper threadbare when she said Confused.

———

I went outside. It didn't feel poisonous just hot and dry. Maybe Dr. Ram was right and Ariel was more susceptible to it. Or maybe we just couldn't feel it. I glanced at the UPS truck down the road. Its foiled windows reflected light reflected by the mirrored domes of the nuclear reactor on the shore. My father and Dr. Ram waiting inside. An eightfoot U-Haul trailer they had fetched from the border checkpoint rested tonguedown on the asphalt beside the Ralphs truck. My father and Dr. Ram had cut off its dryrotted tires and pulled the trailer on its rims up the gentle slope from the checkpoint. That must have been fun.

Ariel had helped me figure out the casting Yan had used to trap a unicorn in a reversible stasis, which couldn't have been pleasant considering what it had already cost her. I took it as a measure of her trust. Or maybe her desperation.

I set a mirrored flashlight bulb on the road and said *bippity bop* and I was in a pentagram. I yelled that I was ready and the side door to the Ralphs truck opened and Ariel stepped into sunlight and onto the road and then unbelievably stumbled. She recovered and then put her forelegs onto the back of the U-Haul trailer and tipped it toward her. She lurched onto it and kept her weight back to keep the back of the trailer on the road with the tongue up and before I let myself think about all that could go wrong I made the passes and recited the incantation and Ariel became a mirrored statue.

My father and Dr. Ram came out of the UPS truck and hurried to the trailer. I broke the pentagram and stepped out of it to join them and we looked up silently at the mirrored figure standing like a lookout in the tilted trailer bed. If my father was upset it didn't show. But it usually didn't.

"It went okay," I said.

He reached up. Hesitated. Looked—embarrassed? Ashamed? Touched fingertips to mirrored flank. "Well. We'll find out, I guess." Fingertips left mirrored fingertips and left no prints behind.

The ground was fairly flat for miles to the north. We put our backpacks in the trailer and two of us pushed while the third held the tongue up by its safety chains and pulled. The rims bumped on the cracked and grassy asphalt. We rotated positions every quartermile or so. It was a lot of work and we didn't say much. We wanted out of there, wanted her out of there. We drank a lot of water and kept to the less encroached middle of the freeway and went as fast as we could. Dr. Ram said that whether the Change or the big quake had caused the radiation to be released, he thought most of it had blown inland because both events had happened in the later afternoon when the wind would have been offshore.

The landscape slid across Ariel. In the trailer she looked even larger than she was and precarious. I knew she could not break if she fell. Nothing in existence could touch her now. But I still did not want her to fall.

When I was pushing instead of pulling I told my father and Dr. Ram about Yan's idea that casting is a kind of software.

"You think the universe is a kind of computer that runs on magic," Dr. Ram asked.

"Kind of. The same way it used to be a computer that ran on physics."

"But the sun still burns," my father said. "That's a nuclear reaction. Gravity works. Electrochemical signals travel along my nervous system. My cells convert food into energy. Old laws weren't replaced or we wouldn't be able to exist."

"Perhaps the rules allow exceptions now."

"Which is the exception. The old rules or the new ones."

Dr. Ram wiped his brow and gulped water and resumed pushing. "The old laws are much more in evidence or else as you say we could not exist. I would venture that the new laws allow local, narrowly defined exceptions."

My father snorted. "So you guys are running IF and UNLESS commands on the universe's OS. Shit."

"I don't really know what that means."

"It doesn't matter." My father looked at the mirrored figure of Ariel gleaming sunlight along its flanks, blue across the top, distorting freeway and brush and world outside it. "Why uranium."

"Give me a lever big enough," said Dr. Ram, "and I will move the world."

I nodded. "Uranium and alicorn have a lot of leverage."

"I never should have let you kids play together," my father said.

About a mile past the reactor was a sign for BASILONE RD SAN ONOFRE 1 MILE. Beyond that the freeway turned slight left and began a mild uphill grade into some low hills. We slogged along among the remains of cars and trucks and bumped over broken pavement and cracks and clots of grass and weeds until the incline crested at the Basilone Road exit. A nearby call box now a bird's nest. SAN CLEMENTE NEXT 5 EXITS. The incline did not slope back down again but merely leveled off. I guess a downslope would have been asking too much.

In the narrow shade of a cracked overpass we rested on an embankment thick with sunbrowned grass. I kept staring up at the crack in the sidewall and thinking that the overpass had stood for nine years since the big quake and telling myself the chances of it collapsing now were astronomical.

My father swabbed himself with his shirt. Dr. Ram just sat with his elbows on his knees and his head hanging down and panted like a hardworked dog. He permitted himself to undo a button on his buttonup shirt. We all tried not to look at Ariel in the trailer.

"Two miles from the reactor," said my father. "How far do you think we should go before we let her out."

Dr. Ram shrugged. "Already the vegetation is more abundant. But I would wait until we begin seeing birds and wildlife. By the time we reach San Clemente, I should hope. I am reluctant to delay us for any reason, but I believe it is important that I find a library."

"There's one about a mile from here." My father stood and helped Dr. Ram up and Dr. Ram helped me up. "What you looking for."

"A *Merck Manual* or *Physicians' Desk Reference*. And after that I think a pharmacy."

Discarded furniture and computers in the parking lot. The laundromat next door piled with knotted garbage bags. Stacked waterjugs, clothesline with flapping weathered laundry. A portajohn between two nearby trucks. Beside the building a PVC-framed shower fed from a hose leading to a cistern or solar shower on the roof. Wheelbarrows and wagons and lawn toys scattered out front. Garden boxes growing tomatoes and who knows what else. Front door propped open. The library looked to have been squatted for a good while.

We left the trailer in the street outside and headed in. Just inside the door my father stopped and Dr. Ram ran into him. He stepped back and started to say something and my father held a hand up and his other hand went to his sword. Then the smell hit me.

My father sheathed his sword as he came back to the entrance and motioned us inside. "Nothing in here's gonna hurt us. But you won't want to stay very long."

We followed him inside. Books still on the shelves. Toy cars and action figures on the floor. Bookshelves knocked over. A fan of blood dried brown against a wall and half a window.

The bodies were stacked in back. It was hard to tell how many.

"Let's find your books and get out of here." My father kept his voice low in the library, in all libraries, as if thoughts that slept there might awaken if he were loud.

Dr. Ram nodded and went to find the medical reference section.

I remembered what Dr. Ram had told me about the squatters who'd killed the Hendricks family. "Who did this."

My father shrugged. "Can't be sure. Happened in the last few weeks though." He tugged his T-shirt collar over his nose and went near the piled body parts and leaned out over the flyspecked custard of bloody carpet and yanked a spear from a woman's torso. I looked away and made myself not throw up.

"Unusual weapon." He held it up and pointed at the gorestreaked point shaped like the nib of a fountain pen. "It's an aluminum pipe that's been funnelcut and filed down. The edges have been filed flat so that the whole striking area is edged. Hate to get hit by one of these." He hefted it. "Long like a javelin but heavy. I doubt I could throw this effectively more than, I dunno, five yards." He frowned at the white geometric designs painted along the shaft.

"Big strong guys did all this by throwing spears?"

"Big strong somethings did."

"Where are the heads."

"We'll look for pikes out back. Meantime—"

Dr. Ram yelled from the other side of the library and we ran.

———

A man and a woman stood between tall shelves. The man held an axe handle in two hands and looked about to swing it. Behind him stood a woman with a hand up before her face as if warding something off. Both were shouting out, or had been about to, facing something that was no longer there. Both were as mirrored as Ariel.

———

An hour later I shook my head and broke the pentagram I'd made before the mirrored couple. "I'm sorry. I don't think there's a password."

"Then they are like this forever," asked Dr. Ram.

I nodded. "They aren't in pain or even experiencing anything. We think there's no time inside the stasis, so they'll never be aware of anything. But it's forever. As far as I know, anyway."

"My son did this?"

My father held up the painted aluminum spear. "I don't think so, Raj."

"Who then."

"Not sure."

Even knowing what I knew it was hard to believe there were two living people beneath those reflections. "Why put them in stasis and no one else."

"I think they were hiding here in the stacks and they got found. This guy comes out swinging, whoever he's swinging at says oh-shit-abracadabra. Boom. Very fast."

"Then the casting had to have been prepared ahead of time and opened with a password. Which means—"

"Yan made the spell even if he didn't cast it," said Dr. Ram.

"Yeah. Sorry."

My father looked closer at the spear. "Someone painted eyes on the point."

———————

Dr. Ram found a *Merck Manual* and we left the library in search of a drugstore. We never found the heads.

My father stayed with Ariel while Dr. Ram and I looked for a pharmacy. The nearest one was pretty cleaned out but Dr. Ram found what he needed there anyway.

Back outside he gave us several foil packets containing pills. "We are most fortunate that potassium iodide has an extremely long shelf life, especially in such packaging. Nevertheless I recommend we double the suggested dosage."

I looked at the packet in my hand. Was radiation here now. Was I walking through it. Was I breathing it. Was it going through me. I didn't really understand it.

We took the pills with water we had replenished from jugs in the library and we turned the trailer around and headed back to the freeway. I felt those two mirrored people behind me the whole way, time capsules awaiting opening in some universe not yet born.

———————

After the onramp we stopped to rest and gulp more water. My father drank a lot and sweated heavily. He looked as tired as I felt.

Dr. Ram squatted in the trailer's narrow band of shade and swabbed his brow with a handtowel. "When was the last time you were in a city, Peter. I am talking about a real one, not this sprawl."

"About five years I guess." He hawked and spat. "San Diego, if that counts."

"There was always some doubt. But did you find it even less populated than after the Change."

"I'd have to say it was pretty much an oil painting, yeah. Why."

"I believe most people have left the cities by now. Cities consumed vast resources from areas outside their borders, you know. Their own food and medicine resources were quite minimal—a few weeks at the most. If we assume one person in a thousand remained after the Change that would leave cities with a reserve of two thousand weeks. Which is just short of forty years."

"Which would leave us nearly ten years. Except that most of those reserves have gone bad by now."

"So over time," Dr. Ram said, "people have left the cities to join farming communes or become farmers themselves. Or formed small fishing communities such as our own. But the cities—" He shook his head. "They are now mausoleums."

"The resources are depleted but the cities aren't empty. People like cities, Raj. That's why we build them. More people lived in cities than didn't."

"Human beings are marginalized and scattered now."

"We were marginalized and scattered fifty thousand years ago. We got over it."

"In fortynine thousand years."

My father cleared his throat and spat again and drank more water. "Sooner this time. We know how to do it now."

Dr. Ram gave him an odd look, amused and sad. "There will not be a need for such development until the population grows beyond the current capacity. Or until things are in such disrepair that they need replacement. Certainly this will not happen in our time."

"Sure it will. People build stuff. They always have."

"But the cities are already built," I said. "They've got more stuff than anybody could use. What do you need that isn't already out there."

"Our children simply take what they need, Peter. They learned it from us."

He looked troubled. "I'm trying to think of what they actually build. What they make. Ron Golecki makes surfboards." He snorted. "I can't think of anything else."

Dr. Ram slowly shook his head. "Nothing that is not built on what is already there."

"Well I'll be goddamned. We didn't teach them how to build cities and they don't want to learn. They'll just keep living in our ruins."

"Dad, you're living in your ruins. Everyone is."

"They weren't ruins when we built them. My point being that we built them. You couldn't do it if you had to. If another ice age came we'd be toast. Shit, Raj is right. Nobody'll build a city for forty thousand years. You kids aren't civilized. You just inhabit a civilization."

"What civilization. The one that didn't adapt to the Change? The one you all keep crying about losing but don't rebuild or replace? The one that's no good to anybody now except to lib shit from? Why can't you just get over it and let us be what we are."

"What, parasites? Graverobbers?"

"Just different. We're different from you, that's all. We don't come from your world. Your rules don't work for us. Literally don't work. Maybe we won't build cities because we'll get good at what does work. Maybe by taking a different road we'll avoid your mistakes while we're at it."

"Ignore our history so you can repeat it, you mean."

"Don't flatter yourselves. Your history is history. It sure isn't anything you're doing in the world I live in. So why don't you just let it fucking go already."

"Let what go. The fact that everything we accomplished will disappear because you kids don't give a shit? The fact that your children will play in our ruins and wonder about the lost gods who built them?"

"Who are you kidding, Dad. You're not worried about your grandkids, you're just afraid of being forgotten. You didn't build those skyscrapers for posterity, you built them for yourselves. You left shoeprints on the moon just so you could say Look, we left shoeprints on the moon. If the Change hadn't happened we'd be cleaning up the mess you left us and trying to keep our heritage from killing us while you all tell us how much better things were when you were our age. You told me you made it so hot the ice-caps were melting, you burned down the forests, animals were dying out. Fuck, look what we just walked through. Thirty years after it got turned off and it still might kill us."

It felt just like the night we'd read each other's diaries. I wasn't in control. He wasn't in control. Somehow we had become symbols for ourselves. He started coughing and I just talked over it. Yet despite my anger I felt a strange spreading calm inside. "What do you want us to do, imitate you? Cut the lawns and fix the windows and glue back the wallpaper and tell you how great you all were? Okay fine: you built a really impressive world. But it's broken now and you won't throw it away and you're mad because we don't want it. You want us to live by rules that have nothing to do with the way our world works and you hate us because we won't. You are lost gods. What's pathetic is you're lost and you're still around and all you do is bitch because we don't appreciate you."

"We're trying to pass the torch before you forget how to make fire."

"Your torch blew out thirty years ago. You go ahead and hold onto it. One day we'll bury it with you. And then we'll go on and live without you in this world, the one you never tried to figure out and couldn't adapt to. It really will be our world then and we'll figure it out just fine. We'll make fire our way. We'll make history our way. So fuck you. Fuck all of you." I looked away and wiped my eyes.

"I've started to wonder," my father said, "if what Yan is trying to do isn't such a bad idea."

Dr. Ram looked astonished. "Peter—"

I matched his tone. "You go ahead and wonder that. While you're at it wonder what happens to her if he does." I pointed at Ariel motionless and perfect gleaming sunlight. The bright rebuttal of her. He looked at her with the startled wonder of someone seeing her for the first time and he said nothing. For what could he have said.

And suddenly I understood why I was crying. Under that cracked over-pass on a crumbling freeway in that dead world. Yan wanted to resurrect their past so he could live in it. But I felt no connection to their past at all. To me it was already dead and buried. At some point recently but without realizing it I had already buried my father, buried his world and buried the whole selfish lot of them, and I was grieving, and grieving all the harder because I knew I would move on. Because all of us would bury them and move on.

TWENTY-TWO

"So what'd I miss." Ariel sprang off the trailer and landed soundlessly on the road as the trailer tongue tipped skyward.

"How do you feel," said Dr. Ram.

She took a deep breath. "Fit as a fiddle, Doc. Air feels good. How long's it been. Ten years? Fifty?" She looked at me. "Howdy. You must be Fred Garey the Fifth. I knew your great great grandpaw."

"It is the next morning now." Dr. Ram didn't smile at her joke.

A furrow appeared between her eyes. She glanced at me and at my father standing back a bit. "All right, what did I miss."

The Camino de Estrella overpass had collapsed. Half an SUV still stuck out from a huge chunk of concrete on the near side, half a surfboard still on its roof.

I had slept terribly. At dawn I'd given up and crawled out of my van and made the first of the canned Yuban coffee. By the time I was drinking my first cup my father had emerged from the back of his Ford. I silently handed him a cup and he leaned against the trailer drinking it and coughing his morning cough and watched the growing light delineating Ariel's mirrored form. He looked as if he hadn't slept any better than I had.

By the time the sun was above the horizon and Dr. Ram staggered from the bed of his Dodge van I'd seen many birds and several lizards and a snake and a rat. Vegetation everywhere. If there was radiation here the wildlife seemed to like it.

My father had looked from Ariel to Dr. Ram and raised his eyebrows a fraction and Dr. Ram had nodded in midstretch and said, "From our surroundings I think it is safe now."

My father had looked at me and I had finished my coffee and flung the grounds and said *defenestrate*.

Now Ariel was looking curiously at me and my father. "Come on. What happened."

"Me and my father had an argument."

"An argument." She glanced at my father, who nodded. "Jeez, I leave you guys alone for—" Her eyes widened. "Holy shit. What time is it."

We looked at each other and shrugged.

"I don't know what time it is. I lost my clock. Fuck."

"You'll get it back again," my father said. "It probably resets itself or something."

"How do you know."

"Okay fine, you won't get it back again. Let's go."

"I see someone woke up on the wrong side of the bed."

He coughed into his fist. "I woke up on the wrong side of my goddamn life. Come on."

We argued about which route to take. In a few miles I-5 would split off to the 405 Freeway and turn inland to head through the dense desolation of Orange County and central Los Angeles. North of that it threaded through the Santa Monica Mountains and down onto the long straight flat route of the California Central Plain. The 405 stayed closer to the coast and ran north through western Los Angeles until it rejoined I-5 just south of the Santa Monica Mountains. Two other occasionally intermingling routes ran hard by the coast, Highway 101 and the Pacific Coast Highway.

My father did not want to take the 5 through Orange County and Los Angeles. "I don't want to scrounge around for everything we eat and drink and keep a lookout for loners twentyfour seven," he said.

"The coastal roads are bound to be more populated," said Dr. Ram. "And certainly inaccessible at points due to floods and landslides."

"There's no shortage of surface streets inland even if they aren't in great shape. You sure these are the real reasons you want to take the Five?"

"What other reasons would there be."

"Well. The more likely we are to get jacked on the road the less likely we are to get to your son."

If Dr. Ram got pissed he didn't let it show. "If that were the case I would not have helped you fight those men in the sporting goods store. I readily admit I would sacrifice myself to save my son but I would not sacrifice you and your son and this wonderful creature."

"Shucks, Doc, I wouldn't sacrifice you for anything either."

"Ariel, shut up."

She looked too startled to reply.

"Raj, what possible reason could you have had to come with us if it wasn't to slow us up or keep us from reaching Yan."

"Perhaps I am here to act as a voice of reason when the time comes, as it seems the supply diminishes as we travel."

"And what do you think we'll be unreasonable about. When the time comes. We're not going to all this trouble to slap Yan's wrist and ask him nice not to be a bad boy anymore. Let's be blunt here. I know he's your son but he's killed people, if only by giving others weapons and incentive to do his dirty work for him. And he's going to kill a lot more if he gets away with reversing the Change."

"We are not certain that is his intention. And last night you did not seem very opposed to such a notion."

I flinched. Dr. Ram didn't swing often but when he did he went for the jaw. I'd have given a lot to know what my father would have replied but Ariel picked that moment to drag a hoof across the hood of a car. Flaking paint and metal shavings peeled up in little curlicues and it made a noise that made me grit my teeth.

"Okay, enough." She turned away from the car and faced my father and Dr. Ram. "I set out on this little journey months ago. I still know why I'm doing it and I still have some ideas about what I'll do if and when we find your son, Mr. Ramchandani. I asked for help from Pete and Fred but I don't recall picking team captains. So here's the deal. I'm going up the coast. If I find some indication Yan is inland I'll head inland. Anyone who wants to come with me is welcome to. Anyone who doesn't is welcome not to. And anyone who wants to slow, stall, or stop me is gonna have hoofprints on his ass. I'm leaving now. I'm going that way." She inclined her horn toward the 405 split up ahead and started walking.

My father and Dr. Ram stared after her but did not move. I hesitated and then threw my gear into my backpack and hurried after her, shrugging it on as I went.

Ariel didn't so much as glance at me when I caught up to her. We walked a mile without a word until I said You are so full of shit.

"But I'm so gloriously full of shit."

"You wouldn't leave him."

Now she looked at me and then looked behind us. "Afraid you'll never know."

I looked and saw my father and Dr. Ram walking half a mile back and twenty feet apart.

We passed a sign that read DANA POINT CITY LIMIT. I studied her. Started to ask a question. Stopped.

"You want to know about what happened in the truck yesterday. Or rather what didn't happen."

I nodded. "Why wouldn't you let me touch you."

"Let me ask you something. Do you think you should be able to."

"I think it depends. On, um, your definition. How strict, I mean."

"I think you're right. And I've run across gray areas before. But you still confuse me, Fred. I don't make the rules. In fact they're not rules, they're laws. Natural laws. So I don't have a choice. And neither do you."

I felt oddly chagrined.

"Don't worry, I won't say anything. It's clear you and Pete have enough on your plate as it is."

We walked through Dana Point and we walked through San Juan Capistrano. The sunbrowned San Joaquin Foothills slowly approached, green patches and black resolved into trees and scorched land, weathered Kentucky Fried Chickens and Carl's Jrs. and McDonald's and Starbucks and Taco Bells, worn gas stations and unbelievable numbers of vitiated cars. Dilapidated car dealerships, vinecovered office buildings, half finished condominiums. Shredded billboards, one with an empty nest on top the size of a car. Malls and marquees and restaurants and shops that would never be used by anyone for anything again but would probably last a thousand years. Thousands and thousands of crows and finches and pigeons and parrots, squabbling gulls and circling hawks and combative mockingbirds, thick rows of guano paralleling drooping powerlines. Crumbled asphalt and sagging facades and sharded windows glinting sunlight. Take this torch.

We followed I-5 as it bent inland to Mission Viejo. Every mile of it looked like every other mile. Hills and embankments brown around us now. We did not stop for lunch but ate and drank while walking. Our shadows shortened and stretched right. Coastroad exits creeping by. We followed Ariel's lead and remained wordless the rest of that long day.

———————

We made another ten miles on the 405 and car camped near the Jamboree Road exit, each of us in his separate vehicle except for Ariel who kept watch. Apparently she only slept when she felt like it.

I had a hard time sleeping. My body was tired but my mind would not shut down. For the first time since I was a little kid I could not hear the ocean. Worry about what lay ahead with Yan had become everpresent. The memory of my father's resentment not just against me but against my entire generation.

You kids aren't civilized. You just inhabit a civilization.

We're trying to pass the torch before you forget how to make fire.

I've started to wonder if what Yan is trying to do isn't such a bad idea.

Where the suffering hell had all that come from.

I stared up at the roof for hours. My mind had actually begun to quiet when I heard a strange muffled animal sound nearby. I held my breath and thought about stasis bottles in my backpack that might be useful. Why the hell hadn't I grabbed any decent weapons along our way. Why hadn't I ever learned to use any weapons period.

I turned onto my side and slowly raised up. Lot of good that did. The windows were so dirtcaked there could have been an army of elephants out there for all I could see. My father had prevented us from cleaning car windows before bedding down. "Might as well hang a sign saying someone's sleeping in here."

I took my recently acquired filleting knife from a flap pocket of my backpack. No biggie, Fred. Probably just a dog. A coyote, a hyena. But how often have you ever seen just one dog, one hyena.

No subtle way to get out of the enormous car. You couldn't open the windows without busting them. I crawled over the seat and grabbed the doorhandle. One two three go.

Cool night air flooded in. Ariel stood beside the truck my father had picked to sleep in two cars back. Her coat the color of phosphorescent wavecaps in the starlight. The truck door was open. What I'd heard was coming from inside. I told myself I needed fresh air inside the car and left the door open six inches.

"I guess I'm dense," came Ariel's voice. "I'm still not clear on what the problem is."

I opened the door a few inches wider and strained to hear.

"Well for starters I'm fortyfour and I'm back on the road."

"Who are you kidding. You're thrilled to be on the road. Your every goddamn muscle is singing its praises. Every step you take is also taken by a twenty year old who loved every inch of it, and a fortyfour year old who's sorry he took it all for granted. Why don't you tell me what's really wrong."

"Maybe you should tell me."

"All right. I think you think you deserved better and didn't get it. I think it's made you angry and bitter. I think it's why you're walled off from everybody. Especially your son."

"No, really, don't pull any punches."

"You asked."

"I did." Long pause. "I don't think I deserved better and didn't get it. I think I had better and lost it."

"Don't take this wrong, but you really should be over me by now."

"Who said I was talking about you."

"Oh. Oh. I'm so sorry." Another long pause. "Fred's mom?"

"Yeah."

"You want to tell me about it? Or you want to tell me to fuck off."

"Fuck off."

"You're not getting off that easy."

His dry laugh turned into another cough. "Okay. Just remember you asked." A light cracking as he opened a waterbottle. His voice was clearer next time he spoke. "I have to go back a bit. Shit, nearly half my life ago. Twentythree. What the fuck could I possibly know." He snorted.

"After—after New York me and Shaughnessy squatted a house in North Carolina. A little bigger than we needed, weathered but nice. Away from things. I became Mr. Handyman and got into fixing the joint up. It distracted me from the fact that I had fucked up something extraordinary over a complete stranger."

"Twentyone years ago, Pete. You can put the scourge away now, dont-cha think."

"I'm talking about then. After a while I realized I was either gonna have to make a go of this thing with this stranger or head back out on my own. I figured if it didn't work out I could head out on my own anyway so why not give the stranger a shot."

"Ever logical the heart."

"I don't recall throwing popcorn from the balcony when you told your story."

"Okay, I'm sorry. Really, I'm sorry. I'll shut up."

"Uh huh. It turned out Shaughnessy'd been thinking along similar lines. In her mind she'd been kind of a homewrecker. The same shadow had fallen over both of us. So we decided maybe change would do us some good. Leave the past, share the present, invest in a future, yadda yadda. I told Shaughn I wanted to write down what had happened. Like if it was a thing, an object out there in the world, then I could leave it behind. So I took six months and did exactly that. I wrote about what had happened to me from the Change up to that point and I put it on our diningroom table with a brick on top and I left it behind forever."

"Or so you thought."

"Or so I thought." Sound of him drinking water. "Me and Shaughn lasted about three months after we hit the road. We made an effort to get to know each other and it turned out we weren't a very good fit. We really were strangers after all. I shouldn't have been surprised. Fact I don't think I was.

"We split up in South Carolina. That was a hell of a thing to do in those days. You had no way of knowing if the person you left that day was going to be dead two months later. But Shaughn wouldn't have it any other way. She was done. We struck the tent and literally went our separate ways. I'm fairly sure she headed back to Charlotte where I'd first met her. Better the devil you know I guess.

"Of course I took it out on myself for I don't know how long. But even while I was telling myself how I was a worthless shitstorm in other people's lives, guess where I headed."

"Washington D.C."

"How could you possibly have known about that."

"I read your book."

Long pause. "Christ, sometimes I wish I'd never written the son of a bitch. I had no idea I was gonna be parading myself around in my underwear for whoever wanted to look, you know?"

"Yes you did. It's just that back then you were someone who would parade around in his underwear if he thought there would be enough drama to warrant it and now you're not."

"Ha."

"I'd say you have a breezy, conversational style punctuated by episodes of self indulgence. Plus there's not enough of me in it by half."

"I never should have taught you how to read. You know, to this day I don't know how that manuscript got published."

"I feel that way about half the books I've read."

"Clearly someone found it and took it to a screwpress operator somewhere. Raj says it's survived because it's the only worthwhile book about the Change." He imitated Dr. Ram's accent. "The others are sterling examples of derivative and polemic amateurs with no story to tell and no gift for telling it." He laughed. "I was just a kid. I wrote it entirely so I could leave the whole thing behind me and the motherfucker followed me all the way across the country."

She made a soft horselike blurt. "No accounting for taste. So you went to Washington."

"Yeah. I went looking for McGee, of course. I had more connection with her in three hours than I had with Shaughn in a year and a half. Not that, you know, I had any idea what I'd do if I found her. Be another shitstorm probably. But I didn't find her. Didn't find any of the people from the collective who'd squatted around D.C. Those who didn't get killed in New York had all gone back to their farm and I had no idea where that was. I looked for a while but finally I asked myself what I really intended to do if I found her. If McGee was alive she was probably paired up. She was a looker and charismatic as hell and not exactly pining for attention. Probably a mom. And if she wasn't dead or paired up or mommed out then she was alone, and if McGee was alone it was because she wanted to be. Who the hell was I to come messing with that. So I changed plans and decided to head back to Florida, maybe even try to search out my mom and my brother. I wasn't very hopeful but I also didn't have anything more important to do.

"I meant to get there, I really did. But somewhere around Savannah I made a right and just kept going. I had about twentyfour hundred miles' worth of west in front of me." He snorted. "You accomplish a lot more when you're young and stupid, you know that? Because if you had any sense you'd know better. You look at a road atlas and think, hell, at ten miles a day I'll be there in two hundred and forty days. Fifteen miles a day?" He snapped his fingers. "Hundred and something days."

"One sixty."

"Isn't math terrific. All you need to walk across North America in six months is a pencil and paper. Shit. I was lucky to do it in three times that. I told myself I came out here because I needed change but my reasons were the same as yours. Me and you had always talked about coming out here, and in the back of my mind I thought I might find you. Who the hell walks across North America because he wants change."

"Someone who wants a lot of change."

"Well. Can't argue with that. So around Louisiana I got sick as hell. Started off like a cold and ended up pneumonia or closer to it than I ever want to be again. I was a walking case of drown until I just stopped walking. I mean literally stopped and fell down in the middle of the road. I got rescued by a group of Vodoun. You know about them?"

"New one on me."

"Voodoo. Ten-thousand-year-old religion brought to Haiti by African slaves, seasoned with some Christianity courtesy of your friendly caucasian merchants and priests. Very magic-based. Sympathetic magic mostly, but animistic, deterministic, shamanistic."

"Will this be on the final."

"Before the Change they were considered very fringe. Threatening. Really it's very communal, very tribal. Drumming, dancing, speaking in tongues, being ridden by the loa—possessed by a spirit. The thing is, a lot of it works now. Works really well."

"I take it you got fairly acquainted with them."

"About a year's worth. They healed me. The head priest gave me drugs those wiccans in Del Mar would donate an organ to get hold of. Two weeks after they found me half dead in the road I was wearing a comfy white caftan and dancing around the djembes and yelling thankyous to everyone I saw. I was the most cured son of a bitch you ever did see. But I was also a—well, slave is too strong and prisoner isn't right. I was mostly free to do whatever I wanted so long as I didn't leave."

"Indentured servant."

"That's closer, because I was giving them a chunk of my life in exchange for them saving the whole thing. And you know what. I didn't mind. It seemed fair to me."

"At first."

"At first. Until I wanted to leave. Which wasn't for around six months. I started making noises about how I'd been heading for the coast when they found me and I would be needing to move on soon. Lewis, the head priest, came to see me. Before you go thinking this was in shacks in the swamp or something, this all happened at Louisiana State University in Baton Rouge. They held ceremonies in a theater called the Swine Palace and lived in nearby buildings. So Lewis comes to see me and I tell him thanks, I appreciate everything everyone's done for me, you've all been so kind but I have to get on with my life now. Lewis was a big guy and when I told him that he just slumped like a big sad bear. He told me that in Vodoun nothing happens by accident and that the loas exist to maintain balance in the world. I owed them a life and if I left before that debt was paid he was concerned about what the loas might do to me. It wasn't a threat. He really was worried that I'd get torn up by demons if I took off. Did I know that several people had stayed with the group after being rescued and they're very happy here and no harm has come to them? I asked what had happened to the ones who left and Lewis just grinned and patted my shoulder and said he had no idea because no one had ever wanted to leave before.

"Let me be clear. No one threatened me. I wasn't even sure anyone would come for me if I just walked out and kept going."

"So what stopped you."

"Three things. One, my conscience. I really did feel like I owed them something. And I enjoyed life there. I was valued. In my world those people were feared and even shunned. People ridiculed their beliefs in one hand and were afraid of their magic in the other. Hell, if you'd asked me about voodoo before I fell down on that road in Louisiana I'd have told you it's a religion where they stick pins in dolls to make people sick and they make zombies for some reason or other and they kill chickens and have fits and speak in tongues and have orgies."

"Did they."

"Well yeah. The same way Catholics celebrate nailing a guy to a wooden beam by eating flesh and drinking blood and get on their knees every week to beg their god not to roast them for eternity for the mistakes committed during their twoscore and ten. Sure I saw ugly things while I was there. Castings that should never see the light of day performed on people out of sheer spite. But I also saw Lewis risk his own life to negotiate with a loa that had been offended by someone. He let himself be possessed by a demon so he could argue with it. The loa said it would settle for a thumb in payment and Lewis cut the guy's thumb off right there. And believe me the guy was happy for it. That thing's teeth were the size of my shoe.

"These people squeezed a lot of flavor from life. They had passion. Their religion helped them lead good lives and be good people without forcing them to. Hell, their religion saved me. In Vodoun everything is connected. All of nature is actors and props playing out this sort of drama that's already set out for them."

"Thing number two?"

"Fuckers had my sword. There was a no-weapons policy and it wasn't hypocritical. I never saw anyone wield a weapon while I was there unless you count magic. But Malachi Lee gave me that sword. No way was I leaving without it. It hadn't been confiscated . . . exactly."

"Thing number three?"

"Danelle."

"Ah."

"Very ah. While I was recovering from whatever had laid me out there was this girl who'd show up sometimes. She was a hoodoo woman, sort of a wiccan and midwife and nurse. Serious mojo. It didn't hurt that she was about my age and awfully easy to look at.

"One day I wake up and she's sitting beside my bed. I'm breaking a fever and she's in a chair reading. I'm sweating buckets and mildly hallucinating and everything looks sort of outlined. Not unreal but too real. And then I see what she's reading and I yelp and she looks up. I ask can I see that book and she marks her place and hands it over without a word. *Ariel: A Book of the Change.* You have got to be shitting me."

"That must have been strange."

"I thought I hallucinated it, I swear. I had to ask her about it next time I saw her. Dannie was no dummy and I guess I write the way I talk. Then there's that whole hi-my-name's-Pete thing. She brought the book back next time she came and asked Is this you. I told her it was. She asked if I'd made it up. I told her sometimes I wish I had.

"I don't know if Danelle traded shifts with other healers who visited me but I started seeing her a lot more after that. Dannie believed in her church deeply but privately. She'd been part of the Vodoun group almost from the start. It had probably kept her alive. Things were really bad for women then. She'd been a junior at LSU when the Change occurred. Awfully smart but almost unbelievably unworldly. It was sort of charming and frustrating. Not only had she not been anywhere, she'd hardly encountered other kinds of people or cultures. There weren't many white people in the Baton Rouge group and none from Florida by way of New York and North Carolina so she asked me a lot about places I'd been, things I'd seen.

"We got to know each other in installments. You got to know most everyone in the group that way. There were a couple hundred people at most and you all ended up together in one way or another at dances and ceremonies and crap like that. Religion since the Change, very community-based.

"Dannie and I liked each other and wanted to spend more time together. So it wasn't hard for that six months to become seven and then eight and then nine. The community thought it was great. Lewis did too. Another tent stake in his newest convert.

"Funny enough it was Danelle who wanted to leave. One night she told me something she'd never told anyone. She'd never been outside of Louisiana and since the Change she hadn't even left Baton Rouge. She wanted to know what was out there.

"Here's the fuckedup part. I was torn about leaving with her. The world had a way of doing ugly things to pretty girls and I didn't exactly have the best track record myself. Life with the group was decent, the people were a pretty good bunch, I seemed to have acquired a smart girlfriend who also happened to be a major hottie. Why move on.

"I told Danelle I'd originally been heading for California and she was all over it. Sure, let's go, tomorrow okay? I told her we needed to slow down and figure things out and have a plan of attack, and in any case I wasn't going anywhere without my sword. She told me the confiscated weapons were kept in Lewis' suite.

"Somehow that got me off my ass. The weapon I was given by the man who gave his life to help me was locked away in someone's fucking apartment while I played house and gained fifteen pounds. I owed the group my life. I did. But I owed Malachi my life a couple times over way before Lewis and company came into the picture.

"I broke into Lewis' and stashed the sword in a shopping cart full of laundry and Dannie wheeled it off and stashed it in a bundle between a hedge and a wall. After dark I met up with her and grabbed the sword and changed into traveling clothes and headed for the Ten Freeway.

"If they came after us I never saw any sign of it. There wasn't any point in hunting us down. We hadn't taken anything of theirs, we hadn't damaged anything, we weren't exactly gonna report them to the cops or anything. If they believed their religion—and most of them did, it wasn't just lip service—then the loas would find us and balance the scales."

There was a pause so long I thought he might have simply finished. I lay down on the seat with my head near the slightly opened door and quieted my breathing and strained to hear. Finally he took a deep breath and said, "I haven't wanted a cigarette in twenty years and now I'm dying for one."

"I can do Skittles."

"I'll live, thanks. Okay. Let me tell it while I've got some momentum, cause I don't want to do this again."

"Okay."

"Dannie turned out to be pretty good road company. If you can travel together you can do anything together."

"I've heard that. It happened to a friend of mine once."

"I bet. So me and Dannie made it across Texas. It wasn't completely awful but I don't want to do it again."

"I've been through southern Texas. No there there. How'd you manage it."

"There's an awful lot of freight trucks between towns on I-Ten. Most of them were unscavenged. It's a bit of a commitment to walk for days out into the desert to scavenge a truck. We lived on beans and franks and water and Kool-Aid and Jack Daniel's and macaroni and ramen and Jiffy Pop from Houston to El Paso and then some. Our big score was a National Guard supply truck full of MREs. I think those damned things will outlive Fred's mirror spells. I also reacquainted myself with a slingshot and hunted rabbits and squirrels. You know there really are tumbleweeds out there?"

"Yeah. They look fake."

"We stayed away from cities mostly. I wasn't on an adventure. I was all done with adventures. Done fighting bad guys and joining causes and correcting bad etiquette."

"So how many altercations did you have."

He laughed. "I had food and water and weapons and I was with a beautiful young woman. What do you think. Sometimes I gave people food and water and sometimes I didn't. Sometimes people just want to fuck with you. We had I guess a dozen runins with serious assholes and probably four or five times as many encounters with people whose kindness either helped us along our way or literally saved our lives. It's the assholes I remember best. Isn't that awful.

"We weren't out of Baton Rouge a week before I was wondering how I could possibly have stayed with the group so long. A year for christ's sake. But it gave me Dannie. I'd set out on a seventeen hundred mile walk with someone I liked, maybe even loved, but didn't really know that well. Sound familiar."

"I can feel you putting on your armor."

"If it was a mistake it was the best one I ever made. What Dannie lacked in worldliness she more than made up for in adaptability. She wasn't afraid of the world outside of Baton Rouge, she was excited about it. She was more nervous about me. Well so was I. Dannie was newer territory than any ground I was covering. We had over seventeen hundred miles to get bored listening to each other and it never happened. At least I never did. If she did she hid it pretty well."

"I think it's safe to say that no one will ever leave you because you're boring, Pete."

"Thanks. I think."

"You're welcome I'm sure."

"The more we traveled the more getting to the coast became less im-

portant than just being together. That reason in the back of my mind got
even further back I guess.

"But one day about a year after we left Baton Rouge we crested a ridge
north of Santa Barbara and saw the Pacific Ocean. By then we had a good
reason to stop wandering because Dannie was pregnant with Fred.

"If we'd headed south about two days we'd have probably found some
nice fishing community and squatted a nice rich-man's cabana with a spec-
tacular ocean view and had our baby and become useful members of society, blah dee blah blah. But except for the Vodoun group I hadn't been part
of a community since the Change, which at that time had happened about
ten or eleven years earlier. I was still a loner at heart. Didn't trust people,
didn't want to rely on anybody else, didn't want to be accountable to anyone. Dannie was curious about other people but also afraid of them.

"So we had some decisions to make. I didn't want to keep hunting and
scavenging. It was risky and I was suddenly a family man. Even weirder I
wanted to be a family man.

"I still camped in libraries whenever I could, still read books to help
keep me alive. I'd read about California and the area around Ojai sounded
good to me. Rich, green, temperate, sparsely populated, and only three or
four days away even if we took it slow.

"Ojai was everything I'd hoped for. Big green fertile valley, rolling hills,
unspoiled. Unpopulated. Fires had gotten to some of it but there's not much
you can do about that anymore. We found a ranch house in salvageable
shape on about eight extremely overgrown acres. Horse stable, vegetable
garden. All of it losing out to overgrowth of course.

"We provisioned from nearby properties and a farm supply and feed
store. Over in Ojai proper there was an agricultural museum and a little
western museum and I libbed a Brabant turnwrest plow and a dogcart, har-
nesses, you name it. Dannie worked on the house while I cleared about two
acres' worth of field. I never, never want to do that again.

"What was left of a cattleranch a couple miles away was a dozen cows
grazing in a wild field. I went and brought one home. Which meant fixing
the fence. I found horses that had gone wild. What I knew about horses
wouldn't fill a thimble and was mostly wrong. I brought one of those home
too. That was an adventure. He had a long solemn face so I named him
Honest Abe.

"I had books on farming and homesteading but I didn't even know what I didn't know. At first I hunted as much as I farmed cause we had to live on something till things grew. That herd of cows was tempting but I left them alone. Dannie worked as hard as I did right up until the day she took off her weeding gloves and wiped her brow and told me we'd better go inside if we didn't want our baby born in a beanfield.

"The day Fred was born something in me let go. Like when you've been clenching a muscle and don't know it till it unclenches and then the relief is almost painful. Fred was like that for me. I'm not sure I could even say what it was I let go of. Wandering maybe. Fear of loving something again. Because as much as I loved Dannie that old fear still nipped at its heels. But here was Fred. And I loved him but I was the world's expert on horses compared to what I knew about babies.

"So I'm Pioneer Pete and I'm busting my ass to learn a way of life I'd never considered and living with a woman I loved and respected more every day, making up fatherhood as I went along—and maybe becoming a bit more fully formed as a human being."

He paused again. Drank and coughed and drank again. "I've had a life of adventures. I really have. They've been amazing and it's even more amazing I lived through them. For a long time you were the biggest one. And after you've had your biggest adventure what do you do with the rest of your life. Look for bigger adventures?" His laugh was sad and bitter, and older than I ever want to sound. "Maybe you redefine what adventure is. Love's an adventure. Making a baby and raising it, that's an adventure. Watching my wife pull our boy away from a fireplace grate while I read about how to brew beer was all the thrill I needed anymore. Eating food from land I cleared and plowed and planted and weeded and harvested was adventure enough. You get biblical doing that. Superstitious. You and the land are connected."

His laugh was genuine this time. "That first year I got my ass kicked by every bug and frost and foraging animal and storm there was. I overwatered. Undergrazed. Lit smudge pots to save our citrus from a January freeze and nearly burned our house down. One thing after another. The second year we started getting on pretty well. The farm pretty much existed to keep the cow alive and the cow returned the favor. Those things are milking and shitting machines.

"This is the part where I'm supposed to tell you that one day I realized that acting out the human drama with hoe in hand from sunup to sundown to keep my family alive had made me happy. By the sweat of my brow did I cleave unto them, blah blah. Well guess what. I fucking hated it. I was a shitty farmer. My every waking moment was chained to two crappy weedy acres. Chickens are the stupidest meanest creatures on earth. I was delighted whenever I ate one of the sons of bitches. The house was falling apart. Even mild winters sucked. I wasn't cut out for that life. What I loved was Danelle and Fred. My wife and my son were my work as much as any field or wall and I was a lot more proud of them than any other thing I built or fixed or grew. I loved having a family.

"Naturally I was waiting for the other shoe to drop. Two years after Fred was born I was still waiting. Three years after he was born I'd finally forgotten about it. And of course it dropped. And it was Fred who dropped it."

Lightning traced my veins.

"One night I'm in bed with Dannie and I ask her where she got that scab on her chest. It was just a scab the size of a pencil eraser. She told me it had happened the day before. I'd been in the barn trying to figure out how anyone ever shod a horse without getting killed. Dannie was out back hanging laundry and Fred was playing in the dirt nearby. She saw him put something in his mouth and told him to take it out. He said no because that's what three year olds do so she picked him up and said give it to me now and he took a rusty nail out of his mouth and said Ha and poked her in the chest.

"This was thirteen years after the Change. Alcohol and hydrogen peroxide and Betadine and all of that had lost their potency a decade before. All the old antibiotics might as well have been jujubes. Mommy couldn't spray your owie and send you back outside. Your owie could cost you a finger, a hand, an arm. A scrape on a fence could fucking kill you.

"But Dannie told me she had put a salve on it right away and she was the big hoodoo woman with the dialed-in mojo so I figured I shouldn't worry. She'd put plenty of salves on my owies in the last three years and I was still kicking.

"Three days later she got a headache. No more aspirin. No more Advil. She made bark tea but it didn't go away. Next day it was worse. I noticed she was clenching her jaw and she told me it was sore. I asked her if she'd had a tetanus shot as a kid. She said What's tetanus.

"I got out my *Merck* and started getting worried. Even a tetanus shot as a kid meant she'd been vaccinated over twenty years ago. The *Merck* recommended boosters after five. I memorized the symptoms and kept them to myself. I debrided the site and put more of her salve on it. Every goddamn treatment the *Merck* recommended was a manufactured pharmaceutical that was useless now. It didn't stop me from looking. The few pharmacies in Ojai had been looted years ago but meds packed in foil in an airtight container in a dark room had to exist somewhere. I grabbed what I could find and made Dannie take it anyway. She thought I was overreacting. Then the jaw stiffness spread to her neck and she started having trouble swallowing.

"The spasms started after that, in her face. It was awful. Like something inside her was fighting to get out. She couldn't control what was happening to her face, but her eyes—it was like she was in a car going downhill and she hit the brakes and nothing happened. And it just got worse. This horrible grin, this insane joker's face, possessed my wife. I think the look on my face whenever it happened scared her as much as what was happening to her. Every muscle in her face would bulge. She couldn't talk when it happened. Then it'd let up and she could talk but usually she just went right out like after an epileptic fit.

"But this one time it hit her and I held onto her and it just went on and on and her teeth clenched so hard they sounded like nails on a chalkboard and finally it let up and she went limp and before she went unconscious she said something that I still dream about as much as I dream about that demon mask that would take over her face. She said They found me."

"The loas."

"Yeah. She thought the loas had caught up to us. She thought she was being punished for leaving the group. And maybe she was, I don't know. It's not a crazy idea anymore."

He was quiet a while and I needed to sniff but I didn't dare so I just let my nose run. When he spoke again his voice was heavy and tired. "The muscle spasms spread. Her stomach and then her back and then her chest. She couldn't breathe when it happened. Every time I thought it was killing her. Everything just, just. . . . She fell out of bed. It threw her out of the bed. She couldn't eat because her jaw wouldn't relax. She lost so much weight. She. She."

"Pete, it's okay. You don't have to say any more."

"I'd shut a door and the sound would set it off. She'd start bucking and flopping and pouring sweat. One night it broke her back. I heard it. Can you, I mean jesus fucking christ her back muscles broke her spine. She was awake for all of it and I couldn't stop it, couldn't make it better. I knew there was only one thing I could do for her and I couldn't do it. Not Dannie. Not my wife. So it took her a week to die. It was the worst thing I've ever seen. One day her muscles locked up and she couldn't breathe and she went unconscious and they stayed locked up. She was thrashing and I was trying to hold her and then everything all let go at once. Everything stopped. Dannie stopped. Just stopped. Gone. And. all I could feel. was relief. So horrible. A rusty nail."

I couldn't hear this. I could not hear this.

"I buried her on the farm. Beside a blighted oaktree she'd kept me from cutting down because she liked the shade. Then I thought about what to do next. Finally I said fuck it what do I care. I took Fred to the library and stayed there a few days and did some reading and then I went back to the house and waited till Fred was asleep and did a Summoning."

"The loas."

"Yeah. The loas. They were scary motherfuckers. What I had on my side was the fact that I didn't give a fuck. I offered them a trade. Me for Danelle. They thought that was funny as shit. What's in it for them. Then they offered me a trade. I could go to their plane and look for Dannie and if I found her I could try to bring her back. If I did we stayed here. If I didn't we stayed there.

"I think I'd have tried it. I was that crazy. But I had Fred. I couldn't leave him and I sure as hell wasn't gonna bring him. So I declined and so did they. By their rules they were being fair.

"So then I thought about going back to Baton Rouge and killing Lewis. But I had Fred. I thought about killing myself because I couldn't live without her. But I had Fred.

"And then I thought what if I didn't have Fred. God help me I did. But at least part of me was still sane enough to know better. Fred didn't cause this. A nail caused this. A spore. A woman who hadn't had a vaccination in twenty years if ever. A world without immunity. Where does the blame stop.

"So I tried staying where we were. Tried to work and take care of Fred and maintain the farm. But I didn't give a shit anymore. I kept telling myself hold on. Just hold on, you'll see what you should do.

"I'd grieved before. When my father died. When I realized I would never find my mom and brother after the Change. When I lost you. Everyone who went through the Change has. But this. I was afraid of myself. Of what I might do to Fred. I started drinking. Antibiotics hadn't lasted but Jack Daniel's was doing just fucking great. Pretty soon everything settled down to an even drone. I worked all day and played with Fred and drank myself to sleep and did it all again next day. Things started falling apart and I didn't keep up with fixing them.

"Finally I told myself that I couldn't just maintain. Just maintaining was no way for Fred to grow up. He'd known exactly two human beings. Now there was just one and that one was a pretty sorry example. So however much I wanted to wallow in my misery or take it out on myself or the world, Fred deserved a better shot. I needed to get him to a farming collective or a fishing village. Some kind of community. Someplace full of people who cared more about being alive than I did. That's what I told myself. Truth was I left our farm because every day of my life I had to look at my wife's grave in ground I had worked for nearly four years and I couldn't take another minute of it.

"In the end it wasn't even a decision. I got up one morning and smashed the JD bottles in the sink and I set the cow loose and opened up the chicken pen. I got my sword from beside the bed and cleaned it and packed my backpack. I packsaddled Abe and put Fred on him and we both said bye to Momma and then we left. Left it all. I thought about burning down the farm. Very dramatic you know, very final. But I couldn't do it. Not with her there.

"I took the One Oh One south and kept a sharp eye out. We made it as far as Oxnard without any trouble. We hit a section of highway that had crumbled from mudslides and I realized we'd have to backtrack and go along the beach for a while but when I turned around there were five guys standing behind us and nowhere for us to go. Nailbats and tapewrapped bikechains. A machete. I'd walked right into it and not smelled a thing.

"They wanted Abe. I took Fred off him and told them they could have him. They took Abe and Fred started crying. Then they decided they wanted my sword and I decided to give it to them. Having your kid with you changes things.

"I was handing it over quiet as a lamb. They didn't smell any trouble. I was an easy score, five minutes' work. And then something happened I still don't understand. One second I'm handing over my sword and keeping an eye on Fred and the next I'm standing on what's left of the road feeling the wind on my face and listening to waves crashing and Fred yelling his head off. I couldn't understand what was wrong. Then I looked around and saw five dead guys. Or pieces that added up to five dead guys. I drew Fred, my sword Fred, and the blade was clean. Clean. I had no memory of a fight. No memory of cleaning my sword and sheathing it. I asked Fred what had happened to Honest Abe and all he could do was point. Abe had gone over the cliffside. I don't know if he bolted or if one of the guys hazed him or what. That poor horse. He deserved better.

"Fred freaked out when I picked him up and I realized I was cut pretty bad on my forearm. The machete I guess. I bound it up and I made Fred hide while I went down the slope and got what I could from Abe's pack. I washed the wound and dressed it and went on. I was more annoyed than hurt. Right then anyway. It hurt like a son of a bitch later on.

"I got a stroller for Fred from an SUV and kept going south. I avoided squat villages and hid whenever I saw anybody. When we got to Del Mar I knew I was done. Done walking, done hiding. Done wandering or farming or being a husband. All of it. I was. I squatted a house away from the beach so I wouldn't have to worry about fighting anyone for it and I kept my mouth shut and raised my boy and locked up my past and threw away the key. I helped people when it was needed but mostly I kept to myself and felt my life get narrower and told myself that was all right by me.

"Then my book followed me out here and a few people put the pieces together and asked if I wrote it, if that was me in it. I'd just change the subject. Mostly I managed to keep my past from catching up to me. Except for dreams. Sometimes I dream about Dannie. In some of them I can't remember her face. Or I dream about what happened to her face after she got sick. Those are bad. And there's nothing I can even show Fred and say That was your mom. He says sometimes he remembers what she looked like. I hope so. Because he's the only piece of her I have.

"So. Six months ago me and Fred have a huge fight and he leaves home. His friend burns down Paypay's shop and then tries to fuck up the whole town. And now Fred shows up with you. My son. With you. And my first thought should have been joy at seeing you still alive and beautiful. At knowing that some important relic of my past had survived intact. That something I had loved wasn't worse for having known me. But I knew that after all this time and pain you weren't here for some reunion. You were here to take me back to everything I'd quit. And what I thought when I saw you was god damn you. God damn you Ariel I was done. You say I love being back on the road. I say I'm fortyfour very long years old and I'm sitting in a rusting car on a fuckedup freeway in a dead world that I turned my back on for over sixteen locked-down goddamn years. You've been a splinter in my heart since I was just a kid. All that time I hoped you were still out there somewhere. All that time I hoped I'd see you again someday before I died. All that time my life got smaller. I got smaller. And now here you are, the thing I injured most in my life standing right next to me, and the person who injured me most in my life is sleeping twenty feet away. And we're all on the road heading toward who the fuck knows what. And all I can say is I will fight for you, for both of you, and maybe even die for you. But I don't know if I will ever forgive you."

———————

Dawn was graying past the overhanging trees. Another sleepless night. I sat up in the musty SUV and watched the sky get brighter and kept thinking to myself So that's it. So that's it.

Ariel had left my father an hour ago so he could try to sleep. He was probably staring up at the roof of his own car and rehashing his own thoughts as the night dispersed.

Before she'd bid him goodnight Ariel had thanked him for his story. For the trust. And then she'd told him, "Pete. My Pete. The world has humbled us. We feel diminished by our very lives. Nothing can make things as they were for us, between us. But our souls are connected. Our lives entwined. You know this. We have walked so many roads together. Yet this is the last. You know this too. We are joined upon this final road in common purpose. Journeys end in lovers meeting, right? And all I can say is that I'll walk it with you to the end. Because of that connection. And because whatever may have happened to either of us along those joined or separate ways you are in my heart and I am your friend."

Then she'd left him to resume her watch and as she passed my car she glanced my way and gave a little nod and I knew this night's unburdening had also been for me.

I suppose it was a gift. Now I understood my father's reticence and anger and my own toward him now seemed pointless and petty. But a consequence of that understanding was that I had gone to bed in a world in which I was righteously angry at my father's resentment and then watched the sun rise on a world in which I really had been its cause. A world in which I had killed my mother.

PART THREE:
CASTING REFLECTIONS

TWENTY-THREE

On the taxiway it stood upon its rounded nose and swiveled gently in the morning breeze, a hundred feet high and painted white, American Airlines logo on its silver tail catching sunlight as it pirouetted hugely. Silent and graceful and unmistakable.

Hard by the John Wayne Airport were scars from an airplane that had left the runway at fourthirty in the afternoon nearly thirty years ago and failed on takeoff and plowed with unimaginable force through a row of low buildings to fireball through a neighborhood before gouging out a big chunk of freeway overpass and carving the embankment. After three decades of overgrowth and weathering the scars could still be traced out.

The airport was still and almost stately. Airplanes nosing into gates and patiently waiting forever on taxiways. Massive energies banked, innumerable journeys interrupted. I had never been this close to an airplane before and I found them less believable in real life than in the telling. They didn't look like machines, they looked like the corpses of blind and massive servile beasts. What kind of energies had thrown these leviathans across thousands of miles of air.

Much less probable was the airplane balanced on its nose and turning slowly in the wind. For several minutes we watched its lazy revolutions. Then Dr. Ram asked Who would go to such effort for something so purposeless.

We all looked at him. Of course we were thinking the same thing. He doesn't see it. He won't see it. Finally I said It was Yan.

"But why would Yan do this. What is the point."

I watched a seagull circle the upended jet before landing on the exhaust of a massive engine. "He's testing himself. I think it's also a message to me."

"Saying what."

"Hey Fred. Look what I can do now."

"Could you do this, Fred," my father asked.

I frowned at the massive airplane turning in the breeze.

"You moved the train car," he said.

"True. I don't know. Maybe."

"He knows we're coming after him," said Ariel. "That's the message."

"Surely someone else could have done this," Dr. Ram insisted.

"Sure. But Yan knows how much I've always wanted to fly."

Out there in the remade world lay toppled buildings fallen to ruin, rusting bridges bending into bay water, foundered submarines on ocean floors. Desiccated skeletons in prison cells and elevators and hospital wards. Silent spacecraft circling round the silenced world. Countless metal cars eroding. Slow vines knitting a green shroud across the body of a civilization. Whales migrating, sea serpents mating. Crashing waves on every beach on every coast. Always crashing.

Out there in the newly undelineate world a wheel will roll, wheels on axles travel but connected gears won't turn. Fire burns but bullets won't fire. Lightning will flash but electricity can't be generated or stored. A pendulum will swing but a springworks will not drive it. Venting steam will turn a turbine but a turbine will drive nothing. Nine hundred ninetynine out of a thousand people had vanished all at once without a trace but none of those remaining ever saw another person disappear.

Out there in the nascent world were lives beginning or ending or fixed forever in bloodstained rooms. Poisoned land emitting broken atoms sleeting through anything alive. Mammoth structures collapsed by sound. An upended airplane turning and turning on its nose in gypsy wind. An unkempt grave beneath a blighted tree on a wilding farm.

Out there in the altered world now parents and their children eye each other like reluctant armies massed before a wary battle. A young man without conscience trying to restore a past existing only in memory and relic and imagination. Three men and one supernatural creature making slow and awkward progress across an illdefined bridge between one world resolving into dust and another wanting resolution. Burdened by more than they carried. Connected by more than they admitted. Memory and relic.

Irvine, Costa Mesa, Fountain Valley. Undifferentiated flatlands scarred by crumbling freeways strewn with squat unwindowed buildings bearing signs proclaiming lost and alien allegiances. Nokia, Chilmark, NEC.

We walked and did not speak much. I wanted to talk to my father about what I'd heard the night before but he'd been telling it to Ariel and not to me, and who knows what he might have withheld had he known that I'd been listening. The image of my mother walked before me like a restless ghost. My father walked tirelessly, surveying our surroundings but returning to a constant inward gaze. He looked preoccupied and gray. Perhaps the lack of sleep was wearing at him. I wondered if the same ghost led him on. Dr. Ram was preoccupied as well, probably with ghosts of his own. Or with their possibility.

That night we camped in an RV beneath an overpass. We ate canned food we passed around and wrapped ourselves in blankets from the RV when the sun went down. Evenings were cool but my father wouldn't allow a fire.

"So what's your story Doc," said Ariel. "Where were you when the Change happened."

"I am afraid it is most unexciting. I was in an elevator."

"Unexciting? I've never been in an elevator."

"This elevator was on the ground floor of my apartment building in La Jolla. I spent most of a day thinking that the emergency telephone would eventually work or the power would come back on or someone would hear me shouting and pounding with my shoe. When I finally got out I simply climbed the stairs to my apartment and went to bed. So I missed all of the excitement of that first night. In the morning of course I saw right away that something more fundamental than a simple power failure had occurred. Cars did not work and the quiet was absolute. At first I wondered if some sort of nuclear detonation had destroyed everything electronic. In those days there was much discussion about the EMP, you know, the electromagnetic pulse.

"But then I saw the balloon. It was several miles inland and backlit by the morning sun. A hot air balloon floating at the mercy of the wind. By the time it was above the Naval Air Station I saw a blimp, of all things, headed straight for it. I thought, you know, someone is trying to rescue those poor fellows up there. But as the blimp got closer I saw that it was very odd. It was brown and covered with spots as if made of leather. I was just trying to figure out if this was some kind of advertising when it opened a large pair of wings."

"Holy shit," I said.

"Indeed yes. They were like bat wings. Or perhaps a pterodactyl. The creature flew into the balloon and opened a set of jaws that could easily have swallowed a sport utility vehicle. There was a terrible tangle of leather and fabric and the balloon went down with the creature. All without a sound. Those poor people."

He shrugged. "Everybody's experience of those days is not so different. Ordinary things had become impossible and impossible things were everywhere to be seen. The lights were not going to come back on. The gas and water pressure dropped to nothing very quickly. There was much panic. It seemed a good time to make myself indispensable so I broke into a pharmacy and several clinics and stocked what I would need to take care of myself and others." He smiled. "I awarded myself a diploma two years early and began a practice."

"You mean you weren't a doctor before?" I said.

"Oh I should say not. I was a fourth year medical student. Even now I am only a doctor in the relative sense."

"Doctor enough for me."

"Thank you, Peter." To Ariel he said, "I did not want to be so close to the city so I came to Del Mar and met Parmita, and now I have a beautiful and wonderful wife and children I love deeply. In spite of much tragedy and hardship I believe my life has been a gift. I know I will never see a fraction of the world you and Peter have seen. And that is perfectly all right with me."

Ariel looked amused. "There's still a lot of road ahead of us, Doc."

During Dr. Ram's story my father had been cleaning his sword. Now he started to put it away but I leaned toward him and something in my look made him glance from me to the sword and back to me. I nodded a fraction and he held the sword before him in its sheath and then held it out to me.

I had never held it before. He'd had it with him all my life and I had never seen him give it up to anyone for any reason.

I spread my blanket out and took the sword and set it carefully on the blanket before me. I knew the curved blade in its sheath should be facing me with the twined handle on the left. Unthreatening and difficult to draw. A position of peace.

I was aware of the three of them watching me. All conversation stopped. I made a shooing gesture and Dr. Ram and my father scooted back. My father seemed tense like a cat in a strange place.

I slowly drew the sword and set it alongside its black lacquered scabbard. It was elegant. Something so beautifully itself that it was both weapon and work of art. My father had told me that the blade was five hundred years old, forged from metal pounded paperthin and folded and pounded flat again, over and over until hundreds of layers formed a strong and unbelievably sharp blade. There was a pattern to its tempering. The round guard was carved with a dragon winding around strange writing. The twined handle's diamond pattern provided a natural firm grip that absorbed sweat. Beautiful and terrible. The essence of sword. As if its purpose and history could be reconstructed from this sole example the way every person contained deep within his cells the essence of all people. Along the edge were several notches that had to have been made by the edge of another blade.

I looked up at my father. "How does it come apart."

He knelt facing me and wrapped the blade in the blanket and used his multitool to push two wooden pins from the handle and pulled the length of tang from the handle and set the handle and carved round guard and several metal discs aside. I thanked him and unfolded the blanket to reveal the naked blade and set it down on the road. I got a mirrored quarter from my pack and spoke a word and sat within a sudden pentagram.

I'd brought a dozen stasis bottles that could do this casting with a single word, but I wanted it done with thought and care the way the sword itself had been created. So I focused on my work and forgot my surroundings and when I was done I broke the pentagram at the cardinal points and invited my father in to reassemble his sword. Newly mirrored and unbreakable, undullable and eternal.

His practiced hands reassembled it with calm deliberation. He slid the blade into its plain black scabbard and sat looking at it.

I began returning items to my pack to disguise the fact that I did not know what to say. That he did not know what to say.

He stood abruptly and nodded and then left us. I think he was trying not to cry.

Ariel watched him go and then shook her head and looked at me. "You're a hell of a negotiator, kid," she said.

Soon we were near the Long Beach Airport, still on the 405. Vinecovered walls twelve feet high lined the freeway and limited our view to the cars ahead of us, the cars behind us, the crest of an occasional brown hill.

That night we car camped in Torrance. It looked like everyplace we'd already been; I only knew where we were was because of the freeway signs. I slept heavily and without dreaming and was grateful for that. Next morning the human members of our party got up and stumbled blinking from their cars and pissed beside them and drank coffee and ate and brushed their teeth and put on their packs and looked at the large unicorn that stood motionless and facing north. She looked worried.

An hour later our packs were off and we were squatting behind a dumptruck in the middle of the broken road discussing what we should do about the oval dressing mirror standing in the middle of a clear stretch of freeway up ahead. We were at the Artesia Boulevard exit which was apparently also the 91 Freeway; I couldn't make sense of the different identities these roads had possessed. The dressing mirror was framed in cherry wood and it reflected morning sunlight onto the pavement and gave me the flatout creeps.

"Any reason we shouldn't just ignore it and keep going?" my father said.

"Yan and I did a lot of things with mirrors."

My father started to ask me a question but something in the mirror started moving and he stopped. A figure in the frame stood waving at us.

I sighed. "We figured out how to make mirrors record what they reflected. Then you could say a key, a password, and the mirror would play it back."

"And so the movie industry returns," said Ariel.

Now the figure was holding something white and square.

"If this mirror needs a password to play back," said Dr. Ram, "why is it playing now."

"Because we said the password. It's another note to us. Yan would make it easy to read."

A hundred feet away the figure in the mirror waved again and grew still and was suddenly replaced by the image of ourselves peering out from behind a dumptruck two hundred feet away.

"Well," said Ariel, "we might as well see what he has to say." She headed toward it but my father hesitated.

"It's just a mirror," I said. "Not a stasis bottle. Not a weapon."

He smirked. "As far as I'm concerned mirrors turned into weapons about ten years ago." He shouldered his pack and went to catch up with Ariel.

———————

Three men on a clear summer morning staring at their reflection in a dressing mirror on a ruining freeway. Ariel looked beyond it with a suggestion of a frown on her alien yet somehow human features.

"Ready?" I said.

They nodded.

I said *yan* and there he was within the oval frame. He stood in front of a white marble wall. He looked the same. Where he was looked cold. Faint mist tendrils glided past him. He'd just finished saying the casting to make the mirror record and you could see a bit of the pentagram on the stone floor behind him. Now he smiled and waved and held up a large sketchpad and flipped back the cover to reveal heavy markered writing on the white paper. HOWDY FRED! He held it out a moment and grinned like he'd told a joke and then flipped the page again. MISS ME?

"Like a zit," I said. Then became aware of Dr. Ram beside me and felt my face get hot.

Yan's image turned a page. IF U R READING THIS THEN U CAME AFTER ME. He shook his head sadly and turned the page. PROBABLY NOT ALONE.

WHO'SE THERE WITH U I WONDER He put a finger to his chin and pretended to consider, then made an Ah! face and flipped a page. HI MR GAREY!

My father smiled thinly.

Flip. ITLL BE NICE 2 HAVE VISITERS ILL KEEP THE FIREPLACE LIT FOR U Yan brightened and nodded vigorously. Flip. MEAN WHILE I PUT SOME HURDELS BETWEEN U & ME TO MAKE IT WORTH OUR TIME Flip. I HAVE EVERY FAITH IN U FRED Flip. SEE U IN MY STATELY PLESURE DOME! Flip. YOU'RE PAL YAN

He dropped the sketchbook and grinned. He looked awkward and self conscious. He waved and then said a word and we were looking at ourselves. I looked like I'd stepped in dogshit.

Dr. Ram turned away from the mirror. "Confidence has always been one of my son's more prominent attributes."

My laugh was almost a bark, loud on the quiet freeway. Then my father joined in and finally so did Dr. Ram, a bit sheepishly. Ariel watched the three of us laughing like idiots. Then her expression changed and I saw movement out of the corner of my eye and looked just as a dozen men on horseback galloped up the Artesia Boulevard offramp and pounded toward us. Then I realized they weren't men at all. Or horses either.

TWENTY-FOUR

A centaur is the top parts of a human sticking up out of the major part of a horse. That's what the books show anyway, and I guess that's what you'd say if you never got closer than a thousand feet from one, which I highly recommend.

The dozen or so centaurs headed for us were gray emaciated stickfigures drawn with rulers, all sharp joints and planed angles. Equine and spindly bodies sprouting skeletal humanoid torsos topped by sliteyed wedgeshaped heads. They looked like something designed to lean into a gale and moved with deceptive grace and speed. The furless hide was pebbled. Their triangular hooves curved inward between the sharp points and wrinkled like turtle heads. Some wore modified motorcycle panniers dangling painted human skulls. They carried painted spears with funnelcut points.

"Well, this explains a lot," my father said. "What do we do."

"Can't run," said Ariel. "They're too fast."

"Guess they're not here to ask directions."

"I think the mirror called them."

My father drew his bright sword and glanced at me. "Bring any centaur repellant?"

I shook my head. "Fresh out." My voice cracked. My knees were rubber and I thought I was going to piss myself.

"Get in a car," my father said. "Lock the doors."

"But—"

"Car. Now. Throw spells."

There was no arguing because they were on us. I grabbed my pack and made for a Land Rover. Bad moment when I found the passenger door locked but through the dirty window I saw the driver side lock was up. I ran to that side and jumped in and fumbled with my backpack's closures while trying to think of what it contained that might be any use. I could open the spells without taking them out but in my near panic I couldn't think of what I'd made and needed to see the talismans to remember. My fingers felt nerveless. A quick flash made me look out the dirty windshield in time to see my father's sword catch sunlight as it slid along a hollow metal spear and cut the holder's fingers from its bony hands.

I flinched as something smacked against the right side window six inches from my head. Heavy plastic tubing clattered on the hood and rolled to the pavement. The point had broken off.

Ariel intercepted another centaur in front of the Rover's blunt hood and parried a spearthrust with her horn hard enough to knock its wielder into the back of the topless Mustang beside it.

I unzipped my pack and turned it upside down and shook things onto the seat. All around me was clatter and banging. I could barely see what was happening. I needed to find a way to help now or get back outside and join in. The three of them couldn't defeat those twelve creatures. Not that four of us could either but—

A loud smack and the windshield spiderwebbed and I jumped back as a blunted spear rolled off the flat hood. My father and Ariel and Dr. Ram formed a triangle facing away from the Land Rover. Not fighting the centaurs so much as fending them off because they were coming after me.

Dr. Ram recocked his crossbow and slid home a bolt. My father's bloodstained sword was steady and pointed at the emaciated twitching figure of a centaur lying fingerless and bleeding from a yardlong smile splitting its gaunt human belly. It pushed up on its gouting stumps and tried to rise and a flood of blood and viscera vomited from the slash. I stared at a bloody stringy ball the size of a grapefruit that I realized was the partially digested head of a child.

Ariel arose from the convertible with half her horn gleaming dark red. The centaur she'd fought lay upended and unmoving in the back seat.

The remaining centaurs fanned out to surround us. One jumped gracefully onto the bed of a once-white Ford Explorer and put its forelegs on the roof of the cab and yanked a crossbow bolt out of its flank. The flared broadhead tore out a plug of flesh and dark red sprayed. The centaur tossed the bolt aside without a glance and raised a silver necklace to its lipless mouth and blew. A whistle sounded and the other centaurs looked its way. It let go the whistle and called out something that sounded like "fregary." Its voice sounded as if its tongue were too big for its mouth.

My father and Ariel looked at me and the hairs stood up on my arms as I realized that the creature was calling my name.

"Fregary. Kmout fregary. Kmout."

I set aside my pack with wooden fingers. Opened the car door. Stood on the siderunner. Surrounding centaurs awaiting their leader's command. My father and Ariel and Dr. Ram at ready.

The leader grinned a toothless black V. "Fregary." His tone was downright cheerful. "Kmout fregary. Kmere."

A breeze blew and I drew a deep breath and my jaw clenched and my mouth went tight and my heart pounded and I wanted to hurt him, wanted to see how much more of that dark red I could conjure from his loathsome body, and I caught myself stepping toward him with every intention of finding out. The wind shifted and I stopped. What the hell was I thinking.

"Fregary. Kmere."

"Fuuuuuck you," I called back.

"That's my boy," my father said.

"Comes by it honest," said Ariel.

"Fregary. Kmon. Hepya frenz."

"Help them how."

"Ya kmout, day liff."

Ariel put her forelegs on the side of the Mustang and parodied the centaur leader's pose by rising over the body of the centaur whose gore still slathered her horn. "Fuuuuck you."

I didn't even see the spear until she flinched and six feet of two-inch-wide pipe streaked by where her body had just been. I swear it hissed as it flew into the Mercedes in the next lane and punched in the quarterpanel.

"Maybe I should go with them," I said. It sounded insincere even to me.

My father glanced back at me. "If they want you it's because they've been told to bring you back or kill you."

"But you guys will be okay. You can go on and—"

"If they've been told to bring you back or kill you it's because Yan thinks you can stop him."

I stared.

My father turned to address the leader. "In any case I'm not in the habit of giving up my children to underfed polo ponies."

The leader spread his long arms. His empty grin looked somehow bigger than his head. "Denwe shitya skulls. Fregary kmon enway. Fukya."

Ariel stepped closer to the leader looming on his pickup truck. "Hey skinny," she called. "How about you and me dance. You win, you get the fregary. You lose, you and your pals trot back to whatever anorexic merry-go-round you escaped from. What do you say."

The sliteyed gaze lowered to her as if just noticing her. "Yoonkhorn." It bent its cadaverous torso forward and spat at Ariel's hooves. The spittle thickened and began inching toward her like some kind of worm. She ground it beneath a silver hoof and it let out a little squeak.

Ariel turned her back on the leader posing on his truck and lifted her tail at him and leapt weightlessly over the convertible. "Worth a try," she told my father.

"Now what," I said.

"Now they try to kill us," my father said.

"We try to stop them though," said Ariel.

"Hey Raj," my father said, "are you—" He broke off.

Dr. Ram leaned against the side of the Land Rover with the crossbow loosely gripped and pointed at the pavement. Shades paler and looking sleepy. Free hand clamped over a dark stain that began midthigh on his shorts and ran down to the pavement where an aluminum spear lay darkly wet along its first two feet.

My father sheathed his sword as he ran to Dr. Ram and took the crossbow and pulled him away from the Land Rover and opened the door and heaved him inside, which left a dark swath on the gray seat. A spear meant for my father slammed the open car door. He turned unhurriedly and shot the closest centaur in the mouth. The head jerked back with the bolt sticking out the back like a weathervane. The gaunt torso arched and then slumped forward. I caught myself thinking it was going to fall off the horse and then remembered that it was the horse. Its legs buckled and it collapsed where it stood.

Then it got back up and reached back and pulled the bolt out of its head.

"The brain's behind the breastbone," said Ariel.

"Which one," my father asked without looking from the creature he'd just shot.

"The horsey one."

"Gotcha." He bent to get more bolts from Dr. Ram.

"Ready set go," said Ariel and went for the leader who hadn't moved from the Ford Explorer. She flowed up the front of the pickup and leapt up from the hood just as the leader jumped out at her. She had the stronger end of the deal and knocked him backward and they slammed into the truck bed so hard the truck rocked on its flat tires. The centaur's mouth opened impossibly wide and clamped onto her neck.

The only reason I was still alive was because other centaurs were watching this too.

My father stayed behind the Land Rover door and reloaded the crossbow. Near him lay the spear that had hit Dr. Ram. I picked it up to throw it at the nearest centaur, which stood broadside to me as it watched Ariel and its leader savaging each other. The spear must have weighed ten pounds. The shaft was painted and the grip was twined. The center had been filled with concrete. I threw it anyway and it arced laughably slowly and hit the centaur between the ribs and bounced off. I got its attention though. It turned and raised its own spear and I got the feeling this one wouldn't bounce off.

I flinched at a twang and hiss by my left ear as my father fired his next bolt. The centaur caught it by the fletchings. At least that's how it looked. But then it yanked its arm and the bolt came with it and dark red sprayed from above the sharp bone at the juncture of human torso and equine breast.

My father handed me the crossbow and brushed past me drawing his sword and ran toward the centaur he'd just shot. The centaur leaned back its entire upper torso and drew back the spear to throw just as Ariel and the leader struggled up from the truck bed and fell over the side and hit hard on the road.

My father hesitated.

I yelled *randori dad* as the centaur threw. The spear hit my father square in his mirrored chest and bounced off. My father toppled backward and hit with a sickening thud.

The centaur leader rose above Ariel and jabbed its sharp hooves down. Ariel knocked them aside and thrashed but did not get up.

The centaur that threw the spear cocked its planed head and stepped slowly toward my father and sniffed at his suddenly mirrored form like a wary dog. Two more steps. One more. The centaur bent toward the distorted image and sniffed beside the mirrored sword.

I yelled *hyperion dad* and my father became unmirrored and completed the block he'd begun with his sword a few seconds ago. He looked surprised when he chopped the centaur in the side of the neck. So did the centaur. Jetting blood it jerked upright. My father recovered quickly and pushed a yard of blade into the creature's equine breast. The toothless mouth gaped wide enough to eat a basketball and let out a yowl that made me feel like I was chewing glass. The dying creature stepped back wobbling like a newborn colt and looked down at its own dark gouting. Its knobby fingers groped the wound and then it realized it was dead and fell down.

The other centaurs charged. I hoped my crossbow would make a good club because I only had one more bolt. I fired and had no idea if I hit anything because something slammed into the crossbow hard enough to spin me around and send the crossbow flying. A spear. Then a blow meant for my head hit my shoulder instead and knocked me sideways into a car. I got back to my feet expecting to be bowled over any second and the pain hit me and the world went white and I put my good arm up to fend off the killing blow that didn't come and didn't come.

I lowered my arm. In front of Dr. Ram my father faced the centaurs with sword ready. Ariel lay still beneath the leader's hooves. Ten feet in front of me a centaur held its spear back to throw. None of the centaurs moved. All of them were looking at a point behind me.

A cold spot crept between my shoulder blades as I turned slowly thinking I would see Yan behind me somehow stepping from the mirror smiling and smug. But it wasn't Yan. It was a girl. Maybe fourteen, shorthaired and skinny, white T-shirt and khaki shorts and red JanSport backpack and the brightest green sneakers I ever saw. She stood on the roof of a Honda with her arms folded and squinted in the noonday sun. A pair of sunglasses hung from a shirt collar. She had no weapons or compatriots that I could see but the centaurs watched her as if she were about to hurl thunderbolts at them.

When she saw she had everyone's attention she stepped down from the car and came toward us. She glanced at me as she went by and gave a little smile. Dark tan and pale blue eyes and freckles, maybe ninetyfive pounds. We might have just caught each other's eye at the vibe for all the concern she showed about the ugliness she was walking into. She paid no attention to the other centaurs as she walked up to the leader and put her thumbs through the beltloops of her baggy shorts and grinned up at him and said, "Hi. Fuck off."

My father and I traded an incredulous glance. He shrugged.

The centaur leader glared at the girl. On her back beneath him Ariel looked at the scene in outright disbelief. Astonishingly the leader stepped back. Ariel got up quickly and put some distance between herself and the leader, ready for anything but doing nothing.

The girl looked at the surrounding centaurs. "All of you. Fuck off." Her tone betrayed no trace of doubt that they'd do anything but fuck off. And the centaurs lowered their spears and looked at their leader.

Who looked at me. Literally trembling with desire to kill me. "Fregary. Snot ova."

I swallowed. "It is for now." I tried to copy my father's up-yours tone but even I wasn't buying it.

The girl made a brushing motion at the leader. "Shoo. Or I cut myself and start giving out free hugs in five, four, three—"

They wheeled and galloped off. Their hooves made an odd soft clicking as they headed back to the Artesia offramp they had come from. The girl stood watching them till they were out of sight. By then we were all staring at the girl.

Ariel moved first. The girl looked away from the offramp and watched curiously as Ariel came to her and lowered her head. The girl bit her lip and her eyes watered and she nodded and stepped forward and put her arms around Ariel's neck and set her cheek against her and ignored her sunglasses as they fell from her collar. Tears came to my eyes as well. I'm not sure I could say why.

Just before she let Ariel go I heard her whisper Please don't tell them.

TWENTY-FIVE

"They hate people," Avy said. "There isn't any reason. They hate us and they want us dead. Period."

I was sitting in the shade of a Chrysler van sharing water with the girl who had inexplicably saved us. My father was dressing Dr. Ram's cut. Ariel alternated between scowling and looking thoughtful.

Avy gave me back the waterbottle and I finished it. I was still pretty shaky and my arm felt like one big bruise. "They hate people but they're afraid of you."

She shrugged. "I smell wrong. They're fucking terrified of me bleeding all over them."

"You smell wrong."

"Some people's smell keeps mosquitoes away. Or fleas. With me it's centaurs."

"And you showed up just as they were about to wipe us out."

She cocked her head. "Are you giving me shit?"

"No. Really no. It's just been a long day."

We fell silent. She pawed at the asphalt chunks in the tufts of grass between her bright green sneakers. I felt idiotic and ungrateful and tried to think of something to say. I watched my father bandage Dr. Ram's thigh and ask him questions and shake his head over the staining gauze.

"I was tracking them." She didn't look at me. "Fuckers hit the port a week ago and killed anything that moved."

"What port."

"Long Beach. There was a bunch who set up there, they libbed shipping containers and shit and started trading. Fucking assholes mostly. Still. They got hit hard. I think two clans joined up to jack them because there were a lot more of them. They split up after. I followed this group."

"How come."

"To kill the motherfuckers in their sleep, why else. Only they don't sleep. Fuckers." She looked like she was about to cry.

"You had people in Long Beach?"

"No."

My father set a hand on Dr. Ram's shoulder and stood and went to Ariel. I left Avy sitting on the curb and joined them. "How is he," I asked my father.

"Not bad for someone who almost got his leg core-sampled. It missed the artery and the bleeding's mostly stopped. Raj says he can sew it up. You want the bad part?"

"That was the good part?"

"It is when you know they wipe their spearpoints with their own shit."

I stared. "That's. That's."

"Yeah. I've only irrigated the wound and taped him up for now. The real fun part comes next. We have to sterilize the wound and sew it up and get some kind of antibiotic into him."

"So what do we do."

"We can't stay here. The polo ponies might come back."

"They will," said Avy. We looked at her as if we had forgotten she was there. "They'll keep their distance and pick us off," she said. "We should find somewhere safe."

"We?" I said.

We put Dr. Ram on a handtruck and rolled him off the freeway to a furniture store that had not been looted or squatted. We barred the front door and made sure the rear loading door was locked and then set up in the upstairs office, a windowless cul-de-sac. We set Dr. Ram on a couch with his leg propped on an ugly green fringe pillow and my father and I left him with Ariel and Avy while we went to lib food and supplies.

"So what's her story," my father asked when we were back outside.

"Most I know is that she says the centaurs wiped out some kind of trading post in Long Beach and she's trying to return the favor."

"You believe that?"

"Why would she lie."

"Cause she doesn't want us to know she was following us."

"Was she."

"Someone was." He shrugged and coughed and drew his sword and squinted at it reflecting afternoon sun. "I couldn't even feel it cutting," he told the blade. "And there's not a mark. Not even blood." He shook his head and sheathed the sword without looking.

"There never will be. Why would she follow us."

My father pointed to an intact Sport Chalet and we crossed the street toward it. "There's a lot of places like that library in San Juan Capistrano," he said as we crossed the street. "When me and your mom followed I-Ten out here, when I came down from Ojai with you, I saw whole towns that looked like that."

I thought of Avy saying They hate us. "They've been wiping out towns for twenty years?"

"Maybe. What I don't understand is why Yan would help them."

"He gave them stasis bottles. He probably didn't think about what they'd do with them. He hasn't seen what you've seen."

"Maybe." He pulled a roll of duct tape from his pack and tore off two strips and made an X on the front door glass of the Sport Chalet and hit it with a broken chunk of sidewalk. The sound echoed down the street but was nowhere near as loud as if the glass had all crashed in. Instead it spiderwebbed and he knocked out chunks and reached in and unlocked the door. "She tell you why they're afraid of her?"

"Her name's Avy. She says they don't like her smell or they're afraid of her blood or something. Like mosquitoes and fleas, whatever that means." I thought about adding what I'd heard her whisper to Ariel but I decided not to.

He frowned. "No kidding."

"What she said."

"Well. Let's shop."

I stuck close to my father in the Sport Chalet which I think he chose to ignore. We found a few boxes of Power Bars. I thought they'd gone bad but my father said they'd always tasted like that. The real score was weapons. Hunting knives, a crossbow and bolts, a compound bow and hunting arrows, bowstrings. New cargo shorts for Dr. Ram. Two lanterns and mesh wicks and little tea candles.

It was nearly sunset when we set our haul on the uneven sidewalk and my father showed me how to load and cock the crossbow. We stacked cardboard boxes and I fired at them from various distances until I felt reasonably sure I could defend myself if I were ever attacked by a cardboard box.

"Hold onto it," my father said. "I'll show you how to set it in your pack so you can get to it fast. Ariel used to carry mine but I doubt she'll let us pull that shit anymore. I'll show you what you can coat the boltheads with too. Maybe your new girlfriend can donate some blood."

I let that one pass. "It's all survival with you isn't it."

"It's all survival with anyone who wants to, you know . . . survive."

I thought we were edging up on the Generation Change vs. Generation Fred issue and shifted tack. "How come the centaurs never attacked Del Mar."

"I thought you'd have figured that out. It's Mr. Papadopoulos."

"Paypay?"

"Sure. Towns don't need casters just to make charms, Fred. What do you think happened to Sudama."

"He was killed by hyenas."

"We told you he was killed by hyenas. And hell maybe he was. We never found him. For all I know he's a mirrored statue out in the woods. But Paypay does a lot of mojo to keep certain things from coming into town. Mostly it works. Del Mar's stable, viable, and everyone wants it to stay that way. It's a mean old world and towns need defending and swords and baseball bats aren't always the best defense. Why do you think I let you apprentice to him. Paypay won't live forever you know."

"I'm supposed to become Del Mar's defender?"

"You were till you and Yan started opening the wrong doors. Paypay doesn't think he has enough time to train someone else. But no one can make you do it."

We scoured a looted 7-Eleven more from duty than in hope. All we took from it was a bag of peppermint candies my father found rather unbelievably hanging by itself on a rack and some coins he took from the register after jimmying it open.

I didn't know what to think about the whole town-defender thing. All my training suddenly seemed colored by it. As we left the 7-Eleven I asked my father why no one had told me about it.

"No reason to until Paypay was sure you had the chops for the job." He was wearing the compound bow bandolier style and carrying a handbasket with lanterns and wicks and Power Bars and peppermints. He put his coins into a newspaper machine and opened the lid and pulled a newspaper from beneath several others. "It's not an issue right now, Fred." He glanced at the headline. GAZA RETALIATION JUSTIFIED, PRIME MINISTER CLAIMS. "We have a ways to go and you don't have to decide anything till you're back. Hell, you don't have to decide anything then."

"How do you know how far we have to go."

"Yan's mirrorgram. His message. White marble, wispy fog, stately pleasure dome. He's in San Simeon."

"What's in San Simeon."

He gave the half smirk I would always associate with him. "Hearst Castle."

Dr. Ram cut the bloodstained gauze with a pair of dainty scissors and poured saline on the bandage to soften the dried blood and carefully pulled the fabric flaps from his thigh. The wound wasn't deep but it looked awful. The spearpoint had scored his thigh and cut out a neat crescent. A fist-sized area around the wound was black.

"Well that's gonna need a bandaid," said Ariel.

I asked him if it hurt.

"Only when I inhale or exhale." He grinned. "Sorry. A very old joke."

"What you need me to do, Raj," my father said.

"I will have to open the wound slightly while you irrigate it with saline to remove any foreign matter."

"All right.

"I would appreciate some help sterilizing it. I believe I can stitch it myself."

"All right." My father tossed Ariel the bag of peppermints.

She let it hit her and land on the floor. "You are a god," she said.

"Yeah. I promise to use my powers only for good."

"And smite. You have to smite."

"Heavy on the smite."

Avy lit lanterns and set them around the room and then set one near Dr. Ram for all the world as if she'd been with us from the start. He nodded at her and then looked up at my father, who knelt before him with a squeeze bottle of contact-lens saline. "You sure this stuff is okay?"

"As long as the seal was not broken it should still be sterile."

"Okay. Ready when you are."

Dr. Ram took a deep breath and put his fingers on either side of the wound and took another breath and pulled the edges of the wound away from each other. The fingerlong runnel immediately filled with blood and my father hesitated. "It is okay," said Dr. Ram. "The blood will help irrigate."

My father nodded uncertainly and began squeezing saline onto the wound. It made a little piddling sound like pissing onto sand and I suddenly felt ill. I started to turn away but my father said, "Mop up as I go, will you, Fred." So I grabbed maxipads from Dr. Ram's pack and dabbed and swabbed as my father sprayed. I tried to look away but the sound by itself was worse.

"Looks pretty clean to me, Raj."

"Let us hope so."

My father set down the saline bottle and held out a handful of vodka sampler bottles. "Name your poison."

"Stoli is good. It has no flavorings or additives."

"Straight or rocks?" He twisted one open and handed it to Dr. Ram, who drank it and handed back the empty. My father grinned. "The patient must be anesthetized. Another round?"

"For the wound this time, I am afraid."

My father twisted open another bottle and handed it to him and he upended it onto the open wound and clamped his teeth and hissed and arched his back like a fish on a deck. I grabbed his hand and my father grabbed his leg as bloody vodka ran down his thigh.

"Bit of a kick to it," my father said.

Dr. Ram laughed. "Alcohol has never agreed with me."

I dabbed around the wound again and got out his suturing kit. He put on a pair of thin white rubber gloves while I swabbed the pliers head of my father's multitool and held it in the lantern flame and then used that to hold the curved suturing needle in the flame. He tried to thread the needle but his hands were none too steady so my father put on a pair of rubber gloves and did it for him. Then he sewed the wound.

At one point Dr. Ram glanced up at me and gave a little smile. "It is not as bad as it looks. There are not so many nerves in the thigh, you know, and if we find one we can just move the needle over and try again."

"I'll take your word for it."

My father pulled the last stitch and tied off the suture and rebandaged the wound. Then he handed Dr. Ram another vodka and opened one for himself. He even offered me one but I passed. My father raised the sampler to Dr. Ram and said Kampai. Dr. Ram raised his and said A la sature. They drank.

"Some ibuprofin and Levoquin and you're all set," my father said.

"I will have to make do with willow bark and goldenseal tea I am afraid."

"Gotta love those wiccans."

Avy set up the campstove and set water to boiling.

Ariel crunched a peppermint she had somehow gotten out of the bag and then out of its twistended wrapper.

My father sat in a leather office chair and leaned back and put his feet on the desk and partitioned himself from us with the front section of the paper.

"Haven't you read that already," I said.

"I like to read it every couple of years just to keep up."

"Everyone like ramen?" Avy said.

I wanted to ask Who are you. What are you doing here. But my father, Mr. Survival, was reading the paper and grunting approval and Dr. Ram was examining his healing wound and nodding absently that sure, ramen would be swell and I thought, well they're older and wiser and besides I like ramen.

Ariel glanced around at everyone and announced that she was going out scouting. She seemed annoyed. My father's hand waved above the paper as she left.

The room got humid from steam while we waited for dinner. I mulled whether to ask my father about something he'd said outside the 7-Eleven: *you don't have to decide anything till you're back.* It wasn't the decision I wanted to ask him about. It was that "you're."

"In Xanadu did Kublai Khan a stately pleasure dome decree," said Ariel.

"That Byron," my father said. "He talked purty."

"He did but that was Coleridge, you person from Porlock."

"No way."

"Yes way."

"Anyway that's one reason I think Yan's at Hearst Castle."

"Because of a Brian poem?" I said.

"Byron."

"Coleridge."

"Whatever." He shrugged. "Yan's a showoff. He wants to be a bigshot, wants to be all nationwide. Bigshots need headquarters."

"What is it with evil wizard guys and famous buildings," said Ariel.

"It was the same before the Change," said Dr. Ram. "Except back then they built their own structures instead of squatting them and named them after themselves."

I folded my arms. "And Yan knows this."

"If he didn't know it before he knows it now that he's there."

We sat in lounge chairs we'd dragged outside the furniture store, drinking coffee in the morning chill and debating where to point our little pilgrimage.

Avy made astonishingly good coffee.

"Why bring me back to him," I said. "Why not just kill me along with everybody else."

"He wants his big wizard battle," said my father.

"I would like to offer another possibility," said Dr. Ram. His bandage peeked out from beneath his new cargo shorts. "When Yan was very little he would loot items from shops. I believe the term now is lib. He would often play with these libbed items in front of me or Parmita. We would ask where he had obtained them and then lecture him about the propriety and danger of young boys scavenging from seemingly untenanted shops. But Parmita noticed that Yan would go out of his way to play with these items in front of us as if wanting us to ask him about them."

My father glanced at me and Ariel. "Um, I'm not following you here, Raj."

"I believe Yan wants us to stop him."

"Not us," I said. "Me."

"You're the Worthy Adversary," said Ariel.

I nodded. "If he keeps anyone else from stopping him so what. If he keeps me from stopping him he's got the universe's approval for what he wants to do."

My father finished his coffee and flung the grounds from the cup. "That is one fuckedup dynamic."

"Which is why it's probably true," said Ariel.

San Simeon lay on the coast about two hundred twenty miles north of where we were, which was about seventyfive miles north of Del Mar, which meant we were only a fourth of the way there. The roadmaps came out again and so did the arguments about our route. I expected Ariel to settle them the same way she had before but it was Avy who decided us.

"The coast roads are all fucked up, washed out here and here." She pointed at Malibu and Santa Barbara. Her finger landed on Oxnard. "There's gangs here that jack anyone who comes through, I think just for the fuck of it."

"I was introduced to them once," my father said. "Do you remember Honest Abe, Fred."

"He was our horse, right?"

Ariel snorted.

"Anyway," said Avy, "the coasts are pretty much fucked for travel."

"No fucking way," said Ariel.

Avy nodded enthusiastically. "Yeah, it sucks, cause it's really fucking pretty."

"Then what the fuck can we do," said Ariel.

My father studied his own shoulder and tried not to laugh as he said, "Fuck if I know."

Avy studied the map, oblivious. She tapped a city just north of us and looked up and said, "We could fucking fly."

TWENTY-SIX

"For all we know there's an army in there."

We lay prone in high grass on the mild slope of freeway berm. Avy propped beside me on her skinny elbows fidgety and impatient. Dr. Ram lay on the other side of my father and squinted at the huge structure. Ariel was somewhere out of sight.

Before us lay a large field gone wild. In the middle a tall orange and white banded pole twined with vines on its bottom third. In the brush beside it a van overcome by weeds. On tall pillars near us a blue sign with yellow letters. GOODYEAR. Owlshit thick on the ground around it. On the far side of the field an enormous building, pale brown with a huge white door, seemed to have grown from the network of creeping vines spreading from what had been a nursery next door. Near us was a cluster of small aluminum-sided buildings. A narrow path had been trampled between the small buildings and the enormous one.

My father lowered his binoculars and glanced at me. "An army of what."

"Centaurs maybe."

"Prescient centaurs who know we're headed for that hangar."

The map said we were in Carson. Why had they named these stretches of land. You couldn't tell one from the other. We were about five miles north of the furniture store where we'd spent the night. Behind us lay the 405 Freeway and before us spread the wild field with its vined pole and hangar and aluminum-sided buildings.

My father looked at Avy. "If you know anything else about this now's the time to say so."

"Just what I told you. There's some kind of ship in that building that could fly before the Change. There's an old guy who lives here who says he could make it go again if he got some help. He's been trying for a long time. He's kind of a—well he's a fucking nut is what he is. But that doesn't mean the ship thing isn't in there."

My father glanced up at the blue and yellow sign. Below the logo it read GOODYEAR AIRSHIP OPERATIONS. "What do you think, Raj."

Dr. Ram shrugged. "Helium is still lighter than air."

"You think there's any helium in that thing after thirty years."

"I think there is an enormous hangar a thousand feet away and inside it there could be almost anything."

"Prescient centaurs," I said.

Ariel came nonchalantly through the high grass. "Well no one's following us."

My father frowned and tapped his sword sheath. He glanced at Avy and said Okay then and got up and headed toward the cluster of aluminum buildings. Dr. Ram shouldered his pack and followed. Ariel gave Avy a look and then went after them.

I hung back with Avy. "What's with you and Ariel."

"What the fuck are you talking about."

"You know what I'm talking about."

"Why the fuck should I tell you."

"How come you're so defensive."

"How come you ask so many fucking questions." She started away.

"You eat with that mouth?"

She stopped and looked back. For a startling moment I thought she was going to cry. Then she gave a barking laugh. "You have no fucking idea," she said and turned away.

———

WELCOME TO GOODYEAR AIRSHIP OPERATIONS
PASSENGERS PLEASE REPORT TO THE OFFICE

We set our packs on weathered picnic tables on an awninged rear porch covered with dead leaves that crackled when we walked. Wild roses grew near two trees beyond the porch. A rusting sign requested PLEASE DO NOT CLIMB THE TREES. No problem.

My father banged on the sliding glass door beside a sign that said OFFICE. "Anybody home?"

"No one but us chickens," said Ariel. She had ignored the office and was watching the huge hangar.

My father grabbed the crossbow from Dr. Ram and went into the office anyway. "Someone lived here," he said when he came back. "Not for a while though."

"Hangar," said Ariel.

"Yah. Here, Fred." He handed me a brochure he'd taken from the office and then grabbed up his pack and felt for the fence in the wall of vines and gave Dr. Ram a boost over it before vaulting it himself. Ariel leapt over it lightly.

I opened the brochure. THE GOODYEAR BLIMP. Unbelievably large finned cylinders floated above stadiums and pastures, moored on fields and dwarfed the people gathered underneath their blue and silver length.

Avy touched my arm. "She knows something about me. Okay? It's nobody's business."

I frowned down at her. Once again I wanted to ask Why are you with us. What are we doing here with you. But she seemed so determined and so frail at the same time and I admired and pitied her. Ninety pounds of solid will. My urge to demand an accounting dissolved. "Okay," I said. She nodded and then jumped the fence without touching it.

The path was worn over what remained of a paved road that curved out to the central circle of broken asphalt and then curved away to the hangar. The banded pole was supported by envined rigging cables. Dr. Ram said it was a mooring mast for the airship. I stared at it as we passed. It was at least thirty feet high. I glanced at the brochure my father had given me. Still couldn't picture it.

I'd wondered how we were going to open the enormous hangar door but there was a regular door beside it half hidden by overgrowth and lost in the scale of the thing. It was partway open and we stopped before it and Ariel nodded at my father and he banged on the door. "Hel-loooo?"

The knock and his voice echoed hugely. Something clanged inside.

Avy took a deep breath and stepped up to the doorway and put a hand on my father's arm. My father stepped back. "José?" Avy called.

My father started to say something but stopped at a twitch of Ariel's head.

Avy opened the door wider. "José?"

The voice that responded echoed so much I could not distinguish words.

"It's Avy. I brought some people."

A thud and then approaching footsteps. Into the trapezoid of doorway light stepped a skinny old lunatic. Mostly bald with wild wisps of gray hair and veiny eyes showing too much white, remaining teeth yellow. Filthy white shirt with epaulets and old jeans sagging off hipbones and blown out at the knees. "Avy. And—" he looked at us wonderingly "—people." And stopped at Ariel.

"What do you say José?" said Ariel. "We're here to see a man about a blimp."

I looked from the majestic flying cylinders depicted in the brochure to the enormous wrinkled filthy bag spread out on the hangar floor and lit by sunlight columns from skylights far above. A twenty-foot hump about six feet high in the middle of the wrinkled bag. The whole bag covered by a nylon net bordered with sandbag weights attached with hooks.

At the far end of the hangar was a wellpreserved flatbed semi. On its bed stood a banded cluster of long thin metal tanks. Beside the rack a tall metal stairway on wheels. Giant metal fins leaning against that. Apart from these the hangar was mostly empty space and a lot of it. Unseen pigeons flapped in rafters high overhead. The floor a riot of dried gray splotches.

Our footsteps echoed as José toured us around the used condom of deflated blimp and pointed out sections and gave long technical explanations and was scarcely able to contain his excitement at our assumed willingness to help him get this empty rubber bag into the air.

I tugged on Dr. Ram's sleeve. "We can still get out of here and find somewhere safe before the centaurs show up," I whispered.

"Let us see what your father wishes to do."

"Are you gonna get in that thing."

He looked thoughtful. "I have learned to be surprised by anything. And unlike you I have fond memories of it flying. It was a local fixture, quite a sight you know. Very beautiful."

"It looks like a skinned whale."

José looked back at me. I didn't much care for the light in his eyes. "Don't judge a blimp by its cover, young man."

"I'm sure this thing's amazing when it's in the air. But that doesn't look like it's gonna happen anytime soon and we're kind of in a—"

"Son, this thing is the *Spirit of America*. And we can have her in the air in a day."

"I was just a kid. Had my light-plane certification, worked twin-engine Cessnas mostly. Grew up right here in Carson. Saw the blimp all the time, didn't pay much attention. Applied for a crew job after I got certified, then forgot about it. Two years later they called, asked was I still interested. Hell yes I was interested. We went everywhere in this thing. *Spirit of America*. The G-Bomb we called it. They flew her as much as they parked her. Built the hangar here after the hurricane nearly wrecked her. Hurricanes in So Cal, you remember that. Global warming, shit. Guess that got fixed.

"Day of the Change she was hangared. Pretty unusual, they usually flew little PR trips on Saturdays. CEOs and cancer kids. But someone ran a RC plane into her, believe that? Left a hole big as me. Lucky thing really. She'da crashed if she'da been out. Not a big deal, crashing. Engines quit, you go down slow. Steering's all linkage anyhow. Envelope wouldn't have survived though. So it's a lucky thing.

"Hear something funny? I wasn't here in Carson. San Francisco. First vacation in two years. Got it cause she'd been hangared. Hungover as a sonofabitch. Fourthirty comes and the whole world changes and I'm puking up shit I ate in third grade.

"First year or two I barely even thought about the blimp. Thought more about not getting killed. You know how that goes. Shacked up with these two Berkeley girls. Don't ever do that. Fun at first but someone's toes get stepped on sooner or later. Then life just kind of kept happening to me. Does that. Worked my way toward Sacramento, became a trapper. I mean blimp and airplane mechanic, what's that get you now. Drink in a trade bar for some stories maybe. I drank em too.

"One day I'm telling G-Bomb stories for Cuervo shots and it hits me.

She's hangared down in Carson. Been telling all these stories and hadn't even thought about it. No reason she couldn't fly. Helium tanks, valves still work. Engines just push her. Don't need em to fly. Can't inflate her alone though. There's a sequence. Can't manage everything by myself. Can't launch her alone either. Well maybe. Wouldn't want to.

"I only thought about it though. Life kept happening. Wife. Kids. No seat time in my future. Trapping, candlemaking, I don't know whatall. Kids lit out for San Francisco when they were old enough. City still sucked em in back then before it all burned down. You know about that? Terrible shame.

"Well not long after Consuela died I'm looking in the mirror thinking Who's this old guy. And I remembered my old friend down in Carson. The *Sofa* we called her. *S of A*. Realized there's nothing to stop me paying her a visit and giving her a lift. Not anymore. I thought hell why not. What else you got to do old man.

"Another year to get down here. Start to measure your life in these big chunks. Couldn't believe it when I finally came back here. I just broke down and cried. She was right like they left her. They hadn't deflated her. Thirty years did that. Nests everywhere in the envelope—packrats, raccoons, you name it. Things had lived in the gondola. Coyote dens in the hangar. Hundred million birds up in the rafters. Crap everywhere. Took my time. Cleaned everything. Inspect and repair and inspect. Envelope's fine. You can cut it but you can't tear it. Go on, try. Strong and light, huh. Rubberized fabric. They had a patent. I started hauling in and hooking up. She's been flightready for months now. Your young man here doesn't believe that I can see. That's all right. Might feel the same way in his place.

"One morning Avy shows up. All beatup, looking for a hiding place. Won't tell who did it. Or what did. Fed her, healed her up. Like a half starved puppy. She'd go away. Always come back though. Home base. Asked what are you trying to do here José. Told her. Showed her pictures. Flying over stadiums and racetracks. I'm even in a couple of em but she don't believe it's me. Can't blame her. Looked like a different person then. Was. Said she'd find me some help and took off. Figured you know she just said it to be nice and went her way. But here she is. And here you are. And a unicorn no less. I seen one of you once, you know that? Long time ago outside the City. Not long after the Change. Second prettiest thing I ever saw. Third now that you're here. *Spirit* flying's prettiest. No offense. You'll see when she's up. I love this thing. I really do. Always did. She's all I got now. Happiest part of my life laying here in this hangar. Wish I'd known it then. But hell. We all got a sob story huh. It's just a mean old world is all. Not why you're here though.

"Thing is I can't gas her up alone and I sure can't launch her by myself. Even if she flies she'll mostly just get blown around by the wind. No engine to push her. Still. Up there, flying. First people in what, thirty years. Avy here says you're in a hurry to get somewhere. And I don't care where we go so long as it's up. So how about it. Want a lift?"

TWENTY-SEVEN

The rushing hiss of releasing helium filled the hangar space. The corpse of the blimp stretched out to either side of me, amorphous in early morning light. A hose ran from the gasbag, the envelope José called it, to the tanks on the semi. The main valve had turned with some help from a pipe wrench and WD-40.

We had repositioned the nylon net over the envelope and moved the weights along its edges. There was a system José said, a sequence in which the weights had to be moved and rehung as the envelope inflated. As it rose from the floor like a blister José directed my father and Dr. Ram in unhooking thirtyfive-pound weights from one end of the restraining net and rehanging them on the other like they were playing some big chess game. As the day wore on the hiss of gas continued in the massive space and the blimp took shape, one end tautening and rising, then the other as the weights were repositioned.

At the far end of the hangar I emptied my backpack and sorted out ingredients, looking for the mirrored button I knew contained a quick pentagram spell.

José had only ever planned to take the blimp up and let the wind push it around until he decided he'd revisited his history long enough and vented the helium and came back down again. "Blimp don't crash. I mean it does but it's slow. Even a big tear takes ten, fifteen minutes to bring her down." When my father told him we wanted to use the blimp to actually go somewhere José blinked and smiled and shook his head as if my father were the crazy one. "Wish I could. Can't. Prop driven. You can steer her fine, there's a manual system they put in for emergencies. But nothing to make her go."

But my father had only clapped José on the shoulder and said, "Fred, you and Yan pushed a train three miles. Think you can get this thing through the air?"

Now I found the mirrored button and stared at it and tried to remember the word that would unlock it.

The blimp was more than twice as long as the Surfliner car. My father claimed it would weigh less than air once it was inflated. That was kind of hard to believe. But if it was true and the push spell worked it would get the blimp over the mountains and across the Central Plain, over the Santa Lucia Range to the ocean and Yan's doorstep if that's where he was. And that was just too frigging cool an idea to resist.

When I'd explained how we'd pushed the Surfliner using a model and sympathetic magic José laughed and left the hangar and trudged across the field to the aluminum buildings and came back with a footlong model of the blimp. "This do?"

Across the hangar the doorway light dimmed with Ariel's distinctive silhouette. She was heading off with Avy to scout and find provisions. The hangar made her nervous. Not hard to defend with a doorway bottleneck and no windows to speak of but if anything came our way we'd be trapped here and it wouldn't be hard to starve us out.

I looked at the blimp model on the concrete floor. Charm it, then pretend-fly it in my hand while we flew correspondingly inside its mammoth counterpart? Hard to picture. The Surfliner had been on rails and we had modeled the territory as well. This though. I shook my head.

But wait. We'd modeled the Surfliner because we couldn't use a basic push spell without it going off the rails. Here there were no rails. Just a lot of sky to push it through. The unsubtle whack of a blunt-force spell might be just what we needed. The blimp would fly, the blimp would steer. It only needed a push. Well, a lot of pushes.

I could do that. I even had what I needed in my pack.

I had opened the pentagram bottle and was halfway through my preparations and thinking what a pain it was going to be to make at least a couple dozen of these blunt-force spells in stasis bottles when I realized I was still thinking oldschool. You don't need to make a couple dozen blunt-force bottle spells, Fred. You need to make a spell that makes blunt-force bottle spells.

The implications of that notion suddenly unfolded before me, the way they had when Yan and I invented macro spells.

I could tell the blunt-force-making spell how many blunt-force spells to make. I could tell it to assign a password to the first spell it made and add a consecutive number to the password of each ensuing bottle. So that *hocus pocus one* opened the first and *hocus pocus two* opened the second and so on. I could build a spell that slipped through the crack of latent password and checked the integrity of a latent macro spell before it played. And if I could do that then by the same method I could enter anybody else's macro spell and check it and copy it and maybe even alter it.

I saw it all with a kind of mad prophet clarity. Macro spells that prevented other spells from being hacked. That translated spoken english into latin for plain-language casting. Spells that would reorder and link macro spells and open them in sequence. That recorded what mirrors witnessed and played it back, like Yan's message to us but also for messages and plays and performances.

Holy shit. Even if we stopped Yan nothing was going to be the same again. The genie was literally out of the bottle. Macro spells were going to change the world. A town had seen us break a stasis spell. The idea would spread. At first only casters would have the training to make the macro spells that thermosed coffee or made unicorn charms or pushed carts on roads or whatever. But eventually all the components for those macro spells would themselves be macro spells. There would be macro spells that compiled macro spells and reconfigured them and customized them. And anyone could use them. Just say the secret word and build a house, sail a boat, make a weapon, fly to the moon.

The world, our world, would be rebuilt. Not in its former image. Built anew. I saw it. Clear as I could see myself in the mirrored buttons before me. The world would change again. Or no: we would change it. By finally using its new rules to our advantage.

Human beings are marginalized now.

I held up a slippery mirrored button. Here was our new technology. The thing that would bring us back from the margins. In ways I couldn't foresee, couldn't even imagine. But there wasn't a splinter of doubt in my mind these mirrored shapes would shape us all. As long as we stopped Yan.

By lunchtime I'd invented the copycast spell and had it make three blunt-force spells keyed to open consecutively. I emerged from my deep reverie surprised to see how much the blimp had taken shape. It was half inflated, a wounded monster recuperating in a grotto. Now the role of the weights secured to the covering net was plain: their hookended ropes were taut, longer on the end nearest me as the farther side evened up with the near, a slow leviathan resisting captivity. I walked its length and marveled. This might really fly. We might really fly in it.

I passed my father who was carrying a pair of weights and told him I was going outside to test the pushing spell. He only nodded and said Don't go far.

Outside was blinding bright and cloudy. I duct taped the bottled blunt-force spells to a treetrunk and stepped back and thought about it a minute and then said *blue wombat one* and was immediately knocked backward as the spell discharged and the entire tree shuddered and rustled and erupted terrified finches.

I stayed on the grass and waited. Thirty seconds later the tree jerked noisily again. Thirty seconds after that it did it again and looked a little off plumb.

I looked back at the enormous hangar looming. Thought about the growing shape inside. Oh man. This might be a rough ride.

Then Avy yelled and I looked to see her astride Ariel in lightning gallop toward me off the freeway and I registered that Avy was yelling Get inside just as I saw the pack of centaurs galloping after them.

TWENTY-EIGHT

"I think technically it's a horde," said Ariel.

My father looked away from hammering tenpenny nails into the two by four he was using to bar the door. "Say what." I could hear Dr. Ram and José nailing in another two by four on the far end of the hangar.

"A group of centaurs. Fred called it a pack but I think it's a horde. Not a flock. Definitely not a pride. A murder of centaurs?"

"A posse," I said.

"Ooh, that's good."

My father looked at us as if we'd sprouted feathers and then shook his head and turned back to his hammering without another word.

The door pounded back.

We were under siege.

Ariel and Avy had made it to the hangar well ahead of the centaurs and we'd had a few minutes to gather everyone and improvise before the doorpounding began. The hangar's windows were high up near the ceiling and for now we could ignore them as a potential entryway and focus on the door. Which the centaurs were doing as well.

My father stepped back from the door and watched it shake from the pounding that boomed dully throughout the hangar. "We'll need someone to watch the doors."

"Me," said Ariel. "Avy."

He nodded.

Dr. Ram and José rejoined us. "She's holding for now," José said. "But she's only as strong as what she's nailed to."

"As are we all," said Dr. Ram.

My father raised an eyebrow at Dr. Ram. "It'll have to do till we find something better."

"Helium tank's empty," said José. "Need to swap her out." He left to switch the valve, in no hurry and seemingly unperturbed about the pack—horde, posse, gaggle, whatever—of centaurs wanting in. But then he hadn't seen them.

"I suggest we use the empty tanks to brace the doors," said Dr. Ram.

"Good idea. Fred, help him get them off the truck."

Dr. Ram and I headed for the back of the hangar. Ariel sped past us to watch the far door. I wondered what she'd do if they got it open.

José turned off the valve and moved the nozzle to a fresh tank while Dr. Ram and I unstrapped the tanks. We climbed onto the flatbed and pushed off the heavy empty and the clang of it hitting the concrete floor was ridiculous. We rolled it to the back door and shoved the nozzle end against the door and chocked it and went back and unloaded another empty and put it beside the first. We wedged the third empty against the front door. We'd have to wait on the next tank to gas out.

With the rolling tanks and thudding doors and venting gas it was awfully loud in that huge space.

Doors secured for now we took stock. José said two men could push open the giant bay doors from outside but that he'd chained and locked them on the inside. A narrow sunlight column shone on either side of the enormous doors and we could easily see whenever one of the centaurs peered in. Dr. Ram nailed one with a hunting arrow Ariel and Avy had brought back and the centaurs stopped peering in. "Homecourt advantage," my father said. "They can't see in but we can see out. Ariel, why the hell did you lead them back here. Couldn't you outrun those assholes."

"They didn't follow us thank you very much. They'd already staked out the joint. We came up on them at the offramp."

"Boy were those fuckers surprised," said Avy.

"I recall you being a bit of a surprised fucker yourself."

She bristled. "Surprised. Not scared."

"Ya got me there, champ. I take it back."

"José," my father said pointedly, "what do we need to do to fly out of here. Skip the frills, just gas and go."

"Gas and go." José thought about it. "Couple more hours to inflate. Use the bosun's chair and pulley to inspect the envelope and hang the stabilizers. Secure the gondola. Fill her up and tie her off. Once everything's checked out we'd usually open the bay and take off the net and walk her out with the mooring lines. Not enough of us to do that I don't think."

"And there's that whole 'centaurs waiting to kill us when we open the doors' thing," said Ariel.

"Fred, your pushing spell work?"

I nodded and did not say that it might work a bit too well.

"How long you think, José."

"Six, seven hours if everything goes okay."

"Twelve then."

José grinned like a skull. "Now there's a man who's been around."

Another empty helium tank braced the front door. Dr. Ram and José adjusted weights on the cover net. My father inventoried weapons and provisions. I used my new copycast invention to make a dozen blunt-force bottles to push the blimp when we were afloat. If we made it that far.

In a few hours the envelope was taut enough to strain at its netting and begin to lift off from the hangar floor to reveal the metal gondola beneath. José halted the inflation and inspected the bolts that secured the gondola to aluminum braces on the envelope. "Lot easier to do while she's not fighting to get away from ya," he said. It turned out the gondola wasn't attached. It rested in a wheeled cradle of yellowpainted metal. "Must've been about to reattach her when the Change hit," said José. My father and Dr. Ram helped reposition the cradle while José ratcheted the gondola back onto the envelope.

By the time the blimp was fully inflated the hangar had grown dark and you could not see the entire shape at once. Our candles and propane lanterns cast small pools of light in the hangar's vastness. My father asked if I could make a light. "Might as well make it bright. We aren't hiding from anything now."

I had found a stack of inflatable mylar toy blimps in José's office apartment and now I filled two of them with helium and put glowspell bottles on them and released them in different parts of the hangar. They floated up into the dark to lodge among the unseen rafters. I spoke the key but the spells did not activate. I said it louder but we stood in the dark craning our heads toward what might have been a starless sky.

"Maybe they can't hear you," said Ariel.

Which got me wondering. How close did you have to be for a key to open a bottle spell. Hearing distance? A hundred miles? Any distance at all? We'd never tested it.

I yelled the key. It only echoed in the ringing dark. Maybe it was too distorted.

I used two more toy blimps and put another glowspell on each and carried them to one end of the hangar and said *formaldehyde* and the world went white.

Jesus fucking christ boomed from somewhere near the blimp.

I clamped my eyes shut and turned my head and let go a balloon and stood there as if plunged into a pool of milk. If my small sun rose to light the hangar's world I could not see it. Bothered pigeons flapped distantly.

Ariel's voice spoke beside me. "Can you see."

I shook my head and then said no.

"Okay. Walk back with me. Avy, grab his hand."

Her rough hand found mine and pulled. Presumably Ariel walked beside us but I couldn't hear her. Great pulsing spots filled my vision. I thought I sensed motion at their periphery but I wasn't sure. "Is it light in here."

"Fuck yeah."

"Take me to the other side. I need to light the second one."

"What for. It's bright as shit—"

Ariel answered for me. "Because if you're working with something between you and the one that's lit you'll be in shadow. Good thinking, Fred."

At the far end I held up the balloon and we turned our heads away and I said *monosodium* and let it go.

"Did it light."

"Oh yeah," said Ariel.

"It's weird it isn't hot," said Avy. "They look like suns." She began leading me back.

"So it's dark out," said Ariel.

"Um, yeah," I said.

"And the moon's full tonight."

I wasn't sure what she was getting at. "Well," I said slowly from my private whiteout, "that should give the centaurs an advantage—"

"Avy," said Ariel.

"What. Jesus fucking christ."

"Are you planning on just surprising everybody while we're busy not getting killed by centaurs."

"No." Her grip tightened on my hand.

"What, then."

"I don't know. Leave me the fuck alone."

"Ow. Hey could you—my hand." I tried to get it loose and couldn't.

"Sorry." The pressure lessened. "Fuck."

"Maybe you two should talk about this privately. Could you give me back my hand a second."

She did and I wrung it and rubbed some feeling back. She touched my shoulder and led me along.

"How come the centaurs are afraid of you," I asked suddenly, suddenly afraid.

"What a swell question," said Ariel. "Tell us Avy why the centaurs are afraid of you. And while you're at it tell us why everyone else should be afraid of you in about three hours."

"Why are you doing this. They like me. You're just fucking it up."

Maybe I was slow. Maybe it was the pulsing spots in my vision. "What happens three hours from now."

"Watch our little friend here. Or look at an almanac."

"Why are you being such a bitch."

"Everyone should do what they're good at. You've got three hours, young lady. You tell them, I tell them, or they find out anyway. That's not a threat, it's astronomy. So don't get your fur up."

———

My eyes were better within an hour. I'd definitely overdone it in the lighting department; the hangar was shadowless stark.

The blimp was big.

"We're getting in that?" I asked Ariel, who was the only other person not helping ready the thing.

"Yes Jonah, we're getting in that. Hey José. What do you call people who fly blimps."

José stuck his head out the open gondola door. He had changed into a white buttonup shirt with a wingpin on the breast that read AIRSHIP. He yelled Ballast and cackled and withdrew. Ratcheting resumed.

"Blimponauts," Ariel decided.

"You gonna tell me what's up with Avy."

"Only fair to give her the chance to. You'll find out anyway." She looked at me. Her focus could be disconcerting. "Hey. Could you make one of those nifty mirror bottles like you put me in."

"For what."

"For Avy."

I studied her. Her tail twitched. Behind her the tautening form of the blimp. Miniature suns in the distant rafters. Avy easily carrying two weights that had to have weighed nearly as much as she did, nodding as she passed my father, one-handing the weights up to hook on the retaining net. Okay, I said.

———————

The unwavering double daylight made the hangar weirdly timeless. I couldn't have said if it was day or night outside. All of us were tired and yawning. I was helping my father work a rope that led through a pulley to a bosun's chair in which José was strapped, absurdly nimble as he stepped off the portable staircase and defied gravity to float across a twelve-foot gap to the rigid surface of the netted blimp.

My father and I ran forward with the rope.

The hissing gas had stopped.

José gave a thumbsup and we belayed the rope and started hauling on another one. A blue and yellow fin began to rise alongside the tail of the blimp. Dr. Ram and Avy steadied it until it ascended from their outstretched fingertips as if they had set it free. They hurried up the portable staircase to steady the end of the suspended fin while we continued hoisting it up to José. They carefully guided it into place and José drew back a section of netting and stepped around rigging to begin attaching the top fin to the blimp.

"You can relax, Fred," my father said. "We're just holding it steady."

I nodded and relaxed my cramped hands and watched José work. "You'd think he did this every day."

"He's probably thought about doing it every day."

"How come the centaurs haven't attacked."

"That what's got you nervous?"

"Lunatic centaurs who throw javelins and want to shit our skulls? Well kind of, yeah."

"I thought it was flying in the blimp."

"I'll take it over the centaurs."

"No, we'll take it over the centaurs. You'll push." He grinned. He looked like a tired boy wearing an old-man mask.

"I see where Ariel gets it," I said.

"How do you know I didn't get it from her."

"Did you."

"By now I have no idea." He watched José working on top of the blimp. You'd think José's feet would sink in but they didn't. "They're hanging back because they don't know what we've got waiting for them in here. But they do know we can't stay here forever. If I were them I'd send out messengers to bring back my bestest centaur buddies."

"Gosh, if that isn't good news I don't know what is."

"It buys us time."

Time. I took a breath to tell him about Avy, not that I knew what exactly to tell him, but José clapped and signaled that he was done and we had three more fins to go.

The gondola was bigger inside than it looked outside. Six chairs counting pilot and copilot. Large, but where were we going to put a very big horselike creature.

José opened a panel in back of the gondola to reveal a compartment with bins that held equipment. "Here."

"She won't fit in there."

"These rear slots come out. She can stand half in there and half in here."

"That's . . . a good idea." I was going to say undignified.

"Show you something." He stepped into the cramped compartment and opened narrow panels in back on either side. He removed two long cables and attached them to fixtures within the narrow panels and then handed me a cable and told me to pull it. I did. Nothing happened. I put some weight into it and the cable paid out slowly.

José grinned. "You're turning the aileron."

"The wholeron?"

"The big fin. That's how we'll steer. Just like a fish fin in the water."

"Like a rudder?"

"There ya go."

"Why can't we use the big steering wheel there."

"Linkage won't work. Too complicated." He shook his head. "Damn Change. They came up with this in case the engines failed. Pretty sweet."

I pictured people frantically pulling the cables after the engines failed and the blimp started crashing. "Sweet," I said.

José must have seen it in my face. "She crashes slow, son," he said.

———————

Dr. Ram found an access ladder and suggested climbing up to the roof to pick off centaurs. My father nodded and gathered their bows. "Every little bit counts." They climbed up. Soon we heard guttural gargling yells outside the hangar doors.

The blimp was inflated and the fins were attached and the gondola was bolted on. I'd made the bottle spell Ariel had requested, and push spell talismans had been duct taped to the back of the gondola. I'd kept some extras in my pack. What else needed doing.

"Gotta figure out how to open the hangar doors without getting killed," said José.

"Any ideas?" I said.

"Not a one. Seems your dad's the sharp one for that kind of plan."

The sharp one and Dr. Ram were climbing down the tall iron ladder bolted to the wall. My father hopped down and dusted his hands. "Got a few," he said. He handed his crossbow off to Dr. Ram.

"What's it like out there," I said.

"Super Bowl for centaurs." When I just stared he said, "There are a whole lot of centaurs. Moon's full though and there's not really anywhere they can hide. We fired till we ran dry."

"We're out of arrows?" I was embarrassed at the alarm in my voice.

"We ran out of the ones we took with us."

"I brought back a bunch with Avy," Ariel said. "Fred, why don't you ask her where she put them."

I started to make a smart reply but Ariel's look changed my mind.

My father glanced around. "Where is Avy."

"My office," said José. "Said she wanted to rest."

"When do we leave," I said.

"Soon as we figure out how to get the blimp out without getting killed," my father said.

José grinned at me. "Told ya."

José's office was a tiny room with a desk pushed against a wall to make space for a narrow mattress. By the dim light from a propane lantern on the desk I saw Avy struggling to fit herself into a tight fur coat. She twisted toward me and I saw she wasn't wearing a fur coat but a coat of fur and I realized I was looking not at Avy but some other creature that had got into the hangar. It turned toward me and its look was beseeching and trapped and then suddenly commandeered. It contorted and bent back impossibly and bared dog teeth and bristled and raised thin claws the length of my thumb.

I turned and ran and tried to slam the office door behind me. The creature leapt across the tiny room and hit the door before it could close. I tried to put some distance between us, running shadowless in the dual light and hoping I could get to my backpack before the creature got to me.

Claws clicked concrete close behind.

I realized I didn't need to reach the backpack, it just needed to be able to hear me. I shouted *salmagundi*. All that happened was that everyone stared at me and at the thing pursuing me. Near the massive hangar doors I heard my father clearly say What. The. Fuck.

Something swiped at my hoodie and I cut left and put on speed.

Ahead of me Ariel stepped out from behind the gondola and said Oh crap.

I yelled *salmagundi* again. Claws behind me and an odd snuffling. Don't look don't look.

"That the password?" Ariel called.

"Yes. Shit. Yes."

She said it and the mirrored paperclip in my backpack in the gondola became unmirrored and the thing behind me hit the concrete floor and rolled with loud metallic tinging and then skidded with an awful teeth-grinding scrape.

I stopped and looked back. A mirrored humanoid statue lay faceup on the floor. Twinned sunlight gleamed fine detail of silvered fur and needle teeth and a long thin mirrored claw protruding from an elongated paw reaching out and reaching out.

I glanced back at Ariel standing underneath the massive blimp and saw motion behind her and started yelling again. Ariel looked puzzled until I pointed and she stepped past the gondola to look at the back of the hangar where the door had been forced open and a horde, group, pack, posse of centaurs streamed in.

TWENTY-NINE

Running for the gondola meant heading toward the centaurs. But what choice was there. I needed my backpack. We all did.

Ariel ran for the centaurs and lowered her head to meet the nearest one. The hangar rang with clopping hooves and trumpeting javelins. A pipe javelin clattered by me. From behind me came a heavy rumble as the hangar doors rolled open, pushed by my father and José and Dr. Ram or by even more centaurs.

I ducked under the netting and ran into the gondola and tripped over stacked bundles and practically landed on my backpack. I snatched it up and tried to run outside but a pack strap snagged a seat and nearly dislocated my bruised shoulder. I fumbled with it and gave up and tore open the main flap and upended the pack. Underwear socks toiletry mirrored items. I scooped up anything remotely shiny and ran from the gondola.

The hangar doors were halfway open and centaurs in the light that fanned outside. My father and Dr. Ram were dragging José between them dead or hurt or just too slow. They'd grabbed up metal trashcan lids and thrust them out behind them as they ran. A javelin hit my father's makeshift shield and knocked it from his grip.

Ariel a white flash amid brown centaurs on my right. Several lay dead or injured already. Another fell and gleaming red swathed Ariel's side.

I picked a mirrored object and stuffed the rest into my hoodie's pouch and ran toward Ariel. Slippery silver button. I held it up and yelled at Ariel and hoped she'd heard me as I threw it high and turned my head and shouted out *encomium.* The world went white around me and my stark black shadow stretched across the floor as a third sun ignited and fell. I shielded my eyes and glanced back. Ariel already running toward me knocking blinded centaurs aside. She sped by nearly glowing in the nearby light, spiral horn and silver hooves slathered with gore and white coat streaked brickred.

Blinded centaurs brandished javelins and slammed each other in violent confusion. I saw two collide and one impale the other who yanked the javelin from his chest and swung it wildly until his forelegs folded under him.

Ariel ran past my father and Dr. Ram to meet the next wave of centaurs running in past their blinded comrades. A flick of her horn deflected a javelin meant for José.

I tried to help my father with José but he shook me off. "Get Avy."

"Where is she."

He looked at me like I was crazy and in the mêlée's lull I felt an utter fool. My father let go of José who was having trouble breathing and ran to the mirrored creature that had chased me. He set it upright and then jumped behind it just in time to use it as a shield against a spear that surely would have run him through. He staggered back and turned and saw us watching and yelled Will you fucking go.

We fucking went. We dumped José in the gondola and Dr. Ram grabbed up his bow and started shooting and I remembered that I'd been after arrows when I'd gone for Avy in José's office all of sixty seconds and a hundred years ago. I looked across what suddenly seemed a vast expanse of hangar floor to José's open office door. A lot of pissedoff centaurs stood between here and there.

My father's way was blocked by a centaur that reared up to tower above him and drew back its torso about to snap forward and drive two yards of funnelcut shitsmeared pipe into his chest. My father used the mirrored creature as a shield again to block the thrust and then stepped off angle and drew his sword and ran forward as the centaur drew back again. His blade sank to the hilt into the centaur's lower sternum. He twisted it a quarter turn and pulled it out again and deep red gouted. Instead of snapping forward the centaur's upper torso flopped back on its own horseback with a crack of breaking bone that I could hear across the hangar. The legs shot straight and the centaur toppled as if made of wood. It was horrible.

I kicked the chocks from the tires on the metal cradle that held the gondola. A spear shot by my shoulder and cracked into a gondola window. My father shoved the mirrored creature into the gondola and ran around the front of the blimp with his sword held level and cut the hanging weights from the retaining net as he ran by.

The curving roof of blimp above me lifted and the gondola tilted up. I yelled at Dr. Ram to grab the trailing rope. He saw the tilting blimp and dropped his bow and grabbed the belaying rope and pulled. The restraining net slid back along the envelope and snagged against the fins. The remaining weights and Dr. Ram were all that kept us from floating to the rafters like one of my sun balloons.

Banging behind me. José in the pilot seat pounding on the front window. He was paperwhite. "Push." He mimed. "Push her."

The centaurs had halted in a dense halfcircle in front of the blimp. They threw spears but didn't rush us. I think the very strangeness and intimidating size of the blimp had made them hesitate but that intimidation would doubtless be shortlived. As would we when they got over it.

Ariel ran toward us and my father ran for the back of the blimp to cut the final strands of netting. I made a decision and ran after him and dug my hands in my hoodie pouch and pulled out mirrored talismans. My father was about to sever the weights that had gathered in a tangle dangling from the tail when I yelled at him to stop. He glanced at me and seemed about to do it anyway. Most of the centaurs I had blinded were still milling around. If they were affected anything like I had been it would be a good ten minutes before they even saw pulsing spots. Those that could see were hot on Ariel's hooves. I hurried past my father and threw a mirrored ring at them and said *æolus* and the ring unmirrored and a blast of wind bowled blind and sighted centaurs backward like dried leaves swept by a gale.

I pointed to the yellow metal release lever on the wheeled gondola cradle. "Push," I said. "Let go when I yell."

He understood and sheathed his sword and bent to the cradle.

I glanced at the push spell talismans I had taped to the back of the gondola. I realized I should have made the push spell increase in intensity over a few seconds instead of giving out a sudden slam. There was a chance they'd just tear the gondola off the envelope when I unlocked them. Oh well.

Up front Ariel stood by Dr. Ram deflecting javelins meant for him.

How he held that rope in the midst of that I'll never understand. I flung a mirrored rectangle and said *tsunami* and the mirror became a nine of diamonds and the centaurs in front of us were knocked backward in a spreading wave that cleared our way. I glanced back and yelled for my father to push. I wished I'd made another sun spell.

My father pushed the cradle and the gondola lurched toward us.

The fallen centaurs picked themselves back up.

Dr. Ram up front, weights in back, my father pushing, massive blimp creeping forward.

We weren't going to make it.

What I did next I did without thinking about its repercussions. I only saw that we needed to get out of there and that with more ballast we could go fast and maybe not float up into the rafters. "Ariel, get in. Now."

She glanced at me and nodded and worked her way into the gondola and said, "José, you wanna get the kid out of the way?" I assumed that Avy had managed to get aboard in the calamity. Was she hurt.

No time. I told Dr. Ram to hang on and yelled at my father to throw the release lever. Ariel ducked low and scuttled into the gondola and the tilt decreased and Dr. Ram took up the slack. I climbed into the gondola doorway and yelled Hold on and then said *vishnu* and a mirrored object taped to the back of the gondola unmirrored and blew us forward and blew my father back among the blinded centaurs.

We skimmed above the hangar floor. I fell back against the doorway edge but kept my grip. Ariel stumbled midturn as she tried to fit herself into the rear storage compartment. She took up a third of the gondola. Dr. Ram was nearly run over by the surging gondola but climbed the landing rope like a spider and held on swinging and spinning as the blimp rushed from the hangar and emerged into the cool gray predawn. The swinging saved him. Javelins shot past him and one cracked through a forward window.

I held on as we tilted up. A javelin slammed the gondola floor. Dr. Ram hung like a plumb bob and in a moment our angle was so sharp that he was able to let go and drop to the front of the gondola. He kicked in the remaining window plastic and lowered himself to the supine copilot's chair. "Fred, Peter is on the—"

"I know. José, can we throw him a line."

"In back." He shook a thumb toward at the storage compartment.

I leaned out the canting doorway. The door had been latched open and I was a sitting duck but the centaurs were throwing their javelins at the easier target of the envelope. Mostly. My father held the netting and dragged along behind us. In a moment he would be among the centaurs like a flail. "Hold on," I yelled down. "We're getting a rope."

Dr. Ram was already clambering down the angled seats as if they were a cushioned ladder. The mirrored creature and most of our gear had slid down the center aisle and wedged against the seats and Ariel who thrashed in the entry to the storage compartment and could not move aside. Dr. Ram looked back helplessly.

The anchored blimp was nearly vertical.

I braced my legs and leaned out the nearly horizontal doorway. Cold predawn air. The ground was a long way down. An enormous centaur fitted an arrow the size of a broomhandle into a recurved bow taller than me and then drew and sighted and released. I felt it hit the gondola. "Climb up," I called down to my father. "Can you climb up."

"To where."

I saw his point. He'd be on the fin and we'd still be weighted down and he wouldn't be able to get into the gondola.

Shit— "Hold on," I yelled again and then yelled *coriander* and an object unmirrored and a blast went down and we shot up. A dull reverberation traveled through the gasbag and I saw it rippling just before I lost my grip and caught myself and heaved myself back into the sideways doorway and looked down.

We were vertical now. We trailed a tail of weighted netting that contained my father several dozen yards above the ground, some airborne whale bound homeward with its human catch. My father twisted in the netting as a plague of javelins arced by him. He managed to unhook a weight and drop it on a centaur's head.

We rose another hundred feet and slowed and began to sink.

"We're getting a rope," I yelled down. "José?"

Redfaced now in his reclined chair José spread his hands. "Rope's in back," he grated.

Ariel cursed a steady stream as she struggled in the plugged opening. She was covered in blood and blood was everywhere in the gondola. I yelled for Dr. Ram to check our packs but he was already going through them.

The netting was on the ground again and we were anchored vertically but still dragging with the early morning offshore breeze. My father had clambered up almost to the tail to get some distance from the centaurs and had nowhere left to go. He was a hundred feet below me and there was nothing I could do. Bright light from the hangar backlit centaurs running toward us.

My father looked up at me and gave a nod and a little smile and then started climbing down the netting.

I said No but he couldn't have heard. It wouldn't have mattered.

A dozen feet above the dawnlit ground he drew his sword and sliced away the netting strands above his head. He gripped the final strands another second as a centaur reared below him and jabbed with its javelin and then my father cut the final strands and dropped and drove his sword into the centaur's upturned chest as he landed on it. He jumped from the dying creature's back even as it fell beneath him and was swinging at another as he hit the ground.

Behind me José yelled that we were loose and rising.

I shifted with the righting blimp and could not affect the scene below. Centaurs everywhere enormous armed converging. The huge dark archer with his eightfoot bow and spearlength arrow sighted on my father and drew. Olympian in the wedge of hangar light.

I looked back at a dull crack and thudding from the gondola and for an awful moment thought we had torn loose but saw that Ariel had gained traction with our righting and had knocked out the partitions to either side of the storage compartment entryway. She wriggled free and struggled forward and Dr. Ram practically fell into the compartment and emerged a second later with a coil of nylon line. He lobbed it and I caught it and fumbled for the free end and loosened it and looked down. And couldn't see my father.

"Do the push," José called from the captain's chair. "Get us out of here."

"My father's down there."

Dr. Ram came up beside me. Ariel kicked out a shard of shattered plexiglass and poked her head out the empty window. We were already fifty feet higher than when I'd last seen my father and the onshore breeze was pushing us inland. Daybreak soon. "Where."

"He was on the netting and he cut it loose. I saw him about to—"

He pointed. "There."

I didn't see my father. I saw a furious knot of centaurs jabbing at something in their midst. I felt dizzy. Dr. Ram grabbed me as I sagged.

Dawn found us before it touched the tumult on the ground. I squinted in the cold wind and waxing orange light and saw a centaur in the bunch go down, saw its upper body caught and used to block an arrow five feet long, saw the body drop and my father running through the break. A centaur leapt from the fray and took aim with a javelin but didn't throw and didn't throw and then buckled and fell. Beside me Dr. Ram lowered his bow and said, "My last arrow."

We had the god view here up high. Where was the path my father could not make out from the ground, the hiding place we could shout out to him, the obstacles and makeshift weaponry revealed by our perspective. Nowhere. There was an enormous hangar spreading a wedge of light across an overgrown field full of centaurs and a mooring pole and some rusted vehicles.

I was going to ask José what might be close at hand down there when I saw Ariel clearly gauging the distance. "You'd never make it," I said.

She glanced at me. "Doc, drop Avy."

Dr. Ram looked startled. "We do not need to jettison ballast and she weighs very little even if—"

"Doc."

He frowned but tossed his bow back into the gondola and picked up the reflective creature and leaned it against the empty window and looked at Ariel.

"It won't hurt her," said Ariel.

Before I could protest Dr. Ram bearhugged the figure to the opened door and let it go. Aimed or not it broke a centaur's back.

"Say the word, Fred," said Ariel.

I had no idea what she meant. And then I understood. The thing we had just jettisoned was Avy. And centaurs were afraid of her. Shit, no wonder.

I leaned out and saw my father throw a javelin at a centaur from three yards away and then heave his sword after it while the centaur blocked the javelin. A yard of unbreakable spinning razor arced into the centaur's ribs and stuck. I yelled *hibachi* and the thing that was Avy unmirrored and only took a second to get its bearings before it bared needle teeth and ran like a wolf and started tearing into centaurs like a dog in a henhouse. She landed on the back of the nearest one and raked thumbsized claws across its upper back. Its torso whipped around to face her and she laid it open breast to belly. Its stuttering scream stopped the other centaurs cold.

Avy sprang into the upper body of another centaur, twenty claws burying into planed face and stalk neck and plated belly and then ripping as she fell twisting to the ground. The centaur just watched her do it. All the centaurs just watched her. They seemed paralyzed in the presence of what she had become. Snarls and stuttered screams drifted up as dawn light touched the field below.

Now a lone centaur shook off its paralysis and galloped after my father and raised its javelin as it bore down on him. We yelled but my father couldn't hear. Now the centaur cast its javelin aside and bent its upper torso low. My father finally glanced back and tried to change direction much too late. Now the centaur lowered a skeletal arm and scooped up my father like a reclaimed doll and checked his swordswing with its other hand and struggling with him galloped west. Now the centaurs farthest from the werewolf Avy shook from their paralysis and abandoned their rived comrades to give chase. Now the centaur carrying my father headed up the overgrown embankment toward the freeway and the others followed or pursued, I could not tell which. Now the morning wind propelled us useless toward the gaining day.

PART FOUR:
STANDING WAVES

THIRTY

We flew. It did not feel like flying. It felt like sitting in a chair in a small room while the world crept by beneath. I looked out the jagged window at what I ought to marvel at and didn't feel a thing. From the ragged ocean mountain shadows shrank across the broken land as dawn picked out a graveyard world. Highways houses buildings burnt by fire, broken by earthquake, shredded by storm, overcome by creeping green. Swaths of hillside char. A dead world interring in its tenanted and unkempt wilding, caught between artifact and reclamation. Between patient mountain and ancient ocean waiting out the ruin that lay between.

We were slowing again and I heard myself tell everyone to hold on and they braced themselves and I heard myself say *megalith* and we surged north.

Ariel studied me as I got up and edged around her and told Dr. Ram I'd take over steering. Dr. Ram handed me the cables and wrung his hands and said You must pull very hard. He put a hand on my shoulder and made his way to the copilot seat to stare in silent dread and wonder at this new perspective on the world he'd known resolving back into elements from which it had been wrested.

Through the cables in my hands I felt the ailerons shudder in the wind.

"We have to go on," said Ariel behind me.

I glanced back to see her looking out the window at the still and silent world. "You telling me or you?"

She looked at me sharply and then relaxed. "Maybe both."

"You're pretty determined to get to Yan."

"You think because of Joe."

"I don't know what to think."

"If Yan reverses the Change—"

"I know. I know what will happen. I don't know if I think he should be stopped at any cost."

"Pete doesn't weigh as much as this does, Fred. No one person does. Including me. That's the ugly truth. It sucks and it's heartbreaking but there it is."

"So that's it then? Okay, that happened, let's move on?"

"I'm talking about what you have to be willing to accept, not what's happened. I've been your father's Familiar and I love him still and always will. All these years I think I knew he was out there in the world alive. I think I know it still."

I stared at her. "I think—" I had to draw a long breath to calm the surge that built inside. "I think you'd tell me that in any case to keep us moving forward."

"He's alive, Fred."

"Disneyland on the right," called José. He laughed bitterly. "Crazies there now. Fighting to live in Fantasyland." He nearly had to shout above the wind that rushed in through the broken windows.

Dr. Ram went to his side and frowned. "Try not to shout," he said. "I think you should rest if at all possible. If these seats recline—"

José waved it off. "Got the rest a my life to relax."

I crouched and looked out the window but wasn't sure what I should be looking at. Inland lay a large triangular patch of land. All that distinguished it was its shape and what looked like a little vine-enshrouded mountain rising up near one corner.

"It is occupied?" Dr. Ram said.

"Sure. Old employees, Disney freaks. Think they're preserving something. Be a religion in another twenty years. Kill you soon as look at you if you set foot in there." He snorted. "Small world after all." He turned forward again and set his hands on the wheel and I knew he wished he could steer us. His face was tomato red and his eyes were bulging and he was pouring sweat and clearly having the time of his life.

We'd started drifting inland again and I pulled a cable. Somewhere huge outside a tall fin turned a little bit. Somewhere unseen down there my father was dead or injured or captured by creatures that liked to eat our heads and shit our skulls so they could paint them and make tassels out of them.

Which I could not keep thinking about and could not stop thinking about. "So," I said to Ariel. "Avy's a werewolf."

"Yep."

I nodded. I thought I was handling all this rather well. "How'd that happen."

"She got it from her parents."

"Her parents made her a werewolf?"

"Her parents were werewolves."

I took this in. "And what happened to them."

"She doesn't know. She's looking for them, partly. She also thinks they're dead."

"Do you."

"Not sure. Probably."

"Well." I felt myself trying not to cry. "Avy's a werewolf. There you go."

"He's alive, Fred. When this is—" She went absolutely still.

"What."

Her eyes were empty as a doll's and her voice was dull and flat and distant as she said It's started.

"What's—"

felt before it   hit

                from out the north   the shuddering sky

                         shudder across blimp fabric

                         bitter metal taste pass through

distant thud door close other world

                    ariel white blur

                       sand attenuate gale

vague

   soft

waver

ripple through her roll

through her see

through her floor

through her pilot seat copilot seat and gone

place in world gone

place in mind gone

dead space of her

of her kind always

never

been

abolished

increate

Then passed

remembered

real once more feel

shudder in the world roll on.

José and Dr. Ram stared blankly out the windows blinking and looking confused. Unnoticed now the transitory world crept steadily below us.

Ariel remained stock still. The blank remove still owned her eyes. Then she looked at me without a shred of recognition. Then she screamed.

"He's warming up. Testing little versions of the spell that will reverse the Change."

"But what . . . happened."

"The Change reversed. The old rules worked. For the smallest moment, the thinnest wavefront spreading from his little trial run, I didn't exist. I don't remember it. But I feel the gap. Like a crack in ice." A ripple went down her flank. "Who knows what happened to whatever was around him. What arrogance. Now do you believe what he's up to, Doc."

"You do not know that it was Yan."

"Dr. Ram. It was. I know it was him. I could feel it. The way I felt it at the vibe that night. It was Yan."

"But you did not express this feeling until after Ariel said it was Yan." I'm not sure he believed it himself.

"You know what else it means." Ariel was looking at me now.

"Yeah. It means we don't have much time."

Sparkling towers in morning sun. Skyward glass and steel upthrust from the restituting earth like jagged bone from a poorknit wound. Ghost encampment wavering in the heat.

José had beckoned to us and pointed out downtown Los Angeles. I thought it looked like a mirage. And it was.

At first I couldn't believe human beings had built this. How could they have needed it. How many of them could there have been. Here was the space they'd occupied, the roads they'd traveled, places they'd worked and slept and eaten and swam. All the people I had seen in my entire life would not have filled half of one of those remanded towers. All the ground between mountain and sea bespoke their mass existence. Retreating though it was. The sight of it was beautiful and terrifying, awe-inspiring and insufferably proud. What gods that had lived here had been alien and aloof.

"We spent generations building our own gravemarkers," Ram said finally, nodding at the downtown towers. "Like the pharaohs."

"It looks new," I said. "Do you think people still live there."

José passed me a pair of binoculars and I put the cups to my eyes and worked the focus. A lightbrown rectangle grayed by distance. Missing windows, earthquake cracks. The other buildings all the same, damaged and weathered and still. The only movement multitudes of birds on rooftop roosts and riding thermal spirals up beside the walls. A nest the size of our gondola. A few buildings collapsed. Shattered overpasses, windgathered trashdrift worn to mulch against groundlevel walls, burnstains, birdshit thick as icing on a cake. My father had journeyed through places like this with Ariel.

José pointed out something on the burned hillside between us and the silent city. Huge block letters blackened by fire crawling with vines and nested by birds. I passed the binoculars to Dr. Ram who studied downtown and then studied the lettered mountainside and lowered the binoculars and shook his head. "Still standing. It is amazing."

"What's that beside it there. To the right and down a little."

José didn't even look. "Griffith Observatory. Long time ago they put it in the mountains so they could look at the stars. City grew around it. Light got so bad you couldn't even see em. People came here to see different kinda stars anyhow. Pretty though. Back in the day."

Light so bright you couldn't see the stars. Isn't that daylight. I studied the spreading ruin from ocean to mountain. Not an inch of it unshaped by human device my father had told me.

My father. Adrenaline surged. I held back sudden tears.

José held out his hand and Dr. Ram handed him the binoculars and he looped the strap around his skinny wrist and told me to hang onto his belt.

"I do not think you should be moving around right now," Dr. Ram said but José flapped a hand at him and leaned out a broken window without waiting for me. I grabbed his belt and held on as he scanned the blimp and saw him frown. He didn't weigh a thing.

"Is there damage," Dr. Ram said.

José lowered the binoculars but didn't come back in. Wind whipped thin wisps of graywhite hair about his head. "Hell yeah there's damage. Spear holes, a tear near the tail." He glanced in and saw my face and grinned. "No worries, Fred. She'll float for hours and come down easy as a dandelion seed. Need a rip like *Titanic* to founder this old girl." His frown deepened. He seemed to be looking past the blimp. He raised the binoculars again and worked the focus and looked at something for a long time.

"What is it," I asked. "What's wrong."

He ducked back in and handed me the binoculars and pointed at the window and sat down breathing hard. His white crew shirt sweatpatched. Dr. Ram grabbed my belt as I leaned out and brought the binoculars to my eyes. Enormous blur of the blimp above, port engine directly before me, propeller turning lazily in the wind. I started to work the focus but José panted, "Four Oh Five." I shifted the binoculars to the broken 405 Freeway below and tried to hold them steady in the wind at my back and work the focus. I slid past motion and reversed and focused on a tiny figure wobbly in the overlapping circles of my vision. Barely visible in the silent distance.

Suddenly taller than the SUV it passed in front of as it ran north on the freeway.

"What is it," said Dr. Ram. "What do you see."

I lowered the binoculars and stared at what was now too far away to see. "It's a centaur. It's following us."

THIRTY-ONE

We could only go so fast. The push spells moved us northward in violent fits like flicking a marble every time it began to slow. An initial surge, a long coast, a crawl influenced by the wind, another surge. The abandon of Los Angeles still rose prominent behind us, burnscarred Hollywood Hills between. We crept above the shallow bowl of San Fernando Valley following the 405 and being followed. Amid the grass and weeds and trees the giant grid of surface streets still discernible by the ordered punctuation of streetlamps and housing rows and phone poles. Up ahead the freeway tangled with several others in a confusion of collapsed flyovers and cloverleafs. Beyond that the San Gabriel Mountains and Cajon Pass.

Getting over it was going to be a problem.

"José, how high up are we," said Ariel.

"Four thousand feet." He grinned like a skull. "Still got the touch."

"How high you think these mountains get."

"Cajon Pass is fortyone ninety."

"So we need a couple hundred feet, yah."

"Envelope's a mess. Engines don't work so we can't fill the ballonets from the air scoops."

"What's that mean in english," I said.

"Can't adjust trim. Can't climb." He shrugged. "Got flaps though. Shove us forward and we can go up."

"So we're okay the way we are?" Ariel said.

"If everything holds together, sure. Kinda worried about the trim."

"Doc?"

Dr. Ram leaned in from the broken window windswept and clutching the binoculars. "I simply cannot tell. I have been able only to see that it is a centaur, nothing more."

Ariel looked at me. "And you think it has Pete."

"All I said was that it looked like it was carrying something."

"We can't afford to turn around or wait. Not unless we know for sure."

"I know." In the air above the mountains in the battered gondola of a wounded airship on my way to confront my former best friend holed up in the ruin of a former castle while he perfects the casting that will reinstate the old world's order I am talking to a unicorn about whether the centaur following us is carrying my captured father. Um, okay. If I made it back to Del Mar who would possibly believe the unadulterated truth.

And thought about my father's tales of humpback whales and dragons.

And wondered when I'd started thinking if I made it back instead of when.

––––––––––

We could not climb. Every time I released a push spell we surged forward and I worked the flaps to José's directions. Every time we surged forward the rips in the massive envelope above us got worse. The height we gained was offset by the lift we lost from escaping helium and our forward progress was slowed by our need to climb.

Then the pass was up ahead and the ground was itself rising up to meet us.

"One good push," said José. "Maybe two in a row. Get her over the hump. Rest is easy. Downhill glide." His skullgrin looking forced. "No worries if we lose height then. Mountainside'll drop off faster than we will."

The frayed double ribbon of Interstate 5 twined up toward us dotted with cars and semitrucks. I could not imagine how such a road had been carved into a stretch of mountain range and Dr. Ram's explanations only made it seem more incredible. And such roads had been routine. Those people had carved themselves into the world and thought nothing of it.

We'd lost sight of the pursuing centaur sometime back. I was worried

I would run out of push spells before we reached the pass. The *Spirit of America* dragged toward it canted and descending. Our approach was slow and oddly silent.

We slowed even more in the wind that gusted off the crest. José had me pull on the ailerons and we nosed up and climbed in the rushing air. "Don't need to move fast over the ground," José called. "Need to move fast through the air. Air moves fast over us it amounts to the same thing." He cackled and then coughed. He looked terrible.

We began to drift and I righted us. The pass wound along the ridge's crest for miles. I couldn't see where it began to descend. The wind off the crest gave us some lift but I didn't think it would be enough to carry us to the downhill side and said as much to José.

"Hell, we'll just ride her wheel then. Bounce and roll till the road starts to drop." He didn't look remotely worried. He looked like someone blading down a long incline with the wind at his back. The gleam in his eyes was not reassuring.

I traded a glance with Ariel. "We can always jump off when we're down," she said.

"I'll bet that won't be as easy as you—"

A shadow passed over the blimp. I didn't think anything of it. A cloud shadow. It was Ariel's sudden cocking of her head and the dawning light in her eyes that made me stop. She glanced around and was just about to yell something when José yelled it for her. "Holy shit hold on."

Something massive savaged into the envelope above us. We were thrown to the right as the gondola rocked with the blimp's violent yaw. Dr. Ram nearly fell out the window but caught himself on a chair. Supplies rained down on the weedgrown freeway.

We swung back to perpendicular but were canted forward now. The ground below filled the broken windows. Dr. Ram scrambled into the co-pilot seat and buckled in. "What is happening," he asked José.

Bulkhead metal had dented where Ariel hit. She struggled upright and shook herself and lowered her neck to look out the port side and said Here it comes again.

Thud and tearing from above. We rolled and righted. Above the sound an oddly girlish cry.

"What the fuck," I yelled.

"Roc," said Ariel.

"Rock? That was a goddamn rock?"

"Are oh see. Big bird."

I thought of the roomsized birdnests atop the gaunt ruined buildings.

"Sit down and buckle up," José said.

He didn't have to tell me twice. I scrambled past Ariel and into the seat behind José. The buckle had just clicked home when we were hit again fatally and hard.

Overhead the envelope shredded and we dropped.

My stomach floated. My heart rose. We were going to hit. I grabbed the back of José's chair. We hit.

The gondola landed on the wheel and the shock absorber collapsed and the tire burst. My forehead hit my hands on the chair. Metal groaned and we bounced. The envelope cascaded around us as the gondola shot up into it. Then we yanked to a stop and my seatbelt dug my lap and we plummeted again. No inflated tire and shock absorber this time. The floor hit hard and buckled. Ariel's legs collapsed beneath her. The gondola tipped sideways. The shredded envelope descended on us softly like a curtain and daylight dimmed. Dr. Ram and José and I hung jackknifed in our seats.

Silence.

A girlish cry from high above.

"Everyone all right?" Ariel said somewhere behind me.

"I believe I am uninjured," said Dr. Ram. "Fred?"

I started to say yes and a stabbing pain on my right side seized my breath. ". . . hurt," I managed.

Dr. Ram unbuckled and fell out of his chair and landed on his hands and knees. He stood slowly and started to reach up to me but stopped and frowned at José hanging limp in his chair in front of me.

"I can undo this thing if you can help catch me," I said.

Dr. Ram nodded and I unbuckled my seatbelt and sort of rolled out into Dr. Ram's arms. My feet hit ground and jarring pain shot up my right side. I gasped and sat down quickly and put a hand to my ribcage half expecting to feel something sticking out.

Dr. Ram unbuckled José and caught him up as he dropped like a flopping doll. He set him on the ground in front of me and he was staring up at nothing and I wrinkled my nose at the smell that came from him. Dr. Ram put an ear to José's chest and listened and put a finger on his neck and held still and then tilted his head back and pinched his nose shut and bent and blew twice into his mouth. José's chest rose and fell and rose and fell and did not rise again. Dr. Ram straddled him and set his hands above his sternum and began to work him like a bellows.

I asked if I could help but he shook his head and kept working on José. It was getting hot in the sideways gondola. I looked at Ariel who had picked herself up after the crash and was watching silently. "Are we safe here, you think."

"We're not safe anywhere. But the roc's probably gone if that's what you mean. Doc?"

Dr. Ram looked up from José's body. "I must continue."

"All right. I'll see if we can dig our way out. Fred?"

I started to get up and a hot wire went through my right floating ribs. I hissed and sat back and shook my head.

"Okay. Be right back." She squeezed through the empty front window and was quickly lost among folds of fallen rubber gasbag.

I scooted closer to Dr. Ram. He was pouring sweat in the hot gondola. José moved in time with Dr. Ram's compressions and I heard something crack in the gondola and looked around before I realized it was one of José's ribs. José stopped moving when Dr. Ram stopped with his hands on José's chest as if waiting for a referee to count him out. Sweat dropped from his nose onto José's shirt.

"Did he have a heart attack."

"It would appear so. I believe he went into arrhythmia when we first took off. There is nothing I can do for him."

I looked from the vacated form to Dr. Ram. "I think he was happy. He got to fly again."

He looked reluctant to abandon his resuscitation even now. Finally he shut José's eyes. "You are a good boy, Fred."

"Excuse me?"

"Yall hear me?" came Ariel's voice.

"Sure," I called back.

"You need to get out of there. Now would be good."

"Should we bring José," I asked Dr. Ram.

"Let us see what is happening. We can always come back for him."

True enough. He helped me to my feet and it hurt like hell and he held my arm as we made our way out the sideways window and batted at the ruined tent of envelope until it flapped open at a tear in front of us and we were suddenly blinking in hot daylight on a weedgrown freeway on a mountain pass.

Our crash's aftermath was hardly epic. Strewn gear and a loose pile of deflated envelope humped at the gondola and flattened ailerons, one lying canted after gouging through the cloth top of a weatherbeaten Jeep. Shredded rubber flapped in vagrant winds.

We had landed a few yards west of the freeway. Wall of mountainside along the east. Ariel stood in the bed of a Ford pickup facing south. Watching something.

"Got your binoculars, Doc?"

"No, I am sorry, I left them in the. . . ." He gestured at the flayed ruin of airship.

"Something coming our way?" I said.

Horn flashed sunlight as she nodded. "Yup. Galloping, looks like."

There was nothing to do but scrounge our meager weaponry and supplies. Dr. Ram and I rolled back tatters that had been a majestic flying thing only a few minutes ago. He searched the gondola while I scrounged nearby. I think he was trying to spare me sight of José.

"It's a lone centaur," Ariel called.

"It caught up to us?" I found my backpack in the tall grass beside the road. It seemed to be in good shape though the flap was open as I had left it. I rummaged through it to see if I had lost any supplies or casting ingredients.

"Maybe we just landed along the Pony Express route. Doc, you find those binoculars?"

"I have just found them, yes." He waved them from the sideways gondola.

"You might wanna bring em out here."

Dr. Ram brought the binoculars to his eyes and looked where Ariel inclined her head and worked the focus.

"What is it," I called.

Dr. Ram held out the binoculars. I limped over dragging the backpack by its flap because lifting it hurt too much, and I took the binoculars and found the blurry horselike form and worked the focus until it resolved into a centaur galloping straight toward us. I lowered the binoculars and glanced at Ariel who said Keep looking.

I kept looking. Eventually the centaur turned to round a schoolbus and I saw the riders who had been hidden by its angular torso. I dropped the binoculars and said holy shit and ran toward the centaur yelling in pain and in relief.

"Thith ith Bob," my father said. "He rethcued me."

"Uth," said Avy.

"Uth."

"Bob-bob-bob-bob-bob," agreed the centaur a respectful distance away.

My father was unharmed. Avy looked beatup but at least she looked like Avy again. Both of them had cotton wadding jammed up their nostrils. I asked why and my father grinned and pulled it out. "Sorry. It lets us be around Bob without wanting to kill him. It's the smell, you know?"

"Oh of course," said Dr. Ram. "Pheromones."

My father nodded. "That's why we hate each other. It's chemical. A chemical reaction. It's not conscious. Hell it's not really even hate."

I looked at Bob and remembered the centaurs' scent. My arm hairs began to prickle and I felt cold violence in the pit of my stomach. I looked away.

"What is your friend's immunity," said Dr. Ram.

"Bob? He got whacked in a fight a long time ago and lost his sense of smell. Gives him perspective."

I set a hand against my taped-up ribs and stood beside Avy as my father and Dr. Ram dug a shallow grave for José beside the wrecked gondola. Ariel and Bob stood downwind apparently conversing. I couldn't get over the sight.

"So you're okay now?" I said.

Avy nodded.

"You should have told us."

She nodded again. "He was a weird old guy," she said as my father and Dr. Ram wrapped José's body in a shroud of gray rubber envelope remnants from the *Spirit of America*. "But I really liked him. He was nice to me."

"You helped him do the one thing he wanted to do before he died."

They put José's body in the broken ground.

"How often do you, you know."

"Every twentyeight days." She laughed bitterly.

"I never heard of one of you before. Not a real one I mean."

"One of me. Yeah, me neither. Can we talk about something else."

"Sure. What's the story with Bob."

Avy studied the unicorn and the centaur improbably conversing amid the ruins of traffic as my father and his friend laid down their shovels and mopped their brows with their shirts. "I was still chasing him when I started changing back. I don't—I never remember what happens when I'm, you know." She held her hands like comical claws. "I just sort of wake up. Come back to myself. I was chasing Bob and he had your father on his back and they were running north on the freeway and the blimp was up in the air ahead of them. I couldn't keep up after I started changing. Your father saw it and made Bob wait."

"Made him wait? Bob wasn't kidnapping him?"

She shook her head. "I think he wants to help us."

"Does anyone want to say anything."

We looked at each other ringed around the mounded rectangle. What was there to say. We'd known him two days, Avy'd known him a little longer. Finally Avy came forward and pressed an airship crew wingpin into the freshly upturned earth and said, "He gave me these when I first met him. He said it made me an official crew member." She touched the wings and stood. "Goodbye, José. I hope you're still flying." And we turned and left the wreck and ruin of that inconsequential place.

THIRTY-TWO

It was still early morning and my father thought we might be able to make it across the pass before dark. Bob followed from a distance downwind as we walked, my father and Ariel talking as we went. My ribs said howdy every time I put my right foot down.

"I don't know how I figured out he didn't mean to hurt me," my father told us. "He grabbed me up and carted me off and I kept doing everything I could to kill him. Finally it got through that he wasn't trying to kill me back. But I couldn't stop myself. Everything in me was yelling that I had to kill him. He had a pretty good lead on the other centaurs and it helped that Avy was following us. I mean what were they gonna do if they caught up to her. You saw how she tore into them.

"Bob pulled some cotton wadding out of his pannier and managed to make me understand he wanted me to plug up my nose. Soon as I did it was like I came up from the bottom of a lake or something. I didn't want to kill him anymore. It was crazy. I couldn't believe the smell of something could influence my behavior that much."

"As a doctor it is hardly surprising to learn that someone's behavior can be altered by something that goes into his nose."

"Got me there. So I figured out he wants to help us but I haven't figured out why."

"His people made a deal with Yan," said Ariel. "Bob thinks they're gonna get screwed."

We stopped walking and looked at her. Behind us Bob cocked his head at an angle that hurt to look at.

"Yan gave them stasis bottles and told them there'd be a reward if they brought him a unicorn, the way he's done for half the west coast far as I can tell. But he also gave them a description of the Fregary and promised them a big rock candy mountain with sugarcoated skulls or something if they delivered him."

"See. He really wants his big wizard battle."

"So if the centaurs had stasis bottles," I said, "how come me and Ariel aren't mirrored statues on our way north right now."

"They used them up first chance they got."

"The library," my father said.

"The library. Reality testing, very important when strangers give you magic weapons."

"Okay so Yan gives them some magic beans if they bring him a cow. But the beans really work. So why does Bob think they're gonna get screwed. I'd want more beans."

"What happens when the centaurs bring Yan a unicorn and he becomes king of the universe."

"They disappear," I said.

"And Bob figured this out?" my father said.

"Naw. He just figured Yan's a human being offering a deal that's too good to be true."

"His head may be flat but he ain't stupid," said my father.

"I told him what Yan's up to and he understands why it's important to stop him. He's in."

"Why couldn't he just convince his people about all this," I said.

Ariel nodded at the waiting centaur. "Why don't you go over to Bob and take a big ole whiff and then let me try to convince you he's here to help you."

"Oh. Pheronomes."

"Yup, the dreaded Egyptian Pharaoh Gnomes. Which reminds me." She shut her eyes and tossed her head and said a word in a language I had never heard. She turned to Bob behind us. "Hey Bob. Front and center."

Bob came forward. I found myself reaching for a weapon, a rock, anything. Bob came closer. My palms sweated and I stood ready to fight. Bob's shadow fell across me. I frowned. I couldn't smell him. I brought my hand to my nose. I couldn't smell it either. Bob's alien face stared down. Slant eyes and patterned scars interrupted by another across his nose and lower forehead.

"I figure yall can live without a sense of smell for a while," said Ariel. "You aren't missing much around here."

Bob said his clan would keep chasing us. We were low on food and water but found plenty of the latter in cars and trucks along the way. The road wound along the mountainside and the going was relatively easy. The pavement was cracked and potholed and overgrown, edge lanes sometimes blocked by fallen rocks or longdried mudslides. Ariel and my father walked to either side of Bob in flanking positions that would be convenient if Bob got a hankering for something ugly. I wondered if he might have more to fear from us than we did from him.

Avy practically collapsed when we broke for lunch. It was plain she was too weak to continue at the pace we'd kept. When Ariel asked if she was all right she only nodded and shrugged and said It takes a lot out of me and wolfed down her Power Bar. She bore no trace of her previous bravado. I wondered if that was as much a part of her cycle as her physical change. Or maybe she was just dispirited. Humiliated at us seeing her secret self.

My father ordered us on our way after only twenty minutes. Everyone looked at Avy and she merely nodded and rose wearily. But before she could resume her struggle Bob stepped beside her and knelt his forelegs and offered her his great dark hand and Avy hesitated only a moment before taking it and looking up into the unreadable planes of the centaur's face and giving a tightlipped smile of thanks and assent and possibly surrender and letting him swing her up onto his long and bony back.

As we continued on our way I noticed that Ariel and my father no longer walked flank to Bob.

6% GRADE

TRUCKS USE LOW GEAR

"If I remember correctly," Dr. Ram said as we passed the sign, "the descent begins in a mile or two."

Ariel nodded. "It's all downhill from there, Doc."

Dr. Ram adjusted his pack's shoulder straps. "I confess I have never fully understood that phrase. Is it meant to be positive or negative."

"Positive," said my father. "Downhill's easier."

"But when a situation goes downhill it is usually not good, yes?"

We thought about it. "Well hell," my father said. "Now I'm not sure anymore."

"There are many folk sayings in english that have never been adequately explained to me. Such as It is the squeaky wheel that gets the grease."

"What's to explain," my father said. "It means that you won't get what you want unless you make some noise."

"I have taken it to mean that if you stand out from the crowd you will be silenced."

We thought about that.

"And if a situation does not work out well did it pan out, or did it not pan out."

"It panned out," my father said.

Ariel laughed.

"It didn't pan out?"

In the next mile and a half we came up with A rolling stone gathers no moss (Does it want to do such a thing," Dr. Ram wanted to know) and The early bird catches the worm (So worms that sleep late live to reproduce, my father said) and a few others. Bob contributed Please don't kill me. After some back and forth with Ariel we figured out it was the "please" that stumped him.

At which point we rounded a long broad curve and the road sloped down ahead of us to wind for several miles until it curved out of sight between the mountains.

My father called a halt and told us to search nearby vehicles for toolboxes. Dr. Ram pointed out a towtruck and we jimmied a side panel to reveal a wide assortment of tools.

"What do you need all this for," I said.

"Oh I don't need most of it. Screwdriver. Pliers. Hammer. Crescent wrench." He named them as he removed them from the truck. "Oh and a jack and—shit, what do you call em, Raj. Cross shaped thing for changing tires. It's been so long."

"Lug wrench," said Ariel.

"Lug wrench," he said fondly.

"Why," I said, "do you need those few tools."

"So we can drive down the mountain, Fred. Why else."

No hydraulic jack would work. Neither would the crank kind. My father just shook his head. "It doesn't make any goddamn sense," he said. "One's just a screw. The other just pushes. Simple machines don't get much simpler than that. How can they not work."

"It is very interesting," said Dr. Ram.

"It'll be more interesting when your shiny head comes out of some centaur's ass because we couldn't outrun them."

"These jacks are not really simple machines the way physics defines it, you know. A ramp or a basic lever and fulcrum will still work. The crank jack uses circular motion to turn a screw which narrows the hinged metal pieces attached to it and causes them to rise. Energy is being transferred in several directions. The hydraulic jack works by—"

"One screws, one pushes, Raj."

"Perhaps adding an element of complexity prohibits function."

"I think it's about intent," I said.

My father looked disgusted. "Intent."

I shrugged. "It's a factor in casting."

"Well, I intend to get under this goddamn car if I have to dig a moat around it."

He had picked a Dodge Intrepid, the chassis so rusty and shitcovered it was hard to tell its original color. "Big car, low center of gravity, aerodynamic, common tire size," he said. We jimmied trunks and removed spare tires that weren't dryrotted. My father inflated them with a footpump from a nearby RV and cursed the whole time that it made no sense that a bike pump worked and a hydraulic jack did not. Dr. Ram suggested that the hydraulic jack had simply bled out over time. My father stared at the footpump long enough to make me wonder if he was thinking about braining Dr. Ram with it. Apparently Dr. Ram wondered the same thing as he found somewhere else to be for a few minutes.

My father set his sword aside and used the lug wrench to loosen the right side tires and we lifted the big car on its left side and Bob propped it up while my father removed the dryrotted tires and replaced them with the good ones. We lowered the car slowly and the tires held. My father loosened the left side tires and we lifted the car again and he changed the tires and then worked on the underside of the car with hammer and pliers, banging and cursing and prying. I asked him what he was doing to it.

"These cars were in drive when the Change happened," he said. "Stick or automatic, they're stuck in gear because the shift lever won't work. I'm taking it out of gear this way." He banged on something with the hammer and looked satisfied and said Who said violence never settles anything.

Ariel watched for a while, I think to be sure Bob wasn't going to drop the car on him, and then galloped off without a word, shadow stretching across the broken freeway in the lowering sun.

Finally my father ducked out from under the car with blackened hands and a smudged cheek and nodded thanks to Bob and joined us in lowering the car slowly. He chocked the front tires with chunks of asphalt.

Dr. Ram emptied waterbottles on the windows and scrubbed the windows with a rag and squeegeed them clean. He and my father kept ducking their heads and smiling in a kind of embarrassed disbelief. I finally asked them what was so funny.

"We're gonna drive a car," my father said and laughed.

Ariel trotted up. "I hope so," she said, "cause Bob's big boys are about three miles behind us and coming fast."

———————

The back seat was roomy. I expected that musty old car smell but it didn't smell like anything because right now nothing smelled like anything. Leather and vinyl had dried and cracked and faded. Dr. Ram had to show Avy how to fasten her seatbelt. I buckled mine and felt it press against what had to be a fractured rib. I remembered when me and Yan would play in cars when we were little kids pretending to drive and imagining what it was like to be in something moving by itself. That was magic to us.

The windows wouldn't roll down so my father had busted out the driver's and passenger's sides from inside with a fire extinguisher. Now he stood behind the opened driver's door, frighteningly calm and amazingly not looking at the ragged line of centaurs heading toward us on the grassy freeway a few miles south.

"You're sure you can do this," Ariel asked for the third time.

He nodded. "Long as we got speed and nothing blocks the road."

"Okay." She glanced back. "Wish we had time to scout ahead. You better get going." She went to the back of the car as my father kicked the asphalt chunks away from the front tires and got in and closed the door. "Race you to the bottom," he called back.

"Me and Bob are gonna race."

"Bob bob," said Bob.

My father glanced at him and then at Ariel. "I got five bucks on you. No offense, Bob."

"Bob bob."

"You won't collect if you don't get your ass in gear. Let's go." She and Bob got behind the car and pushed. We began to roll. My ribs screamed raven calls as I tried to turn to see how close the centaurs were. Mostly what I saw was Bob pushing with his huge hands and Ariel pushing with her forehead against the taillight and her horn absurd upon the trunk. Bob grinned at me through the streaked rear windshield and that was scary enough.

We moved slowly at first and I thought surely we were going to be overrun by berserking centaurs bent on using our heads for saddlebag danglies. The ride was rough and steering seemed to take a lot of effort. It wasn't as if we had miles of smooth paved road ahead of us. It was grass and occasional trees and boulders interrupting the crumbling asphalt. We bumped on broken pavement as my father muscled us around traffic heaps.

"The road is in terrible condition," said Dr. Ram. "I am not convinced we can attain the necessary speed."

Speed. Duhh. I began rooting in my backpack.

My father glanced in his sideview mirror and said We may have to do some shooting.

It was hard to focus on my backpack and not to look out the back windshield. I was sure I could run faster than we were going.

"We got a Plan B?" came from behind us.

I pulled a mirrored toy soldier from the pack. "Think so," I called. I yanked a strip of duct tape from the roll and pressed the mirrored soldier into the middle of the strip and opened my door. Grass and pavement streamed by faster than I'd thought. I grabbed the roof and stood and held out the taped soldier. "Tell Bob to—" I froze. The closest centaurs were a couple hundred yards behind us. Some had long bows. Now I could hear the plaintive whalecry notes of trumpeted javelins.

I recovered because I had to. "Tell Bob to press this against the back of the car."

"He understands english," Ariel yelled at the ground.

"Bob bob," said Bob. He held out a long arm and I handed him the taped soldier and the tape folded on itself. Bob stared at it. I mimed pulling it open and Bob nodded and let go of the car and pulled the stuck tape halves apart too hard and tore the tape in two. Now the mirrored soldier dangled from the edge of one half.

The centaurs holding bows began to raise them. The javelins trumpeted in unison if not in harmony.

"Stick it on the back," I called. "Tape it to the back."

Bob pressed the taped soldier to the flat back of the filthy rusty trunk lid. It was only going to hold for a few seconds.

"Move," I said. "Ariel, Bob, out of the way."

Ariel lifted her head and saw the tape and veered away from the car. Bob veered the other way. A broomstick arrow slammed the trunk. I dropped back into the car and yelled *zimbabwe* and the soldier unmirrored and the push spell I had salvaged from the blimp discharged and the seat slammed into me and my ribs felt like they were being branded as we surged forward and jounced along the broken downhill road.

A semitruck loomed in front of us and we jerked around it. Apparently it was easier to steer if you went faster. The downhill path curved left and we leaned right. The highway wasn't very crowded and we could see what was coming up fairly well. Ariel and Bob pulled ahead of us. Ariel ran between two rusting cars and Bob darted around one. They really were racing. They didn't look back.

I looked back. The centaurs were no longer gaining on us but they were nowhere near far enough away. There were about a third as many as there'd been at the blimp hangar, which was still a couple dozen centaurs too many.

We bounced in our restraints and things creaked and shuddered and we leaned from side to side as we swerved around the inert vehicles. "I take it the brakes do not function," said Dr. Ram.

"Brakes are for pussies Raj."

Now we were going so fast that air had begun blowing into the car. I remembered moving the Surfliner to the racetrack a hundred years ago, the rough and tumble journey that had led directly to this one.

Ariel and Bob rounded the next broad curve well ahead of us and disappeared around the mountainside. It was hard to tell who was in the lead.

An ominous grinding from the front wheels rose as we picked up speed.

"What is that," I said.

"Bearings," my father called back. "Probably dry as a bone."

"Will it be okay."

He shrugged. "Find out."

We rounded the next curve and Avy and I yelled because ahead the grassy road became a ramp that slanted down at least six miles rulerstraight until it seemingly bent up to disappear far out on the vast plain spread before us. The sun was lowering and mountain shadows darkened half the way. The pit of my stomach felt as if I had jumped from a great height but had not yet hit. Avy gripped my hand but did not look at me. Her thick nails bit into my palm.

Dr. Ram glanced at the dashboard in front of my father. "The speedometer does not work."

My father looked at it. "I'm guessing sixty, sixtyfive." He looked in the rearview and for some reason grinned as he said You kids all right back there.

Avy nodded and I said fine. The ride got smoother as we went faster. I glanced behind us again. No centaurs yet.

Dr. Ram stuck his hand out the window and cupped air and straightened his hand and planed it up and down. Brought his hand in and looked at it as if something had happened to it.

Now we were gaining on Ariel and Bob up ahead. Down ahead. They seemed to be running neck and neck.

"Seventyfive you think, Raj?"

"My judgement of such things is not what it used to be."

"Can you believe we used to do this all the time."

"Does it feel strange."

My father thought about this. "What's strange is that it doesn't feel all that strange."

"Like riding a bicycle."

My father nodded and then they both laughed. "I shoulda boosted a convertible. With a high output head unit and twin Infinity Kappa Perfect Twelve subs in a ported enclosure. Boomchik boomchik."

"It is interesting that you can turn the steering wheel but the speedometer does not operate," said Dr. Ram. "The principle is the same."

They could have been sitting on the beach the way they were talking. It was all I could do to keep from yelling myself hoarse and Avy's nails were drawing blood from my palms. Pre-Changers are crazy. Every one of them.

I looked back again. "Still behind us."

My father checked the sideview. "Don't they get tired."

"They can run for days," said Avy.

"Great."

Something glinted up ahead. Near the bottom of the long descent the light had hit something just right. I frowned. "Did you see that."

"See what," my father said.

"Something up ahead. Like a big glass dome in the road. I just saw it for a second."

"Raj?"

"I saw nothing, sorry."

"Know soon enough."

The grinding from the front wheels was very loud now. It sounded like they were about to fall off. My father sniffed and then frowned when he realized he couldn't smell anything at all.

The air grew hot as the valley floor rose to meet us. Backlit mountains on the left stretched shadows across a vast undifferentiated plain bisected by the knifecut highway running straight to the horizon. Ahead and to the left a cluster of buildings that had been a town called Grapevine. The downgrade began to level. How far would we roll after that. A mile? Two?

A few hundred yards ahead now Ariel and Bob veered right and galloped off the road. Something flashed again and this time my father and Dr. Ram flinched. I saw a clear dome shape outlined for a moment huge and lying across most of the road. Ariel made a tight U and came toward us yelling something and I wondered why my father wasn't trying to stop or go around the shape. Maybe we were going too fast for either. Then I realized Ariel was shouting Go straight. Don't turn. Go into it.

And we did. A cold wave swept through the car. Through me. I no longer felt Avy's hand on mine. Tiny pops from the backpack at my feet. Then we emerged from whatever we had passed through and Avy's hand dug into mine and we surged forward as my father stomped the brake and nothing happened and he pulled the emergency brake and we skewed and a choppy screech came from the tires and we kept skewing. Going backward looking up the long incline. Ariel and Bob ran toward us on the grassy shoulder of the road. No sign of whatever we had driven through. Beside me Avy was crying, I thought because she was afraid. Everything drifted to the right and we were looking downhill again. My father fought to hold an over-under grip on the wheel turned in the direction of our spin. We yawed right and something snapped and the front end dropped. Metal plowed grass and asphalt and we slowed into the smoke from our own tires until we stopped.

No one moved. Beside me Avy cried softly.

Ariel ran up to the car. "Everyone all right."

"Think so," my father said. He unbuckled his seatbelt and opened his door but did not get out. I looked at Avy. "You okay."

"I don't. I feel. I'm." She shook her head.

Freaked out is what she probably felt and who could blame her. I unbuckled and got out of the car and waved away smoke spewing from the wheelwells and realized it probably smelled awful. The others were unbuckling. I looked back the way we had come. No glint, no dome. Two dozen centaurs galloping toward us miles up the road.

"What should we do," I said.

Ariel glanced up the road. "We wait. We wait right here."

My father opened his door and held onto it and leaned out over the road and threw up blood.

We stood in front of the wrecked Intrepid and faced uphill and held what weapons we had and waited. Except for Avy who had asked if she could wait in the car and now sat in the back uncaring.

The sun touched the mountains.

"Why are we doing this again," my father said.

"Just watch," said Ariel.

We watched. The centaurs screamed down the highway toward us. When they'd seen us standing ready in the road they'd gone berserk, putting on speed and brandishing bows and blowing long notes on their hollow raised spears.

"They'll probably get off a few bowshots," said Ariel. She eyed Bob. "No way to make em stop and talk this over I guess."

Bob shook his head and looked grim. "Day kimmy fust. Fuh be wit-cha." He stood ready and looked grim. Would he really fight his people with us.

We could hear them yelling now. My father drew his reverted sword. Dr. Ram brought up his crossbow. I had a baseball bat. What I didn't have were any stasis spells. Every mirrored item in my backpack was now in its original state. The spells hadn't been released, they'd been undone. Those pops I'd heard from the backpack when we'd driven through the nearly invisible dome. The dome that lay unseen between us and the charging centaurs.

Even in the waning light the glee on their planed and painted faces unmistakable. We had stopped to make our stand and they would have their reckoning too. Hurtling toward us out of mountain shadow into light. Out of nightmare into life. Spears raised bows drawn yelling as they rushed toward us. Rushed unknowing into the space the dome occupied, and blurred like sand attenuating in a gale, and dispersed, and were gone but for the faint reverberation of their warcries on the mountainside.

A lone thick arrow passed between my father and Ariel and slammed into the Dodge. Nothing else emerged. The wind blew inland from the mountains and all else was quiet.

"What the fuck just happened," my father asked.

"They're gone," I said. Finally understanding what lay in the road before us. What we ourselves had passed through. What the centaurs had just passed into never to emerge. "They're—gone."

"They never were," said Ariel.

A low moan brought us around. We looked at Bob as he turned away and covered his face with a huge thin hand and held the other out as if to ward us off.

"Let him go," said Ariel. "We just murdered most of his clan."

"Will someone tell me please what just happened," my father said. He hadn't sheathed his sword.

"Fred's figured it out," said Ariel.

"It's a bubble," I said. "From Yan's casting this morning." As we'd walked that day we'd told him what we thought had been the cause of that horrible ripple we had felt while we were in the air but I could see he wasn't making the connection. "It's a perimeter. Inside it the rules are different. Inside it is the world before the Change. Your world." Even as I said it the idea prickled hair on the back of my neck.

My father turned to face the thing we couldn't see and slowly lowered his sword. Regarding an idea and memory as much as a thing. Glanced at Ariel who nodded and said, "They can't exist in that space. Under those laws."

My father and Dr. Ram looked oddly childlike.

The unicorn nodded at the unencompassed space that lay ahead. "In there is the world your son is trying to restore. What just happened is what happens to those who don't belong in it."

"Um, Dad."

He turned to me. His unfamiliar expression, I realized, was wonder. I pointed at his sword and he raised it and turned it in his hand and let it glint the dying sunlight. The stasis was gone. He looked from the blade to me and I nodded. "All my stasis spells too."

And then we all realized the same thing at the same time and at the same time turned to look at Avy sitting in the slanting car.

THIRTY-THREE

I woke up staring at blank sky and not sure where I was. I heard breathing beside me and held my own. Turned my head to see a blanketed shape beside me in a panel of moonlit filth that was the rear window of an SUV. Memory flooded. With no better shelter in reach before nightfall and Bob still gone we had decided to camp where we were at the foot of the mountain range opening onto the great San Joaquin Valley. Avy and I had folded back the seats in an SUV and settled in. My father and Dr. Ram slept in another vehicle down the road.

I sat up and looked at the moon. The night was not half over. Glanced from moon to Avy and wondered if that connection still remained. She had hardly said a word since we had driven through—

That undelineated thing out there. And a figure ghostly in the moonlight facing where I knew it lay.

I eased my sleeping bag aside and unlocked the door and opened it as quietly as I could. Cool night air. Mountain cutouts in moonlight.

She didn't move when I came up beside her. We said nothing for a while. Regarding an unapparent border beyond which certain past and possible future lay enmodeled. Finally she said It's the death of me.

I watched with her while the moon sank toward the distant mountains. "Where's Bob."

"Grieving. He has a ritual. I don't think he wants us to see it."

"Is he—is he mad at us."

"How would you feel."

"I can't really put myself in his position."

"Fair enough. I don't think he's going to try to hurt anybody if that's what you're asking. His goals are the same as ours."

"That's why you want him along, isn't it."

"We need help, Fred."

"And you need insurance."

"We need both. When the shit finally hits the fan will you be able to look your friend in the eye and do what needs to be done. Will his father. Your father." She lowered her head. "Or will you want to talk it out. To avoid ugliness." She tossed her head at the unseen perimeter. "Some ugliness can't be talked to."

"You think Dr. Ram might try to keep us from hurting Yan."

"I think any of you might. You as much as Doc."

I shook my head. "No. What Yan's doing isn't wrong like a bad decision. It's wrong like a bad math answer. It's crazy and selfish and, and I don't know, tyrannical. Murderous."

"And no one ever loved a tyrant or a murderer, you think?"

"I think people have stopped people they loved from doing wrong."

"I know you're sincere, Fred. I'm just not sure how honest you're being with yourself. In your heart of hearts you've come along not because you think you can stop Yan but because you think you can talk him out of it."

"I suppose I might."

"I'm betting he thinks you'll try. And that's why Bob is my insurance. Our insurance. He won't try to talk anybody out of anything. He'll try to stop Yan with every cell in his body the moment he finds him. So will I."

I wondered at the anger I felt inside. "Well. We'll see when we get there."

"I trust you Fred but I can't rely on you. I don't trust Bob. But I can definitely rely on him."

And with that I began to glimpse the complexity and depth of her manipulation. "That was some chance you took with Avy today."

"It wasn't a chance at all. You couldn't have stopped in time."

"You know what I mean. How did you know she wouldn't just vanish."

"Some of her did. Why do you think she's so upset."

"If she's upset why are you so sure she wanted it gone."

"If you had gangrene in your arm and Dr. Ram cut it off to save the rest of you you'd still be upset that you had lost an arm."

"What Avy lost wasn't going to kill her."

"It was going to kill somebody. It probably has already. She doesn't want to live with that."

"She didn't get to decide."

She sighed. "I know you're troubled, Fred. I know you want answers. You think I can give them to you. Will it knock me off the pedestal if I tell you that I'm dealing with my own shit here too."

I stepped back. "I'm sorry. I'll leave."

"You don't have to leave. Just—enough with the interview. I'm not an oracle. I'm a fancy pony. Same way you're a fancy ape."

"You think you can hide behind all that glib bullshit."

"Well look who just caught up."

"Fuck you."

"Why don't you ask me what you really came here to ask me."

I thought of how to put what I wanted to say next and she waited with her answer ready.

"You can heal things."

"I can. I have. I even brought him back once. He wrote about it. It's still inside me. That absence. I can't admit it again."

"You could do it but you won't."

Wind blew her mane as she turned her full attention on me and said everything by saying nothing.

"It isn't fair."

"No. It isn't." She turned to look again at that invisible perimeter. "Any fairness is a gift."

———————

Next morning I stumbled bleary from the SUV with my sleeping bag around me to find my father and Avy already up and drinking coffee. I sat down and my father silently handed me a cup and I nodded thanks. We sipped and stared at the small guttering fire with the french press and its compressed sediment layer beside it. I wished I could taste the coffee. I glanced at Avy and nodded good morning and decided not to say anything. At least she nodded back.

I asked where Dr. Ram was and my father waved a hand and I turned to see him walking toward us half a mile up the road and carrying a small bundle.

"Car shopping?"

"Didn't say."

I started to ask where Ariel and Bob were but decided not to.

My father opened a waterbottle and emptied it into the saucepan and put it over the fire. When Dr. Ram got back my father poured the bubbling water into the french press and put the lid back on with the plunger high and set it beside Dr. Ram. Dr. Ram nodded thanks and set his cloth bundle before him and opened it with little shooing motions to reveal a flat plastic box and a longbarreled black metal pistol and a box of rounds.

My father blinked but said nothing. Then he coughed and helped himself to his feet with his sword and went behind some cars and coughed and spat and watched Dr. Ram take the gun apart and set the pieces on the cloth. He shook his head and then began searching cars himself. Dr. Ram examined the gun pieces one at a time. He opened the flat gray plastic case and withdrew a rod and picked up the cylinder and pushed the rod into the chambers and dislodged the bullets one by one. They landed on each other clicking like dead bugs. He tossed them aside and pulled a cylindrical brass brush with a long handle from the case and worked that into the emptied chambers. I watched in silence wondering what he could possibly be up to.

After a while I realized Bob stood watching with the rest of us. He had painted dark red checkmarks along his ribcage and smaller versions on either cheek, part of his ritual of mourning I supposed, and then I saw it wasn't paint. He held a tenfoot length of PVC pipe.

Avy and I got to our feet when we saw Bob standing there. Silently regarded the scarified creature as if beholding some dark envoy come to take us to some unimagined reckoning. Dauntless and unswerving.

Avy moved first. Stepped toward him heeding some unheard call. Strange thin girl fearless and frail before a tall lean nightmare enfleshed from out the human race's troubled slumber. Nearing craned her head at his gaunt height. Impassive facets of his scarred planed face. He did not move beyond the tightening of his grip upon the plastic pipe. Twice her height, ten times her weight. Her nostrils flared trying to smell him, trying to transmit to her the fear she ought to feel. Avy stepped into the centaur's shadow. Put out her hand. Set palm to mottled flank. The undeniable solidity. Then collapsed into that space as if falling onto the proffered hand and suddenly began to sob.

"I'm sorry. I'm sorry, I'm so sorry."

He did not bend to her or move a hand to acknowledge or console. Then his hand did come up and I didn't need to look to know that several cars away my father's hand had closed upon the handle of his sword. But a dark and extrajointed finger only traced itself across an incised checkmark on a hardplaned cheek and lowered to draw a smaller check on Avy's upturned cheek. And raised and lowered and drew again.

And when she leaned away and brought her hands up toward her face the centaur gathered both her narrow wrists in one enfolding hand and shook his alien head and turned her roughly but not meanly till she faced the broad reflective plain. He gathered her into himself and brought up what would become his javelin and pointed it toward the ragged mountains waiting hard to the west across the empty plain, and we knew who our real enemy was and knew that it was time to face him.

But first there were totems to prepare and personal rituals of readiness to devise. Bob removed a kit bag from his pannier and set it beside his length of PVC pipe. It contained a pipe saw, a rattail file, a barrel file, sandpaper, cans of paint. While Dr. Ram methodically cleaned his newfound pistol Bob sawed through the pipe at a sharp angle to form a funnel point like a giant hypodermic syringe and then cut a wedge into that and used the barrel file to curve out the cutaway and form the fountain-pen nib shape I had seen in the library in San Juan Capistrano. Now the business end had two points. Bob filed down the inside surface of the pointed end with the rattail file until the entire edge was sharp from point to point. It was fascinating to watch those extrajointed fingers working.

As Bob did all this my father returned from a car with a small glossy rectangular object he cleaned with the tail of his shirt. His expression was odd. Bewildered and smug at the same time. He tucked the thing into a pocket and sat watching Bob sand the outside of his PVC spear and Dr. Ram clean the pistol.

Bob wiped the plastic dust from the shaft with a cloth and squinted down the length of it and put the dull end to his lipless mouth and blew. A clarion note rang out. He lowered the spear and regarded it a moment and then set it down and shook a paint can and opened it and began stirring it.

Dr. Ram finished cleaning the gun and loaded it and folded the oilcloth and repacked the cleaning kit and set it by the fire's ashes and looked at us directly for the first time since he'd brought the relic thing into our midst. He smiled as if a bit embarrassed and turned away from us and brought the pistol up and pulled the trigger six quick times click click click click click click.

Bob stared at him a moment and then dipped his brush and resumed painting a multicolored dot pattern on the business end of his javelin.

Dr. Ram lowered the gun and looked at my father who looked aggrieved and rose using his sword as a cane again. He tucked the sword through his belt and looked at Dr. Ram. "You should have a target," he surrendered.

They kept taking deep breaths and patting themselves and looking around. Hunting signs of difference. Within, without. Outside the perimeter we looked for differences as well. If there were any they were not visible. My father set waterbottles on the roof of a Honda that might have once been black and set the rectangular object he'd been polishing on the hood and quickly backed away. Dr. Ram looked at the gun in his hand like a man called upon to deliver bad news to a friend. Avy and Ariel and Bob and I stood well outside the unseen border and behind him. He looked at my father who did not even nod and he raised the gun and sighted and lowered it and wiped his brow and raised the gun again and fired. The sound was like the clap of two boards. Loud but not the roar I had expected. Its echo cracked along the hardpan plain. Nothing else happened.

Dr. Ram let out a long breath and inhaled deeply and assumed a straddle legged stance facing the waterbottles with the gun in a twohanded grip. He sighted and fired and nothing happened apart from this sound chasing down the first one.

"Forget the bottles, Raj," my father said.

Dr. Ram grinned foolishly and nodded and raised the gun and fired and the Honda's windshield spiderwebbed and glass blew out the back window and sprayed greenish sunlit jewels across the trunk and road behind it.

We all regarded what he'd done and what it meant.

He offered the gun to my father and my father shook his head. "Not my style."

"Mine either I should hope."

"You kidding me. Right now you're the best shot in the world."

Dr. Ram turned the gun in his hand. "One of my teachers used to tell us that one handgun outweighs six doctors."

"Smart guy."

"A smart woman, yes. Is that an iPod you placed on the car."

"Yep. Found one of the solarpowered ones. Figured it was worth a shot." He went back to the car and picked up the object and pressed it and looked startled. He grinned and held it out to Dr. Ram and Dr. Ram grinned back. Outside the circle I couldn't see what they were grinning at but Dr. Ram said Splendid and my father fiddled with the rectangle for a minute and shook his head and muttered and then suddenly looked pleasantly surprised. He pulled a tangle of white wires from his pocket and untangled them and shoved one end into the rectangle and twisted the split ends into his ears and pressed the rectangle. And looked startled again. Dr. Ram cocked his head and my father gave him a thumbsup and then shut his eyes. And stood there swaying as if remembering some pleasant dream. And then dropped to his knees and put his hands on them and rocked back and forth. I was about to go to him when he opened his eyes and shook his head and said God damn it, just god damn it.

Dr. Ram approached him and put a hand on his shoulder and he opened his eyes. "I'm all right."

"I would like to listen. If I may."

He took the wired buds from his ears. "You might want to but you might not like to. I'm serious."

"I see that, yes. And you are probably right. But still. How can I not."

"True. Okay." He offered earbuds and iPod and Dr. Ram screwed in the buds and did things to the iPod and his expression suddenly changed. He looked like a man in love. My father watched him for several minutes and then looked away. Outside the circle we glanced among ourselves. Avy and I shrugged but Ariel seemed keenly interested.

Finally Dr. Ram pulled out the earbuds and handed the iPod back to my father. "That was enough I think. Yes."

My father nodded slowly. "Fred? Want to see why us old people piss and moan so much."

I glanced at Ariel. "Not really," I told her. "Sure I guess," I called out to my father.

I dusted myself off and stepped into the circle. Brief cold washed across me and I broke out in a sudden sweat. Other than that it felt no different inside that profoundly different space.

"Our benefactor was pretty eclectic," my father said as he helped fit the hard white buds into my ears. "What'll it be Fred. Classical? Classic rock? Electronic dance? Audiobook?"

"I don't know." I looked at Dr. Ram.

"Classical is always a good choice," he said.

My father smirked. "Seven Elevens used to use it to keep kids from hanging out there. But I'm an optimist." He tried to show me how to work the dial on the iPod's face but I couldn't understand it. The print went by so fast I couldn't read it. He stopped at BEETHOVEN—NINTH SYMPHONY and pressed the dial. I waited and shrugged and he gestured at me to wait some more and I was about to say it wasn't working when the sun came up inside my head and a world was born between my ears. Weather formed and shifting landscapes etched themselves from formlessness. Nature spoke to me. To my eyes. My heart. Something given voice I never knew had been struggling to speak. The drums and guitar and chants and singing I had heard before were a child's crayon drawing of a sunset. This was a sunset. This was the thing itself.

I looked at my father looking back. So this was what they could not accept having lost. What they insisted we did not appreciate. Not the buildings, not the moonships, not the big loud cars. This. How humbling to experience the life the corpses of my milieu had once contained. To understand at last how rightly felt those people's anguish was.

In the end I could only give back the iPod and say thank you and know he knew that words could not convey what he'd just shown me.

They asked if I would try to cast a simple spell inside the circle. I got my rig and tried to put a waterbottle in a stasis spell. I lit the propane stove and burned things and made the passes and spoke the old words but all I made was smoke and ashes.

My father looked from my rig to the gun in Dr. Ramchandani's hand. No one said anything but we knew it was time to leave.

Dr. Ram put the gun into his pack and no one asked him why. My father kept the iPod too.

———————

We took the torn and weathered top from a PT Cruiser convertible that had been parked in neutral and replaced the dryrotted tires and inflated them with the footpump and my father steered while Ariel and Bob pushed us up the 5 and straight onto the 99 to Bakersfield thirty miles away. The highways of the Central Plain were not as dissolute as most I'd seen, no doubt because so much less grew here. Dr. Ram said it had been a major source of agriculture but they'd had to import all their water which made no sense to me. Why didn't they just grow the crops where the water was. In any case there was little trace of whatever crops they'd grown. Just barren plain dotted with brown life struggling to stake a claim, the only evidence of growth and harvest the rusted shells and vineshrouded humps of tractors and threshers and combines.

———————

SUN FUN STAY PLAY
BAKERSFIELD

Beyond that a still and weedy sunbaked ruin of parched facades and new growth over recent burn. "It does not look appreciably different," Dr. Ram remarked. I remembered that the band that had captured Ariel's mate had come from here and doubtless she remembered too but we saw no other human beings the whole time we were there. Feral dogs and signs of feral cats, crowflocks dense on sagging powerlines, birdshit and char everywhere.

We found a phonebook in a motorcycle shop and used it to look up a tack and bridle shop and used a city map from a gas station to find that. "My kingdom for a GPS," my father said and Dr. Ram smiled tightly but no one asked him what he meant. We smashed the storefront and stood listening for sound beyond the echo of the crash and heard nothing. "A legacy of broken storefronts," my father said. "Your birthright, Fred." And coughed into his fist and went inside. We followed. Aisles and walls of treated leather mummifying in the desert heat. I wondered what it smelled like but was happy not to know. My father filled a rattling metal shopping cart with harness and buckles and straps.

At a nearby U-Haul we considered trailers and towing hitches but decided against them. We got rope and ramen from a ransacked 99¢ Only store and decided not to take a chance on Home Depot in favor of finding lengths of dowel somewhere else. We finally found two tenfoot lengths of PVC pipe at a plumbing supply. I helped my father while the others foraged. Bob inspected copper and aluminum pipe but apparently decided to stick with his PVC, maybe because of the effort he'd invested in it. The making perhaps a part of his ritual of grieving.

We measured Bob and cut harness and looped and stitched and fitted until we'd made a makeshift dogcart harness with which Bob could pull the PT Cruiser. The hardest part was fitting the dowels on the car. There was just no place to secure them. In the end we drove nails through the dowels and bent the nails with pliers and wound them with nylon line and tied the line around the pillar posts and windshield. "It's not supposed to be pretty," my father said, "it's just supposed to get us there."

By the time he was satisfied the others were long back and the afternoon was waning. We were thirty miles east of the 5 and we'd lost a day of travel. Ariel assured us if the harness worked the time we gained would be more than worth the time we'd spent. My father asked just how much time will we gain when you're in harness and Ariel said aren't you funny. Bob seemed eager to get going, oncoming night or no, and calmed down only after Ariel had pointed out that in the night he'd have little warning in the event of trouble and would find it hard to fight in harness.

I was all for pressing on by night, little warning or no. Bakersfield gave me the creeps.

We bedded down in a Sit 'n Sleep mattress store. No need to smash a window this time, the door had been unlocked for over thirty years. I liked the arrangement better than if we'd decamped in separate rooms in some ruined motel. What it lacked in privacy it made up for in reassurance and us bipeds still got a large and comfy bed each. Still everything was musty and cobwebby and even closed stores somehow still had packrat nests.

Ariel and Bob went scouting. I watched them canter down the street and separate a few blocks away. I shook my head and turned back to the store to see Dr. Ram looking down the street as well. "Strange bedfellows, eh," he said.

"I don't know what that means."

"Oh, it only means that common causes sometimes make unlikely allies."

"Common causes."

If he heard the question he didn't acknowledge it. "Clearly uncommon causes as well," he said and laughed.

Back inside I broke out my rig and asked my father to break down his sword and I put a stasis spell around the blade again. While he reassembled it I studied the deadly perfect mirror of its mild curve and thought about how its original stasis spell had been undone. It bothered me. Here was the impossible solution Yan and I had sought. Not the cheat we had devised by creating imperfect stasis spells but an actual negation of a perfect, perfectly made, and permanent stasis spell. Turned out all you had to do was change some of the universe's laws. There was hope for Froggum and his brethren yet.

My father turned the mirrored blade before him. "The sword that was broken is reforged."

"It wasn't broken."

He smiled. "I know, Fred." He sheathed the blade silently and quickly and without looking. "Thanks. Again." He asked if I'd leave the propane stove out so he could heat water for our ramen.

I put away the rest of my rig and sought out Avy while he made dinner. She was off in a corner trying to figure out how to pack the backpack we'd gotten her earlier in the day and what to pack it with. She had only ever used her tiny JanSport for her few possessions and had only traveled with what clothes she wore, changed them only when they wore out, scavenged what she needed when she needed it. Her life was hard for me to imagine.

"Need some help with that," I asked.

"No." She made a botch of folding a pair of khakis. "Don't need your fucking pity either."

"Well at least you're feeling better."

She folded the pants lengthwise and rolled them up on the bare mattress. "Better than what."

"Better than yesterday."

"What the fuck do you know about yesterday."

"I know that you're cured now but it hurt a lot. Probably still does."

"Cured." She snorted. "Cured of what."

"Of being—what you were. What you would, you know, turn into."

She shoved the rumpled pants into the lumpy backpack. "So I'm all human now."

"That's what Ariel says."

"Ariel." She laughed and I saw she was trying to hold back tears. "So I'm two different animals, right? And the one that's most different from you is the one you had to kill."

"Nobody killed anything."

"Really. Let's ask Bob's friends about that. Oh no wait. We can't because they're fucking gone."

"No one wanted to do that. And no one wanted to do anything to you. It just happened. We drove through it."

"Yeah and I'm cured." She threw the pack off the bed. "I smell wrong now."

"I can't smell anything."

"I've been by myself since I can remember being me. Nothing fucked with me. Fucking centaurs were afraid of me. What the fuck am I supposed to do now that I'm cured."

"Be with—" your own kind, I almost said "—with people. Not be alone anymore."

"Thanks. Thanks, Fred. I'm with people now. I'm real ready for that. Maybe I can come live with all of you in Happy Fucking Valley and fucking bake cookies and trade them for shit."

Behind me a soft cough. "Dinner," my father apologized.

"I'm not hungry thanks," said Avy.

"Your choice. I also wanted to let you know that things'll probably get hairy when we hit the coast. You're not obliged to go through any of that with us. It's our fight."

She nodded. "Can I let you know tomorrow."

"You don't have to let us know anything one way or the other."

"Okay. Thanks."

"Sure. Fred?"

"Coming."

He regarded us a moment and then nodded briefly and left. Avy sat on her bed not looking at me. "I came over here to say I'm sorry you're going through this," I said, "and that I'm glad to help you if I can."

She nodded but didn't look. I watched her a moment longer and then left to go eat dinner.

"You know," I told my father when I caught up to him, "I thought the angry part of her would be gone too."

"You thought that was the nonhuman part."

"I guess."

"You know, the hardest thing to keep in mind about Avy isn't that she's spent the last few years turning into a predatory animal once a month. It's that she's around thirteen. And that's a very pissedoff time of life."

"Well at least we all get past it."

He looked at me sharply and then grinned and clapped a calloused hand on my neck and we shared the first genuine laugh we'd had in a long time.

THIRTY-FOUR

"Consider the cuttlefish," said Ariel.

"Cuddlefish?"

"Cuttle, Fred." Walking beside our steadily moving car she glanced at my father behind the wheel. "Christ, you could have at least taught him to read."

"Kids today," he said. "What can you do."

"You read about cuttlefish," I asked.

"No, I slept with a book about them under my pillow and when I woke up I knew everything about them."

"What's with you," Avy asked her.

Ariel watched Bob pulling us westward at a steady lope on State Road 46. He leaned to his task and never stopped surveying the landscape of peeled and ivied billboards advertising nearby vineyards gone to seed and he never complained. Despite what Avy'd said about centaurs he did need rest sometimes though not often and not for very long.

We were forty miles northwest of Bakersfield.

"The cuttlefish," Ariel continued, pointedly ignoring Avy, "is a cephalopod, brother to the squid and octopus. It's very smart and unbelievably adaptable."

"What an in-ter-esting creature this cuttlefish seems to be," my father said. "Tell me, how smart and adaptable is our friend the cuttlefish."

"Like a lot of creatures," Ariel persisted, "the cuttlefish is very good at camouflage. Unlike a lot of creatures good at camouflage the cuttlefish can change its colors and even its textures and shape to match its surroundings as it travels through them. It swims over mud and it looks like mud. It swims past coral and it looks like coral. It swims over a checkerboard—"

"Let me guess," my father said.

"What does it do if it swims over a mirror," I asked.

"Despite his ignorance and illiteracy the boy has a scientific mind," said Ariel.

"It's what got him where he is today," my father agreed.

"But here's the thing about the cuttlefish—"

"At last," my father said.

"It can change its colors and textures and shape at will. It can put on a show. Light up and swirl patterns and stripes and dots and morph till the cows come home."

"Go cuttlefish," I said.

"It does it to attract a mate and it does it to hunt. It tries to get its prey to stare at it. If that doesn't work it pulls out all the stops and lights up like a christmas tree and mesmerizes its prey and then snatches it and eats it."

"When have you ever seen a christmas tree," my father said.

"On teevee. So here's this fish, see, and it's evolved a perfect quick disguise ability, and that ability specialized to the point where the critter can get creative with it so it can get chicks and grab dinner."

We waited. Ariel said nothing. Finally my father sighed and said And.

"And I think Avy's a cuttlefish."

We passed a roadsign. 5 FWY 2 MILES. On the roadside up ahead an empty U-Haul flatbed trailer rigged for horse harness and tilted hitch side up. Around it campfire remnants and bottles and broken glass.

I sat up.

"Avy changed her appearance to hunt," Ariel said loudly, "and to find her own kind." She did not look at the U-Haul trailer. "She became a predator when looking human would have made her vulnerable."

I stared at the trailer as we passed it and looked for signs of red paint on the road beside it. Any trace of pentagram. Ariel stayed eyes ahead.

"I didn't do it on purpose," said Avy. "It just happened to me once a month."

"You could have turned whenever you wanted to," Ariel said. "But you believed all that fullmoon crap so you obliged it."

I looked at my father. He'd taken no interest in the trailer beyond glancing at it and dismissing it. Not for the first time I wondered if places could contain some trace of what had happened in them.

"You also had a glamour," said Ariel. "It's gone now." She did not look and did not look behind us.

"Glamour?" my father said. "Like fashion model glamour?"

"A glamour is a kind of spell," I said. "Like a charm. It keeps people's attention on you and makes them want to do things for you. Girls ask for them all the time at Paypay's."

Ariel looked at me and didn't look back at the trailer and neither did I and I nodded and she nodded back curtly, all the gratitude she would show.

"I kept wondering how come nobody was questioning why you were suddenly coming along with us," I said to Avy. "How come everyone was so accommodating to you. Including me. Your coffee tasted better, the food you cooked seemed better. My dad and Ariel kept deferring to you."

"So you don't really want me here," said Avy.

My father glanced in the rearview. "You saved our asses when we met you. And you saved my ass again after that. In my book that earns you the right to be wherever the hell you want to be."

"I'm just a kid now."

"So you've been reduced to the rest of the human race," said Ariel.

"I've been reduced anyway."

The rectangle of my father's face in the rearview mirror seemed to stifle a grin. "Kid can fight with her mouth too," he said. He coughed and opened the car door to spit.

———————

Bob did not need to sleep but he did need to rest. The next night we stopped in the remnants of the road at the offramp to the 101 Freeway near something called Paso Robles and folded back seats and cleaned nests out of derelict cars and unrolled sleeping bags and ate dinner and drank coffee and didn't talk much, each of us weighted down by where we would arrive soon and where we had been. For some reason I couldn't stop thinking about José buried up there in the mountains beside the wreckage of his blimp, about the Surfliner reflecting sunrises and sunsets as it awaited my return, about the horrible suddenness with which the centaurs chasing us had been utterly obliterated from the world. The ensuing silence. Opening the office door in the blimp hangar and seeing Avy turning into something else. The rusting tanker broken on the beach in Encinitas. L.A.'s artificial skyline rising proudly from its rubble from afar, its derelict abandonment to ruin and alien occupation from closer up. The difference between those views. Yan's mirrored smirking image. My father's thickening cough.

Occupied with these thoughts I set up a pentagram beyond the light of our small fire and opened my grimoires and thought about what castings I might need for whatever confrontation I would have with Yan. So much of what I'd need relied on what he'd have prepared for me. I knew I was the better caster. I also knew that Ariel was right: I was hampered by conscience, by appeasement, possibly by fear, certainly by hope if not by love. Yan was constrained by none of these. He would act where I might hesitate.

From the darkness Dr. Ram's voice said May I speak with you a moment. Before I could say of course Ariel's voice said I was wondering when you'd look me up Doc.

"You know what I would like to discuss with you."

"It's probably not my famous oatmeal cookie recipe so I'm guessing it's about one of your patients."

"He is worse off than he will show, you know."

"He always was."

"He will not take painkillers, even herbal ones. He has moderate to severe pain all the time now."

"Yes."

They were on the other side of the road behind a car and the wind conveyed their conversation to me.

"I know he used to be a smoker."

"Cigarettes didn't do this to him."

"Do you know what did."

"Texas."

"I am afraid I do not understand."

"That landscape he walked through in east Texas, through Houston. It wasn't just a bad fire that hadn't grown back yet. It was a fifty-mile stretch of oil refineries from Houston to the Gulf that blew up or corroded. Scorched earth and acid rain and toxic particles in the air and the groundwater. Part of the Gulf is still burning out on the water. Three decades, Doc.

It's worse than that reactor meltdown. It'll take centuries to recover. And him and his woman walked through it for weeks. Breathing. Eating. Drinking. Touching. It's like that in more places than you think. You all left your fingerprints everywhere."

"So . . . his wife then—"

"If she hadn't died of tetanus, sure. Probably."

"It is a terrible shame."

"It's your dead world taking its revenge."

"I am angry about that world too, you know. I do not miss it the way the others who lived in it do. But that is not my concern at this moment."

"Don't you think I'd help him if I could."

"I want to think so. He has been my patient for several years now but he has been my friend a great deal longer. Our little community, where we live, you know, they think he is strange and they dispute much of what he claims. But they have no idea how much they are in his debt. I have never been sure if he is the bravest man I have ever known or if he simply does not care."

"I don't really want to be a sounding board for your eulogy rehearsal Doc."

"You have a talent for responding to what lies beneath what is said."

"Yeah, it's a gift from the gods."

"It is an ability I have also acquired. In my profession, you know. People often try to tell you something other than what they are saying. You have to learn to listen for it if you are to really help them."

"Just go ahead and hit me with it Doc."

"You are still angry at his betrayal so long ago."

She laughed. "Him and that goddamn book. It was just his side of the story, you know. I am not angry about that. Never was. Not even betrayed. He was a goodlooking boy in his midtwenties whose best friend in the world was an overdone horse and attractive females of his own species came sniffing around whenever he stopped moving long enough. What was he supposed to do, become a monk. It was heartbreaking and it was tragic but who here thinks that losing virginity isn't pretty much inevitable. That's what makes tragedy Doc. Inevitability. No use crying over spilled et cetera. Look at our little hajj here. You think we aren't acting out a tragedy?"

"I do not think the outcome is inevitable."

"I know you don't. It's one of my concerns."

"If you do not feel betrayed then I don't understand your anger."

"But I do feel betrayed Doc. So does he. So do you. So does Fred. So does Avy. So does Bob. I lost a partner, maybe a mate, who was going to be with me for a hundred generations. Pete lost a partner he was going to be with for the rest of his hard short life. Or hers. Fred lost a mother and was blamed for it by his father. We cost Avy part of who she is. We killed Bob's entire tribe including a female he was courting. And no matter how this turns out you've lost a son."

"As I said, that outcome is not inevitable."

"Even if he wins, Doc, even if he lives through it you've lost him. You've lost him already."

After a moment he said, "Are all of your kind so cruel."

"All of my kind are honest. There's a lot of overlap."

"I only came to you to learn if there is anything we can to do help my friend."

"Let him play his part. That's what we can do. He's on the road again and he loves it and he hates the cause and he doesn't want it to end and he knows it has to and that he's the one who'll end it when it does. Journeys end in lovers meeting, Doc. Let him finish it."

———————

Long after I had put away my rig and the fire had guttered and the others were still in their cars I lay awake in my sleeping bag on the reclined seat in the PT Cruiser replaying that conversation in my mind. It was one thing to undertake a mission however necessary you felt it might be. It was another thing to realize there was no way to see it through without everyone involved paying a heavy price no matter how it turned out. Journeys end in lovers meeting. What can victory mean.

———————

Hours later motion woke me. Avy vaulting from the car and landing quiet as a cat. She put on her daypack and turned to me lying blanketed in my reclined seat. The moon had set. Her small figure cutout from the sky. I nodded at her. A long moment before she nodded back.

She went to Bob so as not to startle him. He stood before the campfire's ashes scanning our surroundings with his javelin at arms. He watched her approach. Fourteen years old at most and tiny there before him. She put a hand out to him and set it against his equine chest and looked up at him. Bob leaned the spear upon himself and drew a long thin finger across his wounded cheeks and covered her head with one great hand to tilt it back. Brought the finger down and traced the flaking lines of dark upon each human cheek. Set both hands almost contemplatively upon her head wondering perhaps like me how this small creature could have spread such terror among them. Or maybe blessing her. Then lifted his hands and took up arms again to resume his watch as Avy turned and left at last into the open world.

THIRTY-FIVE

The next day we passed through rolling country. Wild grapes abundant in unordered remnants of untended vineyards. No one said a word about Avy leaving us or needed to. I wondered would she finally accept her unappended self and seek out some fishing village or farming community where she could find a role among her kind, or would she go in search of that lost wild self on some mission of reconstitution. I wondered which was best. I knew which seemed more likely. Either way I wished her well.

In the afternoon we crested the rise and saw a line of ocean hovering it seemed above the floor of our descent. Distant seagulls on the wing. Roll of mist out on the water. Shipwrecked seatowns poking through overgrowth and compounded mudslides. Wrack of plastic bags and bottles washed ashore and dully winking. The continent's necklace.

I breathed in deeply but smelled nothing. Then memory rolled in and I could smell salt air. It smelled like home. I closed my eyes and took deep breaths and told myself that when I opened them I would be facing the Surfliner precarious on its narrow bridge of track, hot coffee inside waiting to be poured into a thermos and taken to the shore as I watched the sun come down while the offshore wind picked up. Then I opened my eyes and Bob was trotting on the downhill slope and the ride was rougher. My father called to him to halt and we climbed out and continued on foot and left the harnessed car to future speculation. With a gentle decline down to the coast and northward on uncertain ground it made more sense to free the centaur and ourselves to other labors.

By the map we rejoined Highway 1 just north of Harmony. There was little sign of town and road apart from signs themselves. Weather and quake and mudslide and time had substituted new embankment grass and tree for pavement wall and rail. The broken road was wholly washed away in places and we trudged through wild grass beside the shoreline picking our way among crumbling chunks of asphalt. Late summer mugginess and heat. Beneath my pack my shirt slapped wetly with my stride.

Near Cambria we camped. Hours of daylight remained but we were tired and according to our map San Simeon was only a few hours' walk north of where we were and with it Hearst Castle and whatever waited for us there.

What seaside motels remained had moldered and decayed and sagged to children's drawings of their former shapes. Remains of cars were not much better. We found nylon tents in trunks and unrolled them and shook out spiders and pitched the tents on the road and well above the tideline. Debated risk of fire. Sunset and a cold onshore breeze decided for us. My sweatsoaked shirt grew cold and I changed to a dry one. We broke apart half rotted furniture from a nearby motel and piled it in a concrete block firepit nearly submerged in sand and got a smokey fire going as the sun set on the water and the mist invaded and the seasound grew around us.

Dull lightning flashed out on the water to the north. There had been no clouds or sign of rain. We watched the flashes and wondered what they could be if they weren't lightning but had no good answer.

My father and Dr. Ram and I spread sleeping bags around the snapping fire and sat drinking stale coffee. Ariel stood near my father. Bob stood a little apart from us and faced the ocean sagittarian against the muted constellations and staring out over the waves as if waiting for some rising glimpse of sail heralding the return of an argosy long forgotten by all but himself.

My father threw a chair leg on the fire. "Wonder how she's doing."

"You know she'll be all right."

He nodded but did not look at Ariel. "But I wonder how she's doing."

"Should we—" I cleared my throat. "Should we talk about tomorrow."

"Hard to have a strategy when you don't know what you're walking into," said my father.

Dr. Ram surprised us all by pulling a book from his pack. *Hearst Castle: A Pictorial History*. "Perhaps we do not know what we are walking into," he said with a shrug, "but this should help us know where we are walking to."

Ariel and I looked over my father's shoulder as he tilted the book toward the fire and turned its pages. The opulence and splendor of the place were hard to believe. It was a series of spanish style buildings atop a hill at the crest of the Santa Lucia Mountains. Art and architecture from around the world had been brought here piece by piece a hundred years ago, shipped to a private dock in San Simeon and then trucked up a single winding road to the castle.

"But what was all this for," I said looking at reflecting pools and gothic libraries and gilded bedrooms.

My father smiled. "It was somebody's house."

"Somebody's?"

"He was rich. Super mega rich. He owned newspapers."

"You own newspapers."

He smiled. "He owned the places that made them."

"He got all that from making newspapers?"

"Most cities had two or three different companies that produced newspapers, Fred," Dr. Ram explained. "They produced a new paper every day, and at their peak they sold several hundred thousand of them every day."

"Several—" I couldn't picture it. I'd thought they were some big deal, a kind of annual recapitulation of events that was distributed throughout the city. Like the bulletin board at the swap meet in Del Mar. A new one every day? I shook my head. "It's all around me," I said, "and I'll never understand it."

"You will never have to," said Dr. Ram.

"If we're lucky," said my father. He was studying a two-page spread of the castle taken from above it. He glanced up at Ariel studying it over his shoulder and brought a hand up and then stopped suddenly and brought the hand back to the book. "This says his main concern was the view," he said. By firelight he was very pale.

"Maybe," said Ariel, "but he's also got some serious access control."

He nodded. "One road in, five miles long and winding. He'd put his main surprises there." He frowned at the book. "We could try skipping the access road and going up the hillside."

Ariel shook her head. "Tough going. Uphill climb. Easy to spot. The access road's probably our best bet. Even boobytrapped it's probably so overgrown you can't see what's heading up it."

"Wonder what kind of shape the buildings are in."

"Quakes, weather, overgrowth. Can't be good. Kind of hard to imagine anyone setting up shop there now, to be honest. The location can't be worth the effort."

"Depends what kind of help he's got," my father said.

We all looked at Bob.

———————

Another sleepless night with my rig spread out before me. Cool mist and crashing waves. I stared at nothing and no ideas would come.

Coughing behind me. "We sure as shit—" he coughed some more "—aren't gonna sneak up on anything." He came up beside me and pulled scabbarded sword from beltloop and squatted holding it.

"Does it hurt."

"Off and on. Right now on. Ariel and Raj are pissed I won't smoke a joint or something."

"They don't want to see you in pain."

"The R O I with painkillers isn't very good. I need to be alert." He coughed again. I didn't say anything. The breeze was cold. I hadn't brought warm clothes.

My father indicated my rig with his chin. "You're trying to second guess him."

"Not doing so great."

"At some point you have to just trust yourself. You know Yan. You know you. You know your stuff. It'll go or it won't." He grinned. "Sounds good doesn't it."

"I've never been through anything like this."

"There's one school of thought that says worrying doesn't change anything so why put yourself through it."

"Which school did you attend."

"Hard knocks. Worry's about control. It makes you cover your bases. What have you forgotten. What haven't you considered. Sometimes you come up with something. So I say go ahead and stress over it if you need to."

"I'm worried about you too."

"I can take care of myself."

"That's not what I meant."

"I know."

A dozen waves addressed the shore.

"When this is over," I said. "What then."

"Over is kinda fuzzy edged when it comes to big events. But assuming there's an over we go back home. Learn our lessons. Live our lives."

"Me and you and Yan's father and a unicorn and a centaur."

"We'll all be in a better position to reply to that the day after tomorrow."

"You sound just like her. You know that."

"She sounds just like me. I sounded like me first."

I studied him. "You really aren't worried about tomorrow."

"Sure I am. I'm just not worried about me. I gave that up a while back." He set a spread hand on his chest. "Way before this."

"So then what are you worried about."

"My son for one thing. My oldest friend and his son for two others. The future."

"Everything but you then."

He laughed. "I'm a foregone conclusion." He stood and both knees gave distinct creaks. He waved his sheathed sword at my rig. "Don't think about all this too much."

"Sure, no problem. What about you."

"I gotta see a horse about a man." He patted my shoulder and walked away and merged with the dark to leave me wondering if he was making the rounds to give uplifting speeches before the fray or simply saying his goodbyes.

Bob saw it first. In the lead he stopped his fourbeat walk and pointed and said, "Bad wadder." We came abreast of him and looked upshore. Finally Ariel said, "There's something wrong with the ocean."

My father got the binoculars from Dr. Ram's pack and put them to his eyes and adjusted them and just stood there looking. Then he coughed and bent with coughing harder and held the binoculars out to Dr. Ram who put them to his eyes and stood looking at the shoreline. Crashing waves the only sound besides my father's hacking cough.

Dr. Ram handed me the binoculars and said, "I do not understand" as I set the rubber cups against my eyes. I worked the focus and the shoreline clarified. Crescent beach and lonestanding pylons and a short stretch of rotting pier. Gliding seagulls. Crashing waves.

No. Not crashing. Motionless.

The waves stood frozen. Caught midcurl and whitecapped where they loomed upon a beach gone dry. Behind them lacefringed breakers and corrugated swells all motionless. The picture of a shoreline's still perfection belied by flying gulls and waving grass and eddying mist.

So he had figured it out. Stopped not one wave but a shoreline full. Left it here as monument and message.

I lowered the binoculars. "We need more guys," I said.

We had to pass before it. Three men and two supernatural creatures treading silent on a stilled and silent shore. Seagulls strutted pecking the dark green surface of that solid water and glanced incurious and hungry. One aloft dove down and hit that unyielding crumpled surface and lay there unmoving save for feathers ruffled by the breeze.

Farther out mute flickers in the water roiled like sheet lightning. Flashes in the frozen ocean. My father studied the horizon with his binoculars a while before venturing, "I think it's static electricity from friction. It looks like the water's moving normally toward the horizon. Slower a bit closer in. Thick like Jell-O."

"What's Jell-O," I asked.

"Jelly."

"He'd only be able to affect a section," I said. "It'd get weaker at the edges."

"But what is the purpose," Dr. Ram asked.

"To show he can. Like the airplane. Yan and I talked about this once. He said he wished he had the power to stop every wave on the beach."

"So it's another note," said my father.

I nodded.

Ariel moved forward on the dried sand and then stepped out until she stood fully on the surface of the water. You expected her to look unsteady but she did not. She walked out from the shoreline cautious among the hardened corrugations until she stood before a sixfoot wave caught mid unfurl like a sculpted glass backdrop glistening and translucent. "It's slippery but it isn't wet," she called.

I went to the rigid water and bent and touched it. Textured, glassy, gritty with blown sand, warmed by the sun. Flicked it with a nail and heard its dull tick. Stood again to marvel at the unicorn walking on top of the waves.

"Hey Peter," she yelled. "I can see your house from here."

"Will you get the hell off of there," my father yelled. He coughed.

She came onshore tail swishing and unusually demure. "This is heap big mojo," she said.

"It's a stunt," my father said.

"It's a heap big stunt."

"Dad."

He looked startled at the word.

"She's right," I said. "Anyone who could do this. I don't know how I could stop them."

"It's more than just you Fred."

I don't know why that surprised me. All this time I'd looked at Yan as my responsibility. Our discussions, our arguments, our experiments—our friendship—had helped to set him on his course. In some ways I had created him. But as I looked at our small group combined in common purpose before this halted ocean preternaturally silent before the wind and beneath the soundings of perplexed gulls I considered the conjunctions of necessity and obligation and fear and retribution that had bent us to this mission through this remnant stretch of deliquescing civilization. I was not alone and my reasons and resolve were not the only ones and to ignore this was not only arrogant but irresponsible. My friendship with Yan was not the thing at stake here. The safety of my little town was not the issue. Ariel's retribution for the horrific murder of her likely mate was not the reason why we stood upon this frozen shore. Nor Bob's justice for his tribe. The present world would vanish if we did not stop Yan. He and I were barely more than boys and it wasn't fair but there it was. If a child could perform a gesture that would eradicate your city didn't you owe it to your city to prevent that gesture. Even at the cost of the child.

That was my first taste of what my father meant about the haziness of victories and endings. None of us would feel good if we achieved our goal. My father had opened his memoir with a quote that we fight to keep something alive rather than expecting that we will triumph. I think that notion had colored every moment of his adult life. As it now would color mine.

"The nice thing about this view," said Ariel, "is that it'll still be here when we get back and we can light a big fire and toast marshmallows and sing Kum Bah Yah." She nodded inland. "But right now the fog has lifted and I'm looking at one bigass overgrown hacienda on the hill up there."

We turned to look and shielded our eyes from the sun and for the first time glimpsed the shrouded form of the enjungled castle that had been there all along, abiding in decay and half submerged in green as Ariel said, "Can't be many of those around, huh."

THIRTY-SIX

L a Cuesta Encantada, The Enchanted Hill. That's what the guy who built the damned thing called it. If he only knew.

Of Highway 1 there remained no trace save several oddshaped bushes grown around the shells of cars like illformed topiary figures in a ragged line. A vinetraced marker like a dolmen in the wild grass that read HEARST SAN SIMEON STATE HISTORICAL MONUMENT presided over a grove amid the asphalt chunks of former parking lot. Beyond this a planed and faintly mission style building stood brokenwindowed from bird impacts and envined and sagging from decades of wind and weathering. A faded bugspecked sign. HEARST SAN SIMEON VISITOR CENTER. Tall glass entrance cracked and dark. Rusting tour bus carcasses long a haven for raccoons and packrats and squirrels and birds. Fountains and statuary slimed and overgrown, humped shapes cowled in vine and weed and algae.

Beyond the Visitors' Center ruins we teased out the narrow path worn in the winding road that sloped toward what could be seen of the castle poking from its living shroud, forgotten capital of some longlost jungle civilization. Pale orange terracotta, scalloped marble, moorish tile.

Bob rumbled something guttural.

"He says this trail is recent," said Ariel, "and recently traveled, but not heavily trafficked."

"We're sure he's up there?" I felt foolish asking it.

My father rested a hand on the handle of his sword and studied the path ahead and the castle now hidden above. "He recorded his little love note in the mirror up there, I'm sure about that." He frowned. "I suppose he could have moved on, though it hadn't really occurred to me."

I laughed. My father looked annoyed. Ariel snorted. "Well, it is funny," she told him as she stepped ahead and began to lead us up the twisting narrow way.

N O PEDESTRIANS OR BICYCLES PAST THIS POINT. The original road had been wide enough for buses but the trail trod through the overgrowth was not. We walked single file and glanced about continually, senses heightened and gazes darting to every moving branch or cracking twig. The overgrowth was headhigh in places and most anything could be in there. I couldn't help remembering the first time I saw Ariel in the overgrown infield at the Del Mar racetrack the night of the vibe. How long ago. A few weeks. Could that be true. The distances we travel measure more than steps and miles.

Trees had grown to form a canopy overhead and we made our obscured way up the unkempt hill like fabled explorers searching out the source of public myth. Headwaters, temple, tomb.

At one point Bob pulled up short and the rest of us nearly collided as we halted. He put up a warning hand and readied his plastic javelin and stood watching something with his head cocked at an alarming angle. He was three feet taller than any of us and could see out over the tall growth and so had taken up the lead with Ariel behind him.

Behind me Dr. Ram kept whispering What, what is it, what, until my father snapped back Raj will you shut the fuck up.

We stood silent amid rustle and cicadas and plaintive crows.

Then came Ariel's braying laugh which I was coming to hate. She said Take a look and moved aside into the brush for us to pass her by. We crowded ahead of Bob and parted the tall grass and looked out on the wilded hills where a herd of horselike creatures with brushy manes and ropey tails stood grazing striped in black and white. A few stood watching Bob.

"What's he done to them," I whispered.

"They're zebras," said my father. "They really look like that."

"They are native to Africa," said Dr. Ram. "Apparently Mr. Hearst maintained a herd of them."

My father crouched looking at the zebras. "Apparently."

"He used to keep anything else around here?" I asked. "Lions?"

"And tigers and bears oh my," my father said. We stared at him and he shook his head nevermind.

"It's not exactly looking ominous so far," said Ariel.

"And that was when the horror began." My father stood and turned his back to the zebras and stretched and coughed. "If he's here he's got the alicorn and the uranium. Can you feel them."

A furrow appeared between her eyes and she shook her head.

"He could have put them in stasis," I said. "You wouldn't feel them if he did."

Bob guttured something.

"He says it's stupid to talk about it," said Ariel, "when we'll find out if we keep going."

"Point taken," said my father and nodded at the centaur standing in the brush. "Lead on MacBob."

Bob stopped and cocked his head again. He pointed with his spear and we saw something shimmering ahead. I thought it might be another bubble, one of the zones in which the pre-Change laws applied. But as we cautiously neared I saw that it was some kind of netting that had been stretched across the road and put into stasis. There was something odd about the way it looked even apart from the mirroring stasis. It seemed insubstantial somehow.

"Don't touch it," I said. "There's something weird about it."

"Let's just go around it," said my father.

We looked and saw that we couldn't. The net was tied to a tree growing out of a nearly vertical stretch of hillside to our left and another tree growing up from the road's sheer dropoff to our right, about the most effective place on the access road an obstacle could have been placed. We couldn't climb over it and we couldn't go off the road to go around it without having to climb the hill the rest of the way. Which was an option but not one we wanted to explore because the hill would be rough going and we'd be in plain sight to anyone in the buildings on top.

"If it's just a stasis field we should be able to climb it, right, Fred."

I picked up a branch and tossed it at the net. Something buzzed and the branch seemed to go through it. "I don't think it's just a stasis field," I said.

My father raised his eyebrows and picked up a bigger branch and touched it to the netting and the buzzing sounded and it looked as if the net ate the end of the branch. Sawdust fell below it. My father frowned at what was left of the branch and then swung it hard at the net and completed the swing with less branch than he started with. The net didn't so much as waver.

He tossed away the stump. "Can you undo this, Fred."

"If I can figure out how he made it work maybe." I stared at the silvery netting. Looked away. In the corner of my eye the netting seemed to flicker. When I looked straight at it the netting seemed more solid. I asked the others if they saw the same thing.

"It's flickering," said Ariel.

"Like a fluorescent light," my father said.

Everyone but Dr. Ram regarded him blankly.

"Fluorescent lights didn't shine steadily. They strobed, faster than you could really see. The effect was that they were on all the time but they weren't."

Dr. Ram nodded. "I remember you could tell when they were going bad because the flickering became very obvious. Many people got headaches."

"So why does it eat the branch," I said.

Ariel studied the shimmering net. "It's turning on and off all the time. When it's off the branch can move into its space. When it's on it slices the branch where it's touching the net."

"So if we try to push past it or climb it or even take it down—" I said.

"Nnnyyyeeeooowww," said my father.

I looked at the ground along the base of the net. Faint line of fine dust and wood particles and the bones of several birds.

"I wonder if something in stasis could get through," said Ariel.

My father drew his sword and slashed at the netting. The blade bounced off it with a leaden clack and the netting rippled slightly. My father looked at the mirrored blade and shrugged and sheathed it. "I'm guessing no."

"When the stasis is on it's just hitting another stasis," I said. "Two impenetrable objects."

Bob eyed the netting and raised his spear and then lowered it again.

Ariel slowly turned her head left and right, looking at some indeterminate point and studying the netting in her peripheral vision. "A hundred thirteen times a second," she said. "What if your stasis flickered at the same rate."

My father stared. "Sometimes you amaze me."

"Only sometimes?"

"What about it Fred."

"Sometimes she amazes me too."

"I mean the flickering, smartass."

"I know. It's worth a try. I can't work it on your sword though."

"We'll figure something out."

———————

We figured something out. I opened a pentagram casting and put a branch in a stasis bottle and added the timer instruction, modified to turn off and on a hundred thirteen times a second. A shimmering branch lay before me now and I unsealed the pentagram and said, "Okay let's give it a try."

"Okay," said my father. "How do we pick it up."

I stared at the blurring branch on the ground before me. Ariel laughed. I glared. "Sorry," she said. "But it is funny."

———————

I put two branches in permanent stasis and used them as tongs to quickly pick up the flickering branch. It rattled like some living thing in my hand as the flickering stasis hit the permanent one and I flung it quickly at the net. It hit and tangled and hung.

"That's good, right," my father said. "That's what it would've done if it was just a stick you threw at a net."

"I think so."

"Good enough for me." H pulled his sword from his beltloop and set it on the ground and pulled his old Buck knife from a pocket. "My turn."

———————

First I made several casting bottles that would make the flickering stasis fields because it seemed like a good thing to have handy. Then my father stood in front of the net with his sword at his feet and his knife open in his hand and I said *flicker dad* and he became shimmery.

I glanced at Ariel and she raised an eyebrow. That's how it looked anyway.

The shimmering blur that was my father grabbed the net and began sawing with the knife. It was disconcerting to watch him move. You could see him plainly but your gaze wouldn't fix on him. He always looked out of focus.

He cut a slit in the net from as high as he could reach down to the ground and stepped through it and drew it aside. He had to keep moving around because the strobing field below his feet was digging into the road. Dr. Ram picked up his sword and walked through the opened flap. I motioned to Bob and he bent unnervingly forward and my father pulled the flap wider and Bob carefully stepped through.

Ariel looked at me and I gestured at the net. "Ladies first."

She sniffed. "Let's go with age before beauty." She lowered her head and walked through.

I shoved my new bottle spells in my pocket and grabbed up my pack and felt very pleased with myself as I went through the net. As long as Yan kept underestimating me we'd be just—

And then the attack hit and I realized that the net wasn't the trap. Getting through it was.

---

n o fred. freddie. put it down. i said put it down. did you hear me she comes dark big angry full of love. clean sheets drying on the line. stern melody her voice. liquid eyes worried. freddie take that out of your mouth right now you hear me. laughing its a game. okay buddy you had your chance. but smiling as she stoops. enveloping smell of her. im lifted. im lifted. her face my world. give me that now. squeal and wave the hard sharp rusty metal no. honest abe laughs in his stall. support of her strong arm. free hand reaches. dont let her take the rusty metal its a game. she looks annoyed. laugh again and poke her with it. poking tickles but she doesnt laugh. ow she says and slaps my hand and knocks it away. i start to cry.

she says fred that hurt. starts to grin. that hurt fred. she wont stop grinning. eyeballs bulge and mouth stretch wide. lips pull back to gums. her teeth. arms clench. momma i cant breathe. that hurt did you hear me. cant breathe momma. grinning angry staring crazy that hurt momma cant breathe holding me she falls and silence doesnt move doesnt breathe

momma

grip relaxes. crawl out. crawl up. face not angry not laughing sleeping peaceful now

momma

head against her chest no heartbeat hole in her shirt the puckered wound

momma

eyes open terrifying wide crazy white around her pupils

that hurt fred you killed me and it hurt

no momma i didnt

you killed me and it hurt a lot

no i didnt mean it

it still hurts fred it always will

i didnt mean it momma what can i do

always will unless you bring me back fred you can bring me back and take the hurt away

i miss you momma daddy misses you we want you back ill bring you back just tell me how

its easy freddie just trade places with me

trade places

thats all you have to do trade places with me and ill be back and it wont hurt ill be with daddy and he wont be sad anymore dont you want that freddie dont you love me

i love you momma i love you but how can i trade places with you

oh thats easy baby all you have to do is die

i have to die momma

just like momma did for you honey

i didnt mean it momma

no you didnt but you can make it better freddie you can make it all okay again dont you want that baby

momma i miss you so much im so sorry

its okay freddie mommas here let momma help you make it better just relax and let me trade with you

momma im scared

wont hurt baby just like going to sleep

im sca

cool hands on my face. the pale palms the dark backs. her smell. my mothers smell. hands on my shoulders pressing firm. slide to my neck and grip. grip tighter. momma i cant breathe but cant tell her now the words are stuck. momma let me go youre

shhh shh its okay

momma hurting i cant

ill be back with daddy baby and you wont have to feel bad all the time

you wouldnt hurt me momma my momma wouldnt hurt me

let go freddie just let go just go to sleep

my momma wouldnt hurt me you cant be my momma loves me

My hands came up and found her clenching hands. My mother's hands. Dug into her fingers. Into my own neck. Dark spots forming in my vision. Red periphery. Face hot. Highpitched whine. Fight her. Fight it. Fight this thing.

The wide-eyed rictus fell across her face again. "Trade with me Freddie. Trade with me you little fuck. You owe me a life you son of a bitch."

I pried fingers from my neck. Saw her face transforming as my vision darkened. Saw her forehead bulge and split and her teeth lengthen and her pupils split to twinned ovals and her hair fuse into blind worms writhing. All her agony become glee now.

I got her claws off my throat and gagged and pushed her back and tried to say you're not my mother but could only cough.

And felt my hands on dirt and dead leaves and my knees on the dirt road.

And heard my father's frightening distorted voice. "I bind you with the chains of obligation. I hold you to your word as I've held mine. I entreat your masters to remand you and abjure your violation. You have no province here. You have no right. You have no right. You have no right."

My cheeks were wet, my eyes burned, my pulse pounded in my head. Hands on my shoulders. "Breathe, Fred." Dr. Ram's voice. "Breathe." He helped me sit back and I looked up at black spots swimming in daylight patches between overhanging branches. I closed my eyes and thought I felt those clenching hands again and struggled and looked around and tried to stand. Dr. Ram held me down and ordered me to breathe.

I blinked and wiped my eyes and saw my father. Blurred and pacing before some dwindling shape and saying in a voice distorted that You have no right, you have no right, until the shape was gone. I said *unflicker dad* and he came into focus deathly pale and shaken. He looked surprised and looked around. "It's gone," he said.

"You—" I coughed, spat, coughed again. "Saw?"

"It was really here," said Ariel.

"What. Was. Really here."

My father regarded the road ahead. "The loa," he said. "The loa was really here."

"How could he know. I mean I expect ruthlessness, you know. The gloves have been off since his little mirrorgram. But how could he know to do this to Fred."

I drank water but it only made me cough and burned my raw throat. I sat where I had fallen. My father and Ariel stood off to one side talking and he kept an eye on me. Dr. Ram had taken off his pack and sat it at his feet and stood staring down at it.

I coughed and cleared my throat and said, "When we wanted to move the Surfliner we needed some castings. Me and Yan went to the—to your house and took some grimoires. I think—"

"He stole my journal."

I nodded and felt ashamed. "He must have. I told him about our fight that night I left so he knew about it. I'm so sorry."

He only nodded and looked up the remnant road toward the shambled castle on the hilltop. Metal in his gaze. He took a deep breath and did not look at Dr. Ram as he said "Raj."

Dr. Ram had knelt and opened his pack and was staring down into it. "I know, Peter."

"Just don't get in my way. That's all I'll say."

Dr. Ram shut the packflap and stood and put on the pack and buckled the waist and chest straps and looked at my father who did not look away as he asked if I was ready.

I wasn't but I said I was. I got to my feet and put on my pack and wondered what could be holding my father upright now apart from sheer resolve. Yet he seemed impatient to embrace whatever else awaited us ahead.

He suggested I put the flicker stasis on him again so he could tie back the net flap. "We might be coming back this way in a hurry and I don't think we should try to cut it down because we might want to close it behind us."

When we were done with that he looked at me long and hard and asked if I really was okay to go on and I said probably not but let's go.

"Good man," he said. "Let's finish it."

THIRTY-SEVEN

Even overgrown and in decay the castle was impressive. Casa Grande, the main building, looked like a spanish cathedral with two moorish spires. Spires and stainedglass windows were broken and all the structures earthquake-cracked and embedded in vines, thick at the ground and spreading to fine green filigree tracing upward. Freestanding pillars had fallen to be strangled by weeds. Fractured mezzanines and overgrown walkways littered with glass shards and terracotta fragments, fallen stonework and broken corbels shaped like angry elephant heads. Palmtrees flourished where they'd been planted many years before and what had been carefully shaped hedges were now shaggy masses of wild reaching growth.

A nearby flight of steps half carpeted in grass and weeds and vines. Terracotta vases, one broken and one housing brittle dead stalks, flanked a debris laden flight of steps encircling what had been a marble fountain sculpted in deep relief. We climbed cautiously. I kept trying to see in all directions at once. The quiet was unnerving.

"Fred," my father said. "Breathe. Long breath." He took a long breath himself and let it out and then turned away and doubled over coughing as quietly as he could. The day was not yet hot but his shirt was sweatpatched.

At the top of the stairs we found ourselves on a winding esplanade of cracked and broken and upheaved tile littered with guano and leaves and fallen branches and lined with marble posts topped with white globes, most of them toppled and globes shattered, the few still upright bugfilled and dirtcaked.

"So what now," I said in a low voice. "Split up, stay together?"

"Stay together at first," my father said in a normal tone. "Split up if we don't find him."

"You think he isn't here? After what just happened?"

"He could have left that behind for us."

"Well if he's not here how will we know when to stop looking for him."

"Everybody leaves garbage. We don't find trash, we know he's not here."

"He could be hiding it."

Ariel snorted. "He set up shop in a castle. He isn't trying to hide."

Just north of the steps we had climbed was an elliptical marble pool filled with rotting vegetation and sludge, bracketed by parentheses of colonnaded marble walkways slick with algae, all enframing a Roman temple facade that had been a ruin a thousand years before the Change. Atop the columned portico pale marble figures adored a bearded fellow with a trident; Ariel said that he was Neptune. Spaced about were filthy globes that had been lights atop squared columns carved in shapes of men, many of them toppled and broken. I could only imagine what this pool had looked like long ago but it retained a wasted beauty in a ruined autumnal way.

This high up the sun had failed to burn away the final wisps of morning mist. Desiccated leaves crunched underfoot as I walked on cracked and diamond patterned tile to inspect a clouded marble wall. I kicked away a clot of brittle leaves and dirt and frowned at the tiles and used my foot to sweep away some more. The paint had dried and flaked but there was no mistaking that I stood within a pentagram.

I looked at the marble wall. Imagined Yan in front of it flipping pages full of large and clumsy writing, faint mist tendrils drifting slowly behind him. A scene I'd recently seen framed by an oval of cherry wood in the middle of a crumbling freeway just before my first sight of centaurs. I PUT SOME HURDELS BETWEEN U & ME TO MAKE IT WORTH OUR TIME. Guess you did you son of a bitch.

Dr. Ram walked by and saw the pentagram and looked at me with eyebrows raised.

"He made the message here," I said. "The mirror was where I'm standing now."

He nodded slowly. He'd hardly said a word since we'd gone through the net. Angry as I was I felt bad for him.

"Yo!" from Ariel. We hurried across the esplanade and up a long flight of stairs to where she stood beside a metal shopping cart lying sideways atop crushed weeds near an arched portico. My father raised an eyebrow at Ariel. "Reassessing this whole 'evil wizard and his orc army' thing?"

"It does seem kind of dinky," she allowed.

"So the talking mirrors and stasis grenades and centaurs out hunting us down. . . ."

"Trades," I said. "One-offs. Yan's a pretty good salesman."

We looked at each other and we knew what we were thinking.

"He doesn't need an army to change the world," said Ariel. "He just needs a casting that works."

I knew she was right. Yan was as she'd told us, powerful and without conscience. The line he'd crossed back on the access road had not even recognized a boundary. But even so our big heroic mission suddenly seemed none of those things.

————————

We walked around the buildings looking for trash. It took an hour and yielded nothing. I suggested we split up and start going through the buildings themselves but my father said no.

"We're kind of obvious in a group," I persisted.

"Gosh it looks dangerous," he said. "Let's split up."

"How about I go with Fred and you go with Doc," said Ariel. "I think Bob can take care of himself."

He eyed her a moment and then said, "Okay. We'll try the guesthouse thing down there. Yell if you find anything."

"Loud and clear."

We watched them walk down the weedy steps toward the vinedraped guesthouse.

Ariel asked Bob where he wanted to search and the centaur stamped the tile with his heavy PVC spear. It sounded like the tile cracked beneath it.

"Good idea," said Ariel. "Yell if you see anything. Fred?"

She and I turned away.

"You paired them up because you don't trust what Dr. Ram will do if he finds Yan first," I said.

She looked surprised. "See, you get out on the road with someone and they get all cozy with how you think."

"But now you want us to split up because you don't want to be hampered by me if you find him, right."

"I can't find him because I'm hampered by you."

I studied her. She had to know she was also allowing the possibility of me finding Yan by myself too. "Okay," I said.

She nodded and started away and then stopped. "Listen Fred. He stopped the ocean. He just shit on any remnant of your friendship in a way no stranger ever could have. He'll kill us all with a word if we let him. Don't give him the chance to."

"I have a few words of my own."

"Well say yours first." She started away, silent on cracked tile and marble shards. She will find him, I thought. Of all of us she will find him and she won't hesitate, won't let him act or explain or deny. She'll just kill him outright and come back and say, I found him. Or maybe kill him and come back and say, I couldn't find him.

And why shouldn't she. Why shouldn't I.

I glanced at Bob. Brutal argus slowly scanning. As much a chance we'll flush out Yan across Bob's path as find him and confront him. Deep breaths. My father's advice. Insects ratcheting deep within the brush. Glanced around. All right.

Ariel was right. Yan knew me deeply. And I knew Yan. So I headed for the proud and beat cathedral of the main building.

Despite my urgency it was impossible to rush through this luxurious decrepitude. Enormous rooms with ornate carved wooden ceilings. Musty carpets moldering on warped floorboards. Faded tapestries sagging on stained walls. Grecian vases surprisingly intact on heavy wooden shelves adorned with packrat nests and cobwebs. Massive desks and tables spotted with guano and sprinkled with rodent droppings. Paintings oddly pristine but for dust. Greek and Roman statuettes and busts in bronze and marble. I had never seen anything like it and never would again. I could not believe all this had belonged to a single man. It was a hoard. Beautiful and orderly and artfully arranged but a hoard nonetheless. This main building must have held a hundred rooms, each crammed with the cream of many civilizations' artwork gone to anonymity and rot, yearning through the layered dust to find a witness. Living here would be impossibly inconvenient but seeing it I understood why Yan would do it. Whoever lived here was a king. Whoever lived here wanted most of all to be engulfed by art and artifice from that lost world and through some sympathetic magic make that world his own. It even spoke to me though I did not respond or even understand its language. But Yan would. Yan would.

Backpack hanging off one shoulder I went quietly through dirt and dust as if trespassing in a tomb. There was so much to take in and I could stop for none of it. I had some idea where Yan might be. Dr. Ram's picture book had shown an opulent bedroom in each of the towers. The Celestial Suites. I mean come on.

Ten minutes later I climbed a set of narrow stairs and found myself in a small octagonal room lined with gold damask draperies alternating with ornately carved wooden panels that looked out on the misty countryside. On one panel a disquieting painting of a man upon a horse regarding a weathered and noseless stone head upon a desert plain. A chandelier of gilded leaves hung dark and dust-topped from the rococo ceiling. A massive carved headboard and bedposts nearly obscured the gold-linened bed against a recessed wall panel overseen by a marble sculpture of a man in a robe.

The rumpled slept-in bed. Bracketed by gilded candelabra holding long tapers beaded with melted wax. On the pale brown carpeted floor beside it a silver tray with a tea service, empty Aquafina bottle, orange rinds.

I set my backpack on the bed and picked up the tray. The cup empty and the teabag beside it faintly damp. Droplets constellating the interior of the empty plastic waterbottle. Orange rinds slimy with pulp.

One arabesqued wall panel was a door that opened out onto a catwalk running between the towers. To my right the brokentiled circumflex of roof capped a low wall of blue and yellow geometric tiles. To my left stone lions stood hindlegged, paws up and backs against globed colonnades carved in snaking spirals. Birdshit everywhere. Dirt and dead leaves carpeting the catwalk. Across from them a carved door in the north tower beneath still iron bells. The reverting estate and wild hills spread out below me. No wave broke on any shore down there, no sound of ocean carried on the cold salt air. I looked for Bob at sentry on the patchy esplanade but did not see him.

I let go my backpack and wiped my hands dry on my pants and picked up my backpack again and crunched through leaves to the north tower. Grabbed the handle in the carved door and without thinking pulled.

Draperies billowed toward me and I almost used a readied word.

This room looked much like the other. If the mess within were any clue he slept here more than in the other one. Empty bottles and wrappers and cans. A flannel shirt draped over a wooden chair. I crumpled it and held it to my face to breathe him in, forgetting that I could not smell a thing. I dropped it to the floor. Wondered could I do this even knowing that the price of failing to would be my world.

A metallic sculpture on the carpet caught my eye. A winged figure chromed and sparkling, out of place amid the wood and marble and tarnish. I picked it up and held it to the muted light. Not a sculpture but some kind of bird transfixed midflight, its wingbeat never to be finished. My face in that dim room reflected and distorted countless times upon its quills and vanes.

"I can do this," I said to it and fogged my image in its uncorroborating eye.

THIRTY-EIGHT

A few minutes later I found where he'd been working.

A dim hall on the third floor led me to some kind of library or study with lattice-grilled bookshelves topped with sculptures lining trefoil-windowed walls. Vaulted ceiling arches with faded intricate designs gave the impression of being in the hold of some great ship or deep within some wellappointed catacomb. Tinted by the mist outside the light seemed winter harsh.

Near the entrance were bookshelves full of mirrored objects.

Heavy chairs and a couch upholstered in pale gold damask had been shoved against the walls and a heavy round table turned on its side and rolled out of the way. The rug beneath had been rolled up to the relocated furniture and on the dull wood beneath was a pentagram painted in blood and broken at the cardinal points. In its center were a campstove and a pot and several books and an iron candelabrum bearing the severed head of a bearded goat.

Even though its cardinal points were broken I edged around the pentagram as if it were a deep well and could not take my gaze off of the empty slit gold eyes staring ever westward from the painted circle. Could not shake the image of my mother's eyes becoming twinned slit pupils. I think you could have heard my heartbeat in the hall.

On the far end of the room pale shafts of light slanted above a heavy table of dark red wood covered with books, notepads, candles, cups, food wrappers. The floor around it littered with mirrored balls and sculptures and cubes. I set my pack in a chair that had to have been several hundred years old and I looked at the table a while before I read the titles on some of the books and picked up the notebooks and turned bottom-curled pages past arcana, hex diagrams, heavy arrows indicating lines of force, scribbled ingredients and inflection notes. Yan's writing was hurried and his work increasingly obscure. It had a fevered air as if he had been amanuensis to some fast-talking muse that would visit only once.

I set down a notebook and glanced around the room. How could a place so alien to me feel so familiar. And asking the question gave me the answer. It felt like the Surfliner. Our adopted and adapted and relocated sleeping car where we had set up shop and covered every surface with books and notes and ingredients and failed experiments as we began the search for knowledge that had led us by such unexpected pathways to this house of rotting splendor. For some reason I thought of the painting in the tower room of the man on horseback staring at the ancient figure slowly being reclaimed by the desert waste.

The notebook opened to a clumsy drawing of a spiral horn. I felt a shock go through me and began to read Yan's scrawl as best I could. And there it was in careless ink on yellow paper.

The casting to reverse the Change was like some epic novel he'd been working on. He'd written notes and studies and then made changes, erasing and amending and revising. Trying to get it right on paper before casting it in life.

I skipped ahead and studied the most recent iteration.

Yan had reasoned that he didn't need to change the universe's laws for the entire universe. The scale and energy required were unimaginable and probably unattainable. He only needed to change the rules in a tiny area, a point, a collection of atoms. A focused violent casting into a dense and potent mass that would force a few of that mass's molecules to operate in a different state by a different set of rules. Once the effect was achieved he only needed it to spread to surrounding particles. He'd decided that the best way to do this would be to use the Changed particles themselves. They would radiate the elements that altered particles they encountered which in turn would radiate as they Changed, a spreading wave of tiny macro spells changing the state of particles and ejecting more macro spells that did the same to any particles they encountered until there was nothing left to change.

It was brutal and blunt and ugly, and breathtaking. Because it felt right. Because it ought to work. Reading it there on the page I felt it in my marrow. Yan had the materials and the method and the casting that could make this happen, set off a detonation like one of the atomic weapons of my father's time that themselves had torn apart the fabric of the real, the fundamental particles of its composition. Which for all I know is where he'd gotten the idea. But this detonation would spread across the world and change its rules to what they had been thirty years ago. Or in another sense he would spread the germ of the old world throughout the new and infected particles would themselves become agents of change. He'd done it already, on a small scale. We had felt the ripple of that demonstration as we flew above the mountains and had seen a blister it had left upon the slope beside the road where Dr. Ram had fired his newfound gun. The bubble that contained the old world's rules. In that trial run such blisters had been scattered everywhere, pockets within which the old world's rules held sway. One had formed up here as well. His notes referred to it but did not mention where it was.

He was so close to manifesting it. It was there on the page, there in isolated pockets in the world.

As I read I could not shake a feeling that at any moment I'd look up from Yan's notes and see him standing there. Until at one point I looked up and there he was. Walking through the doorway framed within the room's arched ribs like one of the many paintings on the many walls. One hand held a bottle of water and the other held a halfpeeled orange to his mouth. His face gaunt and his eyes hollow and his skin pale and his hair falling out.

He bit down on his orange. He saw me. He stopped short. We looked at each other. We both had words for such a time. Ariel had nearly begged me not to hesitate when I saw him. He had just tried to kill me on the access road with a betrayal pure as any love. He was crazy and ruthless and selfish and on the verge of destroying an entire world. I had every reason to kill him with a word without preamble.

"Yan," I said.

He resumed chewing on his orange. Swallowed. "Hello Fred. I'd about given up on you. Where's your father."

I studied him. Watching for the move. The word. "You stole his journal and found out about my mom and cut a deal with the loas. Where do you think he is."

"Looking for me I'm sure." He held out his orange and I shook my head. "But I'm impressed you got by. Good for you Fred. How'd you do it."

"I don't think I want to tell you."

"All right. What do you want to tell me."

I thought of words I'd have to use. Not yet. "I have a business proposition for you."

"A what." He laughed. I tried not to flinch when he moved to scratch his head. Strands of hair fell out. "You came all this way to give me a business proposition."

"No. I came all this way to stop you from reversing the Change. But I thought the best way to do that would be to come up with something else you'd be as interested in doing."

He spat a bloody clot. "What could possibly be as interesting as taking the world back to the way things used to be."

"Running it."

"Beg pardon."

"Running the world."

He grinned. His gums were bleeding. "You're just stalling till your father gets here."

"I'm trying to tell you this before my father gets here."

He shrugged. "Okay. We're at the swap meet. Sell me in two lines."

I took a breath. "I think spellware is the foundation for bringing civilization back from the margins. I think you and I can apply what we've learned and sell it and ride it all the way. I think—"

"Two lines, Fred."

My heart was hammering. "Okay. What do you think."

"I think it's interesting." He scratched his head and held his hand out. "And I think you don't mean a word of it. I also think my hair is falling out."

"Your—" I almost said Your father. "You're sick. It's radiation. From San Onofre."

"Yes. Ruling the world doesn't seem like a very longterm prospect, does it."

"Neither does changing it back."

"Maybe not." His sickly grin. "Probably not. But ruling this one with you isn't something I can do ten minutes from now. And changing it is."

He bit into his orange.

I said *spain*.

The severed goathead mirrored.

Yan looked surprised.

I said *flout*.

The goathead flew off the candelabrum and crashed into a bookcase and hit the floor. The candelabrum fell over.

Yan stared at me in outright disbelief. He should have been in stasis. Failing that he should have been slammed across the room by a blunt-force spell. Somehow my castings had deflected to the goathead. To be sure I said *despain* and the goathead became unmirrored.

He spat out the bloodied orange pulp and shook his head at the splintered bookcase. "You fucker," he said. He sounded really offended. "I don't believe it." He pointed at me and opened his mouth and I threw a marble paperweight and hit him in the chest as he said *uno* and his arm moved and something hot streaked by my head and set fire to a dusty tapestry on the wall. He put a hand to his chest and opened the other to the blazing tapestry and squeezed and pulled and the tapestry flew off the wall and landed on me just as I said *crib*.

Burning fabric covered me. Moving was suddenly difficult as if I were immersed in some thick liquid. The tapestry's weight pressed down on me but I could not feel the tapestry itself. I felt the heat but not the fire. I strained to move and slowly pulled it off me but the fabric shredded as I touched it. The room had gone blurry. I had put myself in the flickering stasis I had rigged to get us by his boobytrapped net. The world shimmered around me. I flickered in and out of the world. The fire's heat reached me but not the flame. I could move when the stasis flicked off. Momentum carried me to the next off moment. Time and light were behaving oddly. It was like I was wearing a stasis suit and moving underwater.

Yan said another word that came to me distorted and the world went white and faded slowly back still blurred. Whatever he'd tried to hit me with the reflecting stasis around me had been enough to ward it off.

I strained to pull the tapestry off me, to get away from the burning, to speak the words that would undo the stasis. *Crib off.*

The world clarified. Tapestry burning on the floor. Room full of smoke. Yan nowhere in sight. I had no notion how much time had passed.

Ariel had been right. I'd tried to talk him out of it. But I knew Yan. I had thought the best way to make him give up his toy wasn't to fight him over it but to offer him a new one he might like just as much. But at least I hadn't hesitated when I'd known he was past bargaining. He'd been ready for me but I'd given him a chance and he hadn't taken it and I'd struck. I suppose that's something.

I grabbed my torn backpack and Yan's notebook and hurried from the burning gothic library.

––––––––––––––

I stood blinking in sunshine and realized Bob was staring at me expectantly. Ariel stood beside him and my father and Dr. Ram hurried toward us from the direction of a guesthouse. I glanced back and saw what had sent them running my way. Smoke poured from a grated window high up.

"I saw him," I said. "Upstairs. He's been living in different rooms and working in a library. He's sick. Radiation sick. He only knows that me and my father are here. We traded shots and he got away. You didn't see him?"

Bob jerked his head negative.

"I was back where I could see two of the side entrances," said Ariel. "Didn't see him."

My father and Dr. Ram rounded the leaf-filled central fountain and came up. My father was winded and his face glistened with sweat.

I held up Yan's notebook. "He's figured it out. I think he can do it. I think that may be where he's headed now that he knows I'm here. There's one of those zones here, one of those bubbles where the old rules work. If I were him I'd head there. Ariel and Bob couldn't get to him and my castings wouldn't work."

"But neither would his," my father said.

"He'd have stuff ready nearby. He'd set it up with bottle spells so he'd just need to activate them. I'm only guessing, but it's what I'd do."

"He can't have been that prepared," said Ariel.

"Why not."

"Cause me and Bob haven't disappeared."

"Well if he isn't that prepared I'll bet he's not far from it."

"Can you sense one of those bubbles the way you did coming down the Grapevine," my father asked Ariel.

"If we get close enough I can."

My father bent and put his hands on his knees and caught his breath. "Then let's get close enough," he said.

––––––––––––

We'd already covered the seaward side and near the main building and Ariel had sensed nothing so we circled around the inland side. Near the tennis courts her head shot up and her eyes went wide and a rainbow shimmer ran down her neck. "Here," she said. "It's here."

Dead leaves and branches on the fissured tennis courts, creeping ivy on the surrounding wall and fence, lazy smile of rotting court net sagging. "I don't see anything," my father said.

"It's here."

"There is a pool," said Dr. Ram. "Beneath the tennis courts."

My father stared at him. "Jesus christ, Raj, did you memorize that book."

Dr. Ram looked oddly embarrassed. "I used to be a very good student," he said, and shrugged.

––––––––––––

The Roman Pool was a favorite of San Simeon guests in the early evening, when sunlight gleamed from the mosaic tiles of hammered gold and delicate Venetian glass adorning the entire pool, walls, and ceiling.

We studied the photos in Dr. Ram's book and tried to figure out how to get in and what traps Yan might have set. The pool was long and lined with lighted columns. In the photographs the still clear water reflected the ornate ribbed ceiling and made the room look like some gilded ship's hull. I could not imagine it still resembled this. There were entrances at either end and Dr. Ram felt sure the door in the wall on the far side of the tennis courts led to dressing rooms that led down to the pool as well.

My father nodded at the building. The entrance we could see was set with high arched windows, many of them brokenpaned. "We'll be backlit if we try to come in from either end," he said. "I vote tennis court." He stood and wiped his hands on his pant legs. It hadn't been a vote at all of course. "Let's go. He knows we're here and any minute now he's gonna say abracadabra and fuck everything up. Ariel, you and Bob cover the ends but stay outside the zone." He indicated Bob's spear. "Use that if you get a shot," he said, and headed for the building without looking to see if we followed.

I glanced at Dr. Ram and didn't know what to say. It's here I thought. No turning back. But there always was no turning back.

Dr. Ram took a deep breath and nodded and unshouldered his pack and stood clutching it. I nodded back and hurried after my father.

———————

I pictured Yan below us looking up to follow our footsteps crunching through dead leaves as we made our way across the tennis courts and readying some surprise for when we appeared. So what if castings didn't work here. A couple of crossbow bolts would.

Midway across the tennis courts I heard faint pops directly behind me. I whirled and saw nothing. My father came up with his sword already drawn. I looked at the blade and realized what had happened. "My castings were undone," I said, and nodded at his sword. "We're in the zone."

"Shit," he said and sheathed the unmirrored blade. "That your only weapon now?"

I held up my baseball bat. "Yeah. Sorry."

Dr. Ram offered his crossbow. "Please. I am not a very good shot with it anyhow."

I glanced at my father and saw him weighing options. He would have to be up close to Yan to use his sword but knew he wouldn't hesitate to use the crossbow if he got a shot, whereas I might hesitate and Dr. Ram may very well have given up the crossbow to avoid the issue altogether. Should he take the crossbow himself and leave me and Dr. Ram effectively weaponless? But he nodded at me and I dropped my backpack and exchanged my bat for Dr. Ram's crossbow. It had a stock quiver with four more bolts. I told him Thanks.

My father took a deep breath and cleared his throat and wiped his mouth with his arm. "No bargaining. Are we clear."

"Very," I said.

"I understand, Peter," said Dr. Ram.

"Okay then. Let's do this."

T he door opened with some careful prodding. A room on one side was marked for men and the other for women. They used to care about men and women bathing and dressing and peeing in separate rooms, I've never been clear on why. We took the men's side down as quietly as we could, single file with my father in the lead and Dr. Ram behind me. The stairwell was dark but there was light enough below.

Midway down my father held up a hand and we stopped. We had come to a small balcony with an ornate railing that seemed to overlook the pool. The stairs continued down to pool level but my father pointed to the balcony and pulled sword and sheath from his beltloop and held up a hand again for us to wait and crept onto the balcony in a low crouch. He laid the sword on the dusty tilestrewn balcony floor and peered cautiously over the railing. Then he ducked back and turned to us and beckoned and put a finger to his lips. I held the crossbow low and level and duckwalked onto the balcony beside him and peered over the rail.

The room felt like a grotto. Gleaming cool dimlit cavernous sequestered. The floor was littered with fallen tiles and uneven where tremors had cracked the surface. Remaining tiles and much of the wall were slick with dark green algae except where gold gleamed through. The long rectangle of the pool stretched to either side below us. The water had long ago evaporated and the building had protected the tiled pool from all but a sprinkling of leaves and trash. A pushbroom lay beside a large area that had been swept clear. A pentagram was painted on the bottom of the pool.

Ariel stood in plain view just outside the south entrance framed with improbable perfection between marble Roman statues flanking the windows. She probably reckoned that Yan couldn't cast anything her way from within the bubble of pre-Change law he had created here and that she could likely deal with any nonmagical thing he might send her way. I looked for Bob's distinctive silhouette at the north entrance but could not see him.

Other than the pentagram there was no other sign of Yan. I was about to whisper to my father when loud rumbling echoed directly below us in the empty narrow feeder to the pool. My father peered over the rail and I quickly followed. Below us Yan walked toward the pentagram painted on the tiled pool pulling a dolly on which two long narrow objects lay. Dr. Ram stiffened when he saw Yan's sickly appearance.

Yan stopped to catch his breath outside the painted circle and I saw the objects were a yardlong rod of metal and a tapering length of spiral bone. He dusted his hands and turned toward the southern entrance and saw Ariel and stopped cold and said Son of a bitch. His voice reverberated in the pool.

"Hi asshole," Ariel called in. "I'm here about my friend."

He glanced around with such quick panic I don't think he'd have seen us if we'd stood in plain sight. "You can't come in here," he called back.

"Nope. But I can wait here till the sun turns cold. How bout you."

He glanced around again more calmly this time and seemed to relax. "Did Fred summon you."

"I brought him, dickhead. I'm all about the reunions. You and me for instance. Why don't you crawl up out of that slimy pool like you all did about a billion years ago and enjoy the sunshine out here."

Yan's laugh rang around us. "You won't be waiting there long."

My father squeezed my arm and whispered Shoot him.

I glanced down at the crossbow. He was right. I should shoot him.

I brought the crossbow up and set my cheek against the stock and sighted and my father had a coughing fit. I glanced at him and he frantically waved me on and I looked back and saw Yan looking up at us and saw him realize Ariel had just been stalling him. Then Dr. Ram stood and stepped to the balcony rail and Yan looked genuinely startled for the first time.

I sighted. Found the trigger. Held my breath.

And could not kill him while he was looking at his father.

"Shoot him." My father reached for the crossbow. I pulled it away. Numbly thinking He doesn't have a weapon and his casting won't work in here and he's half dead already for godsake. I don't have to shoot him.

I ran past my father and down the stairs followed by his hacking God damn it Fred. I emerged on the narrow slippery tiled walkway edging the pool and headed for the shallow end where Ariel stood looking in.

Above me Dr. Ram said Yanamandra.

Yan ignored him and dragged the rod and the alicorn from the dolly to the center of the pentagram and laid them down in an X.

My father clattering down the stairs.

Bob's silhouette at the northern entrance, spear held ready.

I jumped into the shallow end of the pool and slipped on slick tile and landed on my ass and stood again. I ran as best I could toward Yan and entered the pentagram and briefly wondered how Yan thought he would cast in a zone in which those rules no longer worked and then I was on him. I could have shot him but instead I swung the crossbow at his head.

He ducked and tried to trip me. I swung back but he crowded me and checked the blow. He grabbed me and we went down. I punched him weakly. He punched me in my broken ribs. My breath seized. My father's yells and footsteps echoed all around us. I held Yan and the crossbow and Yan held onto me. All our careful spells and traps and preparations had come down to two teenagers wrestling at the bottom of an empty pool. Journeys end in lovers meeting.

Then he got the crossbow away from me. He aimed it at my middle and didn't even hesitate to pull the trigger. The bowstring thumped and I flinched but felt nothing. The bolt had fallen out as we had grappled. He started to draw a new one from the stock quiver but gave that up and held the crossbow like a club as my father ran past me with sword drawn.

Glass crashed from the northern entrance.

Yan swung and my father blocked and a yard of PVC pipe suddenly jutted from above my father's hipbone.

Blade bit wood. My father yanked Yan toward him. Then his body caught up to what had just happened to it and he turned white and dropped hard to his knees. He held to his sword embedded in the crossbow stock but Yan wrenched the crossbow free and stepped back. Even as my father fell forward onto one hand he swung for Yan but Yan was out of range.

My father swung wildly and I jumped up and the blade passed under me and I sidestepped to avoid the backswing. Yan broke the stock to cock the draw and slapped a new bolt in the groove. His breath shook as he leveled the crossbow at me and then changed his mind and aimed it at my father.

A loud crack like the clap of two boards filled the tiled room and a fist-sized chunk of tile exploded from low on the pool wall behind Yan. The pieces pattered around us. Yan looked at me. Gaunt and holloweyed and strangely balding. He started to raise the crossbow but then lowered it and let it go and didn't look as it clattered loudly and discharged on the tile. The bolt hit the pool wall and bounced off.

Yan just stood there. Fred, he said. He put a hand to his chest and brought it up to look at it and his palm was red with blood. He looked up to the balcony at his father holding the pistol he had found the day we coasted down the mountain to the Central Plain and his eyes rolled and he pivoted and I saw the large red bleeding plug torn from his back as he augered to the floor.

My father made a horrible sound and rolled to his side curled up. His sword slipped from his hands. Only then did I understand he had been impaled by Bob's javelin.

"Pete," Ariel called from outside. I looked up. She stood outside the entrance a helpless world away. "Pete, hold on. Hold on." She sounded afraid. I had never heard her sound afraid.

His face was bonewhite when I went to him. Both hands gripped the painted spear. Tribal designs slathered with his own gore. I knelt beside him and put a hand on his hands but he shook his head and coughed a spray of blood and grated "Yan."

I looked at him a moment but had no idea what I could do so I went to Yan. He lay on his back with a small spot of blood on his chest but a thick dark pool of it spreading behind him on the tile. His eyelids fluttered and one leg kicked and one hand dug at a pants pocket. A stain spread at his crotch.

"Yan."

He tried to say something but all that came out was *luh, luh, luh*.

I heard Dr. Ram run down the walkway toward the shallow end of the pool. "Your father's coming," I heard myself say. I felt made out of wood. "He'll help you." I glanced up as Dr. Ram jumped into the pool. He still held the pistol.

Yan got his hand into his pocket. His eyes were bright. He said *luh, luh*. He brought his hand out holding a tiny mirrored frog.

My heart leapt and I pried the mirrored frog from his fingers. I held it slippery in my hand and thought wait a minute, we're in a zone where the old rules work, this thing should be just a frog. I looked at Yan and he was looking back at me and an awful glee shone in his eyes and I understood that by learning how to change the laws of this world to the old ones he had figured out how to violate that old world's rules as well. The way they had been violated to cause the Change in the first place. The violation itself lay in my hand. Here was the paper strip in the chocolate kiss, the deliberate crack that would undo the stasis spell that was the world. And it didn't matter who was holding it, it mattered what was said to it. And I turned to cover Yan's mouth but he inhaled raggedly and said *logos* with his final breath. And the light in his eyes was nothing but gloat before it dulled to mere reflection. And the mirrored frog became a living animal in my hand as the casting unlocked and the pentagram sealed and the world began to change.

THIRTY-NINE

I heard Ariel yell for Bob to run. I heard her yell for us to bring my father. I watched her look helplessly through the brokenpaned entrance a moment longer and then bolt away. Rod and horn crossed in the pentagram. My father curled around the length of shaft that ran him through, struggling to raise himself on one elbow. Yan staring sightless past the ceiling, wrongly still, the final shape of his last word still on his lips. Dr. Ram still clutching his pistol as he knelt beside the body of his son.

"Dr. Ram. Dr. Ram. My dad's hurt. He needs your help."

His grip tightened on the pistol but I wasn't sure he heard me. He felt Yan's neck for a pulse. Then he yelled and he raised the gun and in a moment of insane clarity I thought he was going to kill me. He fired. I flinched. He kept firing. The sound enormous in the empty pool. Tile fragments stung my arms. Glass blew outward. The gun clicked and clicked long after it was out of bullets and Dr. Ram's yell had become a hoarse inhuman sob torn from his very core.

What stopped him was my father's hand upon his leg. He'd managed to prop himself up on one arm and reach out and Dr. Ram looked dumbly down at him, breathing hard but suddenly focused.

"Ow," my father said.

———————

He screamed when we deadcarried him up the steps at the shallow end of the pool. There was strangely little blood. The javelin corking it for

now. We set him down outside the entrance and I stayed with him while
Dr. Ram went back inside to get the dolly. Ariel and Bob stood watching
near the Casa Grande several hundred feet away. My father panting and
pale.

"Can I do anything."

"Raj."

"He'll be right here. He's getting a dolly for you."

He closed his eyes. I watched the javelin waver with his heartbeat.
"Yan?"

I looked into the empty Roman pool at Dr. Ram hugging the horribly
loose body of his son. Alive not two minutes ago. Moving, breathing, talking. How could that be. "We stopped him. Don't talk." And felt tears and
welling panic yawn a deep abyss inside me.

He craned his head and saw and let out a long breath. "Sorry."

Approaching clatter. I looked up to see Dr. Ram pulling the cart up the
steps and out into the daylight. Arms and chest dark with his son's blood.
Eyes unearthly bright. He looked like someone looking at something very
far away. "He's here now," I told my father. "Hold on."

"Ariel?"

"She's right over there. We're taking you to her, Dad. Hold on."

"Kay."

We lifted him onto the dolly as carefully as we could. It looked agoniz-
ing and he yelled again. Dr. Ram pulled the dolly and I ran alongside and
held my father's hand.

His grip became surprisingly strong. "Fred."

"Right here, Dad."

He shook his head. "Fred," he said and lifted his head to look back at
the pool.

Then I understood. "Let's get you to Ariel first." The smeared and
painted length of spear impaling him incongruous and alien.

Ariel and Bob had backed up to the fountain now. We reached them
and Ariel lowered her muzzle close to my father and said Aw shit.

My father lay back and closed his eyes and said I think it's gonna
bruise.

Dr. Ram set down his pack and pulled things from it and began to
work on my father. I could not imagine what he could do for him. I could

not imagine how he could do it in the face of what he had just lost. As if he had just cut off one of his own limbs.

I straightened and Bob was staring at me. He said something guttural and mimed throwing and pointed.

"He saw Yan get the crossbow from you," said Ariel, "and he threw at him and Pete got in the way."

"I know."

Bob said something else to me.

"He asks if he owes you a blood debt."

"I don't. . . ." I couldn't make words connect. Couldn't make things matter or mean.

"You have to answer him directly. He needs to know if you're going to try to kill him."

"I need to get my father's sword."

"Tell him yes or no."

"Tell him fuck you."

I heard Ariel say something to Bob as I left them. Bob's grunted reply.

Dr. Ram had closed Yan's eyes. Despite my urgency I could not help but squat there in the empty pool staring and trying to find a name for what I felt. The place where I had loved him felt like stone. The darkly clotted blood surrounding him was smeared and shoeprint-patterned. The pentagram—

The pentagram was sealed. Rod and alicorn were fusing. The rift would soon appear and the old rules working in this fixed point would wash across the globe as the world spun into it, spreading west as we turned east.

I kissed Yan's forehead and retrieved my father's sword and sheath from where he'd dropped them at the bottom of the tiled pool.

"Stay with me Peter," Dr. Ram was telling my father.

"Still here. What—" his teeth showed in a horrible parody of a grin "—do?"

He lay curled on his side with the obscene length of javelin topmost.

Dr. Ram looked at all of us as he spoke to my father. "Right now the spear is obstructing the arterial bleeding. If I remove it the bleeding will be very heavy."

"How long."

"Minutes."

"Leave it? Till we—" the javelin shook as he drew a harsh breath "—somewhere?"

Dr. Ram knelt before him. Set a hand on his shoulder. "Peter. This has pierced your bowel. The wound is septic. There will be infection I cannot stop."

"How long."

"Days. It will be very painful."

My father laughed. "Thought the cough was bad."

I looked at Ariel. Who merely watched. I thought frantically about what castings I knew. What forces I could bring to bear. What Ariel refused to do. "I could put him in stasis," I said. "We could bring him back with us."

Dr. Ram only looked down. "Even if we fixed this, with his lungs. . . ." He shrugged. "I am sorry, Fred. But it would only postpone what is going to happen to him."

"Better . . . this way."

"Dad you don't know what could happen." I looked at Dr. Ram. "What would he have, three months? Six? You don't know what we could come up with in six months. What I could come up with."

"Fred," my father said. "It's okay."

"The fuck it is. You're not a quitter." I turned on Ariel. "You could fix this. You could fix all of it, now."

She turned away from all of us and looked out at the ocean and said The waves are crashing again.

"So what. So fucking what. Of course they're crashing. Yan's dead. His casting's started. What the fuck does—"

"It'll come out of the east," she said, still looking at the landless west. "Won't it. The world will revolve into it. We'll revolve into it. A thousand miles an hour spreading west. But we'll be last because we're on this side of the line. It's happening now. I can feel it. Can't you feel it. Tomorrow all your spells and all your stasis castings will be gone. Bob and all his people. Me and all mine. Our world." She turned to me. "Yours."

"What the fuck am I supposed to do. It's already started."

"How do you stop a casting once it's started."

"You don't. Not from outside the pentagram."

"The pentagram is sealed."

"Of course it's sealed. Otherwise the casting wouldn't work."

"What happens if you breach it."

"This is pointless. We need to—"

"What happens if you breach it."

"You're safe inside it when you breach it at the cardinal points. That's how you get out in the first place. You know this, why are you—"

"What happens if you breach it from the outside."

I remembered light and heat and fear the night of the vibe at the racetrack. Huddling in my protected zone while the world around me whited out. The fire geyser rising from the burning infield. "All the casting's energy is directed out the breach. You could do it with a piece of iron but you'd get killed."

We turned at the sound of my father's voice. He had managed to sit up and draw his sword. Its curved metal length shone in the sun as he said How about steel.

———————

"You can't do this," I said.

"Someone has to. Might as well be me."

What argument could I give. How could I refute a yard of shitstained pipe running through him and something in his lungs that waited to claim him no matter what.

"You want this?"

"What I want," he said, measuring his words because each of them clearly hurt, "is to sit in Starbucks with a doubleshot nofoam latte and get a text from my wife telling me traffic sucks and we'll be late for the movie ex oh ex oh."

"I don't understand."

"I know. I want this, Fred." A shadow fell across him and he squinted up at Ariel. "Thousand miles an hour?"

"About that."

"Then someone better get my pack and help me up."

I helped him stand. I expected his yell but it was still terrible to hear. He kept his teeth clenched. "Bob?"

The centaur had been hanging back cautiously but now came forward.

He looked uncomfortable and awkward and I realized his hands wanted a javelin. My father tried to hold a hand up to him but apparently it hurt too much. Instead he gave a thumbsup and flicked a fingernail against the spear that ran him through, which made a loud tick that made me wince. "Not your fault," he said. "Understand?"

Bob looked thoughtful and said something that sounded like throwing up.

"Does the son release the blood debt also," Ariel translated.

I looked at my father. The awful painful mess. "My father does so I do too."

Bob nodded solemnly. Beside me my father muttered Good man.

Bob held out a long arm and my father looked up but shook his head uncertain what was wanted until Bob pointed at my father's sword. My father leaned hard on me and slowly drew his sword and turned the dull side toward the centaur who accepted it and regarded it and then suddenly grabbed the protruding length of javelin and chopped down with the sword. I felt the jolt go through me and it had to have hurt like hell but my father only clamped his jaw and growled as all but six inches of javelin sliced away to reveal a cross section of white plastic.

The centaur turned the blade upright with the sharp end toward itself and held the sword out to my father. He took it but nearly dropped it and I helped him hold it and guide it back to the scabbard.

"Raj."

Dr. Ram came forward and started to reach for him and then thought better of it and glanced at me. I nodded that I had him. "Peter what can I do."

"Lose the gun."

Dr. Ram looked startled. "I am out of bullets anyway." His forlorn smile was heartbreaking. "Can I give you something for the pain."

"Fuck no. Pain's all that's holding me up. Always was. You're a shitty barber Raj."

"Yes I know."

He leaned harder on me and held out his hand. Dr. Ram took it in both of his. "Fred's gonna walk me in. He can bring Yan back if you want."

I felt a sudden horror but then realized that he only meant I could bring Yan's body back with me. Dr. Ram squeezed my father's hand tightly and

I can't describe what went across his face. Grief, anger, confusion, fear. He started to say something but couldn't and just shook his head.

"You did right, Raj."

Dr. Ram nodded and his mouth convulsed and he said It is still horrible. And let my father go.

My father glanced at me and I turned us toward the building that held the waiting pentagram. "Get him home," he said.

I shouldered his backpack and promised him I would.

And then she stood before us there resplendent in sunlight eternal in form ancient in beauty terrible in purity.

They stood silent a moment and I felt his weight shift off me as he drew some deeper final strength from her. "Walk with me?"

"Try and stop me."

Silent communion as we struggled toward the Roman pool. The awful hardness of the plastic bulging as he pressed against me. The bright awareness that my time with him was measured now. That his time would end here at this unexpected borderland.

Then Ariel stopped walking and I saw this was as far as they would go together. She started to say something but he held up a hand and she waited.

"I know you did this," he said.

She looked at him a long time before she said, "I couldn't find a path that led anywhere but here. I tried. I tried so hard. Was I wrong."

"I don't know. I'm tired. I'm ready. It counts. And it's a castle by the beach for christ's sake."

She waited.

"Do you need me to forgive you," he said.

"I need you to believe there's nothing to forgive."

"Well. I'd still share my toothbrush with you. How's that."

"I'd say it's a start."

His laugh rattled. "I'd say you haven't seen my toothbrush." He took a deep breath and stood a little straighter. "This is gonna be really hard."

"You're ready, Pete."

"I mean this part."

"Oh. Oh." She came forward. Looked at me. "You can let him go," she said.

I shifted his weight and steadied him and held a hand against his shoulder and then stepped away. Histories and forces dovetailed here, the intersect of hearts and deeds. All they'd known and done converged upon this point. Journeys end.

She bent her head and he put his arms around her strong white neck. Bloodied fingers clenching cotton mane. Her dark eyes closed and a long deep shudder rippled down her neck and flank and who would ever know what it had cost her to defy propriety and withstand his touch.

"I'm sorry about your crow," he said.

"Oh Pete. I'm sorry about all crows."

He held on a moment longer and then lowered his arms. Her head came up and her eyes opened and she stepped back.

He gave a little shrug. "Goodbye," he said.

She lowered her head until her horn touched the ground.

He sagged and I hurried to take his weight again. "Are you ready," I said.

"Hell no. Come on."

I looked at Ariel and she looked back and I could not tell what she was thinking or what she felt. I got my shoulder under my father and guided him toward the pool and the abiding moment. Broken glass crunched underfoot

At the doorway he looked back at her. "No more a-roving, huh."

"The heart be still as loving Pete."

He snorted. "Fucking Coleridge."

She studied him. "Byron."

"Whatever."

He was smiling when he looked away.

Nothing in the pool had changed. Yan where I'd left him eyes closed and on his back. Gouges in the tiled pool wall, scattered fragments. Crossbow lying askance. Alicorn and rod fused in the sealed pentagram. What else had I expected.

We took the steps down slowly and I think it hurt him just as much to put his weight on me as it did to walk.

Beside the pentagram I pulled his sword still in its sheath from his beltloop and lowered him and set his pack beside him and handed him his sword. He gasped as he leaned to favor one side. "Sorry we named you after this," he said. "Meant well."

Ariel looked down at us through bulletshattered glass.

"I'm not sorry."

He nodded and set the sword down and patted my leg.

"Malachi though. That's another story."

"Got me there. Listen." I waited while he fought a cough and then coughed and then said god damn. "I scrape the circle with the blade and everything goes boom, right."

I didn't feel right talking down to him like this, couldn't take seeing Yan at the edge of my vision. I sat beside him on the tile. "It should."

"How big."

"I don't know. The stronger the casting the more energy comes out the breach."

"Big then."

"I think, yeah."

He studied the pentagram. Apart from the innocuous fusion of horn and rod there was no sign of the power it contained, the world-transforming change that emanated from this point. No light no shimmer no hum. Just a painted star and circle at the bottom of a pool.

He reached for his pack and I hurried to hand it to him. He fished around and just as I was going to ask if I could get what he was looking for he pulled out a tangle of white wire and glossy iPod. He pressed it and it lit and he dialed it and looked up at me. "Piano Concerto Number Five, Emperor," he said. "Thirtyeight minutes. Think you can get a few miles from here in thirtyeight minutes."

"I think so."

"Make me feel better about this than I think so. I won't make it through the Ninth and I'm sure as hell not doing—" he looked down at the tiny screen "—*The Eagles Greatest Hits.*"

"We can do it."

"Better start now."

My heart leapt. "Dad—"

"Thousand miles an hour Fred. I'm good for maybe five hundred."

"I just. I'm sorry. About that day. About Mom."

"Never be sorry about her, Fred. Never. To me. Anybody. Listen to me. My hand's on the switch here and I'm not sorry about a second. Understand me? You. Your mother. Ariel. Del Mar. Dragons. Whales. The road. The whole beautiful mess. I wouldn't trade it if I could live twice as long. My sage advice to my good son. Make a life you wouldn't trade for anything. When I scrape this son of a bitch across that circle your world belongs to you. Figure it out. Make something of it. Don't waste this. Don't live in our shit until it all runs out. Or I swear to god I'll rattle chains and haunt your ass."

"All right." The weight of those two words. Here is the handed torch. "I will. We will."

He nodded. "Good man. I love you Fred. Always have. Now get out of here. Get Raj home."

I told him I loved him and hugged him one last time and then I said goodbye and stumbled numb and tearblind from the pool and from the building.

Ariel stood waiting outside. I said We have to go.

She nodded and looked back at him one more time. "Goodbye Pete," she said.

He'd managed to bring himself to sitting upright on his knees. He drew his sword and held it out. It might have been a salute. I don't know if he saw us. The last thing I saw him do was set the sword between himself and the pentagram and pick up the music player and begin unraveling the tangled cord.

———————————

Dr. Ram and I clung to Bob's back as he galloped down the overgrown pathway winding toward the resumed shore. Even with our weight he darted nimbly through the tall grass dodging shrubs and rocks and junk decayed to anonymity. Ariel picked out a path ahead of us, a white blur with white mane streaming. Zebras fled at our approach. I nearly fell off trying to look back up the hill. Bob growled at me and I stopped. I could feel it behind me. Feel him up there waiting. Listening. I remembered the music I had heard that day on the road declining from the mountains. Sunrise in my ears. Morning in my heart. Such music as I'd never heard. Never imagined could exist. I pictured him being filled with such unspeakable light and beauty as he sat wounded and waiting, rocking in the swell and trough of those exquisite harmonies and staring at the painted sigil that meant the end of everything, the final swordstroke that would flood dark silence.

Ariel called something back and I saw the shimmering net beyond her. I patted Dr. Ram and pointed at it and we hugged Bob closely and Bob craned his upper body forward and rushed into the opening my father had left us. Bob stumbled and recovered and Dr. Ram lost his grip and I caught his backpack strap and yanked him back and held him and ignored the whitehot pain that stabbed out from my ribs until he got his arms around Bob's waist again. The mist tendrils had burned off and the day was bright and warming.

It seemed a long time before we passed the ruined visitor's center and the asphalt-clotted field that had been the highway. Ariel sped on, an apparition on this primal shore. Ahead I saw the waves unfurling on the beach and something in me finally conceded Yan was truly gone. Ariel sped over rocky spill past pebbles onto sand and left no hoofprints as she hurried south along the roaring shoreline. Bob thundered behind her and I could feel him hot and sweating now. I glanced back and caught a glimpse of terracotta on the hilltop. Surely we had come three miles by now. Surely the music had built to its furious and tender peak. What if he had changed his mind, no not changed his mind but simply not hung on, fallen with his sword beside the pentagram. Surely it had been—

The hill blew toward the sky.

FORTY

The sound hit us in a deafening wave that nearly knocked me off the centaur's back. Even Ariel stumbled. She started to recover and then realized what it meant and stopped and turned to regard the sudden roiling column of dirt and smoke and fire that had been an entire hill now thundering upward. It was unimaginable even as I watched it. Its light threw shadows on the beach in defiance of the sun. This faded quickly into coruscating yellows and orange lacing through the boiling smoke.

Dr. Ram and I dismounted and stood leeward to the centaur's bulk and watched the mountain burn. Gradually the roar died down until we heard the waves behind us crashing, always crashing once again. The column spread tendrils that grew hazy in conflicting winds.

Good man I thought but didn't say.

Dr. Ram sat on the sand and put his elbows on his knees and put his head in his hands and said Gone. I didn't know if he meant Yan or my father or the hill itself. Maybe all of it. Gone. I looked at him. At Ariel. Wondered at their somberness and realized I was dry eyed too. Later grief would fill the empty spaces in my heart where my father and Yan had lived. Right now there were just the empty spaces where my heart had been cored.

Finally I looked away from the attenuating bole of smoke and dust and looked at Ariel. She seemed uncertain and not altogether with us in our final congregation. "Did it work," I said.

She looked at me and I stepped back at the wildness in her eyes.

She blinked and it was gone.

I looked at Dr. Ram and Bob but they hadn't seen it. Maybe I hadn't seen it either.

"What," she said.

"Did it work," I repeated. "Is it gone."

"The casting?" She stared, looked inward, grew still. "I don't know. I can't tell. It's like—it is and it isn't."

"Well what does that mean."

Bob said something and she nodded. "Bob thinks that the places that changed back stayed that way," she said. "That's why we feel both."

"But did we stop it. Did he stop it."

She talked with Bob a minute and finally said We don't know.

I sighed and picked up a wavesmoothed stone and threw it and sat down beside Dr. Ram. "Well fuck. I mean—" The dissipating cloud that owned the landscape. Residue of hill, castle, father, friend. "What are we supposed to do."

Dr. Ram put a hand on my shoulder. "We are supposed to wait."

"He's right," said Ariel. "If Pete stopped it or he didn't we'll know for sure in about twentythree hours."

Bob said something and pointed where the hill had been. Ariel said something back and laughed mirthlessly.

"What did he say," I asked.

"He asked if I wanted to bet on whether Pete stopped it. I asked him how he'd collect if he didn't."

Bob came forward and turned to face us. He swiveled slowly to look at us and then turned his emaciated torso all the way around to face the dispersing devastation. He turned back to us and held his long arms out and began to speak, the captain of some alien shipwreck addressing his surviving crew.

"There is no victory to celebrate," translated Ariel. "We must honor our dead instead of merely waiting here like insects waiting for the hoof." Bob pointed at Ariel, me, himself, Dr. Ram. "Lover, family, ally, friend. Tribe. Tonight—" She glanced at him. I saw her fight to clamp it down. "Tonight we celebrate their lives."

We gathered anything that would burn and piled it well above the tideline. Dr. Ram and I filled a blanket with sticks and fragments of weathered furniture and what dregs of gasoline and propane and lighter fluid we could scrounge into a red plastic jug. I had to rest a lot because my ribs still hurt but we managed to drag several bundles to add to the pile.

Bob was breaking two by fours and heaping them on. I wondered if he'd taken apart a motel room somewhere.

We broke for a late lunch even though none of us was hungry. Dr. Ram and I sat on the beach and watched the waves while Ariel and Bob stood nearby. Out of habit I started to ask if anybody'd seen my father and then I remembered.

Dr. Ram threw a final load of chairlegs on the pile. I'd had to stop because of the pain in my ribs when I threw. He dusted his hands and regarded the chest-high pile of wood and fabric and ticking before us and then he nodded and grabbed up the incendiary can. I breathed in deep to smell the fluid and realized that I still could not.

I stared past Dr. Ram at a thin man standing in the water. He was dark and bald and gaunt and waist-high in the waves a hundred yards from shore. There was something wrong with his head. Something wrong with the way he moved. I stood speechless while he splashed himself and scrubbed himself and ducked into the water and came up again. He came toward us and the rest of him emerged and I realized I was watching Bob.

I left my clothes upon the shore and walked into the breaking vastness. The water cold but not as cold as I'd expected. I leaned into the surge and closed my eyes and felt its filigree of seaweed move across me. The bottom rocky and a gentle undertow at my feet. I stepped carefully down the continent's slope until the water reached my chest. Closed my eyes and kept my back to everything I'd known and every place I'd been. My body wavered like an anchored frond.

I leaned back and felt cold water fill my ears. My feet lifted and I waved my arms and let the water carry me.

D r. Ram made coffee as the sun got near the horizon. I took a cup and thanked him and let it warm my hands. I drank and felt it warm my belly. Everything felt ritualized, all deeds symbols of themselves.

Bob joined us at sunset. He had painted dots and angular designs across his torso and planed face. Dark red and deep yellow and dappled white. He had found a length of aluminum pipe and now he set it on the sand beside his pannier and kicked up clots of damp sand as he came to us nodding gravely and declining Dr. Ram's offer of hot coffee.

Ariel joined us a few minutes later. "There's barely even a hill left," she said.

We nodded and I sipped coffee. What had she expected. Nothing, I'm sure. She just couldn't help herself. I wondered if curiosity was a common trait among her kind and decided it was not. I thought I knew where she had picked it up.

We looked into the west and watched the red sun sink toward its molten trench. I wondered why you could not feel your shadow getting longer. It seemed you should. Of course I didn't really care. What I really wondered, what all of us wondered, was whether the rules out there had changed again. If we got on a boat and sailed it west would I be able to press a button and hear that astonishing music. Would Ariel disappear. Was a part of the world that my father and Dr. Ram had known now permanently engraved on mine. Or was it chasing the sunset across the turning world to overtake us in the morning.

The sun reached the water and seemed to swell. The wind picked up and the air turned cold. This final night began to wash across us.

D r. Ram threw a lighted stick onto the pyre and it blazed up all at once and all of us stepped back. I remembered primal silhouettes dancing hand in hand before another bonfire a lifetime away and not so long ago. Everything seemed to conjure something else. Will it always be this way.

Y ou were supposed to tell a story. Not about the person you had lost but a person someone else had lost. The story was for the people who remained behind. At least that's how the centaurs did it. We didn't explain to Bob that our losses seemed congruent. And I think we didn't have to.

Bob led the way and I think we expected him to talk about his tribe. But instead he stood between us and the blazing fire gesturing and holding forth in a voice like a drain unclogging, and Ariel's plainly marveling translation told us incidents and details about Avy that made us wonder how we ever could have overlooked the part of her that died while she was with us. Among the centaurs she had been a kind of boogeyman, a feral stalking creature small but unrelenting yet an unmoored soul searching out its sundered root so that it could find peace. Bob's people had strangely touching tall tales about adventurers who set out to find the better half of this revenant creature and restore it to its wild self so that it would be content and stop its unexplained vendetta. Those stories were among the reasons he had saved my father, he explained, because he'd seen the transformed Avy tearing in among his tribe and recognized a chance that he might act those stories out and be a hero to his tribe. That he had been among us when that savage half was taken from her was a singular unlikely thing, he said, and it would give him major mojo and prestige among his kind were he to be believed. The whole time she was with us Bob was acting out the role of hero in a campfire story and the affinity he felt with Avy was an unexpected gift that he would carry all his days.

———

The fire transformed wood to coal. The hidden depths that lay within all things. The threads you glimpsed you wove into a fabric of meaning and explanation and character. Inadequate and unfair.

———

Dr. Ram turned his back to the crackle and smoke and began to talk about my father. He told stories I had heard before. The time he brought George Fayelle to him after George had spent days clinging to a cliffside root. The time my father dealt with the squatters who had killed the Hendricks family. The hyena hunt he organized when Sudama went missing. He talked about the struggling fledgling village that had been Del Mar before my father showed up towing me in a wagon and told how my father had organized and delegated and berated until there was a sense of purpose and shared commitment. He had worked with Paypay to set wards and keep the region safe. He and Dr. Ram had gone scavenging for pharmaceuticals and books and supplies. He had been the gobetween who got the wiccans bartering with Dr. Ram. Yet despite his full involvement he remained detached from Del Mar somehow, invested but not concerned, a part and yet apart. As Del Mar appreciated him but also found him strange and offputting. Committed but indifferent.

And Dr. Ram told stories from my father's book and in the telling it was plain he had not just read them but had talked with him at length about these things for there were incidents and details not related there.

I basked in this as much as I was warmed by heat and light before me. It took some edge off of the deep abiding ache I felt. The beautiful mess. The trade that lent it weight and worth. A good man gone.

––––––––––

She was glossed by firelight like something freshly pulled from some god's forge. She did not step before us yet to speak. Instead she looked at me.

––––––––––

I brushed cold sandgrains from my pants. The onshore breeze had sharpened and I folded my arms in front of me. Heat against my back. Unpatterned crackle and snap of wood. Bob and Ariel and Dr. Ram. Centaur and unicorn and grieving father. Watching the fire as much as me. I was mostly silhouette I knew.

By centaurs' rules I must talk about someone else's loss and not my own. Out of all that had been lost who should that be. My father. Yan. José. Joe. Half of Avy. All Bob's tribe.

"My mother died when I was three," I heard myself begin. "I knew she'd died of some disease but my father never told me it had been my fault. I poked her with a rusty nail and she died of a disease called tetanus. I found this out about a week ago."

Crackling collapse behind me. Brief cinder constellations.

"I don't really remember her. Hanging clothes on a line my father made. Singing. I think she sang lot. I think I dream about it sometimes. I remember her voice but not the songs. The stories I know about her aren't anything I remember, they're ones my father told me. Is that okay."

Deeply shadowed at the edge of firelight Bob spoke to Ariel who nodded. "Bob says that the person who lost someone doesn't have to be there when you tell your stories, Fred." Her smile was sad and wise and tired. "And the stories you tell don't have to be your own."

"Okay." So I told what my father had told me. How she read to me at night from girly soap opera shojo manga novels that he brought back from his bookstore expeditions. She always wanted more than he brought. He'd laugh and say that there wasn't all that much in english and he had to keep her on a diet if she didn't want to go through it all in five years.

I told about our rooster Mr. Jagger getting into the kitchen and coming after me and my mother fending him off with a broom and yelling for my father who rushed in to find me on the counter crying and my mother standing on a chair swatting at Mr. Jagger with a broom. My father had herded the rooster out the door and then started laughing and my mom got mad at him and said that it wasn't funny. I think she had been laughing too. But soon after that we were no longer chicken farmers.

There were more stories like this but not many and as I told them I realized how few there really were, even secondhand from my father, and how much of my mother who had always been a presence by virtue of her absence was unknown to me. In the sense for which we gathered here I had abided by the rules by which we were supposed to give our elegies. For it turned out in the telling that my mother's death was more my father's loss than mine. He had given up the road for her. I had barely known her. Perhaps that was the lesson in those rules.

And from Dr. Ram's stories about everything my father'd done to make Del Mar viable and safe I understood that he had done all that for me. He had given up the road for her but he had stayed away from it for me. How about that.

———————

The fire smaller now, the night well on and growing cold. The waves enloudened in the bonfire's diminution. The world would change tomorrow, or not.

———————

"I once tried to raise a little girl," she began. "Mila. It's the name I gave her, she didn't know the name her parents gave her. They'd been killed along with the rest of her village and she was scavenging in what was left. She was with me for about nine years."

Seabreeze ruffled her mane. That disconcerting voice emerging from the equine silhouette before the waning flames.

"One day Mila found a half starved mongrel puppy from some feral bitch and brought it back to me pleading please please can't we just keep it. I knew better but I also knew that I hadn't done much different by keeping Mila. And I thought it would be good for her to have a dog. She'd learn responsibility and duty and compassion and she'd have a little companion. As below so above and all that.

"It was a sickly little runt and though it grew, it grew no better. When it didn't whine it yapped and you could hear us coming about a week before we got there. Mila named him Uno. It was a pretty good pun I thought. Perro uno. I like dogs and I have had great experiences with them but I never really warmed to Uno. He was generally goodnatured and Mila loved him and he seemed to be good for her. But the dog seemed genuinely incapable of learning anything. Housebreaking on the road, who cares. But stay, quiet, no, fetch, attack—not a chance. I suppose dogs can be as mentally deficient as any other creature with a brain capable of not working right. But I swear you could look into that dog's eyes and see straight to the back of its head. Every day was the first day of the rest of its life. He nearly poisoned himself more than once because he'd eat anything he found. Mila went hungry a few times because he ate all the food we had with us. He chewed up books and clothes and camping gear. I put up with it because Mila needed to fix it or learn to cope with it. I wanted her to learn how to be a human being, didn't I. One who could rejoin her society and find a mate and have a baby and pass along what culture she'd acquired. Mostly from me which is just pathetic when you think about it. Her prospects didn't seem so hot if she couldn't keep a retarded dog from killing himself.

"One day it was raining like hell and we holed up in a little truckstop on what had been a logging road. Uno had been sick all week and the weather had been lousy for days so I didn't mind putting in for a while. Not like I was late for any appointments. But I kept getting more paranoid as the day wore on and I could not figure out why.

"The place was really just a gas station with a twocar service bay and a tiny diner where the roof had collapsed, and an office with a closet bedroom in back. The forest had mostly reclaimed it and god knows what had nested in it, and a half-overgrown eighteenwheeler with a flatbed full of rotten logs had been parked out front for about fifteen years. Something told me to move Mila and the dog into the little bedroom and keep watch from the office which had an amazingly unbroken window that looked out on the front.

"So it's coming down buckets and it's late afternoon and Mila's letting the puppy chew on her hand in the little bedroom when I see a centaur scoping out the truckstop from behind the eighteenwheeler that's more vine than truck. Shit oh dear. I got the office door closed and the desk pushed up against it before they broke into the service bay. They weren't looking for us or for anything far as I could tell. They just wanted in out of the rain and who could blame them. This was the southern Yucatán and rain there doesn't fall, it geysers down in sheets and solid masses. I have seen it strip trees bare.

"I think we would've been fine. The rain made it unlikely they'd smell us and go ballistic or that we'd smell them, the effect's the same. We probably could have sat tight till they moved on.

"But the fucking dog starts yapping. Half a dozen centaurs fifty feet away and all I hear is yap yap yap yap. I give Mila a look and she tries to shut the dog up but she's just as loud as it is and I hiss at her to be quiet and shut the goddamned dog up. The only reason they haven't heard us yet is because they're scavenging the joint and the rain's so loud it sounds like someone crumpling a paper bag in your ear but sooner or later they'll settle down or the rain will let up and they'll hear that dog and push at the office door and get a whiff of Mila and that'll be it. Nothing personal Bob but it's true. They wouldn't give a shit if there was a whole Girl Scout troop in the woods till they got a whiff of them. And if those Girl Scouts got downwind they'd go all *Lord of the Flies* on the centaurs too. You can't reason with chemicals.

"I had to get us out of there now. So I tell Mila shut that dog up and come out of the office quiet as a ghost and open the window cause it's major byebye time. She stuffs the dog into a stuff sack and he yipes and then goes quiet and she grabs her pack and edges out of there. The window hasn't been opened in fifteen years and she gets it up about six inches but that's it.

"And then the dog starts in again. I tell Mila leave the stuff sack and get back into the bedroom and close the door. She looks scared but she does it. Five seconds later the dog's quiet and she tries to open the door and I glare at her and she closes it again. The centaurs don't come running but they do try to open the office door as part of their scrounge. The door thumps the desk and the centaur pushes harder and the desk slides back an inch. But there's nothing to scavenge in this dump and they're just going through the motions and can't be bothered with a stupid door. They just want a dry place to hole up for the night.

"The next morning the rain's let up and the centaurs leave without ever knowing we were there. I thump on the bedroom door and it opens right away. I don't think Mila slept at all. She glances toward the service bay and I tell her it's okay they're gone and right away she asks where's Uno. I tell her I let him out the window. She gets upset and I say look if I hadn't let him go the centaurs would have heard him and they would have forced their way in here to the office and hurt us and hurt Uno too. This way everyone's okay. Yeah she says but where's Uno.

"We searched for him all day. Everywhere but the office thank god. I was jumpy after the centaurs even though I knew they wouldn't be coming back. We searched and Mila didn't find him and we moved on.

"After that I understood that I had no business trying to teach a kid how to be a human being. What I had to do was learn how to be a unicorn. Because I understood down to my very impure heart that I was about as far away from that as I could be right then. I had to find my own kind. I had looked for them before but now I needed them. Everything changed after Mila—after the dog. The road bent north for me again and here I am."

All of us were quiet. Watching her black shape. Listening. Wondering.

"And here we all are. Converged upon this beach at the edge of this world. Standing watch this final night together as we wait to see what will survive tomorrow. Telling each other stories to celebrate those we've lost. And telling them to tell each other goodbye."

FORTY-ONE

"Fred. Fred? Fred."

I sat up cold and tasting grit and blinking in gray light. The bonfire's smoking remains gave off slight heat. Behind me waves crashed, always crashed.

Dr. Ram squatted before me looking worried.

I yawned. Stretched. Stopped. Looked around.

Ariel and Bob stood talking downshore.

"We have about two hours left," said Dr. Ram. "There is coffee."

I laughed despite myself and he looked puzzled. "I love you, Dr. Ram," I said.

He darkened. "You should not make fun. This is not the time or place."

"I wasn't—"

But he turned away.

I finished my stretch and yawn and stood up feeling stiff and cold and grateful for the coffee.

I hadn't been making fun.

I poured hot coffee and watched the waves and remembered drinking coffee on another beach and watching waves. Revelations and confessions.

I brought Dr. Ram a cup as a peace offering and he accepted it as such. "What are they talking about."

"Ariel is trying to talk Bob into staying."

"Why would he want to leave."

He studied the waves. "This is not where he wants to be if this is his last day."

"Where does he want to be."

"He wants to look for his people."

"In two hours?"

Now he looked at me. "I think the looking is the point."

I took this in. I sipped more coffee and then screwed the cup into the sand and headed toward them.

"Let him go," I told her. "It's his two hours, not ours."

She studied me a moment before nodding. "You're right." She turned to Bob and said something. He touched his scarred cheeks and nodded gravely. One arm cradled the new aluminum pipe javelin he'd angle cut and filed down during our stories and vigil last night. "I told him goodbye," she told me. "They have a lot of different goodbyes. There's a see you later, I hope I see you later, I'll probably never see you again, have a nice death, I hope you see your ancestors soon."

"Give him the hope I see you later from me, will you."

She did. I guess.

Bob nodded gravely again and said something back. I looked at Ariel.

"He would like something from you before he goes," she said.

For some reason I felt sudden fear. "What."

"Your blessing."

"My—" I looked at him and he held out his javelin. That terrifying fountain-pen point like something on a leash that really wanted to come after me.

"I think he wants you to put the whammy on his spear," said Ariel.

I studied him a moment. "He's all about getting back with major mojo, huh."

"Put yourself in his place. He's permanently injured. He's lost his tribe. He took off to help a bunch of human beings and a unicorn. He needs some serious pimp juice to get anyone to take him in."

"Between the javelin and Avy and—" I almost said And killing my father "—and helping save the world I think he's got it covered." I looked from the metal javelin to the creature holding it. "You've got serious balls, Bob." To Ariel I said, "They got different words for that?"

"I'll find some."

All my premade castings had been undone yesterday. I got my kit and lit the campstove and did it up from scratch. After everything that had happened I thought I'd feel funny setting up a pentagram and making a casting but I didn't. Training took over. My hands did the work more than my mind did.

Pentagram on the beach. I wondered would the waves break round it if I kept it active while the tide came in.

Ten minutes later I breached the pattern at the cardinal points and handed Bob a perfectly mirrored javelin that would outlast the world itself, which right now might be a one-hour guarantee. He examined it and held it to his lipless mouth and blew a bell-like note that scattered gulls and rang across the shoreline.

Then he thrust the point into the sand and knelt before me and set his hands on the sand and lowered his head. I was so startled I stepped back. He seemed to be waiting for something and I glanced at Ariel. She shook her head slightly. No idea.

I took a tentative step forward and put a palm against his spadeflat head. It felt nothing like I'd thought it would. It was warm and smooth and alive. I thought about thanking him but it wasn't in me. I could forgive him but I was a long way from anything like gratitude. "Whatever today brings," I said feeling foolish while I felt I was enacting something primal and important with this creature on this shore. "I hope you are with your people again. Travel safely." I lifted my hand and stepped back and he stood and yanked the javelin from the sand and reared to an intimidating height and held the mirrored weapon to the sky and ululated. Then he dropped and wheeled and clamped the javelin under one arm and rode off at full gallop, kicking up sand clots in his wake. He went due south and then cut east and soon nothing remained of him but odd tricornered prints the waves already were erasing.

Three of us on the beach. Blackened remnants of last night's bonfire. I could smell salt air again.

"Let me say goodbye now," said Ariel. "Because in five minutes I'll either be on my way or I won't be at all."

"Where will you go."

"Nobody knows."

"I mean if you're still here."

"Ah." From her tone she knew what I'd meant. "I don't know really. There are others of my kind I want to find. There's a colony of demons in Panama that's a good place to hide and lick your wounds. There's a garden in Yosemite that needs tending."

"There's Mila somewhere in the Yucatan."

She cocked her head. "Not an option."

"Not even curious?"

I swear I thought she was going to cry. "I'd like to answer another question you asked a while back," she said.

"All right."

"I'm willing to give it a try."

For a moment I didn't know what she meant. Then I did and it was my turn not to cry. "Oh. I. I mean. I don't know. It's not—" I held out my hands.

"If you don't you'll always wonder."

Which I knew was true.

So I stepped forward and raised a hand and then hesitated. She waited without moving and I set my hand against her neck. What I felt I felt not on my hand but in my heart. Oh I said. Oh.

And stepped back in mute wonder.

Her eyes were closed. Had it been allowed or had she allowed it. I don't know.

"I believe it is close to the time," said Dr. Ram.

Ariel's eyes opened and her tail swished and she said, "Yall are useless without watches. It was time two minutes ago."

We watched the waves together one last time. Would they ever look the same to any of us again. Then we turned away as one because we knew that it was time to go.

"Doc, I know you don't think so now but we all owe you everything. And you still have a lot to live for. Don't forget that."

"I will try. But there is what you know in your mind and—" He set a hand on his chest.

"You ignore one or both at your peril. I wish there were more like you." She turned to me. "And you. So much to say. I'm honored to know you, Fred. You're a good man. The apple didn't fall far from the tree."

"No," I said. "The tree fell."

She was surprised at my tone. Well so was I. "But they have to sooner or later," she said. "Trees. Crows. Roosters. People. Unicorns. Eventually they fall. That's the way it is. No one can do anything about it. What you can do something about is who you are in the time before that."

"Some things fall. Some are pushed."

"I don't think I'm following you bud."

I took a deep breath and looked her in the eye. "Did you kill that dog."

It was the only time I ever saw her flinch. "Oh Fred." She looked at the water. At the hills. At Dr. Ram. Down at the sand. For a second I thought she was simply going to bolt. Then she took her own deep breath and raised her head to look down hard at me and said There never was a dog.

I thought about that. I think about it still. I swallowed hard. "Then goodbye," I said.

If she felt shame or apology or defiance she gave voice to none of it. She only nodded and said, "All right then Fred. I understand. Goodbye. Goodbye."

And it really was.

FORTY-TWO

We took the coastal route back south and detoured only when the road did not allow our passage. Four men and a woman blocked our way outside of Oxnard within miles of where my father had been set upon years before where Honest Abe had died. They told us to set down our packs and step back. I didn't even reply, not directly anyway. I said two words and made them mirrored statues and we continued on our way. The encounter literally did not last a minute. In a week the stasis spells would time out and there'd be five very confused people wondering how the two men they'd been robbing had just vanished right in front of them. They probably deserved worse but I'd had enough of worse.

The closer we got to Del Mar the more eager Dr. Ram seemed to be to get back. I took this as a good sign. For my part I was neither eager nor reluctant. I could think of nowhere else I wanted to be and Del Mar was home. And I'd promised to get Dr. Ram back safely.

I started a new grimoire on the way back. Yan's notebook had been destroyed with the hill and everything on it and I wanted to re-create what I remembered of what he'd learned that I had read. I wasn't afraid of any of it. Magic isn't any more dangerous than a hammer, than the idea of hammer. Or any less. And it helped to pass the tense and awkward silences that filled our walking days especially at first. But every day we conversed a little more until we were having long discussions again. Still it was noth-ing like our old conversations. Too much lay between us. Too much had changed within and without. And even though we talked at length we did not speak about those things.

Three weeks after we set out we passed the torn and capsized tanker rusting on the beach near Encinitas. It looked pretty much the way it had when I had stalked its canted decks as a child. I found its presence oddly comforting. The decay of the last world was what was stable in my own.

With that relief came overwhelming sadness. I had accomplished what I had set out to but I certainly felt no sense of accomplishment. *Over is kinda fuzzy edged when it comes to big events.* Even Bob had said there was no victory to celebrate.

Near Del Mar I saw something gleaming on the beach and detoured to investigate. It was the surfboard I had set in stasis for Ron Golecki about a hundred years ago. The riding harness he had made so he could stand on the nearly frictionless surface was torn and trailing in the churning water by a single nylon strap.

———————

Dr. Ram's homecoming was the most bittersweet event in this whole account. He'd missed Parmita and Nan terribly and was eager to see them again but he feared seeing them just as much. He himself was the reason he was not coming back with Yan and it would wear at him the rest of his days. They had lost a son already and now this. I'd say life tests the human heart out to its limits but I'm not sure what those limits are.

I wasn't sure what he was going to tell them and he didn't really tell them anything. The fact that he'd come back brokenhearted and without his son was tale enough I'm sure. I followed his lead and said nothing more than I had to, though it was rough when they asked about my dad. Nan I knew could see that there was more than I would say but she said nothing. Her eyes told me to tell her later. I had to look away.

They were gracious and invited me to stay and eat and commemorate our homecoming but I told them I had to go. I had a homecoming of my own to undergo.

———————

I'd forgotten about the racetrack's collapsed roof. The damage that had sent me on my elemental way. In the dark it lay there quiet and massive and undeniable and I could not tell if it had fallen into ruin a week or centuries ago.

———————

Past the field that had been the parking lot I stopped and set down my pack and stared out toward the water and tried to find a word for what I felt.

On its railed bridge it curved out night and starlight, waiting unchanged for my return or the universe's death whichever came first. As if no time had passed it by. As for it no time had.

———————

"Something . . . *surfliner.*" I put my hand against the mirrored shape that warped the starry sky above it. *"Flamenco surfliner. Abbatoir surfliner?"*

I started to laugh and then I started to cry but didn't stop laughing. I had forgotten the goddamn password.

———————

Near dawn I woke up from a dream of endless walking. I was in my sleeping bag and the surf boomed and the air was cold and smelled like home. The mirrored railcar loomed. I coughed and cleared my throat and turned my head and spat and then said *grunion surfliner* and I pushed my way inside.

I smelled coffee.

———————

Two days later Paypay frowned up at his jangling door but said nothing as I came in and looked around the shop. I felt like I was visiting a place I'd known as a child. I was. Finally I looked at him and he folded his arms and said You father?

I shook my head.

He nodded as if that had been the only answer I could give. "Good man," he said. "Good caster."

"Good caster?"

"Sure. I teach him but he know a lot already. He help me with things."

"The wards."

He nodded slowly, gauging me.

"I don't understand. If he was a good caster why did he—I mean, I did all of it myself. I don't. . . ."

He shrugged but did not change expression. "He is good but only good. He knows when to stay out of the way."

I think that was when I began to grieve in earnest.

It was a year before it occurred to me to write this down. I had a lot to do before that.

Paypay showed me what he'd done to keep Del Mar safe. The wards were simple and stressed keeping centaurs away. Nothing dramatic. The closer to Del Mar they got the more nervous they began to feel. My father had taken the lessons from the destroyed communities he'd seen on his travels.

I worked with Paypay in the shop just like the old days except that now there was no question about my duties and responsibilities and investigations. The Mrs. Glosters of the world still wanted their pathetic giftshop unicorns and always would. On a nasty whim one day I made her one that looked just like Ariel and she had no idea what to make of it. She thought I was showing her one I'd made for someone else but had her usual one tucked away somewhere. I went with the program and got rid of it and shat her out a fwuffy widdle unicorn wif big eyelashes. The Ariel lookalike had been a horrible mistake anyhow. It brought too much back.

About six months after I got back I showed up at the shop and it was still locked and Paypay hadn't gotten up yet. I went in back and saw that he wasn't going to. No one knew how old he was. Old. He'd often spoken of things even my father and Dr. Ram didn't remember.

We buried him in Seagrove Park on the cliff overlooking the beach, and on the beach I built a bonfire and invited everyone to come and tell stories about people that other people had lost. It's a good custom I think. Those centaurs aren't dumb.

Dr. Ram resumed his practice and barbering and on the surface everything looked the way it had before he'd left. I visited the Ramchandanis regularly at first for dinners and family occasions and knew that I was welcome as family. I loved them and they loved me. But too many ghosts haunted their dinner table, absences that colored every word and gesture. Eventually my visits tapered off. For all her flirtation and interest I never followed up with Nandita. What I knew about her brother would always lie between us, and even if she was content not knowing, something in me would always feel compelled to tell her.

I still saw them of course. Del Mar is small and we all trade favors and items to get by.

One time I had a casting go wrong on me and burned my hand pretty decently and visited Dr. Ram. He'd been thin before all this but now he was gaunt. He packed my hand in some greasy ointment and bandaged it up and sent me to the wiccans for some herbs. As I left he patted my shoulder and said, "Good as new, and be careful next time, Yanamandra."

I caught my breath and he colored and we looked away from each other quickly. I nodded at him and hurried off but I couldn't help glancing back. He'd shut his door and was pulling down the shades.

Even though he had Parmita and Nan to anchor and console him he'd acquired a preoccupied look that made me wonder if one day he'd wander off into the woods and not come back. So I got him into a discussion about the wiccans and pissed him off by hinting that he was upset that he'd gone to school for years to obtain knowledge that relied heavily on outmoded or unavailable technology, whereas they who had been scorned as superstitious fringe society now knew more useful medicine than he did. After some heated back and forth I suggested that he offer to take on an assistant from their coven and learn their herbal remedies and midwifery and charms in exchange for teaching what he knew. He argued with me but eventually approached them and acquired a sort of reciprocal apprentice in Rowena Gladner. They argued as much as they coeducated, and Dr. Ram began to lose that preoccupied look and I stopped worrying as much.

Never underestimate the motivational power of anger.

———————

One day I mirrored up the Surfliner and met Dub Weston on the highway north of town. He'd brought one of his family's horses, a well-mannered chestnut mare I thought was named Gator until I realized it was Gaiter. I'd brought a backpack and a bag of mirrored shapes. I'd traded a year's worth of favors for this and still I knew what a bargain Dub was giving me.

We traveled north without incident until we reached the public library in San Juan Capistrano. There were still faint brown stains on the walls and weapons on the tumbled stacks. The mirrored couple stood exactly as we'd left them. I made a wheeled sledge and harnessed it to Gaiter and put the couple on it and went east to the freeway and then due north.

The airplane still revolved on its nose.

The blimp hangar had been burned but stood with opened doors.

Near the Tejon Summit we found remnants of the *Spirit of America* but could not find José's grave.

On the long decline toward Grapevine we stopped before a large picket of javelins forming a ring half in the road. An enormous bonfire had burned here and I could only wonder at the stories that had been told. Inside the ring was the Honda with its spiderwebbed windshield.

I set my backpack outside the picket and I pulled up javelins until there was an opening large enough for the wagon. I put my bag of mirrored objects on the sledge beside the mirrored couple and I walked Gaiter into the circle and jumped when I heard several pops and a woman gasped and a man yelled No.

Several frogs and a cat fled from the sledge.

After I'd been back a year I visited my father's house for the first time since that day I'd walked Ariel back into his life. It was overgrown and disrepaired. I stared at the spot in the yard where I'd seen him practicing when I'd first arrived with his past in tow. The damage that had sent him on his elemental way. Weedy kneehigh grass. A red wheelbarrow rusting in the sun.

Dr. Ram once told me that broken limbs often heal incorrectly, and the older you are when it breaks the more likely that is. He said that sometimes doctors have to break the limb again and reset it so that it will heal correctly.

I had broken my father's heart here. Put him back on the path he thought he'd left forever, the path that by its tribulation somehow let him reclaim something he felt he had lost. It had always waited there for his return. I think some fundamental part of him had thought of his life in our little village as one long detour. Despite his complaints on the road I always felt a sense of resumption from him. My father and his road were the tired bodies of old friends embracing, journeys end in lovers meeting. If it had meant not having one last journey with his old Familiar, missing one last road to some salvation, his or the entire world's, would he have stayed home. I doubted it.

Ariel had doubted it too.

Even so it wore me down to bedrock to be among my father's timeworn books and derelict possessions. I looked for his journal but of course it wasn't there. I had thought to reclaim something of my father by returning here but in the end took nothing with me when I left. The things remaindered did not shape the man abandoned and I left there more diminished than improved.

Late that night I was awakened by the pattering of an early season storm. I lay there thinking of the wheelbarrow in my father's overgrown yard filling up with water that would evaporate away. Thinking of Ariel admitting that there'd never been a dog. I have asked myself and asked myself why she would have done it. Why that little girl. Why put my father on the road to his own resolution. And the only answer I come up with is that unicorns are gardeners. Myopic, altruistic, relentless gardeners. And Ariel who had always wandered, who belonged no single place—her garden was the world.

I knew it would be a long time till daylight and I got out of bed and lit a candle and went downstairs and took down my father's book for the first time since all of this began and sat down to read it once again yet in some sense for the first time. Alone in the Surfliner with one steady light and the pattering on the walls and roof I only wanted to hear his voice again and it was bound there in that book. *I was bathing in a lake when I saw the unicorn.*

It occurred to me then that I knew the ending to the story he'd begun. Dr. Ram knew it. Ariel roaming somewhere in this barely salvaged world knew it. But otherwise it remained increate and untold. I thought that if I set it down it would be as if I stood with my back to the biggest, longest-burning bonfire ever.

I libbed a lot of legal pads and a box of ballpoint pens. I led my life and plied my trade and learned my craft and warded off what ill I could. I learned the science of casting. The building blocks to restore a scattered and diminished people. At night I wrote.

Stacks of pads and many pens and one year later it was rainy season again and I was up late staring at a line that read *I think that was when I began to grieve in earnest* and wondering what to write next when I realized there was nothing to write next. Above those eleven words lay the rest of my father's story and my part in it. My own is scarcely written because it is scarcely begun.

Of course I'm tempted to repeat history. To leave and leave the manuscript here on a table in the Surfliner beside a fresh pot of coffee, all of it in stasis and awaiting utterance of a word to free it for its unknown reader after a month or a thousand years. After all I am my father's son.

But I am not my father. He let his story go by leaving it behind and heading out into the world. And decades and thousands of miles later it caught up to him in all the ways his story could.

I will let it go by staying here—for now, for now—and putting the story itself out into the world. Tomorrow I will put this stack of lined and stained and curling notepads in my pack and set out for Carlsbad where there is an old bookshop on Woodley Avenue squatted by a reclusive woman who runs an old screwpress and prints things for a living or for fun or both. They say she's odd. They say she is a witch. I will ask her what it takes to set this scrawl in type and bind it from my heart into the feckless world. Maybe she will not be interested. Maybe she's no longer there. Maybe these words remain in different inks on yellowed paper on a dimlit yellow table while the derailed relic of a crumbling world decays around it, and that pot of coffee waits for its unlocking in a world where words are never spoken and the sun has long gone cold.

I hope not. But I am here to speak before the bonfire, not to shepherd what I've said along some trampled way. Having told my father's story I must move on to live my own, mourning ecstatic wise learning fearful sad and hopeful. As my father's very world has told its story and moved on. As my world will one day as well. For civilizations come and go. The ruins around us, the stories we tell, the graves on which we build our lives tell us as much. Meantime we can only live, but try to live such lives as we would want to make good bonfire tales. For good stories outlive any piles of brick or stone.

I hope you live one too.

ACKNOWLEDGEMENTS

Ken Mitchroney. Adrian Smith. Scott Kelley.

I am deeply grateful to my agent, Richard Curtis, and my editor, Anne Sowards, for their wonderful suggestions for the latter drafts of the manuscript.

Carlos of Goodyear Airship Operations in Carson, California, answered many questions and gave me an extensive hands-on tour of the *Spirit of America* for which I am enormously indebted. Mistakes, exaggerations, and outright impossibilities are all my fault.

DJ Timo Maas (timomaas.com) sent me many mix CDs during the writing of this book, and they kept me company for many hours. I hope this returns a little of the favor.

For convenience's sake I combined the adjoining Southern California communities of Del Mar and Solana Beach, and made a few other rearrangements when geography got in the way.

AFTERWORD: NOTE TO SELF

For decades I swore I would never write a sequel to *Ariel*. You can read more about my reasons in the afterword to the recent Ace Books expanded reprint of *Ariel*, but basically I felt that Pete and Ariel's story was finished. The book ends, and a sequel would have felt like an attempt to cash in on the novel's popularity when in fact I really had no story to tell. Maybe not the smartest career move, but there ya go.

I played with the idea of writing about Pete & Ariel's adventure in the remains of Disney World, alluded to in *Ariel*, but I decided against it because it would have been merely an irrelevant adventure, advancing nothing of character or theme, and also because I have made no secret of my feelings about the Disney corporation, and who wants to accompany Pete & Ariel through some bitter writer's polemic?

I was open to writing more books set in the milieu of the Change but I wasn't really focused on it. Instead I went on to write other things, some of which appeared and some of which did not. I also went on to lead a life filled to the brim with struggle and beauty and astonishing synchronicities. Around 1999 I quit writing for about five years and learned to do other things. My life was much enriched by this decision, and I was and remain startled by that.

So what happened that made me change my mind and write a sequel to *Ariel*?

Life. Life happened.

L ike a lot of writers I have notebooks full of ideas, intriguing paragraphs, bullet lists, titles. For years I'd had this notion of magic as a kind of software written for the universe's operating system. I called it spellware. Earlier I had invented (at least I think I invented it) the macrospell in another novel and used it as a plot device. I resurrected the notion in the framework of spellware and wrote some pages of notes about the implications and potential inherent in the idea. How it might be applied, what kind of economy and society might be based on it. The idea was intriguing and fun. But it was just an idea, not a story. God knows there's no shortage of books and movies that consist of not much more than an intriguing idea (if that), but I had no desire to add one more to that huge distracting pile. For me there's gotta be a story, and it's gotta be about something more than just what happens. So spellware remained in the Unfulfilled Notions file (no, I don't really have one called that).

One day out of the blue I realized spellware not only fit perfectly into the *Ariel* milieu, it accounted for it. It gave the world a foundation. If I projected a bit into the future of the Change it provided an economy, a technology, a resurgent civilization with a basis very different from our own. In retrospect the connection seems obvious, but *Ariel* and the world of the Change I had created back in 1978 were hardly foremost in my thoughts.

But somehow setting it in the context of the *Ariel mise-en-scène* spoke to the writer in me (he was still there, somewhere, probably in the attic wearing slippers and smoking a pipe and reading yellowed newspapers). The old spark bridged the gap and the novel was there in my mind waiting to unspool. Not in minute detail. Not the building but the blueprint. And it turned out that Writer Steve had some stuff he wanted to talk about here.

Much has been written about the joys attendant on flashes of inspiration. The ecstasy when the muse strikes. I've experienced it plenty. But what I felt on realizing that I was going to sit down and write this thing was plain and simple dread. I did not want to write a sequel to *Ariel*. I didn't think I wanted to write, period. I was very busy with a lot of other things, some of them going quite well. I had always loved writing, but having a writing career was a whole nother critter, and it had bitten me enough to make me more than a little reluctant to take it out for a walk again however firm the leash. And in fairness I had not been all that nice to it either. So when I realized (this all happened within seconds of that spark connecting spellware with *Ariel*, you understand) that I really was going to sit down and do this thing, I thought of Oscar Wilde saying that maturity is recognizing your mistakes when you make them again.

I knew that Writer Steve was not going to let this one go. (The fact that I can now differentiate him from other parts of me is the best evidence I can offer for the changes time and experience have wrought.) I also knew that arguing with the guy is usually worse than just shutting up and letting him have his way.

So I made a deal with him: you write the book and I'll stay out of your way. But you *only* write the book, and stay the hell out of my life. I'll make coffee and pay the bills and try to keep the office neat; other than that you're on your own with this. There's your office, there's the keyboard. Deal?

And that's really how it was.

Through a series of events too unlikely and elaborate to detail here, during that stretch beginning in 1999 when I'd laid off writing I taught myself to play the didgeridoo. Which (trust me on this) led to composing electronic music. Which led to learning club-style DJing. Which led me to create one of the world's most popular podcasts, Podrunner. About 150 pages of *Elegy Beach* had been written when Podrunner launched in February 2006, and Writer Steve got shoved aside for nearly three years while Podrunner pretty much took over my life as I undertook a whole new career along with a crash course in a business about which I knew very little.

I had estimated *Elegy Beach* would take about eighteen months to write. That estimate ended up being pretty accurate, if you don't count the three-year gap while I became something entirely unexpected for a living. But during those three years I had peeked in on the novel a couple of times to see how it was going and found myself pleasantly surprised. Writer Steve had something going here after all. I really should be more trusting.

I felt I owed it to the guy to give him room to finish the book. He'd been very patient (well, mostly) about this whole composer/DJ/podcaster business, and enabling him to write the thing had been my part of the bargain, after all. I also knew that if I didn't, I'd never hear the end of it.

So I bullied and cajoled and chivvied and rearranged and did what was necessary to make space for two full-time careers in one full-time life, and occasionally checked in on Writer Steve's progress while he diligently typed and researched and IM'd friends with annoying questions and went on road trips to Del Mar racetrack and Goodyear Airship Operations and Hearst Castle and who knows what all else, all while I myself acquired business partners and sponsors and music label licensing and played gigs in Los Angeles and San Francisco and Las Vegas and Reno and Burning Man and auditioned tens of thousands of tracks and created and updated the websites and artwork and newsletters and feeds and everything else that goes with all of it.

It may sound as if I am complaining but I'm not. I like being busy. And I bless my great good fortune every day. Having squandered it in my talented and ambitious and egregiously ignorant youth.

———————————

I'm skeptical when a writer says he writes for himself. I think Really? How come you went to all that trouble to put it on a page and then send it out to be published? So it's sobering to realize that I may have written a novel not *for* myself so much as *to* myself.

In the midst of all the rationales for magic and talking unicorns and scary centaurs against a postapocalyptic backdrop it seemed Writer Steve had a lot he wanted to talk about. Friendship and love and obligation. The conflicts that arise when they are set against each other. What's good and what's awful about the Baby Boom generation contrasted with what's good and what's awful about this recent generation, which my friend Ken has christened Generation Eloi. How to keep on living after the most important event in your life is over, and then realize later on in life that much of what you lived through afterward was more important still. And about loss and the unentitled beauty of existence.

I think one reason Writer Steve was so insistent about writing *Elegy Beach* was because he wanted it to be a note to the rest of me. I think that the whole time he was in the attic he was also paying attention to the rest of the house. I think he wanted to leave a note on the fridge for the owner telling him the place isn't haunted anymore. Telling him it's okay to revisit some of those abandoned rooms now. Telling him it's okay.

find I don't have as much to say about *Elegy Beach* as I did about *Ariel*. But these things stand out:

I had originally intended for Pete and Ariel to be more peripheral. *Elegy Beach* wasn't conceived as a direct sequel but as a tangential one. Pete and Ariel were supposed to be there mostly to provide a stronger connection to the earlier novel, and the idea was for them to become involved in Fred's story. But as it happened Fred became involved in the end of theirs. He is at least as much witness as he is protagonist. The book did not start out as a direct sequel, it became one as it progressed. And as it progressed I was surprised to find it increasingly about Pete and Ariel and what had happened in their lives to shape what they had become out of what we knew of them from decades ago. As *Elegy Beach* is in some ways about what *Ariel* was and is to me. From its first line to its last.

Ironically enough, most of the ideas I had about spellware and its implications aren't present in *Elegy Beach*. The plan at the outset was to explore where the whole spellware notion might lead, but *Elegy Beach* ended up depicting the foundations of the concept and not its eventual iterations. The book had something else it wanted to be about. That happens sometimes. You ignore it at your peril. But since the potential of spellware was the initial flash of inspiration that made me write the book after years of refusal to create a sequel and indeed years of refusal to write at all, I think its absence from the book itself is pretty damned funny.

Steven R. Boyett
Los Angeles, 2009